# SAVAGE TEXAS
# SEVEN DAYS
## TO HELL

# SAVAGE TEXAS
# SEVEN DAYS TO HELL

## William W. Johnstone
### with *J. A. Johnstone*

**PINNACLE BOOKS**
Kensington Publishing Corp.
www.kensingtonbooks.com

PINNACLE BOOKS are published by

Kensington Publishing Corp.
119 West 40th Street
New York, NY 10018

PUBLISHER'S NOTE
Following the death of William W. Johnstone, the Johnstone family is working with a carefully selected writer to organize and complete Mr. Johnstone's outlines and many unfinished manuscripts to create additional novels in all of his series like The Last Gunfighter, Mountain Man, and Eagles, among others. This novel was inspired by Mr. Johnstone's superb storytelling.

All Kensington titles, imprints, and distributed lines are available at special quantity discounts for bulk purchases for sales promotions, premiums, fund-raising, educational, or institutional use. Special book excerpts or customized printings can also be created to fit specific needs. For details, write or phone the office of the Kensington sales manager: Kensington Publishing Corp., 119 West 40th Street, New York, NY 10018, attn: Sales Department; phone 1-800-221-2647.

PINNACLE BOOKS, the Pinnacle logo, and the WWJ steer head logo are Reg. U.S. Pat. & TM Off.

ISBN-13: 978-0-7860-3807-7
ISBN-10: 0-7860-3807-1

First printing: February 2017

10  9  8  7  6  5  4  3  2  1

Printed in the United States of America

First electronic edition: February 2017

ISBN-13: 978-0-7860-3808-4
ISBN-10: 0-7860-3808-X

# ONE

Spud Barker went to the Sunrise Café in Weatherford, Texas, to chow down on his daily breakfast feed. He didn't know it but his regular routine was about to be rudely interrupted. He was heavyset with a face like a fresh-dug potato: gnarly, lumpy, and none too clean, thus giving rise to his handle, "Spud." He dressed like a businessman and wore no gun in plain view. He was trailed by two bodyguards, Vic Terrill and Chubb Driscoll. Terrill had a face like a horse's clean-picked skull, long, bony, and dead-white. Driscoll was an unjolly fat man with the permanent expression of a colicky baby.

The Sunrise Café was the best eatery in town, in the county for that matter. Which wasn't saying much. To be a regular there meant one had arrived, was an insider. It gave one prestige—so Spud Barker reckoned. He liked to see and be seen there. The food was good, too. Spud was a big eater.

Sunrise Café at weekday breakfast time was the last place he expected to find trouble. This morning trouble would find him.

It was about eight in the morning and the breakfast rush was over. Westerners were early risers generally and Weatherford folk were no exception. About a dozen patrons were scattered among the tables on both sides of the central aisle.

Among them but not of them was Sam Heller, no citizen of Weatherford he. He sat alone at a front table facing a window, which gave him a view of the entrance and beyond to the town square.

He was laying for Spud Barker, and when he saw him coming he rose from his chair and quietly sidled over to the front door, standing to one side of it.

Sam Heller was a yellow-haired and bearded well-armed titan in buckskins and denim. A Yankee born and bred, he was Texas sized, standing several inches above six feet, broad shouldered, raw boned, long limbed.

A Northerner who stood alone in Texas 1867, when the War Between the States was recent history and Yankee-hating by the populace was the rule rather than the exception, had to be able to take care of himself.

Sam Heller was such a man.

No one in the café knew him. They didn't know he was a Yankee, didn't know him from Adam. They were blissfully unaware he was about to set in motion a chain of events guaranteed to generate considerable bad feelings.

Sam felt good about the prospect.

Spud Barker came in first, then Terrill, then Driscoll. None of them spared more than a passing glance at the big galoot gawking at the picture on the wall. Their minds were on their bellies for they were hungry. More, they assumed they were safe on home ground. Spud's bodyguards had perhaps grown too comfortable in the seeming security of familiar everyday surroundings.

They moved toward Spud's usual table on the left-hand side of the dining room, comfortably set back from the strong morning sunlight filtering through red-and-white-checked curtains that covered the pair of windows bracketing the front door.

The first warning Spud Barker had that something was amiss was a sudden sense of rushing motion in the immediate vicinity. That was the sound of Sam Heller coming up fast behind Terrill and Driscoll.

He grabbed each of them by the back of the collar and slammed their heads together, making a loud thumping noise. Chubb Driscoll took the brunt of the hit, eyes rolling up in his head as he went down, hitting the floor.

Vic Terrill went wobbly at the knees but stayed on his feet, stunned, seeing stars. He went for his gun more by instinct than anything else, groping blindly for it, but before he could find it Sam grabbed his gun-hand by the wrist. Terrill struggled but could make no headway against Sam's iron grip.

Sam used the arm as a handle to swing the bodyguard hard against the wall on the left. Terrill hit an empty table along the way, rocking it but not knocking it over, upending several chairs.

Terrill slammed into the wall, crying out. Sam closed in on him, powering a pile-driving right uppercut that connected square on the point of Terrill's chin. Terrill's head snapped back, hitting the wall. His eyes showed all-whites, his face went senselessly slack.

Sam's fist was cocked, ready to deliver a follow-up blow but it was unneeded. Terrill was out cold. He folded at the knees, sliding down the wall with his back to it, falling in a crumpled heap at Sam's feet.

Spud Barker's bodyguards had been put out of commission in less than thirty seconds.

Sam turned, bearing down on Spud. It had all happened so fast that Spud hadn't had time to react. Now he did. He felt the Fear.

Spud's mouth went cotton-dry and his belly felt like the bottom dropped out of it. His hands flew up in front of him in a warding gesture: "No! Don't—"

Chubb Driscoll stirred on the floor, groggy, glassy eyed. Getting on hands and knees and trying to rise.

Sam swerved from his path toward Spud to kick Driscoll in the head. Driscoll flopped down and out.

The distraction gave Spud time to recover some of his wits. He started to reach toward his right-side jacket pocket for an object inside that made a suspicious bulge.

Before he could put a hand in his pocket, he was the recipient of a punch in the face that rocked him back on his heels, sending him hurtling backward. Sam crowded Spud, giving him no time to recover.

Sam grabbed Spud by the lapels, holding him upright and giving him a good shaking.

"W-what are you p-p-icking on me for? I don't even know you—"

"But I know you, Spud," Sam Heller interrupted.

Sam had set his attack inside the café to maximize the element of surprise, hitting his targeted men where and when they would least expect it.

He now wanted to take the action outside where

there was less chance of innocent bystanders being hurt.

The windows flanking the front door caught his eye—and Sam was a direct actionist.

He grabbed Spud's collar by the scruff of the neck, his other hand gripping the top of the man's belt and waistband at the small of Spud's back.

Sam heaved upward, lifting Spud until only the toes of his boots were touching the floor, hustling him toward the front of the building.

Sam was giving Spud Barker the "bum's rush," a technique well known to bartenders and bouncers for ejecting belligerent drunks and troublemakers from the premises with a maximum of haste and a minimum of fuss.

"No!—What're you doing? Stop! You loco? Stop, stop!—" came Spud's wailing cries as he was swept forward toward a window to one side of the entrance.

"No, *don't*—!"

Sam stopped short, using his momentum to help heave Spud headfirst into the window.

It was closed.

Sam manhandled Spud Barker like pitching a hay bale into a wagon. A clean toss!

Spud hit the window in a tremendous explosion of shattered glass, splintered wood, red-and-white-checked curtains, and brass curtain rods—gone, now.

He spewed through the window frame into the outer air, landing with a bone-jarring thud on the boardwalk porch fronting the café.

Spud lay still, unmoving. After a pause he started groaning and twitching.

Sam grinned. He wasn't done with Spud Barker yet,

not hardly. But first he had to make sure his rear lines were secure. That meant ensuring the bodyguards were still out of commission and stayed that way.

Sam turned, facing inward to the café. The customers were townsfolk mostly, judging by their clothes, and a few ranchers. They seemed a fairly prosperous lot.

Now they looked like a bomb had gone off. Sam's sudden outburst of violence had come as unexpectedly as a thunderbolt crashing out of a clear blue sky.

Customers and staffers alike tried to make themselves very still and small to avoid drawing Sam's notice. They looked away, not meeting his eyes.

Well and good. Part of the reason for Sam's shock tactics was to cow them into submission so none would be minded to interfere. Which took some doing with stiff-necked Texas men but so far it seemed to be working.

Vic Terrill lay sprawled on the floor, inert, unconscious. But Chubb Driscoll was showing signs of life.

Driscoll had managed to drag himself to an upright support pillar. The side of his face where Sam had kicked him was bruised with an eye swollen shut. His good eye glared hatefully, rolling this way and that. Sam started toward him. Chubb Driscoll went for his gun, pawing at it. Sam came on, not breaking stride. He grabbed a table chair and threw it at Driscoll. Driscoll had his gun in hand, he opened his mouth to shout—

The chair hit hard, breaking apart, silencing his outcry. Chubb Driscoll didn't break, but the hit didn't do him any good, either. He went limp, slumping to the floor.

Busting up the café was one thing but a shoot-out

was a horse of a different color. Sam took his chances as they came but he'd hate like hell for some luckless breakfaster to catch a bullet right in the middle of his or her ham and eggs.

He took a look at Chubb Driscoll. Driscoll's eyes were closed, his smashed nose and lips bleeding. Was he alive or dead?

Sam didn't know. In any case the first thing to do was disarm him. Driscoll's gun was clutched in a closed fist but hadn't been fired.

Sam stepped on Driscoll's wrist, pinning his gun hand to the floor. Driscoll moaned, wincing and flinching like a dog having bad dreams.

"Alive, eh?" Sam said to himself. "But he won't be getting up any time soon."

He broke Driscoll's gun, emptying it and throwing the rounds out the broken window. He let the empty gun fall to the floor.

Sam absently rubbed the top of his big right hand, where he had skinned a couple of knuckles. He crossed to Terrill to give him the once-over. Terrill lay facedown, motionless in the spot where he'd been knocked out.

Sam grabbed a handful of Terrill's hair and raised his head off the floor to see what condition he was in. Terrill didn't so much as twitch.

Sam liked it when they stayed down after he hit them. He let go of the hair, Terrill's head flopping down.

Sam emptied Terrill's gun anyway. He wouldn't be getting a bullet in the back from either of the body-guards any time soon.

Now he could do his business with Spud Barker undisturbed.

Sam Heller took a last look at the people in the dining room, a long hard look. Had any been minded to show fight, that steely eyed gaze stifled any fleeting impulse toward combativeness.

Sam went out. Unlike Spud Barker, he used the door.

# Two

Weatherford town was the capital of the same-named county. It lay in North Central Texas roughly along the same east-west latitude line as Dallas and Hangtree.

Dallas was a money town, Hangtree was a frontier cowtown, and Weatherford was . . . what, exactly?

Weatherford town and county was a good locale for ranching and farming. It was a good locale for lawlessness, too, far enough away from Dallas to avoid attracting unwanted attention from Federal troops yet close enough to be within ready reach of the U.S. Cavalry when Commanche raiders were on the prowl.

In the war's aftermath Weatherford had attracted a bumper crop of outlaws who preyed on Hangtree, Dallas, and all points in-between . . . The gangs raided neighboring communities, killing and plundering.

No lonely ranch house was too small, no settlement too large to escape their depredations. Travelers and wayfarers were prime targets. Many stagecoaches, freight haulers, and wagon trains had left their burned-out hulks scattered about the countryside.

And the sun-bleached bones of their passengers, too.

Weatherford was a clearinghouse for stolen goods. Outlaws from nearby counties disposed of their loot in town. Rustlers, robbers, bandits, and brigands all came knowing their plunder would find a ready market in the merchants of Weatherford. They paid pennies on the dollar but it added up.

People being people and times being hard, buyers and sellers alike were none too fussy about little things like titles and bills of sale for goods and livestock that changed hands.

Any fool could see that the newcomers thronging Weatherford were outlaws dealing in stolen goods, but only a bigger fool would call them on it. Such great fools tend to be short-lived.

That was Weatherford: a lot of folks doing all right by doing wrong. Making it of interest to Sam Heller, a soldier of fortune, bounty hunter, and more. Much more.

A class of men, and some women, too, had sprung up who served as contacts linking town merchants with the bandit chiefs.

These middlemen—or fences, to call them by their right name—insulated the merchants from the tricky and dangerous business of dealing directly with the outlaws in the field, providing much-needed protection for the townsmen to avoid being robbed and killed while trying to exchange money for stolen goods.

The fences took a fat cut of the profits from buyers and sellers in exchange for brokering the deals.

One such middleman was Spud Barker, making him of interest to Sam Heller.

Sam was even more interested in Loman Vard, Spud's partner. Spud took care of business in town but it was Vard who had the contacts with the outlaws. Spud was a businessman and politician, and Vard was an outlaw and killer.

Sam very much wanted to get his hands on Loman Vard, but Vard was a tough man to corner. To get at him, Sam needed a middleman: Spud Barker.

Spud Barker didn't know what hit him. Literally.

He came crashing through the café window into the fresh clean brightness of a spring morning, one he was unable to appreciate at the moment. Somehow he managed to rise to his hands and knees, head hanging down. Pieces of broken glass that had gotten stuck to his clothes fell off, making little chiming tones when they hit the wooden plank board sidewalk.

His vision swam in and out of focus. He raised his hands to his aching head. The backs of his hands and forearms were all cut up, covered with hairline bleeding scratches—his face, too. His hat was lost somewhere along the way between café and sidewalk, but that was the least of his worries.

He made quite a sight in that heretofore-quiet street scene, though there weren't too many people around to see it.

The Sunrise Café stood on the west side of the town's central square, which was lined along the sides by some of Weatherford's leading establishments. There was a bank, a hotel, the town hall, a dry goods emporium, a feed store, and so on. Also a couple of more or less respectable saloons and various shops and stores.

A few people were out on the street, mostly towns-folk running errands or doing some early shopping.

They stopped what they were doing when Spud Barker exploded out the café window onto the boardwalk sidewalk. They paused to see what it was all about, staying a safe distance away.

A fancy two-wheeled buggy drawn by one horse rolled north, its driver slowing it to a halt when he came abreast of the café. The driver had a long bushy beard reaching to his collarbone. He wore a white shirt, black vest, and dark pants. He stared open mouthed, goggling at Spud Barker.

Spud stood on his knees, gingerly feeling around at the top of his head for damages and in the process dislodging more pieces of broken glass. He winced as his fingers discovered a goose egg–sized bump atop his aching noggin. The pain brought tears to his eyes. He blinked away the wetness until he could see clearly again.

Spud didn't like what he saw. A pair of boots had stepped into his field of vision. His gaze traveled upward, taking in the figure of the man looming over him—the wildman who had knocked eight bells out of his bodyguards and thrown him through the window.

Seeing Sam Heller come out of the café to hover over Spud Barker, the driver of the two-wheeled cart snapped the reins to get his horse moving up the street and away.

Sam Heller cut an impressive, even formidable, figure.

Beneath a dark, battered slouch hat his yellow hair fell to his shoulders in the go-to-hell style favored by certain U.S. Cavalry scouts, of which he had once been. That long hair taunted hostile Indians, *"Take this scalp if you dare!"*

By contrast Sam's beard was close cut, neatly trimmed.

He wore a gun, a .36 Navy Colt tucked handle out into his waistband over his left hip. But that was not his main weapon. That was a Winchester 1866 repeating rifle, chopped down at barrel and stock. A weapon commonly known as a mule's leg. It rested in a custom-made leather holster on his right hip.

Sam also carried a Green River knife with an eighteen-inch blade, secured on his left side in a belt-sheath low-slung enough to avoid blocking access to the Navy Colt. Like the famed Bowie knife, the Green River model was also balanced for throwing.

His blue eyes were as cold as polar seas.

Sam didn't like standing with his back to the café, his broad back a tempting target for anybody inside wanting to take a shot at him.

"Let's have some privacy, Spud," he said, grabbing the other by the back of his collar and hauling him to his feet.

Spud Barker's face swelled above the choking collar, reddening under Sam's tight grip. Sam hustled him away from the café to the south end of the wooden sidewalk. The sidewalk and building fronts were raised three feet above the ground. A short flight of three wooden steps with no railing angled down to solid ground.

Sam booted Spud Barker down the stairs. Spud's too-solid flesh clattered and banged on the stairs, counterpointed by his howls of pain and outrage. He hit the ground sprawling.

"You trying to kill me?" he demanded.

"If I do, you won't have to ask, you'll know it," Sam

said. His ready boot toe none too gently prodded Spud to his feet.

"Stay on your feet, Spud. I'm getting tired of picking up your sorry carcass. If I have to do it much more you might just as well stay down permanently," Sam said.

An alley mouth opened at the bottom of the steps. The passageway stood crosswise to the street and ran between two blocks of wooden frame buildings.

Sam muscled Spud fifteen feet deeper into the alley, propping him up and slamming his back against the wall.

"That's better. Now we can have a nice private talk," Sam said.

"I've got nothing to say to you!" Spud Barker blustered.

"No?" Sam said, chuckling.

"No! . . . Why, I know what you are! You're a Yankee, a damned Yankee!" Spud Barker accused, his fleshy jowls quivering with indignation as he stabbed a pointing forefinger at Sam.

"How'd you figure that out?"

"You talk funny," Spud spat. "You know what's good for you, you'll hightail it out of town quick and don't look back. We don't rightly care for your kind in Weatherford, Billy Yank. It's none too healthy for outsiders of the Northern persuasion."

"Not for the sons and daughters of Old Dixie, either, going by all the burned-out wagon trains and stagecoaches I've seen scattered around the county," Sam said.

"Northerners, every last one of them," Spud declared, chin outthrust defiantly.

"Lots of Southerners packing up and heading for California and points west these days. Anyway, how would you know if the missing wayfarers are Yankees or Rebs?"

"The devil must have a special sauce for Yankees, to make them so mean."

"Probably, but we'll get to that later. First, I want to make sure you're defanged." Sam reached into Spud's right-hand jacket pocket, pulling out a four-barreled pepperbox derringer. "Standard issue for the well-dressed Weatherford businessman," he said. "This little beauty can make a real mess. Too much gun for you, Spud—you might hurt yourself. I'll put it away for safekeeping."

He dropped it into a pocket of his buckskin vest. A further pat-down search yielded a set of spiked brass knuckles, a penknife, and a wad of greenback bills. Sam tossed the knuckle-duster and the penknife farther back into the alley and held on to the greenbacks.

"Enough frogskins here to choke a horse," Sam said, thumbing through the wad. "Big bills all the way through, with no little ones to pad it out. It'll go toward covering my expenses."

Sam pocketed the bills while Spud Barker sputtered with impotent outrage.

"Damn you! This is robbery! Robbery in broad daylight, no less!"

Sam tsk-tsked. "Makes you wonder what the town is coming to, eh?"

"You must be mad. The marshal's office is straight across the square and he's probably on his way here right now with his deputies. If you value your skin you'll give me back my money and make tracks out of here as fast as you can—"

"Not to worry, Marshal Finn and company are otherwise engaged. I'm afraid he's going to be a no-show."

"How can you know that?"

Weatherford's notoriously corrupt town marshal, Skeates Finn, upheld the law with sterling evenhanded impartiality, allowing every outlaw who cut him in on the take the right to sell stolen goods in town.

He and his deputies were equally merciless to any badmen who refused to pay, or cheated the lawman out of what he regarded as his fair share. Such offenders were usually shot dead out of hand.

Sam said, "While you and the rest of Weatherford's good citizens were sleeping, Chuck Ramsey's bunch was making a predawn run of stolen goods into town for delivery at Banker Drysdale's warehouse off Town Square. Real first-class merchandise, from what I heard—this ring any bells for you, Spud?"

"Not a bit; I don't know what you're talking about." But Spud did know, if the flicker of recognition in his sick eyes was any indication, and Sam Heller reckoned it was so.

"Here's something you don't know. The Ramsey gang ran into an ambush and got shot to pieces, every last man-jack of them, dead," Sam said.

Spud Barker looked even sicker, face wrenched out of shape by a spasm of strong emotion, as if he'd taken a bite out of an apple to find half a worm.

"It's a sin and a scandal how cheap these owlhoots hold human life," Sam went on. "Maybe they figure such killers and scavengers ain't really human . . . or maybe it takes one to know one, as the saying goes.

"Now here's the part that'll really gall you, Spud.

After going to all that trouble of bushwhacking the Ramseys, the hijackers set fire to the wagons and burned up all the goods."

"*They-burned-them-up?!*" Spud Barker said every word carefully and distinctly.

"Burned them up," Sam repeated cheerfully. "All those plundered goods, turned into a heap of ashes. It's like burning up money, don't you think? A lot of money, I heard."

"You hear a lot," Spud said, looking daggers at him. "Too much."

"I get around," Sam said modestly. "Some good Samaritan passing through stopped by the warehouse to give them the bad news. Banker Drysdale being one of the big men in town there was nothing for it but for Marshal Finn and deputies to saddle up and gallop put pronto out to Hansen's Pass where the ambush went down.

"Now just between the two of us, Spud, and don't let on where you heard it, but I suspicion that when Finn gets to the pass, he's going to find some clues and a set of tracks that lead right straight to Lem Buckman's camp on the far side of the ridge."

"Buckman!" Spud said, startled into angry vehemence. "Buckman would never cross Ramsey, they've been stringing together since the war! They're like brothers! It's all a put-up job to point the finger at Buckman and away from whoever really did the job—"

"Buckman didn't do it, eh, Spud? You would know."

"I don't know a thing," the other said dully.

"Lord, I hope Finn doesn't go off half-cocked and ride into Buckman's camp shooting! A lot of fellows could get hurt . . . Here's a puzzlement: If Buckman and his bunch didn't jump the Ramsey gang and burn the wagons, who did?"

"You tell me," Spud said in flat, clipped tones.

"Loman Vard," Sam suggested brightly. "Why not? Who better? Vard could be going behind your back and everybody else's, trying to take over the town—"

"You madman!" Spud Barker had reached the breaking point where fear gave way to rage, greed, and frustration. "It's not Vard who's sneaking around doing the back shooting and burning, it's you! You lowdown no-account good-for-nothing Yankee jackanapes! Who are you? What do you want? What're you trying to do to this town, destroy it?" Spud Barker was all but shrieking.

"I'll do that and more if that's what it takes to get what I want," Sam Heller said quietly.

"If it's money you're after, I'll pay you to go away and leave me alone. I'll pay you one hundred—no, five hundred dollars in gold!"

"Glad you upped the ante, because there's more than two hundred dollars' worth of greenbacks in your billfold alone, Spud."

"Five hundred dollars in gold, in your hand within the hour, if you'll leave me alone and ride out."

"Sure, let's take a stroll over to the bank and you'll take it out of the petty cash drawer. What could go wrong? I trust you. Who wouldn't trust a receiver of stolen goods plundered from robbed and murdered travelers and emigrants, men, women, and children?" Sam mocked.

"We'll work out a way to get you the money that doesn't put you at risk," Spud insisted.

"I like money as well as anyone else, Spud, but it's just incidental. What I want is information."

"You won't get it from me; it'll take more than a lunatic lone Yankee storming into town, beating innocent people within an inch of their lives and slandering blameless businessmen like myself to make me betray my sacred trusts!"

"I'll make you talk, Spud."

"I've had a bellyful of your damned cat and mouse games—"

"Cat and rat, more like."

"Blast you, speak plainly and say who you are and what you want!"

"The name's Heller, Sam Heller, if that means anything to you."

It did. Blood drained away from Spud Barker's florid complexion, leaving it a sallow white. His eyes narrowed, calculating. He chewed tiny flecks of skin from his quivering lower lip.

Spud felt quite the fool. Had he not been so intimidated by his assailant, the mule's leg on his hip should have been a dead giveaway to his identity. The notoriety of the Yankee bounty man with the chopped-down Winchester was widespread throughout North Central Texas and beyond.

"The Yankee bounty hunter who kills for gold," Spud said. He tried to speak forcefully but his voice cracked, causing him to finish with a near-whisper.

"Guilty as charged," Sam said.

"Y-you're wasting your time sniffing around here, Bluebelly. There's no price on my head!"

"That's because you haven't got caught yet. You may not be a wolf in sheep's clothing but you're no lamb, either . . . A polecat in sheep's clothing, maybe."

"Quit name calling and tell me what you want."

"Loman Vard, that's who I want."

Spud Barker waited a long time before replying. "Never heard of him."

"Stop it. If you're going to lie—you might as well put some feeling into it. There's not a man, woman, or stray dog in Weatherford who doesn't know who Loman Vard is," Sam said. "Loman Vard, your partner in the stolen goods and livestock business. Ring any bells yet?"

"Oh, *that* Vard!"

"Uh-huh, that one. Loman Vard—there's only one," Sam pressed.

"Sure I know him, er, ah, that is I mean I've heard of him, certainly, yes," Spud said, stalling for time. "I got confused for a minute—who wouldn't be, after getting beaten up, thrown through a window, and terrorized by a maniac Yankee? But you've got the wrong man, mister. I'm not partnered up with Vard or anyone else in the stolen goods business. I'm an honest dealer in used and secondhand merchandise—*oof!*"

This last reaction was occasioned by a sharp stiff jab that Sam Heller popped into Spud's soft belly. It was not a particularly hard hit, for Sam wanted the other to be able to talk. But Spud still staggered under the blow.

Some color had been returning to Spud's face, but the jab turned it pasty-white again.

Sam grabbed a fistful of Spud's shirtfront, tearing cloth and sending buttons popping. "Better talk while you can, Spud. If Johnny Cross gets hold of you, your life won't be worth a Confederate dollar," he snapped.

"*Johnny Cross!*—what's he got to do with me?!" Spud Barker was near-hysterical. White rings circled his eyes, fear-dilated pupils swollen to black disks.

"Vard sent Terrible Terry Moran to kill him— You're Vard's partner! Cross'll kill Vard but he won't stop there, he'll clean up on the whole gang and everybody tied in with Vard, then he'll burn down Vard's house to warm his hands by!

"The only chance you've got of coming out of this alive is to give me Vard first. If I get him before Johnny does, I can keep you out of it. But if Johnny gets to Vard first, you're a dead man. You can start running now, but no matter how far and how fast you go, some fine day you'll find yourself looking at Cross from the wrong side of a gun."

"This is madness! You've got the wrong man, I tell you." Spud Barker's shoulders heaved and he knuckled his eyes as though wiping away tears.

Sam noticed that Spud's eyes were both dry and that Spud was peeking at him over the tops of his hands, looking to see if Sam was buying his story.

"It's no good, Spud. I'm not guessing, I *know*. I tracked down Fly Norvine, the only member of Moran's gang to escape the gundown. He spilled his guts by the time I was through with him. He told about Moran and all the rest of it, how you and Vard were thick as thieves with Jimbo Turlock in the run-up to the Marauder raid on Hangtree . . ."

Sam's voice trailed off. Something had changed. A moment ago, Spud Barker had been panting for breath as if he'd just run a mile. Now his breathing had slowed almost to normal.

"You overplayed your hand, Billy Yank," Spud said, smirking. "You had me going there for a while, I'll give you that. But you made a mistake."

"Oh, really?" Sam said.

"Yes, really," Spud returned with hateful mockery of Sam's words and tone. He actually seemed to be enjoying himself now. "If you had Fly Norvine, you could have taken him to Fort Pardee, sworn out a warrant, and come here with the Army to crush this town. But you being here all by your lonesome tells me that you've got nothing, nothing at all."

"That's a horse on me, I reckon," Sam said in a conversational tone, after a pause. "But you know, Spud, there's also such a thing as being too damned smart to live."

Spud tried to put across a reasonable tone. "See here, Heller, I can hardly tell you what I don't know—"

Sam drew his knife and held it up to Spud Barker's face.

Spud's stream of words came to a dead stop. The formidable Green River knife with its eighteen-inch blade tended to have a chilling effect on conversation. Rays of morning sunlight set the blade ablaze with a white-hot glinting. The knife bore the seal of authenticity, the Green River maker's mark stamped into the metal of the blade near the hilt.

Spud Barker stared at the blade as if hypnotized. "W-wuh-wuh—what're that for?!"

"You would have it this way, Spud." Sam sighed. He played with the knife, turning it this way and that, causing its glaring reflected light to shine directly in Spud's eyes, dazzling them.

"Funny thing about nicknames, they get right straight to the heart of the matter," Sam began. "You get a fellow called Shorty and he's going to be short. Man they call Long Nose will have a long nose, and so on. You get the idea. Now what do they call you?— '*Spud.*' That's right on the money because your head does look like a potato. All lumpy, skin rough and patchy like a potato skin, eyes that're little black holes like a 'tater's eyes . . ."

"What're you going on about, Heller?" Spud Barker's words were brittle with rising hysteria.

"I'm through playing with you, Spud. Tell me where Vard is or I'll peel you like a potato."

"You're crazy!"

Sam didn't answer, he just kept playing with the knife, throwing the sun-dazzle into Spud's eyes.

"You can't get away with this!"

"I'm getting away with it, Spud. The law's out of town so there's no help for you there. Your fellow citizens are famously minding their own business, so they won't interfere. You can't stop me. So what's it to be, Spud? Talk? Or get peeled?"

Sam's free hand shot out, grabbing a fistful of Spud Barker's greasy hair, holding his head upright for the knife.

The sudden action caused Spud to cry out in fear. He started wriggling.

"Hold still, Spud, you'll do yourself a mischief," Sam warned. He touched the other's taut neck not with the sharp end of the blade but rather with the squared-off edge running along the top of the knife.

Spud stopped wriggling.

"There's more than one way to peel a potato. I'm going to scalp you, Spud."

Too undone by terror to speak, Spud could only make a croaking gasp by way of protest.

"Scalping won't kill you. It'll put you in a world of hurt but it won't kill you," Sam said brightly. "Every now and then you run into a fellow that's been scalped. More than you might think. They get left for dead and don't die. Scalped man usually keeps his head covered all the time with a hat or head scarf or whatever. For good reason: The top of the head is a mess of scars from crown to ears. It ain't pretty.

"Back when I was fighting Sioux up on the North Range I got to be a pretty fair hand at taking scalps. They made a practice of lifting the hair of our people, men and women both, so we scouts figured turnabout was fair play. Now this Green River blade is no scalping knife but it'll do the job right handily—"

"No, no! . . . Don't!"

"Ah, you can speak after all, Spud. Thought the cat got your tongue, you were so quiet for a while. Long as you can talk, why not tell me where Vard is and save yourself a heap of grief?"

"I can't tell what I don't know!"

"Shh! Not so loud. You'll startle me. If my hand slips I might put out your eye by mistake. Lord knows you'll have misery enough without adding to your troubles."

"Oh, why won't you believe me when I tell you I don't know where Vard is? Why, why?"

"Because you're a liar, Spud."

"I'm not lying—"

"What else would a liar say?" Sam asked reasonably.

"But so would a man telling the truth!" Spud insisted.

"Vard would have given up and thrown you over as soon as I started leaning on him, but you're too dumb to do it to him first," Sam said.

"Vard will kill me if I talk," Spud whispered, wringing his hands. "Not that I know where he is," he added quickly.

"If that's your song, you're stuck with it. Too bad for you," Sam said, touching the knife blade tip to the right-hand corner of Spud's forehead where the hairline met.

"Now I'll tell you what I'm going to do," he went on. "First, I'll mark out the area to be cut along the hairline, down around the ears and then across the back of the neck at the collar. Done right, I can just sort of slip the flat of the knife under the top layers of skin, working it in deep, back toward the crown. Work loose a nice flap of scalp big enough to get a good grip on and, with a bit of luck, I'll peel the whole scalp right off the top of the skull all in one piece!"

Sam pressed the knife blade tip a bit harder against Spud's flesh, pricking it. A tear-sized, ruby droplet beaded at the surface.

Spud Barker shrieked. He went limp, eyes closed, head bowed. Sam thought the man had fainted but Spud was still on his feet. He slapped Spud's jowly cheeks several times, trying to rouse him.

"*Oww!* That hurts," Spud complained.

"You won't even notice it once the scalping starts," Sam said.

"To hell with that, I'll talk!"

"Ah, now you're showing good sense."

"First you've got to promise me something."

"You're sorely trying my patience, Spud. We're not horse trading here. Tell me where I can find Vard and you won't get scalped. That's the only deal on tap today."

"No conditions here, no strings attached. This is something you'll want," Spud Barker said, gripping Sam's arm—not his knife arm. "You've got to kill Loman Vard first chance you get."

"I'm looking forward to it," Sam said, taking Spud's

hand off his arm. No need to tell him that Sam meant to take Vard alive. Vard was a storehouse of information about outlaw alliances and criminal conspiracies in Texas and throughout the Southwest. Sam Heller would squeeze him dry of all he knew before sending him on to swing on a rope in Hangtree.

"Vard will know I've talked, and if you don't kill him he'll kill me."

"You'll be safe enough, Spud."

Spud Barker nervously gnawed on a knuckle. "Vard's hard enough to kill man-to-man, but he won't be alone. He surrounds himself with top guns: Big Taw, the tinhorn they call Acey-Deucy, Kurt Angle, and his cousin—they're a pair of right bastards—Ginger Culhane, the Mex. Everyone a killer and that's not the half of them. Are you sure you can take him? What can you do? One lone man . . ."

"Chuck Ramsey had a five-man gang of stone killers siding him. They went down in a couple minutes shooting at Hansen's Pass," Sam said. "With a rifle you don't have to work close."

"I know you're a sharpshooter, you can pick off Vard at a distance. You don't even have to show yourself. That must be nice," Spud said, not trying to hide the envy in his voice.

Color was coming back to his cheeks as he took heart. "You side Johnny Cross, a one-man army all by himself! If you could bring him in on this thing, Heller."

"Better if Johnny doesn't get involved . . . better for you," Sam said. "Don't forget that bit with Terry Moran. If Johnny finds out you had a hand in that, he'll skin you alive.

"Which is what I'm going to do to you, Spud, if you don't quit stalling and steer me to Loman Vard—and quick!"

"All right, I'll tell you. Between you and Johnny Cross, Vard is finished. If you don't get him Cross surely will."

Sam Heller heaved a sigh of relief when Spud Barker wasn't looking. He'd been afraid he'd really have to start scalping to get him to talk.

Spud Barker opened his mouth to speak but before he could do so a voice demanded:

"*Let-Spud-go!*"

# THREE

Sam Heller stood with his knife at Spud Barker's throat. That's the position in which he'd been surprised by three gunmen.

Careless, Sam thought with bitter self-disgust. *Stupid.* He'd made a slip, one he might pay for with his life.

In the run-up toward making his move against Vard via Spud Barker, Sam had gone some thirty hours without sleep, with little water and less food. That was one of the drawbacks to playing a lone hand: Too often he found himself in the position of a one-man-band, trying to do too much with too little.

Keeping the knife at Spud's throat, Sam edged around to one side so he was partially facing the gunmen. They stood shoulder to shoulder in the street outside the alley mouth.

Sam recognized them. He had a mighty-minded memory for faces and names where man-hunting was concerned, and he'd amassed plenty of information during the near two years he'd been plying his trade here in North Central Texas.

The triggermen were Haze Birnam, Chris Latrobe, and Walt Palenky, stalwarts of the Vard-Barker coalition who were more closely allied with Barker than Vard. Which might explain why they were in town instead of out in the field with Vard—unfortunately for Sam.

Birnam, Latrobe, and Palenky, hardcases all:

Haze Birnam was a strongback brawler who switched to guns when he found out he could kill more people faster with a six-shooter than with his fists. "Burn 'Em Down Birnam," some called him. He was built like a bear but said to be cat-quick.

Chris Latrobe had straw-colored hair, close-set beady eyes that tended to look cross-eyed, and a long turnip nose. Thin and shrunken chested, he suffered frequent colds and had a permanent runny nose.

Walt Palenky looked like an Indian with his thick black hair, long slitted eyes, high cheekbones, and flattened nose. But his roots were Slavic, of East European descent; he was a bit slow witted with oxlike stolidity.

Birnam, Latrobe, and Palenky. They each had a gun in hand except for Latrobe, who wielded two guns. They had the drop on Sam Heller. Not even the fastest gun can beat a gun that's already drawn.

"Looks like we got here just in time to save you from a close shave, Spud," Latrobe said, sniffling. His nose was red and his upper lip glistened with wetness.

"Drop that knife if you want to live, stranger," Haze Birnam said.

"Tell your friends to back off if you don't want a cut throat, Spud," Sam said.

Funny how things work out or don't work out. The trio thought they had come along just in time to save Spud Barker's neck. In reality they had arrived at the moment when Spud was about to betray Loman Vard and by extension themselves, along with the rest of the gang.

Timing really is everything, Sam thought. For him, it was a case of bad timing.

"Tell them, Spud," Sam prompted.

Here was something Spud didn't have to fake . . . his fear was all too real. As well it might be, for he had a very good chance of being killed if his men opened fire.

Which could be a problem. Gang chiefs who show yellow command little respect among their underlings.

Ash-gray Spud tried to speak, choking on the first attempt, his mouth cotton-dry. "D-do what the man says, b-boys."

"Can't do that, Spud," Haze Birnam said, shaking his head. He was taking the play, Latrobe and Palenky deferring to him.

"We stay put," Birnam told the other two. "We got the whip hand here. Billy Yank dies if he cuts Spud and he knows it."

"Move wrong and Spud dies first," Sam said.

"Huh! Fat lot of good that's gonna do you . . . you'll be dead, too," Birnam said with a sneer.

"That way nobody wins. Put up your guns and I'll let him go."

"Drop the knife and you can go."

"I need something more solid than that."

"No guarantees in this life, Bluebelly. You're already on borrowed time."

"Aren't we all?"

"What I see is a man with a knife going against three

men with guns," Birnam taunted. "What'll you bet I can drop you before you get that knife into play?"

"Spud's life."

"And yours—don't forget that, Yank."

"It's a standoff then," Sam said.

"That's all right, we got plenty of time," Birnam said.

He was right. Time was on the side of the trigger-men. The longer this went on, the less Sam's chances got. Time for more of the gang to arrive and close the ring around Sam. Time for Marshal Skeates Finn and his crew to return from Hansen's Pass.

"Why don't I just shoot him in the head and put an end to it, Haze?" Latrobe suggested.

"Which one," Birnam drawled, "the Yankee or Spud?"

Walt Palenky looked startled. After a pause, Latrobe burst out laughing.

"Damn you!" Spud Barker said.

"Just joshing, Spud," Haze Birnam said in a real mean way that seemed to say he was dead serious.

"Maybe I could shoot the knife out of his hand," Walt Palenky said.

"You ain't that good a shot, Walt," Birnam scoffed. "You might hit poor ol' Spud."

"Maybe he should try it at that," Latrobe said brightly.

Birnam laughed this time, Latrobe joining in to laugh at his own joke. Walt Palenky frowned, confused.

Spud Barker found his voice at last. "I'm not forgetting this, you two."

"Ooh," Latrobe said.

"Hard words, Spud. You ain't in no position to be making threats," Birnam said, a loose smile playing around his lips, but cold eyed.

"Keep your chin up, boss, we'll get you out of this," Palenky said, ever-loyal.

"Maybe even alive," Latrobe snickered.

"Hell, let's get to it," Haze Birnam said, thumbing back the hammer of his gun with a sharp metallic *click*.

When a man widely known as "Burn 'Em Down Birnam" commits to action, the crisis has arrived. Sam Heller acted accordingly.

Sam sidestepped, putting him partly behind Spud Barker—at the same time he threw the knife.

Sam Heller was an expert knife thrower and handler. He'd taken to the blade in boyhood days and had spent countless hours of practice at the art over the years. He could throw a knife by the blade or the handle with equal facility as long as the weapon was properly balanced, as was the Green River model.

This cast was thrown by the handle.

Much of the secret behind hitting the mark with a thrown knife depends on knowing how many turns and half-turns a particular knife will make en route to its target.

Lightning-fast mental calculations had come to Sam with the ease of long years of expertise.

The knife was a silver pinwheel spinning toward its man. It hit Haze Birnam square in the chest.

As soon as the knife left Sam's hand he was in motion, pulling with a cross-belly draw the .36 Navy Colt from where it nestled butt out in the waistband over his left hip. He was in too-cramped conditions to loose the mule's leg from its holster rig on his right side.

Sam kicked Spud Barker's feet out from under him, sending him sprawling even as opening shots were fired—not by him but by Walt Palenky.

Sam threw himself backward toward the ground, returning fire in midair at Palenky. Palenky's gun was leveled and shooting, cutting empty air scant inches above Sam's upturned face and chest as he fell.

Sam put two shots into Palenky, one below the rib cage in midtorso, the other a few inches above the belt buckle. Palenky crumpled.

It all happened in a handful of seconds.

Sam hit the dirt, landing in the alley on his back. He fought to stay loose and not tighten up, but the impact was jarring. He took much of the fall on his upper back and shoulders, absorbing the impact. As soon as he hit he rolled to one side, away from where Spud Barker lay heaped.

Haze Birnam, unsteady with a knife in his chest, let his gun fall from his hand. He groaned, sounding like a massive vault door with rusted hinges being forced open.

Spud Barker huddled on his knees head down and rump raised. He looked like he was bowing down to some unseen heathen idol. His arms were crossed in the dirt, pillowing his head, face buried between them.

He panicked when bullets tore up the turf beside him. Rising up to stand on his knees, he frantically waved his arms about, shouting, "Don't! You'll hit *me*!"

A slug creased Spud, causing him to shriek like a mare gored by a longhorn. He flopped facedown and lay flat on the dirt, kicking and sobbing.

Bullets from the same shooter now kicked up dirt from the ground where Sam had landed and would have hit him had he not rolled away an instant earlier.

Chris Latrobe was the shooter, hammering out lead with a gun in each hand. His aim might have been more deadly accurate had he not become entangled with mortally wounded Haze Birnam.

Dying on his feet, Birnam stumbled into Latrobe as the latter tried to nail Sam Heller to the ground with hot lead. Birnam groped for something to hold on to, to keep from falling down into death.

Latrobe's face was a mask of revulsion as he stepped backward to avoid the dying man's lunge. The maddening obstacle kept him from cutting loose on Sam as Latrobe had planned.

Birnam's clutching hands pawed the air, still trying to grab on to Latrobe.

Latrobe batted them away with the guns held in each fist. He finally managed to get clear of Haze Birnam, giving him a shove that sent him toppling earthward. "Die, you son of a—!"

Birnam fell facedown, the force of his own weight driving the knife still deeper into him, to the hilt. He gave a final shuddering spasm as he threw off the last of life.

Latrobe forgot one thing: When he finally got clear of Birnam, he was no longer covered by him.

Sam Heller took advantage of the opening to carefully draw a bead on Latrobe. Shooting accurately with a handgun is difficult when you're on your back, so Sam took pains to make sure he was on target before firing.

He pointed the Navy Colt at Latrobe and squeezed a couple of shots into it.

Two bullet holes appeared on the left side of Latrobe's chest. They were grouped tightly together, each shot a man-killer to the heart.

Chris Latrobe fell hard with a thud that could be heard now that the guns were silent.

Sam rose, standing upright. He stuck the Navy Colt into his belt on his left hip. He swore because the barrel was hot and he could feel it through his denims. "Not as hot as it's going to get for those three Down Yonder," he said to himself, forcing a laugh.

# Four

Sam Heller shucked the mule's leg out of its holster and held it leveled for action. Winchester Model 1866, lever-action repeating rifle with a sawed-off barrel and chopped stock shaped to a pistol grip. It felt good in his hands, *right*.

The heavy artillery, he thought. Still, he hadn't done too badly without it.

Now, though, he was loaded for bear and ready for all comers—

There were none. Birnam, Latrobe, and Palenky were done. Spud Barker had stopped crying and lay where he had fallen, twitching and moaning.

Sam Heller reckoned he'd been luckier than he deserved. If the trio had simply shot him from behind instead of trying to brace him first, he'd be a dead man, his story come to a sudden end.

But they'd wanted to have their fun toying with their intended victim, giving Sam the opening he'd needed to slip the noose.

Still . . .

*Dumb luck, just pure dumb luck saved my skin,* he

marveled to himself. What a fool he'd been to go charging in like a wild bull on a rampage instead of taking proper precautions to stay alive!

He should have come in silent as a cloud shadow, stealthy as a Comanche. But he'd liked the idea of taking Spud Barker in broad daylight in his own town and busting up his bodyguards. The reality was even sweeter.

Dealing out justice to those who deserved it was a heady experience, rich, intoxicating. A man—lawman, especially—could get to liking it too well and that was dangerous. One could grow careless and wrong-headed, character flaws that could bring on a violent and untimely end.

A vital lesson for Sam Heller to remember if he wanted to stay alive to bag his prey of killers, corrupters, and conquerors who believed themselves to be beyond the law . . .

A gray-white haze of gunsmoke now hung in the air, swirling and eddying around Sam as he went to the alley mouth to eye the streets of Weatherford.

He cautiously ducked down and peeked around the corner of the left-hand side of the alley facing the street, looking north toward the Sunrise Café. No bushwhackers in sight. He repeated the process on the right-hand side of the alley: All clear, or so it seemed.

People were there if you knew how to look, Weatherford townsfolk who'd come to see the show of violence, then scrambled for cover when the action got hot.

A hand drew back the curtain of a second-floor window to look out, letting it fall when the hand's owner had seen enough.

Pale ghostly ovals that were faces floated into view

behind smeary windowpanes looking out into the street to see if the killing had stopped or if there was more on tap.

Hunched figures bent almost double ran scrambling for the cover of recessed doorways, side passages, or alcoves with shadows thick enough to hide a man. Others flattened their backs against walls. A couple of tow-headed kids hid under a boardwalk sidewalk.

Somewhere in the middle ground an unseen dog barked, mindlessly yip-yip-yipping away. Even the dogs know to keep their distance, Sam thought.

He'd scanned the street east of the alley but what about west?

Sam went to the opposite end of the alley. He'd been caught napping once this morning and had no intentions of falling for the same trick twice.

The alley's west end opened on unfenced yards, vacant lots, and sprawling empty fields behind the backs of the rows of buildings lining the west side of the street.

Sam had tethered his horse Dusty to a short scraggly mesquite tree behind the block where the café stood. He was more than a little relieved to see that the steel-gray stallion was still there, browsing tufts of green grass.

Dusty lifted up his head and looked at Sam for a moment, then went back to his grazing.

Sam looked west. The town ended here. Beyond the patchwork of lots and fields lay endless prairies.

Stretching west across the vast sprawling flat lay the Hangtree Trail, a dirt road running straight as a ruler across the plains under the Big Sky.

In Weatherford they called it the Weatherford Trail.

Sam Heller toted up the day's score so far, not counting the ones he'd manhandled, like Terrill and Driscoll. He'd cleaned up on all six members of the Chuck Ramsey gang, Chuck Ramsey included; plus Birnam, Latrobe, and Palenky.

Nine dead.

Yet he still hadn't succeeded in obtaining his main objective; namely, getting a line on Loman Vard's whereabouts.

First things first, though. Sam went to Haze Birnam and turned him over on his back, exposing the knife that lay buried deep in his chest. Sam bent down to retrieve it.

He gripped the handle and pulled but the knife fought him, not wanting to come out. Sam stepped on the dead man's shoulder and chest for better leverage. A hard tug and the Green River came free.

Sam wiped the blade clean on a fold of Birnam's shirt and returned it to its belt sheath. Then he went to see about Spud Barker.

Spud had bled a fair amount; he wallowed in a puddle of the red stuff. "I'm hit, I'm hit!" he gasped, sobbing. "I've been shot in the back!" he wailed.

"Serves you right for trying to run away," Sam said.

Spud had been hit in the back, though . . . so to speak. There was something funny about that wound but if Spud was unaware of it Sam was in no hurry to enlighten him; he might be able to work it in his favor.

Spud Barker lay prone on the ground, head tilted upward to keep his face out of the dirt. He blubbered away, fat oily tears leaking from his eyes. His face was wet with the stuff, mixing with the dirt on his face to form a kind of gray-brown clay paste.

Sam hunkered down beside him, eyeing the wound, inspecting the damage but not too closely and most definitely not laying a hand on it. His carefully composed expression was solemn as a church usher's. He gripped Spud's shoulder, shaking it to get the other's attention. Spud Barker's nerves were strained so taut that he cried out at Sam's touch.

"Spud—Spud!"

"H-help me, Heller, help me . . ."

"Nothing I can do for you, you're way beyond my help. You need a doctor—quick!"

"Oww-wow! I can't bear to look at the wound—is it bad?"

"Bad," Sam echoed, "bad."

"Heavens above, you've done for me! This is all your fault!" Spud's tone was accusatory, tinged with hysteria.

"Palenky shot you, not me," Sam said. "If you'd have told me where Vard is earlier I'd have been on my way and you wouldn't have gotten shot at all."

"You used me as a shield, you dirty bas—"

Here between choking sobs, Spud Barker launched into some derogatory remarks about Sam and his parentage.

"Tsk-tsk," Sam said, "you don't want to meet your Maker using language like that."

"Am I—am I going to d-die?" Spud asked, his voice a whispery, breathless hush.

"You might pull through if you get to a doctor in time, before you bleed out."

"What are you waiting for, you damned fool?! Get me to Doc Gisborne. He's got an office here in town . . . I'll tell you how to get there. He'll patch me up; it's not too late yet!"

"First things first, Spud: Where's Loman Vard? Tell me where he is and I'll get you to the doctor in double-quick time. But don't wait too long—each heartbeat is pumping out more of your lifeblood."

Spud Barker took a deep breath before taking the plunge. "All right: Vard's out on the road east of town with most of the gang."

He blurted out the revelation panting, breathless, as if he'd run a marathon.

"Why?" Sam asked.

"A Special job."

"Special job." Those were code words among the gang for a paid killing, Sam knew—murder for hire.

"Vard brought along twelve of the boys," Spud went on.

"Twelve? What's he doing, hiring on for a range war?" Sam said.

Spud shook his head. "A Special job, I told you," he said, voice prickly with irritability.

"How many is he supposed to kill?"

"One man. *One,*" Spud said, holding up a lone index finger by way of underlining his point.

"Who's the target, General Phil Sheridan?" Sam made no attempt to hide his disbelief.

Sheridan was a Union Army war hero now serving as Superintendent of the Western District, otherwise known as Texas. Simply put he was the commanding officer in charge of the postwar Federal military occupation of Texas.

As such he was the most powerful, most hated, and best guarded man in the state.

"Don't waste time while I'm bleeding to death. It would take a lot more, a hell of a lot more than even the likes of Loman Vard and twelve Weatherford pistol-fighters to get Sheridan."

"It's about as serious as whatever cock-and-bull story you're cooking up, Spud. Don't waste what precious time you've got left telling any tall tales."

"That's the hell of it. The truth is so utterly fantastic that nobody will believe a word of it. But I know it's true because of all the money that's flying around the deal," Spud Barker said, greed temporarily banishing fear from his face.

"Here's the naked truth: Vard and the twelve are set east of town, laying in wait for one man—just one—and he's not even a full-grown man at all but some punk kid who's not even got his full growth yet, a Texas young gun named Bill Longley," Spud said with the air of a stage magician pulling a rabbit out of his hat.

"Bill Longley?" Sam Heller said the name out loud, trying it on for size, finding that it rang no bells. "Never heard of him. If you're trying to pull a fast one—"

"Wait! Just wait, hear me out. I never heard of him, either, but somebody has, somebody who's paying Vard big money to make sure Longley doesn't reach Hangtree. Now what do you think of that?"

"You've got my interest, Spud. Keep talking."

"Vard got a telegram the other day. It was from Clinchfield, Texas. Don't know it, huh? Me, neither, so I looked it up. Clinchfield is the capital and county seat of Moraine County on the Blacksnake River.

"The Blacksnake's on the East Texas Gulf Coast. Swamp country, a part of Texas that's more like the Louisiana bayous than anything else. During the war it was a kind of no-man's land or neutral zone where Southerners traded contraband cotton for much-needed medical supplies, firearms, ammunition, and such. There was a big luxury trade in tobacco, brandy, perfume, that sort of thing.

"It's still a smuggler's paradise for luxury goods with no customs duties or excise taxes. No local state or federal taxes. Where there's smugglers there's money, big money. You with me so far, Heller?"

"So far, Spud. So?"

"So Vard got a telegram from Clinchfield few days ago. It was one of his Specials. Again—you know what that means."

"Murder for hire," Sam said.

Spud Barker nodded. "That's Vard's business and his alone. I don't touch it. He wouldn't let me get in on it even if I wanted to, which I don't. I don't fancy a date with the hangman. I knew it was a Special because it was in code, a lot of double talk about Aunt Hattie taking a boat from Shreveport at such and such a time, and can Uncle Lester meet her at Water Oak, and what kind of trunks she'll be carrying, and so on.

"It's a coded message offering a contract for murder. I don't know the code but Vard and his associates do. It's sent out over the regular telegraph wire. That's how I know the message was from Clinchfield, because that part's not in code. The rest I picked up from Vard and the gang. This was a rush job and they were in a big hurry to get it done, so they weren't too particular about talking it up and making the arrangements and all. From what I got this Longley kid is in a big hurry to get to Hangtree for some reason or another.

Something almighty important, a matter of life and death." Spud took a slow, shallow breath.

"The client in Clinchfield is equally determined that this Bill Longley never reaches Hangtree. He hired Vard to make sure that the kid doesn't get there, ever. Longley's supposed to be passing through Weatherford on his way to Hangtree sometime today. Longley's coming from the east along the Hangtree Trail through Weatherford. Vard and the boys made up a welcoming committee to take Longley outside of town."

"They'll kill him," Sam said.

"That's right. There you have it. You want Vard, you'll find him laying for Longley on the trail east of town. Vard and the boys, all twelve of them. Even a bad *hombre* like you might have your hands full tacking Vard and his twelve best guns." Spud laughed, a low mean dirty laugh.

"Of course, I guess a sharpshooter with your skills could pick off Vard from a long way off. Whatever you're going to do, I don't want to know about it. They hang accomplices to murder, too. Vard's not well liked but he's a power in this town and whoever takes him is going to have a whole heap of instant enemies. That's your lookout, Heller. I've done my bit. Now you do your part. Get me to Doc Gisborne's quick and don't spare the horses because I'm feeling mighty poorly."

Spud Barker passed a hand over his face, voice going all quavery. "I feel weak—must be from loss of blood . . . Lord's sake, Heller, get me to the doc while there's still time! I spilled to you, keep your end of the bargain—"

Sam made ready to take his leave. "Thanks, Spud. Getting information out of you is like pulling teeth, but I think I got what I need to know. I can find Vard from what you gave me, I reckon. If not—you'll see me soon and next time it won't go so easy on you."

Storm clouds gathered on Spud Barker's face. Sam started to walk away.

Spud Barker became agitated. "Hey, wait!—where are you going? You can't walk out on me now! You said you'd get me to Doc Gisborne— Y-you can't leave me here to die!"

"I'm not," Sam said.

"B-but you're walking away!"

"I'm leaving, Spud, but you ain't dying."

"I will if I don't get to a doctor!"

"I exaggerated a bit when I said you were hurt bad. You were hit all right but no place fatal. The bullet tagged you in the caboose."

"Huh?— Wha?" Spud Barker did a double take, and he didn't know whether to be relieved or infuriated. What he did was look confused. On him it looked natural.

"In plain English, you got shot in the ass. I reckon there was no missing a target that big. It's a flesh wound and you're bleeding like a stuck pig, but you'll live," Sam said.

"You wouldn't lie to a dying man . . . ?" Spud said falteringly.

"You'll survive—as long as your brains don't leak out. See for yourself if you're not too much of a yellow-belly to take a look," Sam invited.

"Can it be true?" Spud Barker heaved and squirmed, grunting and groaning with each move. He managed at last to raise himself up on his elbows and, under visible strain, looked back over a shoulder.

There was indeed an ugly blue-red bullet hole

piercing his pants and his right buttock, his one and only wound.

"It's true!"

"Uh-huh," Sam agreed without enthusiasm, "and I sure don't envy the doctor with the task of patching you up back there, but that's his lookout. And now enough of this disagreeable subject. We're done, Spud," Sam said with a tone of finality. He started walking away.

Spud wasn't listening. He flopped back down in the dirt, laughing and crying at the same time. "I'm going to live!"

"Not if Vard gets to you before I get to him," Sam Heller said over his shoulder. It took a few seconds to sink in but when it did it got a reaction.

"What did you say?" Spud Barker demanded, startled. "Hey, wait a minute! Come back here, you! Hey wait, wait!"

Sam went to the back of the alley. He paused at the west end of the alley mouth, hesitant to step clear of its shelter and cross the field.

He wanted to make sure no danger lurked in that seemingly innocuous crazy quilt of unfenced backyards with clotheslines stretched out bare of washing, vegetable gardens that had yet to show signs of life, weedy fields, and wide expanses of hard-packed turf flats.

Weatherford had that effect on him. Sinister. It was the kind of town where you expected to find a hostile Indian lurking behind a seedy vine-covered trellis or a disorderly vagrant peering intently into someone's window.

Or maybe that was just how Sam Heller saw it, having narrowly escaped three guns trying to kill him.

He still had the mule's leg in hand. If trouble showed he didn't want to waste time drawing the weapon from its rig.

Dusty was no longer browsing tender green shoots on the tops of nearby bushes. The animal stood facing the back of the Sunrise Café, gazing intently at it. His ears were standing straight up at the top of his head, their pointed tips quivering and swept back.

A window stood at shoulder height to one side of the back door. It was open. The window shade was pulled down. Sam thought he remembered its being raised when he came out before. He'd noted then that the window needed washing and was too dirty to see through.

Sam stood, watched, waited. His line of vision was such that he could see the window but he could not be seen by anyone at the window inside.

At such moments as these he had the terrible patience of the hunter.

The window shade rustled as if being disturbed from inside. Was that a shotgun muzzle he saw nosing its way past the shade?

Sam turned and went back the way he came, through the alley toward the street.

He passed Spud Barker now sitting on the edge of the boardwalk sidewalk, perched so his weight was on his unwounded buttock.

A number of people clustered around him, eager to hear his story of the violent clash that had left three dead.

When they saw Sam they all fell silent.

"As you were," Sam snapped in passing as he climbed

the stairs to the boardwalk sidewalk, closing on the Sunrise Café. Its owner and proprietor, Mikey Costaine, and two of his staffers stood in front of the building, eyeing the damage to the window.

The helpers ducked back inside when they saw Sam Heller coming but not Costaine, a feisty bantamweight with a rooster-tail haircut.

He stepped in front of Sam, barring his way. Veins stood out on his red face, his neck was corded, and his hands were clenched at his sides. He was unarmed and seemingly unfazed by the sight of the mule's leg being toted by Sam, held barrel-down at his side.

"Hold it, you!" Costaine demanded. Sam had already come to a stop to avoid having to run down the man.

"Who's going to pay for the damage?" Costaine said, indicating the empty frame where the window had been. He jabbed the air in front of Sam's chest with a pointing finger, saying, "You, that's who! You're the one who threw Spud Barker out the window. Do you know the trouble I went to getting those glass panes freighted in by overland delivery? What it costs to have the grid framework built and installed? Do you?"

Sam reached into his vest pocket and pulled out the billroll he'd taken earlier from Spud and handed it to the surprised Costaine. "This should cover it."

Costaine opened the roll of bills, thumbing through the greenbacks, their number and denomination smoothing out some of the hard lines in his face.

Getting an idea of how large a sum it was, Costaine quickly folded it in half and stuffed it in one of his front pants pockets before Sam could change his mind and ask for some of it back.

Sam stepped around him and entered the café, Costaine's voice—but not Costaine—following him:

"Where do you think you're going? You're banned from the Sunrise for life, you hear? *Banned!*"

The customers in the café looked at Sam Heller as if they'd seen an open grave, then quickly looked away.

Sam determinedly stalked down the center aisle, his long-legged stride taking him swiftly toward the rear of the building. He straight-armed open a swinging door and entered the kitchen, the door swinging shut behind him.

The space was hot and steamy, confined by tall shelves filled with pots and pans and other cooking utensils. A cook stopped scolding a white-clad helper, both frozen in place as Sam circled around them.

Chubb Driscoll and Vic Terrill, Spud Barker's battered and discredited bodyguards, stood around the back door, waiting and watching for Sam so they could ambush him when he went to his horse.

Terrill stood at the back door, gun in hand. The door was open a few inches and he was peering outside, keeping close watch. Chubb Driscoll was posted at the rear window, holding a shotgun whose barrel rested on the windowsill.

Terrill and Driscoll were so caught up in their surveillance that they were unaware of Sam Heller's presence until he was almost upon them. Sam could have gunned them down right then but he didn't want to shoot them in the back . . . that would have been bad form.

"*Over here!*" Sam shouted, leveling the mule's leg on the two.

Terrill and Driscoll jumped straight up, then fell all over themselves in their haste to react.

Terrill's nerve snapped. He tried to run. He flung open the back door and stood framed in the doorway as Sam levered him with Winchester rounds, ventilating him. Terrill staggered outside and fell facedown.

Chubb Driscoll wrestled with the shotgun whose barrel was sticking through the open window. It was an unwieldy spot and posture and Sam reckoned he could have made a sandwich in the time it took Driscoll to step back, haul the shotgun out of the window, and start to swing it around.

Far enough. Sam put the blast on Driscoll. Driscoll rose up on tiptoes as if somehow that would lessen the impact of the slugs ripping into him.

Muscular reflex—a twitch of the death nerve—caused Driscoll to jerk the shotgun's trigger, loosing a blast that blew a watermelon-sized hole in the back wall.

Driscoll hit the floor so hard he bounced. Not much but it was a true bounce.

Where did Driscoll get the shotgun? Sam wondered. From Costaine? If Sam had known that, he wouldn't have been so quick to pay off on the busted window.

Or maybe not Costaine. Sam couldn't see the proud, feisty little restaurateur knowingly allowing his kitchen to be used as a shooting platform for a couple of ambushers. The shotgun could have been laying around the kitchen, ready to hand. Texans never liked to be too far from a weapon, not even when they were rustling up some chow.

The question of the shotgun's source must go unanswered. Sam considered his account with the Sunrise Café as marked *Paid in Full* and the ledger closed.

A bin full of apples on a countertop caught his eye. He stuffed a couple of them in his vest pockets, a reward for Dusty. The horse's unease about the kitchen had set off alarm bells in Sam's head, tipping him to the presence of the vengeful bushwhackers.

Sam paused for a last look. Chubb Driscoll sure had a lot of blood in him, Sam decided, and it looked like he was spilling a goodly part of it on the kitchen floor.

Sam hoped they could get the mess cleaned up in time for the noonday rush lunch crowd.

He exited by the back door.

# FIVE

A hunted man, like all men, must eat, drink, and rest.

Young Bill Longley was eating and—mostly—drinking in a saloon in Mineral Wells, Texas.

It's midday of the same day Sam Heller hit Weatherford. Bill had skipped Weatherford, detouring around it entirely. Judging by the reception committee waiting for him on the road east of town, he was not likely to find a welcome in that town.

A gang of strangers was massed on the road. They seemed ready to welcome him with open arms. Unfortunately they were holding guns and knives at the time.

Bill saw them before they saw him. He didn't know who they were, but he knew trouble when he saw it. During his relatively short span of time on earth Bill Longley had already seen—and made—more trouble than most men know in a lifetime. More recently in Moraine County on the Texas Gulf Coast a not-so-small private army had done their level best to kill him.

So Bill was already walking soft and peeking around

corners before showing himself by the time he came on Weatherford, Texas.

He'd swung wide to the north where there was more cover, a run of tree-covered hollows and rises.

The Vard gang (for so they were, though unknown to Bill) moved to intercept him, but they'd been too late, save for a couple riders who got too close to him. Too close for them, that is. They found out the hard way that Bill Longley was made for trouble and armed for it, too. He shot two of them out of the saddle making his breakout run.

Bill managed to shake pursuit in the brush. He rode west the long way around Weatherford town and continued his trek. A native Texan, he'd never been in this part of the state before, but he had a keen sense of direction and was able to strike the Hangtree Trail with little difficulty. There wasn't much else out here in this great emptiness.

Besides, the trail stretched directly west out of Weatherford town across the plains. When he hit the trail the town was far distant, out of sight and there was no sign of his pursuers.

Bill rode west, frequently looking back for signs of the gang. The sky was yellow-white, the air still, dead. Not a breath of a breeze. Seemed like heavy weather coming in.

A couple of times he glimpsed a pale brown smudge on the eastern horizon that might have been a dust cloud kicked up by a pack of riders, but he kept out-distancing it and after some hard riding the smudge dropped from sight.

Noon was nearing as Bill Longley came on Mineral Wells in Palo Pinto County west of Weatherford.

Mineral Wells lay midway between Weatherford town and Hangtree.

A flyspeck on the map, Mineral Wells was a loose handful of ramshackle wooden buildings set in the middle of a wide, open flat.

It owed its existence, such as it was, to a rock-bound spring whose mineral-rich waters were thought to have curative powers. They were bottled and marketed in this and neighboring counties.

In postwar Texas times were hard, doctors were few, and not many folks had the money to pay medical bills, so homegrown remedies were popular. Mineral Wells' water had a reputation for being "good for what ails you," allowing the small business to develop. A barnlike structure where the waters were bottled and stored stood beside the spring.

The town proper lay along the trail a hundred yards farther west. It was a one-street town, with a saloon, a general store, and several other shaky establishments. A quiet little place, out in the middle of nowhere, where not much happened apart from just plain folks struggling hard to keep going and make the necessities.

And then young Bill Longley came riding in.

He pulled his horse up, coming to a halt at what passed for the town's main drag.

If he hadn't stopped short he'd have been out of town almost as soon as he'd entered it. Here was a place too small to have its own lawmen. That was all to the good so far as Bill Longley was concerned.

Not much of a town, no, but the saloon drew his gaze like a magnet. Bill eyed it, smacking dry, suncracked lips.

He looked back the way he came, along the trail that stretched east to Weatherford in the next county.

It was empty, not a soul to be seen in that direction under the big sky. No dust cloud in the distance to indicate approaching riders.

Bill stepped down from the saddle, leading his horse by the reins to a watering trough that fronted the street.

He walked with the stiff, slightly bowlegged gait of one who's been on horseback for many hours . . . days.

The trough was filled with plain everyday creek water. Nobody was giving away free mineral water to the horses. Or anybody else.

Bill's horse, a big quick bay with plenty of bottom, was powerfully thirsty. He let the animal have a decent-sized drink but not too much, he didn't want to slow it down by overwatering it. He had to pull up hard on the halter to get the horse's head out of the trough.

The bay looked at him reproachfully with big brown eyes. Bill shrugged, looking sheepish.

"Sorry," he said, "but it's for your own good. Mine, too." He fastened the horse's reins to a hitching post in front of the saloon.

The saloon was a single-story wooden box. It was a warm day, and the front door was wide open, the doorway opening on an inviting cool dimness. The scent of meat cooking on a fire and raw whiskey fumes wafted out of the place, tingling in Bill's nostrils. His stomach rumbled.

Bill Longley wore two guns, both big-caliber six-shooters. He hitched up his gunbelt and stepped inside. Bill was in his late teens, tall, rangy, with a long sharp-featured face, black hair, dark eyes, and a wispy mustache and chin whiskers. Those hard dark eyes of his were as bold and direct as two gun muzzles pointed directly at the beholder.

He'd been doing some hard riding and it showed. Lines of fatigue were carved in his face. He was powdered with trail dust from head to toe. He smelled of man-sweat and horse.

Harry Hoke, owner and proprietor of the saloon, was balding and big eared. He stood behind a bar made of a couple of wooden planks supported by an upright hogshead barrel at either end.

Two men, locals, stood on the other side of the bar drinking their lunch. They glanced over their shoulders to see who had entered.

When they saw Bill they quickly looked away, finding renewed interest in the contents of their cups.

They knew a maverick when they saw one. Bill's youth had nothing to do with it. Young guns were often the most dangerous, being long on nerve and short on pity.

Harry Hoke nodded at Bill, acknowledging his presence with a ready grin. Rowdy youth or not, Hoke needed the business.

Bill stepped up to the bar, standing sideways so he half-faced the entrance and could keep an eye on it.

Now, there were places in Texas where the name of Bill Longley was not unknown. He was blooded, he'd killed his man, more than one, raising plenty of hell along the way.

But Texas is vast and its bad sons legion. Mineral Wells didn't know Bill Longley from Adam. Yet.

Harry Hoke and his two customers knew the type, though.

"What'll it be?" the barkeep asked.

Bill fished a gold coin out of the breast pocket of his shirt, slapping it down on the bar where it rang with a musical chime. "Bottle of whiskey."

"Coming right up, sir," Harry Hoke said, his smile widening. That gold coin rated a "sir" and then some more.

The yellow gold was a spot of brightness in the saloon's dingy gloom. It erased what few last doubts, if any, that the three locals might have had about Bill. No honest youth and damned few grown men in these parts carried that much cash money in their pockets. In gold, no less.

Harry Hoke made haste to fetch a bottle down from a back shelf, setting it on the bar along with a wooden tumbler cup.

Bill reached for them, licking his lips. "Any chance I can get something to eat?"

"I can grill you a side of beef on the cook stove," the barkeep said.

Bill nodded. "Don't overcook it, I like it with the blood dripping. And make it quick."

"Coming right up," Hoke said cheerily.

"I'm in kind of a hurry," Bill added.

On the dodge, Hoke said to himself, as he hastened to comply. Not before scooping up the gold coin and pocketing it, though.

Bill toted bottle and cup to a corner table. He took a gun from his holster and laid it on the tabletop before he sat down facing the door.

Bill held the bottle up to a shaft of sunlight slanting in through a crack between the wallboards. Red whiskey, with a nice bead on it. He knew his whiskey. Like many badmen on the frontier—like many men—he was well on the way toward being a confirmed alcoholic.

A tremor of eagerness went through his hands as, breathing hard, he pulled the cork.

He frowned, disturbed at his reaction. That wasn't so good. A gunman needs steady hands.

Bill took a deep breath, let it out, setting the bottle down. He held his hands out in front of him. Steady, by God! Not a quiver. That was more like it.

Bill filled the cup to the brim, lifted it to his mouth, and tossed it back, drinking deep, draining it to the last. It hit like a mule kick. Bill gave an all over shudder, like a dog throwing off water.

Liquid fire blossomed in his belly, spreading through him, filling him with welcoming warmth.

He refilled the cup, sipping it, drinking it slowly.

On the far side of the room, on a cast-iron stove, Bill's steak was sizzling on the grill. Harry Hoke hovered over it, tending it with a long-handled two-pronged fork. He paused, crossing the floor to set down some items at Bill's table: a basket of bread, knife and fork, oversized red-and-white-checked napkin that was none too clean.

Bill barely took notice.

"You want that steak rare, ain't that right, friend?"

"What I said," Bill told the barkeep.

"That's what you git," Hoke said, whisking back to the stove.

Bill sat brooding, turning his situation over in his mind. Turning the whiskey tumbler around in his hand. He'd raced halfway across Texas in recent days at a breakneck pace on a desperate mission against overwhelming odds.

He was nearly within reach of his goal. "No stopping me now," he muttered under his breath.

The thought that he had stopped himself never occurred to him. He craved food and drink and that's the way it was.

Harry Hoke brought Bill's steak to the table. Bill moved cup and bottle to make room for the plate—moved them, but not too far away. Hoke set it down.

The two men at the bar gulped down their drinks and went out.

"So long, boys," Hoke called to their retreating backs.

The steak was a thick slab of meat whose edges overhung the plate. A slice down the middle revealed a red center, juicy and dripping.

"Rare enough?" Hoke asked.

Bill nodded yes, holding a knife in one hand and fork in the other. The gun was to the right of the plate, ready to hand.

"Anything else you want, just sing out," Harry Hoke said. Bill waved him away. Harry Hoke went to the bar and began wiping it down with a dirty wet towel.

The aroma of hot roasted meat dripping with blood juices rose up into Bill's face, causing his belly to twist up in knots. He'd forgotten how hungry he was. It had been a long time since he'd eaten a real sit-down meal.

He tore into the steak with knife and fork, carving big chunks out of it and wolfing them down. A third of it was gone before he slowed down, the keen edge of his hunger blunted but not yet satisfied.

He washed down the meat with a long, long drink of whiskey.

Noise and motion on the far side of the saloon jolted Bill, and the gun was in his fist quick as winking before he saw that the intruder was some woman entering by the side door on the north side of the shack.

She was heavyset and as old as his mother. Except that his mother was a nice lady and not a whiskey-crib whore. Nothing there worth a second glance, he thought.

The newcomer went to the bar, her walk unsteady. She'd already gotten a start on the day's drinking. She leaned on the bar, resting both meaty forearms on the countertop.

"You're up early, Lurline," the barkeep said.

Lurline was the saloon's in-house whore. She plied her trade in a crib in a shack that slumped against the rear of the saloon. Harry Hoke rented it to her in return for half her earnings; they weren't much.

"Gimme a drink, Harry."

"You buying, Lurline?"

She called him a dirty name. He chuckled, the gold coin in his pocket buoying up what passed for his good nature.

"Just one," he said, "a small one."

He poured her a shot of raw brown whiskey, not the good red stuff he'd sold to Bill. Lurline tossed it back with practiced skill. She set down the shot glass and caught sight of Bill, her small round red eyes glinting in a puffy face framed by a rat's nest of dun-gray hair.

"Hmm, things are picking up around here," she drawled.

"Don't bother the gentleman, Lurline," Harry Hoke said tightly, his smile gone.

"No bother ay-tall." Lurline pushed herself off the bar and hip-swayed her way to Bill's table. She faltered a step when she saw the pistol on the table. There was only one chair at the table and Bill was occupying it.

Lurline stood, hands on hips, looking down at him as she swayed more than slightly. That irked Bill because she was blocking his view of the door.

"Buy me a drink, handsome," Lurline demanded.

Bill got a good look at her. He took another drink, a stiff one. His Southern gentleman's code required him to be polite to women, effort though it sometimes might be. "I'm not looking for company, ma'am," he said.

"Buy me a drink anyway," she said.

"Hey, barkeep!" Bill called.

Harry Hoke came over, not happy. "Don't bother the man, Lurline."

"Set her up one on me," Bill said.

"That's more like it," Lurline said, giving Hoke a sassy so-there look.

"Drink it at the bar," Bill told her.

"Huh! You ain't very friendly, sonny."

"I said, I'm not looking for company, ma'am." Bill gave her a hard look with those gunsight eyes of his. If she'd been less hungover the sight would have chilled her to the bone, but as it was it didn't register.

Harry Hoke took hold of Lurline's upper arm, fingers digging into flabby flesh. "Say thank you to the gentleman and come get your drink, Lurline."

Lurline let Hoke hustle her away across the floor.

"You ought to drink some more yourself, sonny; it might make you more sociable," she said over her shoulder to Bill.

"Ma'am, there's not enough whiskey in the whole wide world to make me that drunk," Bill said.

Harry Hoke barked off a short mirthless laugh.

At the bar he put his mouth close to Lurline's ear and said, low voiced, "Steer clear of that one, Lurline, he ain't funning."

"Huh! Some stuck-up punk kid who thinks a gun makes him a big man?" She spoke loud enough for

Bill to hear her. "He's lucky I didn't slap him down and take his little popgun away from him . . ."

"You'll be lucky if I don't slap *you* down."

"You? I'd like to see you try!" Lurline's brayed laughter was mocking.

Harry Hoke reached under the bar for a billy club he kept handy for handling quarrelsome drunks.

"Shut up and behave before I put you out cold." He spoke pleasantly, his barkeep's mask of smooth impersonal geniality seemingly returned.

That scared Lurline more than his earlier dark menacing looks and hostile tone.

"When you wake up you'll find your ass kicked out of here for good," Hoke said, smiling.

Lurline pulled in her horns. "Where's my drink?" she demanded.

Hoke stowed the billy club in its place. He poured Lurline a modest-sized whiskey. She gripped the tumbler, turning toward Bill and raising the glass in a toasting gesture.

"Bottoms up!"

Bill ignored her.

"You're no gentleman," she accused.

Hoke reached under the bar again.

Lurline drank, setting down her empty cup.

"Better shuffle off to your crib now, Lurline."

"You ain't no gentleman, either," she said self-pityingly.

Bill sat upright, intent, listening. From outside came the sound of fast-approaching hoofbeats.

Lurline heard them, too.

"More company," she said, brightening. "Maybe one of them knows how to treat a lady . . ."

"What good does that do you? You ain't no lady," Harry Hoke said sourly.

The hoofbeats neared, an ever-loudening drumbeat pounding the ground.

The riders pulled up short outside the saloon in a flash of motion and cloud of dust. A horse half-neighed, half-shrieked in agonized protest as a hard-pulled bit cut painfully into its mouth.

Bill Longley rose, filling his hands with guns: the one on the table and another in the holster on his left hip. He counted one—two—no, three riders.

Gunmen. From the band that had tried to take him outside Weatherford, no doubt. Whoever the hell they were.

A pause, then two men came rushing into the saloon.

They had to come one at a time because the door was too narrow to fit more than one person. The first man in was big and burly, the other short and scrawny with red hair and beard.

"That's his horse, Kurt," the little man said.

"I know it, Ginger," said Kurt.

Bill's table was in a dark corner at the back of the room. Coming in out of the daylight into the saloon's gloom, the newcomers failed to see him at first. Their attention was on Harry Hoke and Lurline in the foreground.

Kurt demanded, "Where's the owner of that bay hitched out front—?"

"Here I am," Bill said.

He wasted no time cutting loose. Gunfire flashed in the shadows, lighting up Bill's face. He was grinning.

Kurt's chest was shattered by a row of slugs before

he could pull his gun. He went down. That cleared Bill's firing line on Ginger.

Ginger clawed for his sidegun. He managed to clear leather but before he brought the gun level to shoot, Bill drilled him with lead.

Paralyzed from the shock of being gut shot, Ginger stood frozen in place for an instant. Reflex action and gravity took over. He jackknifed, dropping floorward.

Bill's next shot took off the top of Ginger's head, causing his hat to fly into the air, along with a lot of blood, bone scraps, and gray matter. The hat flew out the door into the street.

Bill advanced, crossing the floor. Kurt was still alive. Gray faced, drowning in the blood filling his punctured lungs, he glared up at Bill, hating, unable to do anything else.

Bill's gun pointed downward, delivering the kill shot.

Circling around the bodies, Bill approached the doorway at an angle to avoid being outlined. Standing against the wall to one side of the portal, he dropped into a crouch, peeking around the edge of the door frame.

There was a big commotion out front. The trio hadn't bothered to tie up their mounts before making their move.

Kurt and Ginger had gone in, leaving the third man to hold the horses. He was a tinhorn-looking dude in a dark suit, white shirt, and fancy gold-colored brocade vest of a type favored by flashy gambling men.

He had his hands full. One held a gun while the other fisted the trailing ends of three sets of reins belonging to their mounts.

Agitated by gunfire, blood, and death the horses

fought to break free. They kicked up plenty of dirt and grit, hazing the street front with a billowing dust cloud.

The tinhorn was jerked from side to side, continually in danger of losing his footing and going under trampling hooves. He cussed the horses to kingdom come, which didn't gentle them down any. The buffeting kept him from seeing inside the saloon.

"Kurt! Ginger! What's going on in there?" he cried.

Bill reached around the door frame and shot him. The tinhorn vented a wordless outcry. The bullet hole blossomed red on his white shirtfront like a crimson carnation. Pretty, but Bill had been aiming for a more lethal result.

The churning horses had yanked the tinhorn to one side, causing the bullet to miss its fatal mark. His fist opened, letting go of the reins, loosing the horses. They ran, scattering.

Bill stepped outside. The tinhorn stood wide legged, swaying, trying to stay on his feet. His free hand was held pressed to his wound, blood streaming between his fingers, staining them red.

He saw Bill. Bill put him down with a couple of center shots. The tinhorn lay sprawled in the dirt, limbs thrashing.

Bill fired again. The thrashing came to a dead halt, along with the tinhorn.

Bill sure admired that gold brocade vest; it was a shame to ruin it. But that's how the deal went down.

Dust kicked up by the horses drifted down to earth, falling like fine brown mist. Bill looked east along the road to Weatherford, unable to sight the rest of the hunting party. The three he'd killed must have been the advance guard. The rest would be along presently, sure enough.

What few townsfolk there were must have gone to ground when the shooting started, for there were none in sight. The three horses had scattered and were long gone.

Too bad, Bill thought, he could have used an extra to provide relief for the bay. He went to his horse. The bay was where Bill had left him, tied to the hitching post. Its walnut-sized brown eyes were wide and rolling and its pointed-tipped ears stood straight up but it was otherwise unharmed.

Bill patted and stroked the animal, gentling it down—which didn't take much. It was an outlaw's mount, no stranger to gunfire and sudden death.

Bill opened the top of one of his saddlebags. In it were some loaded handguns. The guns he'd used during the fight were low on ammunition. Reloading took precious time, especially with cap-and-ball revolvers, even though that was state of the art for the time and place.

Bill always kept several fully loaded guns within reach at all times, a veteran pistol-fighter's tradecraft.

Now he swapped the guns he'd just used for some fresh ones, putting the empties in the saddlebag. He filled both twin holsters and had a third gun in hand.

Harry Hoke peeked around the hogshead bar upright behind which he had taken cover. Lurline stood by the bar, white faced and quivering. She panted for breath like she was running a race.

She screeched when she saw Bill with the gun. *"Oh, lawd, he's gone kill us all!"*

Lurline turned and ran for the side door, bearing down on it full tilt. It looked like she meant to plow straight through it, but at the last instant she flung the door wide open and ran out. She kept on going until she was out of sight.

"Didn't think she had it in her to run that far," Bill mused. It showed what folks could do when they put their minds to it.

He wagged the gun at Harry Hoke crouching behind the barrel. "Come out of there," he said.

The barkeep rose, holding his hands up in the air. "Don't shoot, mister, I got no quarrel with you."

"You can put your hands down," Bill said, sticking the gun in his belt.

"Obliged," Harry Hoke said, lowering his hands to his sides. He stared at the dead men. He puckered his lips and tried to whistle, but only a breath came out. "Lawd-a-mighty, that was some shooting!"

Bill smiled with his lips, dark eyes blazing. "Know them?"

"Never saw them before," Hoke said. After a pause he said, "Lawdy, man! Don't you know who they are?"

"They're part of a bunch that's been dogging me since Weatherford. Why, I don't know," Bill said. But he could guess: *Barbaroux.*

"Thought I'd lost them but they must have picked up the trail," Bill continued. "They've been nipping at my heels ever since."

The barkeep swallowed hard. "You mean—there are more of them?"

"Hell, yes. These *hombres* got ahead of the pack," he said, indicating the corpses. "For all the good it did them."

Bill crossed to his table. The whiskey bottle was about a third full. He drank deep, draining it.

Harry Hoke called to him: "I could use a drink."

"Help yourself, it's your place," Bill said.

"Just letting you know what I'm up to . . . I don't want you to think I'm getting up to any funny business."

"Do as you please."

Harry Hoke took a bottle off the shelf, uncorked it, and took a long pull from the neck. "I must be getting old, I ain't so used to killings as I used to be." He took another drink.

Bill readied himself to leave. He tilted his hat to the angle he liked and squared his shoulders. "That the road to Hangtree?" he asked, indicating the trail.

Harry Hoke nodded. "Due west as the crow flies. You're a fair piece off yet."

"How far?"

"Good half-day's ride yet."

"Give me another bottle of whiskey for the road."

Harry Hoke took down a fresh bottle of the good stuff from the shelf and set it down on the counter. Bill reached into his breast pocket, fishing around for a coin, coming up empty.

The barkeep held up a hand, palm out. "That gold piece you gave me covers it."

"Thanks," Bill said.

"None needed, you paid for it already. You done me and the rest of the folks hereabouts a favor when you gunned those varmints. We got us a bellyful of them Weatherford badmen shooting up the county."

Bill started for the front door.

"Keep your guard up in Hangtree Trail," Harry Hoke called after him. "It's full of outlaws, too."

"I hope so," Bill said.

"How's that again?"

"I'm looking for one particular outlaw. I've come a long way to find him."

"Good luck."

Bill went outside. The locals were still out of sight. He stowed the bottle in a saddlebag and mounted up.

There had been a change in the weather. A wind was rising out of the northwest, blowing scrums of dirt across the ground. It felt good after the dead breathless stillness earlier.

A dust cloud showed in the east.

*They want me dead but they'll have to work at it,* Bill said to himself. *We'll see who lives and who dies!*

Harry Hoke stood in the doorway of the saloon, grinning. "You put Mineral Wells on the map, son!"

Nothing like a bloody shoot-out to spread the fame of a place. The notoriety should be good for Harry Hoke's business, too.

"What's your name, son?"

"Bill Longley."

Harry Hoke nodded. "I'll remember that."

"Everyone will, some of these days!" Bill Longley shouted, riding west, tearing along the trail.

Harry Hoke got busy stripping the dead men of their valuables.

# Six

*"Hellhounds on my trail!"*

In childhood days Bill Longley was haunted by the hellhounds.

Now as a young man, Bill was being hunted by a different kind of hellhounds, one that was trying to take him down and might very well do so.

Bill first encountered the hellhounds when he was a little boy growing up on the family farm in the small town of Evergreen, Texas.

It was on a hot spring night when the Longley family went to a revival meeting featuring Reverend Jenkins Vale.

The Longleys went to church every Sunday, just like everybody else in town. Reverend Jenkins Vale was a traveling preacher, one of that large breed of wayfaring preachers of the Gospel who journeyed most of the year 'round, making the circuit of small towns in the South and West.

Preacher Jenkins Vale was widely held to be "mighty in the ways of the Lord," as Bill's ma put it, and so she believed. Ma Longley was powerful strong for religion,

Daddy Longley less so, and that was a trial to her. Not that Daddy was not religious. He was a God-fearing churchgoing man, but he also liked to drink and smoke with his card-playing cronies, all of which strengthened Ma's devotion to the Word.

On the night of the meeting, Daddy and Ma and Bill and his brothers and sisters piled into a wagon and rode to the field outside town where the meeting would be held. Most of the residents of Evergreen were present. Apart from the good a revival meeting would do preaching the Word and restoring flagged spirits, it was a kind of entertainment in its way, a show, and as such a big event not to be missed.

A small wooden platform for the preacher had been set up at on a rise at one end of the field. A crowd of a hundred and fifty men, women, and children, virtually the entire population of Evergreen and its surroundings, were grouped facing the platform, sitting on blankets spread on the grassy ground.

When Preacher Jenkins Vale stepped up to the platform to open the meeting, little Bill was disappointed. He'd heard so much about the evangelist that he expected a giant of a man eight feet tall with long gray hair and a thick beard, like one of those old-time biblical prophets whose pictures hung on the walls of his Sunday school classroom.

Preacher Jenkins was a decent enough looking fellow, middle aged, of middling height, with a medium-sized build. He wore a dark frock coat, light gray shirt with black ribbon tie knotted in a bow, and gray trousers.

Little Bill Longley was forced to revise his opinion of Preacher Jenkins Vale dramatically upward the moment the evangelist opened his mouth to speak.

What a voice the man had! It was rich, resonant, and rumbling with the Power and the Glory. The voice was a gift, and the preacher used it to the fullest. It was a voice to make believers out of doubters. It had a hypnotic effect, taking those who heard it out of themselves and carrying them away to an otherworldly realm where all that mattered were the eternal truths of Salvation and Damnation.

Vale liked to remind his audience that he preached "the old-time Gospel of hellfire and brimstone." So he did, devoting much of his time to lurid depictions of the temptations of the flesh and the terrible tortures of hell awaiting those who yielded to the devil's lures. Little Bill was too young to understand much of the adult content of which Jenkins Vale spoke, but he thrilled to its passion and conviction.

During a lull in the torrent of words, Preacher Vale made some conversational remarks about the changes in the weather, a sure sign that the deer-hunting season with its simple joys and pleasures would soon be upon them and how much he was looking forward to spending some time outdoors with gun and dog in hopes of—"Lord willing"—bagging some fresh-killed venison for the cooking pot.

This homely note struck a sympathetic chord in the audience, especially among the men, who virtually without exception were dedicated lifelong hunters as their fathers were before them and as their sons were in the process of becoming. A successful hunt meant the difference between a full belly and a meatless meal that left the whole family hungry and craving more.

Jenkins Vale's casual observation was the gateway by

which the hellhounds would invade the imagination of little Bill.

The devil was a hunter, too, Preacher Vale reminded his audience. He called the devil by the familiarity of Old Scratch, conjuring up a word picture of a foxy grandpa type with a pair of nubbins for horns peeking out from under a hat and oddly misshapen boots deformed by the cloven hoofs he had in place of feet.

He further reminded them of the old saw, which held that to mention the adversary by name was to summon him up. Jenkins Vale was rewarded by the sight of many crowd members casting covert glances at their neighbors, or sometimes even an openly hostile and searching scrutiny of those around them, a reaction that seemed to amuse the preacher.

But that foxy grandpa sitting quietly on a nearby blanket might be nothing more or less than a foxy grandpa, the preacher said, for Old Scratch could transform into the likeness of anyone he pleased, be it an old crone, a straitlaced maiden aunt, or fresh-faced young boy. On mention of this last, little Bill had the uncanny feeling that Jenkins Vale was looking directly at him when he said it. He also felt sure that at this mention Ma had cut a quick sidelong at him, looking away just as quickly. Little Bill squirmed, red faced.

Don't be too sure Old Scratch hadn't taken the form of a comely young miss or handsome lad, Preacher Vale cautioned, quoting the passage from Scripture that states, "The Devil hath power to assume a pleasing shape."

That shape need not be human, either, for Scratch could take the form of any living creature, be it a bird of the air, beast of the field, or creature that dwells in the water. No doubt he had a special fondness for snakes, descendants of that serpent who tempted Eve in the Garden. The best defense against the Devil was faith and trust in the power and ultimate triumph of the Lord. The struggle was long and hard though, for Old Scratch was a mighty hunter, the preacher man said, returning to the main theme of his sermon.

"He hunts the biggest of all game: human souls. Just as you or I might trail our quarry by the tracks it leaves, Old Scratch gets on the trail of his human prey by the smell of the sins he or she has committed. For a sin is a stench in the nostrils of the righteous and an offense to the Almighty," said Jenkins Vale.

"A mortal man uses a pack of hunting dogs to sniff out the trail of the beast he seeks. Trust Old Scratch to have himself a pack of hunting dogs unlike anything in the natural world this side of heaven and earth, that unholy brood of relentless, unstoppable, insufferable sin-sniffers, a foul brood of four-legged fiends: *the hellhounds*!"

Hellhounds! The very name sent shivers along little Bill's spine, making his blood run cold. With ever-mounting dread he sat still, rigid, as though the least little motion would call the hellhounds' wrath down on his head.

In fascinated horror, little Bill heard the preacher tell the tale of how the hellhounds came to reside in the Kennels of Chaos amid the Eternal Inferno.

Each hellhound was as big and tall as a pony. Their paws were larger than human hands and equipped with razor-sharp talons, each curved like a crescent moon. Their bones were iron and their hides tough as armor plate. They came in such colors as coal-black, blood-red, bile-green, jaundice-yellow, pumpkin-moon.

Their ears were triangles pressed point-up at the sides of their skulls, and their eyes were burning coals. Gaping maws were fitted with multiple rows of teeth that were little daggers. Their nostrils were complex bundles that could smell out even the smallest sin.

"Once a hellhound gets a whiff of sin, the brood trails that sinner until his or her dying day—and beyond. Other people can't see them, only the sinner. With cruel patience they wait and wait, always there so the sinner can see them but invisible to all others. Pity these poor sinners who can never know a moment's peace. Haunted by the knowledge that when they draw their last breaths, they will find not the peace of the grave but the never-ending torment of a nightmare that's only begun, for death's door leads them only into the bloody-fanged jaws of the hellhounds, to whom they belong now and forever. Amen!" Preacher Vale said breathlessly.

"Think on that before you yield unto temptation and fall into sin, you who stand on the brink of a cliff, hesitating before taking the final plunge from which there is no return, no salvation! Think on that, you weak-willed sons and daughters of Adam and Eve, and repent!"

Preacher Vale continued. "Repent, Repent! For once you fall into the jaws of the hellhounds, it's too late, nothing can save you! Repent!" At this, he triumphantly concluded his sermon, leaving his audience stunned and silent.

Then someone shouted, *"Hallelujah!"*

Another joined in and then another until the crowd

was transformed into a shouting cheering mass, chanting *"Hallelujah, Hallelujah, Hallelujah!"*

Little Bill sat stiff and shocked. A sharp poke in the ribs from Ma broke the spell, bringing the youngster around to a sense of himself and where he was.

Little Bill Longley took up the chant, shouting as loud as he could for as long as he could.

That night back at home in his bunk he fell into a black bottomless pit of sleep, mercifully free of dreams.

The next night the nightmares began. He woke up screaming in the middle of the night. Ma and Pa were quite cross with him. The following night when it happened again he got a whipping.

It happened the next night and the next, hell-hound nightmares, then a whipping. After eight or ten days and nights he got himself under control so he remembered not to scream when he started awake in the dead of night from a dream of burning coal-eyes and razor-sharp teeth that ripped and tore . . .

The screaming stopped, but the nightmares continued for another month before they began to taper off.

Longley mastered his fear of the hellhounds but he never forgot them.


Now running for his life in what might perhaps be the last few hours of his life—minutes, even—Bill Longley found himself tormented by a new breed of hellhound.

The hellhounds of yesteryear were the product of a child's overactive imagination. Today's hellhounds were stark reality, relentless man-hunters who'd been dogging Longley since they first clashed early that morning east of Weatherford.

Bill had managed to thin the bunch, taking down two outside Weatherford and three in Mineral Wells. He didn't know the ultimate fate of the Weatherford duo, but they were definitely out of the hunt. The Mineral Wells trio, he knew, were dead.

The rest of them had stuck close to him ever since Mineral Wells. There were eight of them and they had him pinned and they were gaining on him.

They were hellhounds for damned sure. He'd been thinking of them that way for a long time now as the day wore on. He was aching to turn the tables on them but it simply wasn't in the cards, not yet and not as far as the eye could see. Which was pretty damned far on this sprawling seemingly endless Texan flat.

He toyed with the idea of turning around and coming at them with both guns blazing. It was a loco idea and he knew the pressure must be getting to him. At eight to one that would be a suicide run.

Bill didn't like running; it went against his grain. If he only had himself to consider he might have tried it anyway. But he had to stay alive because he was on a mission bigger than himself.

He hadn't come so far, crossing hundreds of miles from the swampy East Texas Gulf Coast lands to North Central Texas to be stopped when he was so close to his goal.

But the choice might not be his to make. It was now mid-afternoon and the new hellhounds had been in sight of him for some time. Bill calculated that at this rate they'd soon be within shooting distance.

On he raced west on the Hangtree Trail, a trail he had come to passionately hate. Was there no end to it?

A ribbon of dirt road stretching across plains varied by low ridges and shallow hollows, gorges, and tiny rounded hills that seemed like giant ant mounds. Gray clouds hemmed it in from horizon to horizon.

The bay was a fine horse with a big heart, speed, and stamina. But it had been ridden too hard for too long with little real rest. The bay was fading, nearing the end of its endurance.

The hellhounds' mounts were fresh by comparison. They'd only been at the chase for one day only, and not a full day at that!

The pursuers were steadily closing the gap. Two lead riders were less than fifty yards behind and coming fast. The others weren't too far behind them.

On Longley rode. Time passed. He didn't know how much. All too soon crackling noises broke out nearby.

Gunfire!

Bill glanced back. The two lead riders were now within shooting distance, popping away at him with pistols.

Bullets whipped past Bill on all sides with angry thrumming bumblebee noises. His immunity couldn't last forever and didn't.

"*Ahrghh!*" The shot grazed him, leaving its brand on his flesh. He shuddered from the impact of its passage.

"It'll take more than that to stop me," he vowed.

They had more.

Ahead was a low rise. As Bill neared the top a hammer blow slammed his left shoulder, blowing off a chunk of it. The hit knocked him sideways. Bill felt himself going off the saddle, but he was helpless to stop the fall.

He dropped, tumbling to the ground on the far side of the rise. He rolled head over heels, taking a pounding. The turf-covered ground spared him some of the worst of it.

The bay kept right on going, so used to running that it didn't stop.

# SEVEN

The two lead riders who had downed Longley halted at the top of the rise, looking at the body sprawled facedown and motionless.

They were of Loman Vard's Twelve, now reduced to six. Plus Vard made seven.

Hampden Bray was big, thick featured, with a loose oafish mouth. Milt Mills had sleek silver-gray hair with a well-trimmed mustache to match.

"*Haw!* Got him!" Bray crowed.

"*I* got him," Milt Mills said.

"Like hell you did!" Bray got hot fast; money and bragging rights were involved. "My shot brought him down!"

"I want to see what I got," Milt Mills said, starting his horse downhill.

"What I got," Bray insisted, doing the same.

The two halted near Bill Longley's body.

"So that's what all the fuss was about! He don't look like much now," Bray sneered.

"He was good enough to do for Kurt, Ginger, and

Acey-Deucy in Mineral Wells," Milt Mills said, "and they wasn't none of them shot in the back."

"He must have took 'em by surprise."

"He wounded two of ours back in Weatherford and knocked one of them clean out of the chase."

"Beginner's luck," Hampden Bray said. "The chase is over, and I ended it."

"I did!" Mills countered.

Bray gave the other a hard look, Milt Mills returning the stare impassively. Here were two hardcases well schooled in giving hard looks.

It was Hampden Bray who was the first to break eye contact, climbing down from his horse. "What's the kid's name? I forget."

"Longley—Something Longley," Milt Mills said. "Or maybe Longley Something," he added after a pause.

Hampden Bray went to the body as a third rider came downhill. The newcomer, Big Taw, was a hulking brute, a man-mountain riding a dappled gray the size of a quarter horse.

"You got him," Big Taw said, and grinned.

"I sure did!" Hampden Bray said, chest swelling with pride.

"I did," Milt Mills said.

"I don't give a good damn who got him so long as he's got. My tailbone's sore from all that riding," said Big Taw.

"You'd give a damn if it was you who got him," Hampden Bray said.

"Me," Milt Mills said, indicating himself by pointing at himself with his thumb. "I took him."

"Fun's fun but I ain't funning," Milt Mills said.

"The kid probably killed hisself so he wouldn't have to listen to you two jawboning." Big Taw laughed.

Bill Longley lay facedown with his right arm under him and his left stretched out at his side. Hampden Bray went down on one knee beside the body.

He took hold of Bill's left arm at the elbow and roughly rolled him over on his back, saying, "Let's have a look at you, sonny."

Bill had a gun in his right hand pressed against his chest. He'd been playing possum. It took all he could do to keep from crying out from the pain of Bray manhandling his left arm with its wounded shoulder, but it was all worth it for the look on Bray's face when he saw the pistol.

Bill Longley put a bullet in the middle of that face at point-blank range. Bray catapulted backward.

Milt Mill, still in the saddle, drew his gun and fired. The horse sidled and danced, throwing off Mill's aim. Several rounds tore into the ground near Bill.

Bill rose on his side, breath hissing through clenched teeth from the agony that motion wrung from his shoulder wound. He returned fire, tagging Milt Mills in the middle with a couple of rounds.

*"Oww!"* Milt Mills crumpled, dropping his gun. He gripped his saddle horn with both hands to stay on his horse.

Big Taw had already stepped down from the saddle. Gun raised, he rushed Bill from behind. Bill couldn't turn around fast enough to stop him.

Big Taw savagely sent the gun barrel crashing down against the back of Bill's head, sending him rocketing off into darkness.

Big Taw rubbed his lantern jaw thoughtfully as he stood over Bill Longley. "No shooting for you . . . shooting's too easy."

# EIGHT

Loman Vard and the rest of what was left of his band of Twelve, strung out in a loose arc, came on to the east slope of the rise.

They were five: Vard and Narcisco Velez, Ryland Fenton, Duff Toplin, and Dick Stratton.

This was after Longley had been downed and Bray, Mills, and Big Taw had disappeared behind the low wall-like ridge—between eight and ten feet tall—that extended nearly as far as the eye could see.

A fresh outburst of gunfire broke out on the far side of the ridge. It was almost over as soon as it began.

"Now what?" Vard spat sourly. His sharp-featured face showed rattlesnake eyes and a skinny mustache that smacked of the tinhorn. There was a lot of tinhorn in Loman Vard but more of the killer.

"Mebbe they're finishing the kid off," Dick Stratton suggested.

"I counted about a half-dozen shots. It only takes one to shoot somebody in the head," said Vard.

"Somebody got restless, maybe," Stratton said.

"Here comes Milt," said Duff Toplin, suet faced and

heavyset, a sometimes Weatherford deputy marshal. He wore no badge when riding with the Twelve. "He'll tell us what's up."

Milt Mills rode his horse over the top of the ridge, starting down the near slope. He held on to the saddle horn with both hands, the reins trailing near the ground. His head was bowed forward, his hat hiding his face completely.

"He don't look so good," Narcisco Velez said.

Vard took out a long skinny cigar that looked like a brown twig, stuck it between his jaws, and lit up, puffing a rank-smelling cloud of smoke smelling of burned cherries.

Milt Mills came on toward the band, bent almost double over the horse's neck. Somebody hailed him, calling him by name but receiving no response.

His horse advanced at a slow steady pace, closing on the others, its course taking it near Vard.

"Look at Milt's front, it's all blood!" Stratton gasped.

Milt Mills drew abreast of Vard. He would have kept right on going had Duff Toplin not leaned over in his saddle and grabbed the reins of the other's horse, halting it.

"Lord, Milt, what happened?" Toplin demanded.

Milt Mills slowly lifted his head, showing glazed staring eyes in a blue-white face. Whatever those eyes were looking at, it was not of this world.

"I'm dead," he said.

Toplin was so taken aback that he let go of the reins. The horse started forward, going a few paces before Milt Mills fell off.

Dick Stratton dismounted, hunkering down beside the fallen man.

"He's dead now," he announced.

Velez cursed, pulling his gun and spurring his horse up the slope. When he reached the top he saw Big Taw standing over Bill Longley's inert form.

"Longley's taken! . . . alive!" Velez shouted back down to the others, waving to them to come on over.

Bill Longley returned to wakefulness, sputtering, coughing, choking. He lay on the ground, ringed by Vard and the remnants of his band. Duff Toplin stood over Bill, emptied the contents of a canteen into his upturned face.

Bill pawed at the stream of water with his right hand, trying to brush it away.

"Back to the land of the living." Toplin laughed.

"But not for long." Velez grinned, showing a mouthful of gleaming white teeth centered by a gold front tooth.

"Not too soon, either," Ryland Fenton said. They called him "Rile" because of his ornery disposition. It was on display now as he glared down at Bill with murder in his eyes.

"This lowdown dirty son killed blood-kin of mine. Kurt Angle was my cousin. Longley's gonna pay for what he done, pay hard!"

"He killed a lot of good men today," Big Taw said. "Some was friends of mine."

"So what? Acey-Deucy owed me a hundred dollars' gambling debt," Duff Toplin said mournfully. "I'll never see that money now . . ."

"You got your priorities wrong-way around, lawman. People is more important than money," Rile Fenton said.

"Not when it's my money," Toplin hurled back.

Rile Fenton actually felt the same way but he liked to needle Toplin and make him look bad.

"You'll have your fun, boys," Vard promised. "All in due time. Don't rush things."

"Mebbe we better hurry," fretted a worried Dick Stratton, "what with that twister showing."

"It's a long way off, beyond the far rim of the basin. No guarantee it's going to head this way," Loman Vard said.

They were to wind around of the eastern ridge, inside the basin. The ridge was part of an oval ring several miles in diameter. It enclosed the site of a dry lake bottom with walls some ten feet high.

"Mortlake," it was called on maps and surveyors' charts, from the French, "Morte du lac."

They were all wrong, from the French trapper and explorer who first named the site several hundred years earlier to the modern-day, up-to-the-minute Texas locals of Year AD 1867 who called the site "Dead Lake."

The hard-packed ground was shot through with cracks, creating a kind of natural pattern looking like a giant spiderweb. Weeds grew in the cracks. The Vard gang's horses were hitched to gnarled scraggly shrubs that looked like dwarf trees.

In the far distance at the basin's western rim, a vast charcoal-gray cloud bulked over the horizon, blotting out the sun. A narrow gray whirlwind extended like a feeler from the cloud's underside to a point beyond the western rim wall. It spun like a top, whirling, widening, narrowing, then repeating the cycle.

"It's a damned tornedo!" Dick Stratton cried.

"I see it, Dick," Loman Vard said. "What of it?"

"Let's get out of here!"

"It's far away on the other side of the basin, moving north. We're safe here."

"Yeah, hold on to your guts, Strat, if you got any," Rile Fenton said.

But Stratton's fears were not so easily gentled. "Gunning down some punk kid is one thing, but you can't shoot down a twister," he cried.

"You want to run, run. I got me some evening-up to do." Rile Fenton spat down at Bill Longley. "I'm sticking."

"We're all sticking. Everybody sticks," Loman Vard said. "If the twister changes course and starts this way, we can ride clear in plenty of time."

And that was that, the command from their chief. Dick Stratton got a grip on himself, not without effort. "You know I'd never run out on you boys."

"Damned right you won't," Rile Fenton said in that hateful taunting way of his, significantly slapping the side of his holstered gun to underline his point.

"None of that," Vard said. "Strat's sticking. We've got enough dead today without fighting among ourselves."

"Yeah, and there's the mangy cur responsible," Rile Fenton said, indicating Bill Longley.

"When do we go to work on him?"

"Now," Vard said. "Get him on his feet, Top."

Duff Toplin reached down a meaty hand, grabbing a fistful of Bill's shirtfront and hauling him upright. Cloth tore, buttons popped, but enough of the shirt held together to give Toplin a handhold propping Bill up.

Bill Longley had been tagged twice: creased on the right side, which wasn't too bad, and hit around in the left shoulder. Blood darkly stained much of his shirt on the left side. He had little use of his left arm but he could still wriggle his fingers. Cold comfort that, since he could see his finish drawing near. All he could do was keep his sand and look for a break so he could make a move. If he could only get hold of a gun!

Loman Vard threw away a half-smoked long skinny cigar and lit up a fresh one.

Big Taw stepped away from a cloud of cigar smoke. "*Phaugh!* That smells like the devil's hindquarters!"

"Tastes bad, too."

"Then why do you smoke it?"

"To bother folks."

"I believe it." Big Taw chuckled. "It's working."

Loman Vard went to Bill Longley and blew smoke in his face. Bill was seized by a coughing fit. The cigar's glowing dot tip was reflected as twin orange-red sparks in the pupils of Vard's eyes. His eyeballs were yellow like ancient decaying ivory. Below each eye was a triangular wedge of flesh with the tip pointing downward: snake eyes.

"Bill Longley . . . I never heard of you," Vard said, breaking a long silence. "You can shoot, I'll give you that. But so what? Texas is filled with young red-hots who can shoot. More coming up every day to replace the ones who couldn't shoot as good as they thought they could. What makes you so special that my good friend Commander Rufus Barbaroux wants you dead and will pay good money to get it done?"

"Try and find out," Bill Longley challenged.

"I will," Loman Vard said. "Have no doubts about that, and don't think I won't enjoy it. You cost me a lot of good men today. Barbaroux's big money can't make up for that. You'll beg to tell me before long. When I'm done the men will have their fun. Then I'll cut off your head and send it in a keg of whiskey to Barbaroux. He'll like that. Hell, he'll probably drink it."

"I hope he chokes on it," Bill said. He summoned up what he had—which wasn't much—and tried to hang a hard right fist on Vard's chin.

"None of that, you!" Toplin said, his big arm easily blocking the blow. He shook Bill till his bones rattled.

Vard laughed. "It's good you've still got some fight left in you because you've got to last a while."

He told Toplin, "Make it last, I don't want the show over too soon. Soften him up first, Top. He makes out like he can take it, but it could be all front. Let's find out. But make sure he's able to talk because there's a few questions I want to ask him."

"I know what to do," Toplin said.

Vard nodded. Rile Fenton had been standing off to the side waiting for Vard to finish talking. Vard didn't like to be interrupted. Now he saw his opportunity.

"Let me take first crack at the kid, Vard. It's only what's right and proper. What the hell, he killed cousin Kurt."

Vard shook his head. "You'll get your turn later. Toplin's got a sure hand in these sort of things. He's cracked plenty of prisoners at Finn's jail and made them open up and spill their guts."

"He put plenty of them in the graveyard and more in the hospital. The mayor was complaining to Marshal Finn that Top busted up so many jailbirds that they can't get a decent-sized convict work gang together to tend to repairs around town."

Rile Fenton had little liking for anyone who was not Rile Fenton, and sometimes when he saw himself in the mirror he experienced a profound loathing for the man scowling back at him in the looking glass. But he disliked all others far more.

"Get to it, Top," Vard said.

"Right, boss."

Vard was done talking. He went to check on the horses.

Fenton seethed with the urge to lay into Longley, giving him a beating he'd remember for the rest of his life, which wouldn't be much longer. Fenton burned at the way Vard had cut him off on the matter of who had the right to lay into Longley first.

Toplin got to work on Longley, frog-marching him off to one side where there was room enough to knock him around. The rest of the outfit gathered around to watch the fun.

Vard and Big Taw stood over by the horses. Big Taw's quarter horse had a stone caught in its iron shoe. Vard removed the stone, using a picklike attachment on his pocketknife.

"That Longley kid sure turned out to be quite a handful," Big Taw said.

Vard agreed. "If I'd known how much of a handful I'd have doubled the fee."

"You still can . . . why don't you?"

"Barbaroux warned that Longley was dangerous, authorized me to use how ever many men I needed. I thought the Twelve would be enough . . ."

"Half our men gone, burned down by one punk kid . . ."

"Nobody has to know the details. We can cover that up."

"But there's no hiding we're six men short."

"No. Our troubles are just beginning, Taw. Having

twelve deadly guns on call all the time gave us the whip hand in our dealings with Barker, the marshal, the mayor, and all our other so-called friends. They won't be so friendly now that our firepower is cut in half."

"There's plenty of guns for hire, if you've got the money," Big Taw said.

"It may have to come to that," Vard answered. He hadn't missed the too-casual way Big Taw had mentioned money.

Vard had money, lots of it, hidden in a place that only he could find. The prospect of spending a good part of it to recruit new shooters was unappealing. There was a time factor involved, too. He needed those new men fast. When Vard's enemies found out he was running a shortage of killers, they'd be tempted to strike, while the iron was hot. Vard had many enemies.

He wasn't so sure about his friends, either.

Yes, he had plenty of money hidden away. Then there was the money from Barbaroux for the Longley job. Five thousand dollars, a tidy sum. He was carrying two thousand of it on him right now for emergency money, like buying his way out of an arrest, bribing a politician, or what have you. Not so tidy a sum if he paid the rest of the gang their share. According to the articles of the outfit, if any of the Twelve was killed on duty, his share would be divided among the surviving members.

Numbers: Six men dead meant six extra payout shares for the Longley job to be divided among the six surviving members. Plus him, Vard, made seven. Seven men in all. Six plus seven made thirteen. An ominous number. How many steps to the gallows? Thirteen?

Vard liked the number one better, much better. As,

Looking Out for Number One himself, Loman Vard. No splitting the loot that way!

He wondered if Big Taw had come to the same conclusion. Taw might be as big as an ox but that didn't mean he was as dumb as one. Vard had an advantage, though. He knew where the money was, the money Barbaroux had paid for Bill Longley's murder plus the money Vard had squirreled away since coming to Weatherford.

Big Taw had to take Vard alive to get the money, but Vard labored under no such compulsion where Big Taw was concerned. Another advantage for Vard. Vard's best bet would be to team up with Big Taw, make a deal with him to kill the last six members of the Twelve.

He would have to act fast because the best time to kill the rest of the gang was when they were still well outside Weatherford. Nobody would miss the likes of Rile Fenton, Velez, and the others. There might be some fuss about Duff Toplin because he was a lawman, one of Finn's deputies, but Vard would make it look like Toplin had been killed trying to arrest the gang members. Toplin would get a hero's funeral.

Big Taw would get his when the others were safely dead. Loman Vard would clear out of Weatherford, clear out of Texas completely, if it came to that. Nothing was keeping him here. California seemed like the place to be, from all he'd had heard about it. He could live very well in San Francisco.

The sooner he finished his business here, the better.

# NINE

Duff Toplin went to work on Longley while the others watched. Bill was already shaky from having been shot off his horse, knocked out by Big Taw, and being given a preliminary roughing up by Toplin as a kind of warm-up for the real beating that was coming.

Toplin had a fistful of Bill's shirtfront by which he held him upright and at arm's length. He and Bill stood face to face, though of course towering Top had to lean far forward to bring his face level with Longley's. Bill was tall for a youngster his own age; he stood tall in the company of a group of full-grown adult males as he did now. Toplin was taller still, though, looming over him.

Toplin was laughing and joking with some of the others when Bill struck first, catching Toplin unawares with a looping right hook over Top's brawny arm that was holding him up. Or maybe Bill hadn't caught him unawares after all. Toplin shrugged off the blow unfazed, his head hardly recoiling more than a few inches from the hit.

"Was that a punch? Or was it a fly buzzing 'round

my head?" Toplin smacked his lips, grinning hugely. "What I do to flies—I swat 'em. Here, try some of mine—"

Toplin held Bill up with his right hand. He cracked Bill across the side of his face with his left hand. This was no slap, it was an open-handed strike, a brutal blow. Toplin's hand was cupped to amplify the impact.

Bill shuddered like a struck gong. A violent shock ripped through him from the top of his head to the soles of his feet, rebounding off the ground and rocketing upward to explode through the crown of his skull.

Bill's aching bones were still vibrating when Toplin rocked him with another one, this time on the opposite side of his face, hitting him with a backhand.

A succession of such blows followed, coming hard and fast, slamming Bill's head this way and that, a booming slap with a meaty cupped palm, followed by a blistering backhand; forehand, backhand, forehand, backhand—

Sweat ran off Toplin's low brow into his eyes, stinging them. He pressed his forehead into the crook of an elbow, wiping the sweat off there, only to have it instantly replaced by a fresh layer of the stuff.

"Whew! Beating this boy is hard work, I'll tell you," he said, looking up, grinning loosely.

"I'll spell you if you're tired," Rile Fenton said, rising from the rock on which he'd been sitting.

"Who's tired?" Duff Toplin said quickly. "I'm just giving this pup the beating he deserves. He come a long way to git whomped by me and I aim to make sure he ain't disappointed. Nothing wrong with a good healthy sweat," he added.

"You must not be able to smell you."

"You ain't no lily of the valley yourself, Rile Fenton."

Longley couldn't breathe through his nose; it was stuffed full of blood. The taste of it was in his mouth, a coppery metallic tang.

Toplin moved toward Bill. Bill blew a mess of blood into Toplin's face, splattering it with a misty spray of blood droplets.

Toplin used his bandana to wipe his face. "That don't bother me one little bit, sonny. Reckon I'll have plenty more of your blood on me before we're done here."

Toplin tore into Bill again, more savagely than ever. He switched hands, alternating from right to left and back again because he always needed to use one hand to keep Bill on his feet. Bill was too weak and dazed to stand by himself.

The beating was knocking the sense out of Bill's head, making him unable to think straight.

Toplin lowered a burly shoulder, piledriving a hard left into Bill's belly. Bill jackknifed, doubling up. His shirt tore loose from where Toplin was holding it, leaving the bruiser with a fistful of shredded cloth. The force of the blow knocked Bill backward a man's length. His feet got tangled up and he fell but that was all right, he couldn't have stayed on his feet anyway. Loman Vard moved in for a closer look, smoking one of his brown twig-looking cigars. Little lights that were reflections of the cigar's orange tip danced in Vard's dark pupils.

Cruel laughter and nasty remarks sounded from others in the band but Bill couldn't make them out, overpowered as they were from the roaring swell of fading consciousness.

Bill struggled to his hands and knees, head hanging down, blood dripping from his nose and mouth.

Toplin stood over him, rubbing skinned knuckles. "Not so sassy now, are you, sonny boy?"

Bill hawked up a mouthful of blood and spat it on Toplin's boots.

"No problem, I'll just wipe it off," Toplin said. He kicked Bill in the middle with the top of his boot, lifting Bill up in the air so he came crashing down on his side. Bill lay there, legs together, knees bent.

Rile Fenton pushed forward, crowding in on Toplin. "Let me have some of that while there's still something left to have. I got it coming. That pup owes me a blood debt for killing Cousin Kurt."

"Let him have a go, Top," Vard said. Toplin shrugged, stepped aside.

Fenton pulled his belt knife from the sheath. It was a skinning knife, used for dressing and cleaning deer carcasses.

"Damn it, Fenton," Vard said.

"I ain't gonna cut him up too bad, boss, not on this go-round," Fenton said quickly. "Just whittle on him some so he comes around and don't pass out on us."

"All right," Vard said, "but walk soft, Rile. We don't want this to end too soon and I know all of us, me and the boys, we'll take it poorly if Longley gets his throat cut or bleeds out before he's had a chance to hear from each and every one of us."

In reality Loman Vard didn't want the torture game to end too soon because he needed the time to think of a foolproof way to rope in Big Taw on his plan to kill off the gang. His brain was working furiously to come up with something.

Rile Fenton, knife in hand, stood over Bill. He leaned over, grabbed a handful of Bill's sweat-soaked hair, and hauled upward on it, saying happily, "On your knees, boy!"

Dick Stratton and Narcisco Velez exchanged wary glances, as if saying to each other, *What is Rile Fenton up to now?*

Some of the others looked on uneasily. Torture and murder were fun and games, but there were some lines that shouldn't be crossed, not even by outlaws and killers.

Bill Longley grimaced, neck cording from the painful pressure of Fenton pulling his hair by the roots to force him to rise up.

Breath hissing through clenched teeth, he somehow managed to get his legs under him and rose till he was indeed standing.

Rile Fenton lovingly brandished the knife in front of Bill's face, making a few near-passes at Bill's face and tautly straining neck.

"This here's a skinning knife, boy," Fenton said. "I'm gonna skin you alive."

Bill's right hand thrust upward, grabbing Rile Fenton between the legs and holding on tight. He pulled and twisted as hard as he could.

Rile Fenton shrieked madly in pain. Twisting and whooping like he was going to jump out of his skin, he raised the knife to stab Bill.

A shot sounded from somewhere in the near distance.

Rile Fenton was pierced by a high-velocity slug to the chest.

Blood splattered Bill's face, neck, and shoulders like stinging red hail.

Loman Vard and his band went into action, slapping leather and filling their fists with six-guns, crouching low and turning this way and that in an attempt to see where the shooter or shooters were.

Another shot sounded—

# TEN

Sam Heller was up on the east rim, shooting down into the basin of Dead Lake. He had been dogging Loman Vard and his band for most of the day. He'd missed them on the road east of Weatherford town. He'd circled around from the south while they were on the north side of the trail racing west in pursuit of Bill Longley.

Looking beyond, Sam saw the whirling twister at the far side of the basin. That gave him pause. A tornedo was not to be taken lightly. Sam took some reassurance from the fact that the vortex column was tracking north.

Still a twister was anything but predictable. It could alter its course at the drop of a hat and come surging east toward the basin.

Sam had a more immediate problem at hand, though. Loman Vard was at the top of Sam's personal Wanted list, and he wanted Vard alive. Vard had answers to mysteries that had been haunting Sam for months.

Sam planned to bag Vard by shooting his legs out

from under him. That should slow him down! With Vard pinned, Sam would have a free hand to deal with the rest of the gang. Them, he didn't need alive. Quite the contrary.

Down below Duff Toplin was batting around the captive while the others stood around watching and laughing.

So much the better; it would be easier to take them when they were preoccupied.

Now Toplin made way for Rile Fenton. Fenton loomed over Longley, menacing him with a knife. Things were fast getting out of hand, Sam thought.

Time to get to it.

Then Bill Longley thrust a clawlike hand into Rile Fenton's crotch, clutching, twisting, and tearing.

Fenton's agonized scream made some of the gang's horses jump. And a few of the men, too.

Fenton's knife hand was upraised to strike down Bill. Sam shot him.

*That puts him out of his misery,* Sam said to himself.

The gang was electrified by the mystery gunfire, hauling out their guns, trying to look every which way at once to see where the shot came from. Sam swung the rifle toward Vard to pin him down next. Big Taw stood between Vard and Sam's rifle, blocking the line of fire.

Loman Vard caught on quick. He knew there was only one place the shooting could be coming from: "Up there, there on the ridge—shoot!" he cried.

Big Taw was huge, taking up a lot of landscape. He unknowingly provided a lot of cover for Loman Vard, who was ducking behind him.

But that worked two ways. He also blocked Vard from getting a shot at Sam. Not that Sam was showing much of himself to shoot at, firing as he was from a prone position with head and rifle protruding above the rim.

Dick Stratton went into a funk under fire, losing his nerve. He broke and ran for the horses.

Vard caught sight of him in the corner of his eye. Keeping under cover out of Sam's line of fire, Vard carefully took aim and shot Stratton in the back. Dick Stratton threw up his arms and cried out, stumbled, and fell. No further signs of motion were seen from him, no further signs of life.

Big Taw fisted a big-caliber pistol as he craned for a shot at the rifleman. Sam shot him, drilling him square in the center of his blocky torso. Big Taw lurched, staying on his feet. Sam put another round into him.

Big Taw remained upright.

Velez and Toplin blasted away at the ridgetop in Sam's general direction. Some shots came close, kicking up dirt near Sam's face. He slitted his eyes against the grit.

Amazingly Big Taw was still standing. That irked Sam, who shot him again. Big Taw finally went down, blindly firing his gun into the air before crumpling into a heap.

Sam had a split-second to choose between Vard and the kid: Who lives and who dies?

"Oh, hell!" Sam said, making a choice:

He shot Toplin.

It was a rough shot because his sightlines on Toplin were minimal, so he was only able to wing him, clipping him in the side.

Toplin howled when he was hit and started dancing around like a crazy man, hopping first on one leg, then the other, never both at the same time. It would have been comical if it weren't so grotesque. Bill grabbed Toplin's gun.

"*Vard!*" Bill yelled. He wanted Vard to know who was taking him down.

Meanwhile, Velez opened fire at Sam, missed. Sam shot at Velez, not missing, putting a bullet right between Velez's eyes.

Bill's gun, that is, the one he'd taken from Toplin, was empty. He didn't have much left, either. Exhausted, played out, he slumped to the ground.

Toplin continued to weave around, doubling loops in a figure-eight pattern. He vented shrill staccato cries like the yipping of a small dog. That was the last straw for Sam, who silenced the other with a well-placed shot.

On the far side of Dead Lake basin the twister moved on to the north and away.

# Eleven

Sam went down into the basin, rifle in hand. He was not one to leave things to chance, especially not this day when he'd barely survived such a scrape as he'd had earlier in Weatherford.

First he made sure that all the fallen were really dead. Loman Vard he checked first. He lay on his back, eyes open and staring. An expression of rage and disbelief marked his face as if he couldn't believe he'd been shot dead.

"Takes his secrets to the grave," Sam murmured. Too bad, but that's the way the deal went down. Sam had admired Longley's nerve and had decided to give him a break. By shooting Toplin before he could gun the kid, Sam opened the way for Longley to kill Vard. Sam shrugged.

Sam went the rounds of the rest of the gang but they were all dead gone. The kid was another story. Bill Longley lay where he'd fallen after blasting Vard, Tilson's gun still in hand. Sam took it from Bill's unresisting grip.

It was empty. He tossed the gun away. Bill stirred, moaning. Still alive . . .

Good, he might have some answers. Sam was powerfully interested to learn what brought Loman Vard and the kid together. Vard had been out to kill him, but why?

Sam went down on one knee beside Bill. Bill looked like hell. He'd been shot twice, fallen off a horse, been beaten and kicked.

He'd taken his hardest hit with the shoulder wound. It had bled plenty, soaking through much of his shirt.

Longley needed patching up but he was in no danger of bleeding out yet. He was breathing regularly and his pulse was steady if not overly strong.

One eye was swollen almost shut and the other was slitted open. It was watching Sam.

"Still with us, huh?"

"Who're you?" Bill asked through smashed, swollen lips.

"Your guardian angel, looks like," Sam said.

"I don't see any wings on you . . ."

"You ain't likely to be wearing any, either."

"That's okay . . . I'm in no hurry."

"Not ever, I mean."

"That's okay, too . . . you the shooter?"

"That's right."

"Why?"

"I didn't like Vard," Sam said.

Bill Longley nodded slightly, as though that made perfect sense.

"Vard's dead?" he asked.

"You did for him," Sam said.

"Good . . . The others?"

"They're dead, too."

"A clean sweep? Better still."

"Why was Vard after you?" Sam asked.

"Can't talk—mouth dry," Bill said after a pause.

Sure, Sam thought sardonically. Longley could talk until Sam asked him a question he wanted to know the answer to.

"I'll get you water," Sam said. "I'm going to get my horse, then I'll be back. Sit tight."

"Nothing else I can do," said Bill.

Sam rose, brushing dust off the knees of his jeans with his palms.

"Hey," Longley said.

Sam halted, waiting.

"You're a Yank," Bill said. It was not a question.

"Yup. That rankles in your craw." Sam's remark was not a question, either.

"I can live with it."

"Mighty big of you."

"I think so."

Sam went off, shaking his head, a sour smile playing on his lips. He climbed the easy slope of the rim wall and went down the other side. He went to his horse by the stream, mounted up, and rode back to Bill Longley in Dead Lake basin.

He tethered the animal and crossed to the youth. A folded blanket under the back of Bill's head raised it clear of the ground.

"Water . . ." Bill croaked from between cracked, parched lips.

"I'll check your wounds first." Sam wanted to make sure the other wasn't gut-shot. He didn't seem to be but best to be certain. A drink of water was bad for a gut-shot victim. Yet if Longley were gut-shot there was a good chance he'd die before getting somewhere where he could get proper medical treatment . . .

Bill's shirtfront was ripped, torn open. Sam used a pocketknife to cut away the cloth from the shoulder wound. There was a bullet hole in his upper left shoulder, an ugly thing that was a puckered hole thick with coagulated red-black blood.

"Lucky . . . looks like the round missed the bone and went clear through," Sam said.

"Lucky . . . that's me," Bill said, sarcastic-like. "Takes more than that mangy bunch to do for Bill Longley."

Sam cut away the rest of Bill's shirt, baring him from the waist up. The youth was lean with a long ropy torso. There was no fat on him and hardly much meat. Ribs were outlined against the skin.

His flesh was piebald with ugly purple-brown-yellow bruises sustained both from his fall from his horse and the beating from Vard's gang. A long finger-wide furrow along the ribs on the right side marked where a slug had creased him.

Bill gasped as Sam's fingers probed the area adjacent to the wound. "You're damned rough!" His face was pale under his tan and beaded with cold sweat.

"Checking for any cracks or breaks—can't find any, which is all to the good," Sam said. He unknotted his bandana, folding it into a square, and wetted it with water from his canteen. He wet Bill's smashed lips with it, got an arm under the back of Bill's head tilting it upward so the other could drink.

Sam held the canteen spout to Bill's mouth. "Easy— a little at a time."

Bill got some water down his throat. "More."

Sam upraised the canteen and Bill drank deeper.

"That's enough for now, got to get you patched up," Sam said.

He went back to the doctoring. He soaked his bandana with water and used it to clean the wounds, starting with the shoulder first. Bill Longley took it as stoically as he could, but an occasional moan escaped him.

Sam said, "There could be fragments in the wound. You'll have to have it looked at by a real doctor. They've got a good one in Hangtree, Doc Ferguson."

Bill stirred, restless and heaving not with pain but unease. "Hangtree—how close?"

"A couple hours' ride for a healthy man but that's not you. You're not going anywhere for a while lest the wound open up and start bleeding again. That's the last thing you need."

Sam had a spare shirt in one of his saddlebags. He used his knife to cut it up into strips and squares. "Make-shift bandages but they'll do . . . they'll have to," he said.

Sam fished a metal flask out of a hip pocket, unscrewing its chain-fastened cap. Potent alcohol fumes laced the air.

Bill Longley sniffed, his good eye glinting. "Whiskey! Let's have a taste."

"Later, maybe, if there's any left. I need it now to wash out the wounds so they don't get infected. Particularly the shoulder," Sam said.

"Don't be stingy, man, I've got a full bottle in my saddlebag."

"Oh? Where's your horse?"

"The big bay, you can't miss it."

Sam eyed the row of tethered horses. "I don't see it."

"Damn! He ran off when I was shot," Bill said, crestfallen.

"You've got your pick of the gang's horses for a replacement."

"Sure, but no whiskey."

"Uh-huh. Well, let's get to it." Sam held a twig in front of Bill's face. "Here, take it."

"What for?"

"Bite down on it; it'll help fight the pain."

"I don't need it," Bill said, waving it away with his good right hand.

"Think not? The whizz'll burn like fire."

"Do your worst, Yank."

"Brace yourself—this'll hurt," Sam said, not without a certain zest. He carefully poured some whiskey directly onto the raw bloody shoulder wound. Bill Longley gurgled his agony in the back of his throat, held back by clenched teeth. Breath hissed out from him like steam from a boiling kettle.

"You all right?" Sam asked. Bill nodded tightly.

More whiskey went to wet down a thick folded oblong of cloth that would serve as a bandage. It was long enough to drape over the top of Bill's shoulder, covering the bullet's entry and exit holes.

"Hold on, this won't be any fun," Sam warned.

"Hard to believe . . . it's been such great sport till now," Bill said, grimacing.

Sam pressed the cloth in place, covering the wound. Long thin strips of cloth tied over and under Bill's shoulder and underarm held the bandage in place.

Bill Longley was stone still throughout the procedure. When it was done his knotted muscles went slack with relief.

Sam checked the knotted bindings and found them good. He eased Bill's head down on the pillowed blanket. For an instant he thought the other had fainted, but there was Bill's one good slitted eye glaring up at him.

"This rig should hold all right, so long as you don't work it too hard," Sam said.

"What a waste of good whiskey," Bill said.

"You never had an infected wound go bad on you or you'd be singing a different tune," Sam answered.

Bill sank back down to the mass of leafy branches and boughs that served him as a bed. "How bad are they? My wounds, I mean."

"You'll live," Sam said. "Most likely," he added.

"Most likely? That's a hell of a way to put it, Doc," said Bill.

"I'm no doctor," Sam said, "and I'm not in the business of writing guarantees, either. You're young and strong and with any luck you should pull through."

"I will—I got things to do."

"Such as?"

"That's my business," Bill said, smiling grimly.

"Something to do with why Vard was chasing you?"

"Ordinarily I hold no truck with snoops, definitely not Yankee snoops, but since you saved my bacon I'll just say that I'll mind my business and you tend to yours."

"Fair enough," Sam said.

# TWELVE

With shadows falling Sam Heller made camp in the basin. Sam set up the site near where the Vard gang had tied up their horses and upwind from the dead men. The corpses already stank of death. Sam camped where the air was fresh and clean. Light winds from the west helped keep it that way.

The storm had broken up and gone away as suddenly as it began, taking with it the oppressive air pressure and stifling humidity. The air was light and cool. It proved anew the truth of the old saying: If you don't like the weather in Texas, just wait fifteen minutes.

Longley was resting as comfortably as his wounds allowed, which meant not too comfortably at all. He was in no condition to be moved this night and no shape to do much more than sit up in the bed of boughs where he was nesting.

Sam decided it was a good time to do some snooping, as Bill had accused him earlier of doing. There was truth in his words. He had been snooping, digging for information. Every man-hunter was a kind of snoop, sticking his nose in other folks' business. The same could be said of every hunter.

Sam's first priority was to search the body of Loman Vard. Sam's searching fingers worked deftly around the gore as he turned Vard's suit pockets inside out, at first yielding little. Initial disappointment was offset by the discovery in an inside breast pocket of Vard's jacket of an oblong waterproof billfold-type pinseal document carrier thick with hundred-dollar bills— twenty in all—two thousand dollars in new bills.

Sam experienced a rising of the hallucinatory excitement that inevitably accompanies the finding of free money. Sam reasoned that his responsibilities as an undercover investigator were in no way compromised by his finding the money. Part of his undercover role as a bounty hunter required him to collect bounties on the heads of the Wanted outlaws he killed. He couldn't refuse the money or try to return it; such out-of-character actions would expose his role as a covert investigator.

Confiscating Vard's cash fell into the same category, Sam believed with all his heart. If this was money stolen from a bank or bilked from a welfare fund collected for widows and orphans, he would have found some way to return it without compromising himself. That would be stealing. That was where he drew the line.

But Loman Vard's cash was murder money and Sam felt no hesitation in confiscating it. Sam had been probing Vard's clandestine activities for several months without being able to put together the final piece of the puzzle. Spud Barker had supplied that final piece today when he identified Loman Vard's Special line as murder for hire.

What turned his supposition from theory into fact was the no-less-exciting discovery of a telegram that lay folded and hidden in a secret pocket in the lining of the document holder containing the money.

Spud Barker had told how Vard used the telegraph company's national facilities as a vehicle for his murder-for-hire operation. It all made sense to Sam now. Even though lacking the code key used for communicating covertly, Sam had a pretty good idea of what the telegram was all about.

Sam didn't know if the two thousand dollars on Vard's person was a partial payment or payment in full. From the size of the operation and number of men involved, Sam thought it was partial payment: Vard was likely skimming the cream to have some ready money for any unforeseen expenses.

The telegram was a vital clue, a storehouse of information that could unlock a national murder-for-hire ring with extensive dealings in Texas and the West. The code breakers in the Department of the Army's secret Black Bureau cryptography group would really go to town on this message.

Too bad the telegram contained no clue as to why it was so important that Bill Longley not reach Hangtree alive. But he was alive and Sam had him, so that promising avenue of exploration was still very much open.

Sam went to check on Bill, who lay uneasy and restless under some blankets on his bed of boughs. Grinding pain left Bill irritable and short tempered— or maybe he was always like that, Sam didn't know him well enough to say.

Sam left Bill a full canteen and resumed his chores, tending to his horse Dusty first.

He unsaddled the animal and gave him a good rubdown with handfuls of weeds clutched in his big fists.

The saddle contained a secret compartment concealed between a pair of leather flaps. What looked like extensive stitching and binding was merely for show, the overlaid flaps coming apart when tiny interior metal snaps holding them closed were unfastened.

Longley had no clear sightlines on Sam or Dusty from where he lay at the campsite, but Sam kept the horse's body between him and the young gunman as an extra precaution.

Darkness was drawing in. Sam used a dead shrub branch set afire at one end to serve as a torch while he tended the badmen's horses. His, Sam Heller's horses now, by right of possession.

"Two thousand in frogskins and a string of fine horses—not a bad day's work," Sam said to himself. Not bad at all.

Not to mention taking considerable inroads on thinning out Weatherford's outlaw herd.

The horses were posted among enough fresh greenery to keep them fed for the night.

His work here done, Sam set out to tackle an unbroken mustang: Bill Longley.


Sam sat beside the fire warming himself, from time to time puffing on a corncob pipe. Bill Longley lay on his back on bush boughs, with several blankets covering him from shoulder to toe. The blankets had come from bedrolls carried on saddles from some of the Vard gang's horses.

Now he came out of it, forcing himself to a sitting

position, not without many a gasp and groan. When he got his upper body upright, he was white faced, his dark eyes standing out against his skin like ink blots. "Hey, Yank . . ."

"How do you feel?" Sam asked.

"Not so good . . . sick, hollowlike—another drink might set me right."

"Eat something . . . it'll keep up your strength."

"What've you got?"

"Beef jerky and parched corn."

"No, no," Bill said, making a face. "I can't eat, not that stuff . . . *Gaah!*"

Bill let himself be persuaded into having some parched corn, downing a couple of handfuls of it.

"This'll wash it down," Sam said, handing him a canteen.

Bill gulped eagerly, just as quickly spitting out the mouthful with an expression of unlimited disgust. "Water!"

"Redeye's in the other canteen," Sam said, taking the canteen from him. "I'll take that, water is too precious for wasting. I'm not taking any water runs tonight."

"You know where you can run to, Yank . . . and there ain't no water Down Yonder from what I've heard tell."

"No whiskey, either— That's the hell of it."

"I'm glad you're having fun." Longley glared. "If I only had my gun . . ."

"But you don't," Sam said.

"Not yet."

"You'd be hell in a showdown, Bill. You can't even stand up."

Sam hefted the canteen containing the whiskey. "They say redeye loosens the tongue, but your case is different. You've got to loosen your tongue for the redeye."

"If that's not a Yankee for you! Tormenting a wounded man, bargaining with him for a lousy drink! A Southern man would have more human kindness."

"Loman Vard was one of your own, a natural-born Son of Dixie and a native Texan, too—how'd that work out for you? Rile Fenton, too. As for human kindness, I used up mine saving your hide."

"Who asked you? Besides, you didn't do it for me, you did it for yourself, so you could get to Vard," Bill said.

"What's in Hangtree?" Sam asked. "Why did Vard have to kill you before you got there?"

"Ask him, Yank."

"You fixed it so I couldn't."

Bill laughed without mirth. "Now ain't that a damned shame!"

"It sure is," Sam said. "It means you go without a drink until you talk. The kind of drink you want, that is. You can have all the water you want anytime."

"Choke on it," Bill said. He was shaking, partly from fury but more from the effort of sitting up. He sank back groaning to lie at full length in his bed of boughs. "I'm through talking, I've got nothing to say to you. I'll do my talking with a gun. And I'll get one sooner rather than later, Yank."

Sam shrugged. "It must really burn you to be beholden to a Yankee for your life, eh, Bill?"

No reply.

Sam chuckled to himself.

# THIRTEEN

The hours of night rolled on, the moon rising high only to vanish behind a veil of clouds. The air was cold, the temperature of a Texas spring day sometimes dropping by thirty to forty degrees between the hours of daylight and darkness.

The fire kept back much of the cold but some managed to creep in as the flames burned low.

Sam slept light, especially when out in the field. He was on duty this night, watchful not only for perils that come under cover of night but also to monitor Bill Longley.

Bill writhed in troubled sleep. He shuddered and shivered under the blankets. His moans, groans, and sighs were punctuated by words, fragments of phrases. He was talking in his sleep.

Sam leaned close to hear what he was saying. Sleepers let slip curious fragments that they never would have uttered aloud during the day. But Bill's words were too garbled and Sam couldn't make any of them out at all.

Sam knew from wartime experience that the

halfway point between the hours of midnight and dusk is the time that most sick or wounded patients die, a fact well known to doctors, nurses, and hospital workers. Something in the human spirit becomes weakest at those times and most likely to slip across the threshold from life into death.

The moon came out from behind the clouds, shafting silvery beams across the nightscape.

A coyote howled somewhere out in the distance, a lonesome mournful sound to raise the hairs at the back of a man's neck, as it did Sam's.

Bill started awake. "I'm burning up!" he blurted out to no one in particular.

Bill wriggled under the covers, trying to toss the blankets aside. Sam reached over, holding them in place. "Don't—you'll catch a chill," he said.

"I feel like I'm on fire!" Bill was agitated, the one eye he could open fully showing a wild look.

"Easy, easy," Sam soothed. "Want some water?"

"Lord, yes! . . . Mouth's dry, throat's closed up . . . I feel like I'm choking!"

Bill's hands trembled. He seemed lacking in the strength to hold the canteen up by himself. Sam held it for him. Bill drank deeply. Raising a hand to show he'd had enough, he sank back down, head resting on the folded blanket serving as a pillow.

The wildness was gone from his expression. He looked around, experiencing a moment of clarity, aware of his surroundings.

"I don't know if I'm going to make it, Yank," he said quietly.

"You will," Sam said with a positivity he was far from feeling.

"Stop lying."

"Sure, all Yankees are liars but you'll live."

"I've been hurt before, shot before, but not this bad. I feel something trying to pull me under, away . . ."

"That's just your imagination," Sam scoffed. But inwardly he wondered, *Just keep holding on and fighting it.*

"Listen, if I don't make it—"

"You will."

"Let me say my piece now while my mind's right, before those crazy fever dreams come back," Bill said. "The things I've been seeing, not knowing if they're real or not . . ."

"They're not, that's just the fever making your mind play tricks on you."

Sam Heller was playing a game himself, a double game. He very much wanted to hear what Bill Longley had to say, particularly if Bill thought he was on his deathbed, which he just might be. The statement of a dying man could be vitally important, most people not wanting to go into the Great Dark with a lie on their lips.

Bill Longley said, "This is important. There's a man in Hangtree name of Cross . . ."

"Johnny Cross!" Sam said, surprised into an involuntary remark. Should this matter involve Johnny Cross, it was important indeed.

Now it was Bill Longley's turn to be surprised. "You know him? *You?*"

"I know of him," Sam said. In truth he knew Johnny Cross very well indeed. "He's one of the town's leading personalities," Sam added dryly.

Bill Longley was silent, seemingly deep in thought. "Then there's still a chance," he began, sounding stronger and more determined than before. "If I don't make it tell Johnny I had a message for him. Tell him that Cullen Baker's set to hang in Clinchfield at the first of the new month."

Cullen Baker! There was a name known to Sam, if only by ill repute. Cullen Baker, a gunfighter and outlaw, "a real bad un'," as Texans say about such men, and they said it of Baker, a drunken brute and heedless killer. From what Sam knew of him, hanging Cullen Baker seemed like a good idea.

"You can tell Cross yourself when we reach Hangtree. We'll be there tomorrow," Sam said offhandedly, as if the subject was of little interest to him.

"I'm feeling powerful bad," Bill said, his voice thick.

"Fight it!"

Sam turned away, picking up some broken branches to throw on the fire. Bill sat up, gripping Sam's forearm.

"Remember: Cullen Baker hangs in Clinchfield the first of the month," Bill rasped.

"If the worst happens, I'll see Cross gets the message," Sam said.

"Don't pass it along for somebody else to tell him and you wash your hands of the matter. You tell him yourself."

"Why me?"

"If you say you'll do it I know it'll get done."

"Thanks—I think."

"Don't flatter yourself, Yank. If there was anybody else I could rely on I'd use them but there's not, so you're elected. You could have killed me anytime here and made yourself a sweet payday because there's them that want to see me dead real bad."

"I kind of got that idea," Sam said, a tilt of his head indicating where the Vard gang's bodies lay sprawled.

"Remember: *Cullen Baker hangs in Clinchfield on the*

*first of the month*," Bill repeated. "That's all of it. When Johnny hears that, he'll know what to do."

"I got it," Sam said. "You can let go of my arm now; it's gone numb."

"Huh? Oh, right," Bill said, loosing his grip on Sam's forearm. He sank back down into his bed of boughs, exhausted by the effort he'd just made. He closed his eyes, tumbling instantly into sleep.

Throughout the entire episode, Bill Longley had not once demanded a drink of whiskey. That struck Sam Heller as the most worrying sign of all.

*That boy is in bad shape,* Sam said to himself.


Several hours passed, Bill Longley's fever spiking higher. Sam hovered over him during the watches of the night, listening closely as Bill's ravings become steadily more outlandish, the stuff of opium dreams . . .

There was a kingdom in the swamplands ruled by a modern-day Caesar, a red-haired red-bearded tyrant who lorded over the bayou with his own private army and an armored steamboat that was a floating palace. "*Barbaroux!*" Bill whispered.

A name that evoked a memory in Sam of a routine wartime briefing by Union Army and Navy intelligence officers reporting on certain black market kingpins and profiteers operating in the Greater New Orleans and Mississippi River delta zone, who were amassing fortunes dealing in contraband cotton and other smuggled goods; the name of one Barbaroux being on or near the top of that list.

Bill Longley's feverish rant touched on other such matters, of river pirates and waterfront melees, pitched battles between gunboats manned by the authorities

and swamper smugglers, betrayals, poisonings, a
fortress that was also a prison, hangings, and hired
killers—

There was a woman in it, at the heart of it—there
always is, thought Sam with a wry grin common to
those who believe themselves to have outgrown such
foolishness—Bill's voice taking on a soft and tender
tone those few times he said the name: "*Julie.*"

Master of the swampland, Barbaroux wallowed in
extremes of luxury for himself and his inner circle
and terror for all those outside it, carrying on like an
emperor of Imperial Rome. Barbaroux surrounded
himself with wanton women, hulking bodyguards, musicians, flatterers, fools, flunkies, even a fortune-teller
or Conjure Woman as they were called on the bayou.
Her name: "*Malvina.*"

Hearing that name, *Malvina*, Sam suddenly knew
with a shock of certainty that what he'd thought to be
the ravings of delirium were nothing but the naked
truth, that Something Had to Be Done and that he,
Sam Heller, was going to do it, come hell or high water.

# FOURTEEN

Bill Longley awoke in a misty limbo.

He had had a rough night but found himself still alive as darkness ebbed and the scene was lightening. His fever had broken, which meant the worst of it had passed.

He sat up suddenly, groaning as pain from his shoulder wound spasmed through him, leaving him breathless and gasping.

Gray-white fog surrounded him, swirling in banks and sheets. Its touch against his skin felt clammy, damp. The haze was thick, like being inside a cloud. Bill could see only a few paces in front of him.

Confused, disoriented, he whipped his head from side to side in search of some touchstone to reality.

The sight of the campfire nearby was something to hold on to, restoring his sense of balance. Its low-burning flames were a muted palette of pastel yellows, oranges, and reds.

A manlike outline floated into view. Blurred at the edges, phantomlike, it came onward, plowing through the fog.

It hunkered down beside Bill, revealing itself to be Sam Heller.

"Oh, it's you," Bill said.

"Who'd you think it was?"

Bill's right hand knuckled his eyes one by one, rubbing the sleep from them, using a very light touch on his narrowed left eye. "For a flash I thought I'd died and gone to heaven and was floating on a cloud. Then I saw you and knew it couldn't be. No damned Billy Yank will crash those pearly gates."

"What're you worried about? You're headed in the opposite direction anyway," Sam said.

"Not today."

"No, I reckon not."

Sam held a battered tin cup. Steam rose from it, carrying the earthy smell of fresh-made coffee, rich and aromatic.

"Think you're fit enough to handle this?" he asked, holding out the cup to Bill.

"What's wrong with it?" Bill asked sharply.

Sam took a long sip, gulping it down. "Nothing's wrong with it, you suspicious fool. Save for that poison I put in it. Don't do me any favors. If you don't want it I'll drink it. I had my morning cup while you were sleeping, but I could always go for another."

Westerners do crave their coffee and Bill was no exception. Its rich scent made his mouth water.

"I'll take a chance," he said grudgingly. "If Vard and his gang couldn't kill me, I reckon I can survive your cooking."

"I always carry a coffeepot and pound bag of coffee in my traveling kit. I can do without a lot of things, but I've got to have my morning coffee," Sam said, handing the tin cup to Bill.

Bill took it with the air of someone accepting it as his rightful due. Sam noted, not for the first time, that the youth was not one for saying, *Thanks*, or, *much obliged.*

Bill eased back into his bed of boughs, leaning against a fallen log that served as a backrest while he was sitting on the ground. He raised the cup to his mouth, then paused, thoughtful.

"One more thing—watch who you're calling 'fool,' Bluebelly."

"I'll keep that in mind," Sam nodded, straight-faced.

"See that you do."

He took a sip of the steaming black brew. It gave him a jolt—the hair on his head felt like it was standing straight up.

"Whew! I take it back, your coffee might do me in at that," Bill said.

"Puts hair on your chest," Sam said brightly.

"You must have a pelt like a brown bear." Bill nibbled away at the brew, taking small sips over the rim of the cup. It made his heart race and his pulse pound, clearing away some of the cobwebs left strung across his mind by a night of troubled sleep and delirium dreams.

"How about some redeye to brighten this brew?" Bill asked hopefully.

"All gone, I drank it last night," Sam said.

"You *would.*"

"Had to do something to pass the time."

Bill sat there sipping his coffee. With his wits about him, Bill grew more mindful of his mission. Cullen Baker's date with the hangman loomed ever larger in his thoughts, overshadowing all other concerns.

"When do we get moving?" Bill asked, all at once antsy and eager to be gone.

"Have to wait till this mist comes undone. Can't break camp when you can't see what you're doing," Sam said.

He took a tobacco pouch from an inside breast pocket of his buckskin vest and opened it. Inside the waterproof carrier bag was a corncob pipe, package of shag tobacco for pipe smokers, match container, and a few other odds and ends.

He stuffed some tobacco in the pipe bowl, tamping it down with a thumb. He struck a white-tipped Lucifer match against one of his boot soles.

Sam drew contentedly on the pipe, puffing away. "Something else I can't do without is tobacco. That first morning pipe is the best."

He held the pipe out to Bill. "Smoke?"

"No." Bill must have realized that sounded rude, even for him, for he added, "Not a pipe smoker."

"Too bad, you're missing something."

Bill remembered that he had a couple of cheroots still unsmoked. He unbuttoned his shirt breast pocket and reached inside, fishing around with his index and middle fingers held together. Instead of finding a pair of the six-inch square-cuts he habitually carried, he encountered a mass of loose tobacco leaves all shredded and crumbled.

The cigars must have gotten broken sometime during yesterday's dust-up with the gang. Bill Longley swore bitterly. The loss of the cheroots burned him as badly as anything that had happened to him in the last twenty-four hours.

"Something wrong?" Sam asked.

"Broken cigars!" Bill said curtly.

It's the small slights that really sting a man, Bill brooded, like ticks and chiggers that burrow under the skin and nest inside to make a proper job of bedeviling a fellow. He hadn't realized how much he was looking forward to a smoke until the instant he fully realized that small comfort had been snatched away from him.

"Sure you won't have a smoke from the pipe?" Sam offered.

"No," Bill said sharply. "That is, yes, I'm sure I don't want any, thank you very much."

Bill's vexation amused Sam, but the latter kept his face blank and his thoughts to himself.

Bill was not so easily balked, he was mule-stubborn when he set his mind to some purpose. Surely there was a piece of a cigar, some fragment large enough to be smoked.

Sam sat puffing away on his pipe, looking anywhere else but at a red-faced and ever-more frustrated Bill Longley hauling piece after piece of broken cigars from his pocket to toss them into the low-burning campfire when found unsatisfactory.

Finally Bill found a piece that looked like it might do. At last! he thought, fumbling it in fingers grown thick and clumsy by stiffness that was the product of rage. He almost dropped it in his eagerness but made a quick recovery—a gunfighter must have fast hands, after all.

"Match?" he asked Sam, Sam handing him a Lucifer. As usual, no thanks acknowledged the granting of his request.

Somehow smoking this piece of cigar had become of vital significance to Bill Longley, as though it were a magical rite that would open the gateway for a return to normality and the righting of his world. A world that had gone so wrong starting on the day a couple of Combine men had come to the landing at a river called Torrent to demand the weekly taxes they were now required to be paid on the barge crossing operated by Cullen Baker and Bill . . .

The Combine was the name of the holding company that provided the business and financial umbrella for all of Barbaroux's operations now that he had crowned himself the supreme power in Moraine County. Clinchfield was the capital, the county seat of Moraine County and the locale where Barbaroux had set up headquarters.

The Combine's tax-collecting team for this wild region of the swamp was a duo named Deeter and Thissel. Deeter was a river rat version of the tinhorns Bill Longley knew all too well from the gambling hells of the Texas honkytonk districts, the ones who idled their hours away steadily losing at the card tables and roulette wheels and getting money by crimes of violence associated with the sporting milieu.

Deeter had a widow's peak whose pointed tip came near to touching the space between his bushy eyebrows. Oily dark hair was slicked back from his forehead, long, wide sideburns ran down to his jawline, and he had a thick dark mustache and goatee. Very little bare skin was left showing on his face.

He was a would-be dandy who wore flouncy white shirts with ruffled fronts, tight pants, and cream-colored custom-made boots. His arms were so long they gave him an apelike appearance.

Thissel was Deeter's exact opposite. He was small, quiet, orderly, and unassumingly dressed. He peered at the world through steely wire-rim glasses with round

eye frames and circular lenses so thick that they gave
him a froglike appearance, magnifying his eyes so they
appeared unnaturally enlarged and goggling in silent
amusement at the world around them. He had a thick
neatly trimmed sandy-brown mustache; the tips were
waxed and turned up, like a cat's whiskers. He habitually carried a leather-bound pocket notebook into
which he was constantly writing with a gold pencil.

Deeter and Thissel arrived on horseback on a weekday in mid-afternoon at the landing on the east bank
of the Torrent River, the site of a barge that ferried
passengers back and forth across the river, a barge and
line jointly owned and operated by Cullen Baker and
Bill Longley.

Cullen Baker was big, well over six feet tall, raw-
boned and strong-armed, with the powerful sloping
shoulders often seen on heavyweight prizefighters. He
was shaggy haired, thick featured, and red faced, with
pale eyes set well back under an overhanging brow. His
nose had been broken several times and never properly reset. He was clean-shaven, more or less.

Cullen Baker was known as a "booze-fighter." This
does not mean he was anti-booze, or a Temperance
man. It meant that he was a brawler who got drunk
and into fights. Lots of them. He won most because he
was a formidable fighter with considerable physical
resources.

"It's not that I get into fights, it's that the fight gets
into me," he liked to say.

"The hooch gets into you," his first wife used to fire
back at him. There was nothing he could say back to
that except laugh, because it was true. Martha Jane,

her name was. She was quite a gal. He didn't intimidate her, not one little bit, and she never hesitated to say what was on her mind, no matter the circumstances. That was one of the things he'd liked about her, courage being the virtue he admired most.

"She sure had me pegged dead to rights," he'd say when he thought of her, which was more and more infrequently now. He'd married her in 1854, back when he was a pup and she a mere slip of a girl, damned pretty, too.

He never expected to outlive her, he who followed the gunman's trade and rode the outlaw's dark trail for most of his life. No doubt Martha Jane thought the same. She was always going on to him about what it was like to be an outlaw's wife, never knowing when he went out the door if that was the last time she'd ever see him alive. What would happen to her and their two daughters if he was shot dead during some holdup?

Martha Jane caught the sickness and died. She must have been surprised as hell to realize that that no-good badman of a husband of hers was going to outlive her. Cullen had tried to bring up their two daughters by himself after her death, but it was no good. He was an absentee father at best. He left the girls with his in-laws in 1862 to be raised by them. He wondered if they ever thought of their daddy, if they even remembered him?

Cullen's second wife was named Martha, too, a funny kind of coincidence. She had died little more than a year earlier, of natural causes. Strange . . . you heard about how hard life was for men on the frontier with all its perils of hostile Indians and bandits, and wild animals. Yet it was just as hard for the women, who faced all these threats plus the mortal dangers of childbearing and raising a family, keeping the children fed and clothed and healthy, all that in addition to the never-ending round of chores and hard work that was the lot of all ranchers and farmers and their families.

He'd never planned to be a much-married man, outliving not one but two wives and now hitched to a third. That was the way it worked out. No matter how you planned and schemed trying to shape your fate, life kept happening to you.

He certainly never expected to be living in obscurity under an assumed name in the swampland, living a life of hard work and toil as a bargeman running his own small ferrying service, yet here he was, mostly because of Julie.

Julie Morgan, now Julie Morgan Baker. She was a beauty, reminding him of those rare and lovely flowers sometimes found blossoming amid the marshes and bogs of the swampland.

Cullen Baker and Bill Longley had been on the dodge, running from the law several years ago in the aftermath of the breakup of the old Baker gang. They had fled deep into the bayou heart of the Blacksnake River, coming to roost at last in the remoteness of the Torrent River country along the border of Moraine and Albedo Counties.

The two were known on the Blacksnake but strangers to this still-further-removed adjunct to the territory. Baker here went under the alias of "Mr. Montgomery"—from his full name, Cullen Montgomery Baker.

Smuggling was a way of life here, and feuding, too, and with their ready guns Baker and Bill Longley established a place for themselves in the local milieu.

The Law was thoroughly uninterested in shoot-outs between smugglers' gangs or the vendettas of feudist families. As long as no banks were robbed, river traffic harassed, or legitimate riverfront businesses preyed on, the authorities kept out of the Torrent district.

There was also some confusion about whether Moraine or Albedo Counties had jurisdiction over the borderland between the two, where property lines that were drawn on the map ceased to exist in the mazelike tangle of rivers, bayous, and cross-channels. Lawmen on both sides of the line said the hell with it and stayed away.

Cullen Baker wanted Julie Morgan the first time he saw her at a chance meeting in Highwater, the Torrent's leading (in fact, only) market town. She had pale blond hair, a fine-featured face with dark blue eyes, and a slim shapely body that was nicely ripened in all the right places. The object of much attention and rivalry between local Romeos, she frustrated would-be swains by remaining elusively, hauntingly beyond their reach.

She was an orphan, her parents long dead. She'd been raised by her sole living kin, a bayou near hermit known as Crawdad Kate due to her facility in netting great catches of the river shellfish, a delicacy much esteemed for cooking in gumbos, seafood soups, and stews, and étouffées.

Kate was a Morgan by blood, but she and Julie were so physically unlike that one might fancy that they were members of two different species. Julie was a delicate beauty, fair haired, pale, long, and lithe. Kate was dark haired, swarthy, brawny, and buxom, as strong as many men and more dangerous than most. Living by herself in the swamps, Kate vigorously defended herself and her rights by shotgun, gaffing pole, or fisherman's filleting knife, each of which she wielded with lethal proficiency.

Fiercely protective of this orphan girl she had come to love and cherish, Kate had proved to be an effective deterrent to would-be seducers and swampland toughs used to taking what they wanted.

"I had to marry Julie, I knew Kate would come after me with a shotgun if I didn't," Cullen Baker liked to say during their get-togethers after he and Julie were wed, his remark only half in jest. The two of them were alike in many ways and understood each other.

"I may yet, if you don't treat my girl right," Kate would reply, and she and Baker at least knew she was only half-joking, too.

Cullen Baker came courting in the proper old-fashioned way of country folk way, and when the time was right he asked Kate to consent to the marriage. Kate said her Julie would never be wed to an outlaw and gunman, that Cullen Baker had to get himself a respectable way of making a living.

Baker had plied the bargeman's trade years before while living in South Arkansas near the Texas border. He knew the ferrying trade inside out. It had often struck him that a ferry across the Torrent would be a natural and much desired local improvement, saving travelers from having to make long and tiresome detours to find a place where the narrow, swift-running Torrent finally widened and slowed enough to allow a crossing through the shallows.

Cullen Baker marked out a spot high upstream on the Torrent where the river thinned to its narrowest, a site that was ideally suited for a landing. No one had ever developed the locale, though a long-abandoned hunter's cabin stood in a clearing overlooking the water.

Getting a sturdy barge line built to span the river was the hardest part of the job, a Herculean labor to which Cullen Baker harnessed all his furious energies and prodigious strength. Bill Longley was part of the enterprise from the beginning. He'd strung with Baker steadily since the dissolution of the old gang. Bill greatly admired Baker and was intensely loyal to him; for his part Baker had a great liking for Bill, seeing in this reckless go-to-hell red-hot and fellow Texan a younger version of himself, "only better looking and smarter," Baker said, "and maybe even faster with a gun, too."

"Hell, Cullen, you're the fastest, the all-time champion. Nobody can beat you," Bill Longley said with every sign and appearance of deep sincerity, yet there was a still small voice in the back of his mind that wondered if, maybe, he really could shade Cullen on the draw. What an achievement that would be, to best the man who many considered the originator of the new fast-draw, pistol-fighting style that had come into prominence during the war and afterward.

Cullen Baker, not immune to flattery, was greatly pleased with the youth's words, which he considered not flattery but only rightful recognition of his skills. "Keep at it, Bill, keep practicing and someday you'll be the fastest gun in Texas, which means the fastest gun there is," Cullen Baker said.

"Especially seeing as how I'm now retired from the gunfighting game," he added.

"We're both retired. We're bargemen now," Bill Longley said.

It was true, they were bargemen. Once the upright support towers with their flywheels and spinning gears for the line had been built on both banks of the river and the cable line spanning the Torrent put in place, the rest of the project had come together. Modest landing docks were put up on both sides and a flatboat rafting barge constructed.

Baker and Bill did their share of the work but it was too much for any two men so they hired local workmen for much of the carpentry, hauling, and donkey work. They used money they had amassed earlier when selling their guns to smugglers and feudists. When cash ran short during construction, Baker and Bill stealthed their way downriver to Halftown and Clinchfield, donned black masks, and robbed any number of prosperous businesses at gunpoint.

The barge line was open and inaugurated with a big party at which Kate officially gave her consent for Julie Morgan to marry Cullen Baker. They were wed as soon as decently possible. The barge line filled the demand Baker had seen and began turning a profit from the start. Profits and traffic increased as the word spread that the Torrent had been spanned.

Cullen Baker and Bill Longley were making money and socking it away. Baker was as happy as he'd ever been as he enjoyed his newlywed bliss, and Bill Longley reveled in the luxury of going about in broad daylight without a price on his head and total strangers itching to gun him down.

It was too good to last and couldn't. One sunny afternoon trouble arrived in the form of a dark cloud who called himself Mr. Deeter, along with his seemingly less offensive partner Mr. Thissel.

Deeter stalked around the landing site on the east bank of the river, shouting the name of Mr. Montgomery at the top of his lungs, bawling himself red faced. He wandered around, calling for Montgomery, growing increasingly vexed by his inability to find anyone to talk to at the seemingly deserted site.

Cullen Baker lay slung in a canvas hammock strung between two trees. The hammock was on a shady knoll above the landing, screened by a line of tall hedges.

Baker had tapped into a not-so-little brown jug of whiskey that morning and was sleeping off a drunk in the post-noon heat when Deeter came calling. Literally.

Deeter was shouting in a voice more suitable for selling fish at the Clinchfield open-air fish market down by the docks, or for spieling out the action on the turns of a Wheel of Fortune game in a crowded gambling hall at the midnight rush hour. For an as-yet-peaceful and shady barge landing on the east bank of the Torrent River during the mid-afternoon lull, it was distinctly overloud and overbearing.

It didn't do Cullen Baker's hangover any good, either.

He rolled out of the hammock, nimbly landing on his feet. The straw hat that had been shading his eyes, he now clamped down firmly atop his head. He wore a blue denim bib overall with shoulder straps, his upper body bare beneath it. Few persons could have looked less like he was owner-operator of a barge line.

He went down to the landing to see what the noise was all about. Deeter stood in the foreground with hands on hips, exuding an air of impatience. Thissel stood near the little dockside wharf, eyeing it, making an entry in his red notepad with a golden pencil set.

Deeter did not so much introduce himself and his partner Thissel as announce their arrival: "You must be Mr. Montgomery!" Deeter bawled, crowding Cullen Baker. Deeter was a big man, bigger than most, and the aura of potential violence that oozed off him was often intimidating to others, especially those he encountered carrying out his official duties.

Deeter saw Cullen Baker coming downhill and went to confront him, marching toward him.

"You are Mr. Montgomery?" Deeter shouted at Cullen Baker, now universally known throughout these parts by the alias he had adopted.

"Who wants to know?" Cullen Baker demanded.

"I'm Deeter, from the Clinchfield County River Commission, Excise Department. That is my partner Mr. Thissel, he said, indicating the little man with the goggle-eyed glasses by the wharf. Thissel bobbed his head with a friendly nod.

"I'm Montgomery but I didn't get that last part. You are who again?" Cullen Baker asked.

Deeter repeated himself, only louder this time. Bill Longley came along. He'd been downstream, tending a baited fishing line.

Thissel scuttled up from the wharf, making the group a foursome. He stood several paces away in the background, a leather diplomat-type portfolio tucked under an arm. Bill noticed Thissel's ears came to little points at the tops, giving him an elfish look.

Deeter launched into a prepared speech he had memorized, congratulating Montgomery on being inducted into the Greater Moraine County Area's Riverine Revenue Enhancement Association. As a member of the association, Mr. Montgomery would now have the privilege of paying a certain weekly fee to continue operations, said payments to begin this day, now, with ongoing payments to be made once a week every week.

When Deeter finished, Cullen Baker was frowning. "I ain't sure I got all of that but what I did get I didn't like. Is that little fellow over there your translator?" he asked, indicating Thissel. "Because if he is, maybe he can give it to me in plain English this time."

"He said Moraine County wants us to pay taxes for running our barge," Bill Longley said sharply, all dark-eyed and serious.

"Is that right? Is that what you said, mister?" Cullen Baker asked.

"That's about the size of it," Deeter said coolly.

"Moraine County wants to collect taxes on the barge? Our barge?"

"That's right."

"You're from Moraine County. That's *Moraine* County I'm talking about now."

"Yes."

"And Moraine County wants to tax our barge?"

"You hard of hearing, Montgomery? Moraine County's taxing your barge so pay up if you want to stay in business," Deeter said, starting to get tough.

Cullen Baker's laughter was long, loud, and insulting.

"I'm glad you find this so damned funny, mister," Deeter said.

"You will, too, when you get the joke. This ain't

Moraine County, it's *Albedo* County. Everybody but a plain damned fool knows the Torrent is in Albedo County," Cullen Baker said. "I don't pay no taxes to Albedo County anyhow and I sure ain't gonna start not paying taxes to Moraine County, too. Ol' Rufus Redbeard don't cut no ice up here on the Torrent, boys."

"Mr. Barbaroux thinks he does," Deeter said ominously. "The Torrent is tributary to the Blacksnake River, and every business on the Blacksnake has to pay taxes to the Combine. You're running a business on the Blacksnake, so you have to pay."

"It's the law, Mister Montgomery," Thissel said timorously.

Cullen Baker stopped laughing. "I ain't no Combine man, I have to work for a living. So why don't you boys just run along and bother somebody else who's got the time to put up with your nonsense?"

"You're not getting the message, farmer," Deeter said, contemptuously eyeing Cullen Baker in his shapeless straw hat, blue denim overalls, and bare feet.

Bill Longley thought then that it was easy enough for somebody to mistake Cullen for a farmer, especially when he had his work clothes on as he did now. Cullen wasn't wearing a gun that day, either, although there was a half-dozen or so of them, his and Bill's, ready to hand on the barge and around the landing.

"We're busy men and we don't have time to explain the facts of life to yokels like you," Deeter went on. He stood face to face with Cullen, less than an arm's length distance between the two of them. He came up to about the same head height and outweighed him by twenty-five pounds or more, though a lot of that was fat not muscle.

"We don't waste time on hardheads. You get one chance to start making your installment payments. This is your one chance, here, today, now."

"And if I don't pay?" Cullen Baker asked, smiling tightly.

"Then we take action and no fooling around. *I* take action," Deeter said. "If you don't catch my drift by now—and some of you farmer boys and manure spreaders are dumber than fence posts—here's something that'll get the message across."

Deeter made a big show of sweeping back his jacket flap on one side, baring the Colt .45 holstered on his hip and resting the palm of his gun hand on the gun butt. The gun was a fancy showpiece with inlaid white horn handle plates and the metalwork gleaming with a shiny silvery finish.

"See this?" He smiled toothily.

Cullen Baker was smiling, too. He made a fist, bringing it up to shoulder height. It was as big as a milk bottle, a mass of bone, sinews, and tendons, dominated by a row of knuckles that looked like kids' round playing marbles sewn up inside the flesh.

"See this?" Cullen Baker asked.

If you'd been watching closely that day like Bill Longley had, and knew what to look for as Bill Longley did, you would have seen Baker getting set and ready. His big feet were shoulder length apart, right foot leading by about a half a step. His left hand hung down by his side, all loose and relaxed.

Deeter saw Baker was in motion and went for his gun. Cullen Baker lashed out with a wicked right-hand jab.

When he delivered the blow he rose up on the balls of his feet. There was a slight but telling twist of the hips that put the entire force of the body and his considerable weight into it.

There was an audible *crack!*—the sound of Deeter's jaw snapping under the blow. More than a broken jaw, it was fractured, broken in several parts.

Deeter flew backward and fell down, marshy ground cushioning the impact, absorbing the shock. Mercifully he had been knocked out cold, for the pain would have been excruciating—

Thissel turned his head to watch his partner go down for the long count. When he looked back, Bill Longley was standing there with a gun in his hand, held leveled on Thissel, gun cocked and ready for action.

Bill had tucked the gun into his pants at the small of his back, covering it with his shirt before coming to see what the two strangers were all about.

Thissel raised his hands into the air slowly.

"How about you, buddy? You got something you want to show me, too?" Cullen Baker said.

"No, sir, that is, nothing but the sight of me getting away from here as fast as I can," Thissel said quietly.

"You got guts, friend"—Baker laughed—"and smarts, too."

Bill went to Thissel and patted him down with a quick search that yielded nothing of interest but a small-caliber pocket pistol, a notepad, and a thin billfold.

"They make me carry a gun for the job, but I've never used it," Thissel said.

"I believe it; this is a piece of junk," Bill said, tossing the pistol into the river.

"Let him keep his money. Tax collector with that little cash must be honest," Cullen Baker said.

Bill returned the billfold and notepad to Thissel,

then went to Deeter to search him. "I think you busted this fellow's jaw, Cullen."

"I believe I did!" Cullen Baker said happily.

Bill fished out a fat wad of cash, thumbing through it. "I knew this one couldn't be honest. Must be a couple of hundred dollars here!"

"You can go," Baker told Thissel, "and take your trash with you." He indicated Deeter. "We don't want him around here littering up the place."

"Yes, sir!" Thissel hesitated, anxious.

"Something bothering you?" Cullen Baker asked.

"Sorry, sir, I can't move him by myself. Sorry."

"We'll give you a hand."

Baker and Bill slung Deeter facedown across the saddle of his horse while Thissel held the animal's reins to steady it. Baker tied the unconscious man to the saddle so he wouldn't fall off during the ride.

Thissel mounted up. "I must say, you gentlemen have been quite decent about this whole unfortunate affair. You have my apologies. I'm a hireling and I must go where the county sends me.

"Since the recent change in county governance with the Paulus administration going out, the situation has become most deplorable. My 'partner' as you call him, Lester Deeter, was forced on me by the new board of directors—all of whom who were personally installed by Commander Barbaroux himself. This oaf Deeter knows nothing about economics, tax tables, or even basic fundamentals of civics."

"That makes two of us," Bill Longley cracked.

"Yes, sir, but you are not a tax collector," Thissel pointed out.

"Lord forbid!" Bill said, shocked. "Sorry, I said that without thinking. No offense."

"None taken. Those in my profession are used to it," Thissel said sadly.

"If they was all polite and well spoken like you, there wouldn't be no problem," Cullen Baker said.

"Thank you, sir. Very kind of you to say so."

"We still wouldn't pay, but there'd be no cause for anybody to get a busted head," Baker said.

Thissel tsk-tsked. "I fear we'll hit a new low with the people the Commander is bringing in. Why, for example, this man Deeter is more than incompetent, he's an out and out crook!"

"He'll be out of commission for a good long time with that broken jaw," Baker said with grim satisfaction.

"There'll be more like Deeter to replace him, many more, and some possibly a great deal worse," Thissel said. He leaned forward and down in the saddle, toward Cullen Baker and Bill.

"A word of warning, gentlemen. I'm afraid you've made yourself a very bad enemy today."

"Who, Deeter?" Cullen Baker scoffed.

"No, not Deeter, he's nothing. I mean the Commander, Barbaroux himself. He's a dangerous man, more pirate than county administrator. Some of the things I've seen in the last few months would be almost unbelievable if the war hadn't hardened us to all sorts of horror.

"I tell you, gentlemen, this Barbaroux will stop at nothing. He was able to take over the county so easily because so many of the old administration died off suddenly, very suddenly, all at once."

"Yes, word of that even reached us up here on the Torrent," Cullen Baker said, nodding. "Food poisoning, they said, but nobody buys that. I never heard of so many people dying so fast, not rich folks with clean kitchens and the best food and drink—and doctoring—money can buy."

"You're right to be suspicious, sir," Thissel said. "The victims were all top men in the Paulus administration, attending a political banquet at Patriot's Hall in Old Clinchfield. Barbaroux was expected to attend but canceled at the last minute. Most fortunate that he did so, because twenty people died outright of food poisoning, not least of whom was County Administrator Paulus himself. Dozens more were seriously ill and weeks in recovering.

"Most of those killed outright at the banquet were high-level office-holders, backers, and donors belonging to the Paulus administration, including Paulus. County government was unable to function with so many vacancies in the top offices. Barbaroux simply stormed in and had his people installed in the posts. The rumor is that Barbaroux bribed the chief of staff in the governor's office to make the appointments—the *state governor's office, the governor of Texas*—to secure the takeover."

"I believe you, but nobody will ever prove it. Not when the county judges here all answer to Barbaroux," Cullen Baker said.

"True, which is a pity," Thissel went on, "because the most damning piece of evidence in the case has never been investigated or even put on the record. The fact is that a woman who was hired on at the Hall to help with the cooking the night of the banquet, a vicious old crone named Malvina, helped prepare the fatal seafood gumbo which caused the illnesses. Malvina was hired on the express recommendation of Commander Barbaroux. Since then she has been his honored guest at the so-called Great White Boat, living in luxury in that floating palace, the *Sabine Queen*, the steamboat moored at Clinchfield docks where Barbaroux resides with his fancy women and his entourage of flatterers, toadies, and thugs.

"Malvina the Gypsy now styles herself as the Conjure Woman. Where she entertains the guests and turns a tidy profit by giving private fortune-telling sessions on the boat: 'Have your future read by the Conjure Woman, Sees All, Knows All'—that sort of thing."

"That's a hell of a story, friend, but I wouldn't worry too much about me and young Bill here. We don't get invited to too many banquets," Cullen Baker said.

"We sure don't!" Bill Longley agreed, laughing.

Thissel's face was set in hard lines, eyes narrowed. "Poisoning is reserved for those Barbaroux considers too important to be removed by the ordinary means of assassination. Others get the gun, knife, strangler's cord, or the common everyday blunt instrument.

"Beware the Combine police patrols, they're worse than any gang of brigands or river pirates. That's who Barbaroux uses for his dirty work, the rough stuff. When he comes at you he'll use them. When the Combine police come for you, shoot first if you want to live!"

"That's good advice, we'll keep it in mind," Cullen Baker said.

Thissel said his good-byes and rode off, leading Deeter in tow across his horse. Cullen Baker and Bill Longley watched them go.

"Nice fellow," Baker said.

"Wonder why he spilled so much to us?" Bill asked.

"He's probably been aching to unload on someone he could trust. We went against Deeter and the

Combine, so we fit the bill. He put out a lot of good information, but I think he worries too much."

"I'm not so sure," Bill said. "You haven't been going into Halftown or Clinchfield much since you've been married."

"With good reason—I'm still a newlywed!" Baker cracked.

"But I have and I'll tell you this: I've been hearing a lot of talk, too, along the lines Thissel was giving us. Now that Barbaroux has Clinchfield in his pocket, he's looking to expand along the river. And now comes Deeter looking to enroll us on the tax rosters and shake us down. They're closing in on us already."

"They don't know who they're messing with, Bill."

"No, but they're liable to find out when they start looking into Deeter getting whomped, and they will come looking!"

"You worry too much, Bill. When they come in force, then I'll start worrying with you and not before," Baker said. "Hey, you think Julie will like that fancy-Dan pistol of Deeter's I kept?"

"Julie likes anything you give her, Cullen. She's crazy about you," Bill said.

"I know. I don't deserve it," Cullen Baker said blandly. "Ain't I a dog?"


Bill Longley returned to the present that had been the beginning of Cullen Baker's private war with Rufus Barbaroux. The most recent installment had come just yesterday, when the Vard gang, acting at the behest of Barbaroux, had attacked him at Dead Lake basin.

Bill had managed to get the stub lit. The cigar smoke tasted raw and harsh in his throat at first, but now he was getting to it and it was starting to ease his jangled nerves.

Sam Heller sat nearby, staring out into the distance, thoughtfully puffing on his pipe.

Now was a good time to bring up a subject that had been bothering Bill since he first awoke. The fact was that the long hours of fever-racked delirium last night were a blur in his head.

"I went off my head last night, the fever and all," Bill began tentatively, lightly probing. "Reckon I said a lot of crazy talk that made no sense . . ."

"Who could tell? It all sounded like gibberish to me. I couldn't make heads nor tails of it," Sam said like he meant it.

But did he? Bill couldn't be sure because he didn't remember what he'd said and done the night before.

The hell with it, he decided. He'd just carry on the way he had and assume he hadn't cracked to a thing, that he'd kept his secrets.

"Whatever I said, you just pay no never mind to it. It didn't mean a thing, not a damned thing," Bill Longley said.

# FIFTEEN

The mist began to thin out and break up. Great rifts and gaps opened up, like canyons and ravines of emptiness in a low-hanging cloud, so that within a quarter-hour the basin was clear of all but a few scraps and shreds of mist.

It was very early in the morning. The moon had long set in the west and the stars above were paling, fast giving way to a thin wash of brightness steadily creeping in from the east. Blue-black shadows pooled in the basin, looking like real water. The air was still cold, causing Bill to huddle deeper into the blankets covering him where he sat by the fading fire.

Sam Heller watered Dusty with several hatfuls of canteen water. He saddled the horse and mounted up.

"Hey, where you going?" Bill called to him.

"See that hill rising over the south rim wall?" Sam asked, indicating a wooded hilltop that thrust up above the ridgeline in its southeast quadrant.

"I see it," Bill said, his tone challenging. "What of it?"

"I'm going to cut some wood there for a traveling rig."

"Traveling rig?"

"To transport damaged goods."

"If you say so. What about me?"

"You stay here."

This easy assumption of dominance and command irked Bill. It more than irked him; it burned raw along his nerves. "Not afraid I'll run out on you?"

"Run? You can't even stand up," Sam answered.

Which burned Bill all the more but he kept a poker face. Damned if he'd let this arrogant, high-handed Billy Yank know he was getting to him.

"You're not going to leave me here without a gun?" Bill asked in a voice of disbelief.

"I am," Sam said.

"What if some Weatherford friends of Vard track us here and come on me? Or some hostile Indians happen along?"

"I'll be up on the hilltop, I'll see them coming from a long way off."

"You're staking me out here like live bait!"

"Not a bad idea," Sam said, chuckling.

"What if a rattlesnake comes along and me unable to get away?" Bill said.

"Bite him," said Sam. "My money's on you against the snake."

Sam rode to where the Vard gang's horses were picketed. He cut Big Taw's dappled gray quarter horse out of the bunch, fixed a lead rope to it, and went south to the rim wall with the quarter horse in tow.

They climbed the inner slope, crested the top, and disappeared on the far side.

"You'll be laughing out of the other side of your mouth before I'm done, Bluebelly," Bill muttered, watching Sam go.

He didn't have to make plans. His course of action

was ready made, the only move he could make. He needed a gun. He felt naked without one. That feeling of helplessness was repellent to his deepest nature. Bill Longley had spent most of his life since age twelve if not before arming himself for trouble.

He had no idea of what Sam Heller was all about. The man was a mystery to him. Bill couldn't get a handle on what Heller's ultimate goal was. True, he had saved Bill's life more than once, but not out of the milk of human kindness. He kept Bill alive because he wanted to know why Loman Vard was dogging him. Heller had been hard on Vard's trail, that was clear, but the reason why was cloudy.

The Yankee was playing a deep game, but to what end?

Had Vard squirreled away a prize of gold, riches in stolen loot, that Heller was determined to find? But then if Vard had that kind of money hidden away, why would he bother hunting down the likes of Bill Longley? Greed, to squeeze out another payday? It was possible, some badmen were greedy beyond the bounds of all common sense, but Bill didn't read Vard that way based on their brief acquaintance.

Vard had wanted to know why Barbaroux wanted Bill dead. Maybe it all tracked back to Barbaroux in some way . . . ?

Sam Heller was in the dark where Barbaroux was concerned, or so it seemed to Bill Longley. That's where Bill meant to keep him. Barbaroux was a hole card for Bill to draw upon if and when needed. Until then he'd hold the secret tightly to himself.

Bill's status with Heller was unclear, at least to himself. Was he the Yankee's prisoner? Heller wore no badge, was no lawman, and had no more legitimate authority over Bill than the guns he had and Bill lacked. In the real world, though, that counted for plenty. Heller was calling the shots; he could move Bill around on the board pretty much as he pleased.

There were too many unknowns in this game, and trying to sort them out was giving Bill a headache. What he needed to do was act, not think. But he couldn't make a move yet, he still had to play a waiting game, vexatious though it might be.

After what seemed a too long while, Bill saw a pair of blurred dots emerge into view from below the south rim wall, climbing the north slope of the hill Sam had pointed out earlier. The moving dots that were Sam and the trailing quarter horse angled upward to the wood's edge, entering it and vanishing from sight.

Time for Bill to make his move now that he was free from Sam Heller's watchful eyes. He needed a gun. The Vard gang had guns, lots of them. From what he'd seen the day before, a number of them carried more than one gun. Surely there was a loaded gun to be had among the bunch, and Bill meant to have it.

All he had to do was make his way to where the gang lay dead, secure a gun, then make his way back to the campfire so he'd be waiting when Heller came out of the thicket.

The bodies were about fifty yards distant, and downwind of the campsite.

First Bill had to do something pretty tough—stand up.

He flung aside the blankets, a bravura gesture. He paid for it, too. The effort sent sharp pains knifing through his upper body, firing all the aches and pains from having been shot. He squirmed around on his bed of boughs until the agony lessened.

Not such a good start. He found he was very shaky indeed. He could get upright, he felt, but he wasn't so sure about his ability to stay that way.

He rummaged through what remained of the wood for kindling, finding a three-foot-long stick with a fist-sized knob at one end. It looked sturdy enough to support much of his weight if he used it as a cane.

Bill rose shakily to his feet. He felt hot, dizzy, and breathless.

His left arm hung down along his side like a piece of meat. He could wriggle his fingers, but he couldn't do much else without the risk of starting his shoulder wound bleeding again.

Bill Longley pointed himself toward the bodies of the dead men and started forward. He moved slowly and carefully, shuffling along, parsing every step. A misstep could spell disaster.

A flicker of motion overhead caught his eye. A couple of flying V-shapes wheeled around way up in the sky, circling high above Dead Lake basin.

Vultures, thought Bill. That was only to be expected. They were overdue. Yesterday's Vard gang kill-down had happened at twilight, with darkness swallowing up the bodies before the buzzards could get to them.

With daylight now burning, the scavenger birds had begun to make the rounds, scouting the territory in search of something with which to fill their bellies.

Blackbirds, too, were eaters of the dead. A number of them were arrowing into the site from all directions of the compass. Their numbers steadily increasing, they darted into the basin, circling, lowering, their harsh cawing cries making a considerable racket.

Bill ignored them, concentrating on cutting the distance between himself and the dead men. He crept along at a snail's pace. He was exhausted. His legs trembled from the strain. He wanted to relieve them by sitting for a while but feared that once he did so he would be unable to get back up. He paused frequently, leaning hunched over forward, putting a lot of weight on his knob-topped walking stick.

The black birds were well in advance of Bill when it came to reaching the corpses. Considerable numbers of them had come down to earth and were grouping around the bodies.

They were a feisty lot, strutting along on the ground, heads bobbing, shrieking out warning cries when one got too close to another, making aggressive display of fluttering winged plumage, darting sleek shiny heads to peck at each other with their sharp bills, screeching their outrage.

Bill thought seriously about turning back, but by now he was closer to the bodies than the campsite. Having invested so much time and energy in his quest he couldn't quit now. He pushed on, numbing himself to revulsion.

The scene had taken on a hellish aspect as the black-birds mobbed the corpses. Some of the bodies could hardly be seen for the number of birds swarming them. Upturned leather boot toes protruded beyond the edges of seething crow mounds.

Yet Bill Longley was within reach of his goal, the nearest crow-covered mound being only several paces away. It was the body of Big Taw, Bill having marked it well before the invasion of winged carrion eaters.

That was the most unnerving part of the encounter for Bill. Any assumptions he might have had about human beings' innate mastery over the animal kingdom were exploded at first contact with the ravens and crows. Not only were they unafraid of the looming two-legged intruder, they were actively hostile, as though they expected him to get out of their way.

Crows were constantly underfoot, nearly causing Bill to trip and fall over them. He kicked out at one bird, the bird darting a savage peck at his offending foot. Had he not been wearing tough leather boots the thrusting beak might well have done him a mischief.

Bill kicked again at the crow, which dodged his assault and flew away. It did not go far, fluttering to a safe landing beyond his reach.

Bellowing his outrage, Bill advanced on the mortal remains of Big Taw, laying on with his walking stick into the collected crows, striking and slashing.

One blow was nowhere nearly enough. They all but ignored it. His angry cries, meant to frighten and intimidate the birds, sounded thin and unconvincing even to his own ears, especially when weighed against the shrill stridency of the crows' piercing volume.

The walking stick was a far more formidable persuader. The crows erupted up and outward to escape it, loosing a violent outburst of black beating wings and shrieked derision. They flew aloft in a fan-shaped vortex of swift, whirling motion. They came so close that Bill recoiled with a start, nearly losing his footing. Dagger-sharp bills and ripping talons surged toward his head, causing Bill to cross both arms in front of his face to protect it.

He stumbled and felt himself falling, forestalling a tumble by dropping in a huddle to his knees. Bill beat the air over his head with the walking stick to ward off the birds.

Big Taw was momentarily uncovered. The crows had made an unholy mess of his exposed flesh. Bill wasn't squeamish but couldn't help looking away from the red ruin of what had been Big Taw's face.

Such weakness could be his undoing, Bill knew. Steeling himself, he scuttled forward on hands and knees to the body. Big Taw was a two-gun man, which Bill had taken note of yesterday. He was on Big Taw's left side and grabbed for his holstered gun.

There wasn't any . . . the holster was empty.

That was a setback but not one that Bill would allow to slow him down. He reached over the body, battening on the holster on the big man's right-hand side . . .

It, too, was empty.

That was a setback that did give Bill pause. Where were Big Taw's guns? He couldn't have lost both at once, could he?

He came face to face with a raven perched on Big Taw's head, yellow-orange talons digging into the top of his skull. The bird was much bigger than the crows Bill had already learned to be wary of.

Eyes like flat black beads regarded Bill with cool hostile intelligence. Its inky plumage glimmered with iridescent highlights.

Clamped between the upper and lower halves of its long needle-sharp bill was something round and white—

A human eyeball.

"*Gaaah!*" Repulsed, Bill instinctively thrust the walking stick at the bird, trying to lance it.

The raven took wing, lofting itself into the air and out of Bill's reach. It flew away, cawing its mockery.

Shaking his head as if to clear it of that nightmare image, Bill set himself to the task of finding Big Taw's guns.

He crawled around the body in a clockwise circle

searching for the weapons. The ground was hard packed, there were no layers of dirt for the guns to get lost in, no weedy growths to hide them.

When he came around to his starting point he reversed direction and began again, this time moving counterclockwise, once more scanning the ground for the hard bright welcome gleam of metal and finding none.

There were no guns within a wide radius of Big Taw's body. Yet Bill was sure that this was the place where he'd seen the big man go down.

Bill Longley gnashed his teeth in frustration. Here was a complicating factor he hadn't reckoned on. What were the odds of finding Big Taw minus not one gun but two? Of all the rotten luck!

Yet Bill Longley would not, could not, give up. It was a case of letting himself be defeated. Big Taw was only the first of more than a half-dozen dead gunmen. Where there were gunmen dead or alive, there were guns.

Bill Longley moved on to the next body, the one that lay closest to him.

Perhaps because of its nearness to Bill the vultures were keeping their distance from it and him.

Bill hauled himself to his feet, standing there gathering his strength. He stood leaning forward, gripping the tops of his thighs. He was breathless and panting from the exertion of rising up on two legs.

The clamor of many-throated harsh raucous cawing and the buffeting of squadrons of wings beating empty air was a constant din in Bill's ears.

The blackbirds took flight at his approach, perhaps sensing he was seriously off-kilter. Bill stumbled over the corpse and fell, the corpse breaking his fall. The tumble didn't help his open wound any.

Blackness began creeping in around the edges of his vision, but Bill continued his search. The results on this third try had the same yield as the previous two: zero.

No gun. Empty hands, empty holsters, ground bare of firearms.

The light of dawning realization broke in on Bill. It would have come to him sooner if he wasn't so worn down, played out, used up.

The gunmen didn't have any guns. Someone must have taken them away. Who else could have done that but Sam Heller, if only to make Bill Longley out even more of a poor damned fool than ever?

Bill rolled off the corpse, using the momentum to rise to his feet and take a few staggering steps forward. He looked around, scanning for the campsite. He had trouble making it out because he couldn't see so well, what with the shades of blackness that kept rolling and unrolling up and down his field of vision.

He found the site at last and started toward it. He had taken no more than a few steps before he fell down, and out.

# Sixteen

"You've got a lot of sand, my friend," a voice said. "But that's no substitute for brains."

The voice was Sam Heller's.

"What happened?" Bill Longley asked, now fully returned to consciousness.

"You went for a walk to visit Vard and the gang. Your wound opened again. You passed out. I came back down the hill and found you there, brought you back, and patched you up. So here we are again," Sam said.

Bill had been returned to the bed of boughs beside the campfire, now cold and dead. He sat up with his back propped up against a fallen log. He was bare from the waist up, his torso wrapped with fresh home-made bandages, to which Sam had just completed the finishing touches. A folded blanket was draped across his shoulders.

"We won't be here long," Sam added. "The birds are a signpost pointing straight to us."

With an upward tilt of his head he indicated the sky above them. Bill's gaze followed the other's lead. The heights over Dead Lake basin were thick with low-flying vultures circling the site.

Sunlight now slanted directly into the basin, the light of midmorning.

"You're an active fellow, Bill. Too active. A man could get tired playing nursemaid to you," Sam said.

"I didn't ask for help, I can take care of myself," Bill said.

"So I noticed," Sam said with a sardonic grin. "You sure were riding high, wide, and handsome down there in the dirt with the dead men and the vultures and the crows . . ." He laughed. "Strange place for a morning stroll, but to each his own, I reckon. I've got to take some of the blame. I should have told you about the guns."

"What guns?" Bill said sharply.

"The gang's guns. I took care of them yesterday. I gathered up all their weapons and disabled them, busted the firing pins so they wouldn't work."

Anger pasted two red spots on Bill's cheeks. "What'd you do that for?"

"Couldn't leave them laying around where passing Comanche or outlaws could find them, somebody might have got hurt. I covered them up with rocks and brush lest some enterprising badman take them to a gunsmith to get the firing pins replaced to put them back in working order."

Bill swore, long and feelingly.

"Feel better now that you've got that out of your system?" Sam asked when Bill was done.

"No. What'd you do with my guns?"

"They must have got lost in the shuffle. Don't worry, you'll be able to get some new ones in Hangtree. No shortage of guns there. Anyhow, the last thing a man in your condition needs is a firearm."

"My condition? What do you mean?" Bill demanded.

"Youth—you've got too much of it," Sam said. "Though you seem to be doing your level best to use it up, and yourself, too."

"That's my lookout," Bill said.

"So it is," Sam agreed. "Best we clear out of here quick. Hangtree's a-waiting."

The basin had no trees to speak of, only scrub brush, dwarf mesquite, and the like. That's why Sam had gone to the thicket on the hill, to cut some wood for poles, which he had then brought to the campsite on the back of the quarter horse.

He used the poles to build a travois. The travois was a Plains Indians horse-drawn carryall for transporting cargo. The travois consisted of two long poles with several crosspieces tied to them by lengths of rope. The two main poles were each about ten feet long. They were tied together at one end and open at the base to form a triangle shape. A horse blanket was secured sling-style to the wooden framework to serve as the carrying platform. The sledgelike construction was capable of carrying weights of up to several hundred pounds for long distances overland.

Big Taw's quarter horse was pressed into service to haul the travois. The animal was strong, and broad beamed.

Sam Heller gave the travois a final inspection and found it good.

"That's your traveling rig?" Bill Longley was interested despite his resolve to remain aloof from the Yankee and his ways.

Despite which he wore a shirt that came from one

of Sam's saddlebags. It was too big for him, especially in the shoulders, hanging on him like a tent.

"You said it was for damaged goods. What goods?" Bill asked.

"You," Sam said, pointing a finger at Bill.

"Huh? Wha—?" Bill was taken aback.

"Your chariot awaits," Sam said, indicating the travois. "Get on, we're moving out."

Bill's gaze went flat, hard eyed. "I'm not riding in that."

"What are you going to do, walk?" Sam returned.

"I'll ride one of the gang's horses. I'm sure you won't begrudge me that, hardhearted Northerner though you are."

"I wouldn't mind if you could sit a horse for more than a couple of minutes without falling off it."

"I'm the judge of that, not you."

Bill was pacing back and forth around the campsite to show how vigorous he was when a wave of dizziness overcame him. He sat down hard on the ground to keep from falling. He leaned far forward, head hanging down near his crossed legs.

Several minutes passed before the dizzy spell subsided. Sam handed Bill a canteen.

"You want to get to Hangtree in one piece? You've got something to do there, something important? The travois is what's going to get you there," Sam said.

"I'm not going to ride in that; it's for squaws and sick old men." Bill showed a face of disgust.

"You're a shot-up young man, and if you want to get much older you'd best haul ass into the travois before some of Vard's pals come looking for him and find us."

"You've got all the answers, don't you?"

"That's how we Yankees are."

"I know you think so." Bill looked up, studying Sam's face. "How come you're so all-fired anxious to get me to Hangtree?"

"I like to help people," Sam said blandly.

"Uh-uh," Bill said. "I don't have time to waste jawing with you. If that's what it takes to get out of this charnel house I'll do it."

Their section of the basin quadrant where the vultures were feasting was pretty gamy now with the sun's heat coming on.

"Give me a hand and let's get out of here," Bill Longley said. *I'm played out for now,* he admitted to himself, but not out loud.

He went along as Sam helped him to his feet and half-carried half-walked him to the nearby quarter horse and the travois yoked to it. Bill eased himself into the rig.

"There's a rope here for a safety line to hold you in if you need it. Try not to fall out, I don't want to lose you," Sam said.

"You won't be rid of me that easily," Bill said. "How about a gun? If we're attacked I want to defend myself."

"If we're attacked I'll give you one," Sam said.

Sam hauled a metal flask out of his hip pocket. "This is the last leg of the trip so let's start it off right."

Bill sat up straight. "So you had some left after all you son of a—"

"Ah-ah," Sam said, wagging a cautionary finger.

"Gun, you son of a gun," Bill said.

Sam uncapped the flask. There were about two solid belts left. Sam had a good enough idea of Bill's character to drink first so there would be sure to be enough for him.

"Health," Sam said, "and you sure could use some." He tossed his drink back, then passed the flask to Bill.

Bill gulped greedily. "Ah . . . that's good."


Sam Heller was mounted up on Dusty at the head of a string of horses that formerly belonged to the Vard gang.

Bill Longley had described his missing bay, but the animal was nowhere to be found. After Bill had been shot out of the saddle the horse had kept on running, clear out of the basin. It ran off for parts unknown and failed to return last night or this morning. For all Sam knew it was still running.

He promised Bill to keep an eye out for the bay and try to rope it in if he saw it, doubtful though he was that there was much chance of that.

One end of a long lead rope was tied to Sam's saddle horn. The rope stretched out behind him, trailing a string of Vard gang horses each of which was secured to the lead line so as to proceed in single file.

Big Taw's oversized quarter horse followed next in line after Sam and Dusty. Bill Longley was nestled in the travois harnessed behind the big horse. Bill had to eat only the dust churned up by two horses, Sam's and the quarter horse.

Sam pointed Dusty's head west, urging the animal forward. The line of horses advanced, crossing the basin floor.

Sam glanced back for a last look at the Vard gang, but all he could see were the vultures massing them.

Sam sighed. As a bounty hunter he was leaving a lot of money on the table in the persons of Loman Vard and a couple of his top henchmen, all of whom had prices on their heads.

But duty called. Malvina the Gypsy was at the top of the Department of the Army's Most Wanted list. Any lead to her whereabouts had top priority and must be followed to its source.

Let the buzzards have Vard and company.

When the last scavenger bird quit the scene, Sam knew, hardly a trace of flesh would remain behind on the dead men's bones.

But the evil they did would live on . . .

It would be Sam Heller's mission to track down the source of that evil and wipe it out, branch, stem, and roots.

His mission, his duty, and his pleasure.


It was late afternoon when Sam Heller's caravan came to a long low rise. The slope ahead was over a mile long, but the incline was a slight one of only a few degrees.

The horses made the climb with no difficulty, not even breathing hard when they reached the top.

To the west lay a deep narrow valley that ranked as a gorge. A watercourse ran north-south through it. It was called Swift Creek, but it was more of a river than a creek. It ran fast and deep with a treacherous current, rushing south through the gorge, then across a flat for several miles before feeding into the Liberty River, a major watercourse stretching southeast for several hundred miles.

The west bank of the gorge was crowned by a wide flat-topped summit bristling with a thicket of woods. The woods screened the view of what lay beyond, veiling it.

Sam got down from his horse to have a word with Bill Longley.

"We cross Swift Creek next. Hangtree is on the other side."

Bill nodded, forcing a grin. It looked thin, skeletal. He'd suffered a relapse during the long hours of travel. Glazed eyes stared out of a sallow face.

Sam checked Bill's shoulder wound. It checked out okay, not having reopened. But his fever had returned. His forehead was hot to the touch and his teeth chattered. He was suffering from fever and chills at the same time.

"There's a good doctor in Hangtree, so hold on," Sam said.

"I didn't come this far not to make it now," Bill rasped.

"Good man," Sam encouraged.

"Not so's you'd notice," Bill joked feebly.

Sam went to the head of the line and stepped up into Dusty's saddle. They started forward, the rest of the string following.

The gorge was thick with dusky shadows and filled with the sound of fast-rushing water. Sam Heller led the procession of horses down a trail that switchbacked across the eastern bank. A low stone bridge spanned Swift Creek, its side rails barely rising to knee height.

Sam dismounted to oversee on foot the string's crossing of the bridge. The Swift's waters were dangerous. Few who fell in ever came out alive. Holding on to Dusty's halter, Sam started across the span.

The steel-dust horse advanced without hesitation, but some of the animals farther back in line grew restive and balky. Alternately coaxing and cursing the horses, Sam eventually got them across the bridge to the safety of the other side.

"Nothing to it," Sam remarked in passing to Bill stretched out on the travois.

"How come you're sweating?" Bill said.

Ignoring the comment Sam returned to the head of the line and mounted up. The string of horses threaded a switchback trail on the west bank, following it to a flat-topped summit. The crest was covered by a narrow band of thick woods, pierced in the center by the westbound trail. Sam's string entered the gap, continuing through to the other side.

Below the ridgetop, the far side of the slope made an easy descent for about a fifth of a mile before spilling on to a vast tableland. The trail followed the downgrade into the flat where it became Trail Street, the east-west centerline and main drag of Hangtree town. The settlement spread north and south on both sides of Trail Street.

The setting sun cut a scarlet razor line above the western horizon and below the bottom of black thunderhead clouds with slate-colored edges that towered into a darkling sky.

Hangtree was a vista of yellow lights floating in purple-black shadows.

# SEVENTEEN

Sam, Bill, and the string of horses rode downhill into Trail Street and the town proper. Lights glowed behind shaded windows and in lanterns hanging from ridgepoles and projecting building beams.

The eastern mouth of Trail Street opening on the west was bracketed by two old stone structures: a three-story courthouse on the right-hand side and a one-story flat-roof jail with iron-bar windows on the left.

At the opposite, western end of town, where Trail Street petered out and once more became the Hang-tree Trail, the thoroughfare was braced by a pair of sentinel-like landmarks.

On a rise to the left was a white-painted church whose lofty bell tower was topped by a slim octagonal spire. A piece of land adjacent to the building served as the church graveyard. Its neat orderly grounds with well-kept plots and upright tombstones and markers was bounded by a black iron spear fence.

On the right-hand side of the street-turned-trail stood a shaggy knoll dominated by a gnarly, towering dead tree, ancient and blasted black and charred by multiple lightning strikes. This was the Hanging Tree, which served as the gallows from which condemned prisoners were hanged by the neck until dead.

The same Hanging Tree that had given its name to the county and the town that was its capital.

Sam reined in in front of the Golden Spur Saloon on the north side of Trail Street, a few lots west of the courthouse.

The saloon was a big two-story structure sitting solid and foursquare on its lot site and fronting on Trail Street. Its interior glowed with rich yellow-brown light.

From behind batwing saloon doors came the tide-like rise and fall of talk, laughter, crowd noises, the clink of glasses and bottles, the rinky-tink notes of a piano, the humming whirr of a spinning Wheel of Fortune, and jaunty percussive clatter of a metal ball racketing through the slots of a roulette wheel before coming to a silent halt.

Sam got down from his horse and secured several animals in the line to a hitching post, enough to anchor the entire string and ensure they would not go wandering off.

He went to Bill Longley in the travois. Yellow-brown light from the saloon washed over the youth. He looked gaunt, haggard. The hollows of his eyes and cheeks were thickly shadowed. His mouth gaped open.

Sam wondered if Bill had passed out. But in the dark blots of their sockets his eyes were open, intent.

"Where are we?" Bill's words came as a harsh croak. He took a deep breath, swallowed hard. His voice sounded stronger, clearer on his second try as he asked.

"This is the end of the line for you, the Golden Spur

Saloon in Hangtree," Sam said. "It's owned by Damon Bolt, a friend of Johnny Cross."

It was that last that did it, the name of Johnny Cross. Bill summoned up his willpower, making a conscious effort to fight through the strength-sapping fires of the fever racking him.

"You *knew*! You knew all the time," Bill accused. "How?"

"You told me," Sam said gently.

"I never," Bill began.

"You told me last night, during a break in the height of your fever."

"I don't remember." Bill rubbed his face with his hands. "I couldn't tell the dreams—the nightmares—from what was real. Come morning it was all a jumble in my head."

"You didn't say anything discreditable, just that you had a message for Cross you had to deliver. Matter of life and death, you said. It happens that Johnny Cross and I are acquainted. We've done some work together," Sam said.

Killing work, he thought but didn't say. He didn't have to. Bill got the idea, Sam could tell by the look on his face. Simple logic, really. There was only one kind of work on which Johnny Cross and Sam Heller were likely to find common ground.

"Johnny and you . . . a Yankee? Hard to believe!" Bill said, shaking his head.

"Why not? The war's over," Sam said.

"Says who?"

"Robert E. Lee, at Appomattox in sixty-five. That ought to be good enough for even the most stubborn of you diehards."

But even as he said it, Sam knew it was a long way

off from being generally accepted by the embittered Southrons, Bill Longley very much included.

"I'm going inside to find Damon Bolt and tell him what it's all about. Once I've got you squared away I'm going to send a messenger out to Cross Ranch to tell Johnny you're here," Sam said.

He was in a hurry to get things moving. He turned, preparing to start into the saloon when Bill thrust out an imploring hand and cried, "Wait!"

Sam paused in midstride, arrested by the urgency in the other's voice. Bill motioned for Sam to lean in closer. Sam did so.

Bill had the air of one with something confidential to say. Sam tilted his head, putting an ear close to Bill's mouth so he alone could hear.

"For God's sake get me out of this thing!" Bill said, his voice hushed, urgent. "Don't leave me lying here looking like a damned fool!"

"All right," Sam said solemnly, indicating he understood the gravity of the situation. And he did.

Bill Longley regarded himself first and foremost as a Southern gentleman and would do what he had to do to maintain that hard-won status, that precious sense of self. It was part of an unwritten Code of Conduct.

To be a gentleman, to hold oneself as such and to be so regarded by one's peers, was literally a matter of life and death. A gentleman did not allow himself to be cheated, insulted, made a fool of, to have one's dignity or honor impugned—these were literally killing matters, worth fighting and dying for.

To be secured in the travois in the wilderness was a matter of enduring an uncomfortable situation to save one's life.

But to arrive in a new town, a Texas town, a stranger,

to be on public display in a conveyance associated with "squaws and sick old men," as Bill had earlier so witheringly described it, would be to undergo extreme humiliation.

To play the fool, gawked and jeered at by passersby in the street, would be well nigh unendurable.

Ridiculous? To an outsider it was, but Sam Heller understood. He'd often found absurd some of the touchy pretensions of these hypersensitive Southern gentlemen, ever alert for a slight or insult to their honor.

Yet was he so different? There were certain insults to his sense of rightness that he could not abide and was ever ready to take up arms to wipe out said offense in spilled blood—

No, Sam understood the likes of Bill Longley and his kind all too well.

Sam took Bill's good right arm over the elbow, helping the other to his feet, half-lifting him out of the travois. Sam was a powerful man with great bodily strength, so it took no real effort for him to hustle Bill up the wooden stairs accessing the boardwalk sidewalk fronting the Golden Spur.

Several wicker armchairs, high backed and deep seated, were lined up along the wall to one side of the entrance, for the use and convenience of patrons who might wish to enjoy a social glass of beer or spirits or simply pass the time while enjoying the outside air and the passing parade.

This being the dinner hour, the chairs were empty. Sam eased Bill into the middle chair. A shaded window was above and behind the chairs. In the rich bronze light shining through the glass, Bill could be seen sitting huddled in the chair, white lipped and trembling from the strain of being moved. He was fighting to show no sign of weakness or give vent to his sufferings aloud.

For this, too, was part of the Code.

Low voiced, discreet, careful to make no fuss that would draw undue attention to Bill and himself, Sam asked, "How you making it?"

"Better now—that I'm sitting up. Damned near busted my tailbone in that blamed carryall," Bill said tightly.

"You can joke. Good. Sit tight, I'll be right back," Sam said.

"I'll be here."

"Make sure nobody steals the horses."

"I couldn't stop them from stealing *me*!"

"Well, try."

Sam Heller went into the Golden Spur Saloon, batwing doors swinging shut behind him.

Bill let out the breath he'd been holding. He was hurting. He rested the back of his head against the top of the chair and closed his eyes . . .

"Longley, Longley!"

Bill didn't remember falling asleep but the next thing he knew, he was being gently shaken awake by Sam Heller.

Bill opened his eyes. A group of people was gathered around the chair in which he sat.

There was a gambling man with jet-black hair and mustache, clad in a dark brown velour jacket and a maroon cravat. Standing beside him, holding on to his arm, was a lean woman with brick-red hair in a green dress. Her long horsey face was saved from plainness by bright green eyes and a vivid red-painted mouth.

There was a large-sized barkeep, his curly hair parted in the middle, and a small neat black-clad man, who wore the green visor shade of a house card dealer, and was pale with long-fingered hands.

Sam handled the introductions, brief though they were. "Damon Bolt and Mrs. Frye, owners of the Golden Spur," he said, indicating the couple.

"And these two stalwarts are Mr. Morrissey and Ace-High"—the barkeep and the card dealer, respectively.

"Pleased to meet you," Bill murmured.

Morrissey and Ace-High helped Bill to his feet, shaky and unsteady though he was on them. They held him, keeping him upright. Sam had one last surprise for Bill. He held a gunbelt with two holstered guns. "These are yours, Bill, the ones you had at the basin," he said. "They're not loaded, so don't get any ideas."

"I'll hold them," Damon Bolt said.

Sam handed the guns to him. "I've done my bit. I'll leave Mr. Longley in your care."

"I sent for Doc Ferguson," Mrs. Frye said.

"Good." Sam turned to Bill Longley. "You made it to Hangtree. Congratulations," he said, starting to move off.

"Hey, Billy Yank!" Bill called.

Sam paused, looking back at him.

"Thanks," Bill Longley said.

"Anytime, Reb." Sam gave him a two-finger salute and went down the wooden front steps to the horses.

"Let's get him inside," Mrs. Frye said.

Morrissey and Ace-High started to steer Bill to the

front entrance. Bill dug in his heels, drew himself up straight, "I can do it by myself."

Morrissey and Ace-High let go of him. Smiling jauntily, Bill took a step forward. His eyes rolled up in his head, showing only the whites. Bill shut down, blackness felling him like a scythe. He was falling before he knew what hit him.

Morrissey caught him before he hit the veranda. He scooped up Bill in his brawny arms, holding him as easily as if he had been a sleeping child. Morrissey carried Bill through the swinging doors into the saloon, the others following.

"Put him in one of the guest rooms upstairs," Mrs. Frye said. "He'll like that."

Two drunks who'd been thrown out of a saloon on the next block over came staggering along Trail Street, pausing in front of the Golden Spur. They were as plastered as two boiled owls, leaning on each other for support. They watched as Morrissey caught up Bill and carried him into the saloon.

"There's something you don't see every day," one drunk said.

"What's that?" queried the other.

"I've seen plenty of them carried out like that, but this is the first time I've ever seen one carried in!"

# EIGHTEEN

Johnny Cross went into the Golden Spur Saloon. It was mid-afternoon of the second day after the night Bill Longley came to town.

Bill was just about the last person Johnny expected to encounter in his hometown of Hangtree, Texas. The last time he'd seen Bill had been almost two years ago in Halftown in Moraine County on the Blacksnake River. They'd both been riding then with Cullen Baker's gang. That had been a bad time in Johnny's young life, a low point. He'd been drinking too much, brooding too hard, and shooting too quick. And the Blacksnake had been pure hell.

Johnny hated the swamplands. You wouldn't think that a patch of East Texas near the Sabine River and the Gulf of Mexico could be so much like the Louisiana bayou country.

It had all the disadvantages of a swamp—heat, humidity, mud, insects, gators, venomous snakes—and none of the attractions of the Louisiana bayou such as good food and drink, good times, and good-looking gals who were sweet and willing.

It was what the Blacksnake country didn't have that made it attractive: lawmen. It didn't have lawmen. No federal occupation troops, U.S. Navy patrols, National Police Bureau detectives, federal marshal fugitive chasers, Pinkerton men and suchlike, and damned few Home Guards, vigilance committees, bounty hunters, and organized networks of paid informants.

None of them wanted to go into those trackless swamplands with their intricate mazes of rivers, lakes, bayous, and back channels so useful for hiding out and evading man-hunters; roads and trails hemmed in by abundant jungle foliage so advantageous for bushwhackers and ambushers; and their bogs, marshes, and sinkholes so handy for hiding bodies so they'd never be found, no, not in a thousand years.

Johnny Cross had appreciated those features of the Blacksnake River country then, for he'd been a Wanted man, a most Wanted man.

He had ridden with Quantrill's guerrilla raiders for practically the duration of the war, and the members of that band had specifically been denied amnesty after the surrender at Appomattox but instead had been posted with open warrants with no expiration dates or statutes of limitation on them.

In Oklahoma, Kansas, and Arkansas, Johnny Cross had racked up further numerous charges for bank and mail robbery, pillaging weapons from government arsenals, robbery, and murder. That the "murders" were killings of troops and lawmen intent on killing him did nothing to lessen the charges against him.

He'd fallen in with the Baker gang and for a time it had been a good fit. Moraine County's Clinchfield and Halftown, base of operations for the Baker gang, were at the heart of Blacksnake River country and very welcome it had seemed to Johnny Cross at the time.

Cullen Baker seemed designed by nature and inclination for outlawry. Of Herculean strength, he was a fast draw, a dead shot, vicious brawler, and tireless rider. He had raw, reckless courage and a criminal brain seething with schemes.

Johnny got along well with Cullen Baker, no mean feat, for the bandit leader was too often ill tempered and suspicious. He could also be surprisingly generous when it came to distribution of loot.

He was an incurable alcoholic whose vile temper when under the influence would prove to be his undoing time and again.

Johnny got along well with Cullen Baker for most of their six months they rode together. Part of the reason was that Johnny could match Baker shot for shot, bottle for bottle, during their many prodigious drinking bouts. The hulking Baker marveled how Johnny, athletic but of medium height and compactly made, was able to match him despite his far lesser bulk.

Johnny was careful never to outdo the bandit's drinking during these contests. This was the key to getting along with Cullen Baker: never try to outdo him. Not that Johnny had any fear of Baker, knowing that if it came to a showdown, he had confidence in his own abilities to see him through. But he liked him well enough not to want to have to kill him.

Johnny had shown no inclination or desire to challenge Cullen Baker's leadership of the band. This was easy for Johnny to do because in truth he had no such aspirations. He was content at this stage of his career to remain in the background while letting others bask in the limelight. Experience had shown him that the limelight made one a better target.

Cullen Baker had saved Johnny's life at risk to his own more than once, exhibitions of raw nerve in the service of friendship that had ensured Johnny's gratitude. Perhaps that was why Baker had performed them. There was no telling for sure. For all his elemental drives and sometimes crudeness, Cullen Baker was a deep one.

Bill Longley was a wild youth in his midteens when he began riding with the gang. From the start he held his own and more than matched the performances of older, more veteran outlaws. Something in Bill's nature and Johnny's own clicked, causing them to string together at work and play. Bill's prodigious, unquenchable thirst for alcohol excited Cullen Baker's admiration as much as the teenager's undoubted ability with a gun.

Things went sour for the band in the end. A few big schemes came undone at the same time; bad luck caused the gang to ride into a deadly ambush that wiped their numbers in half. Some blamed Baker's rampant drinking for their problems, but Johnny figured the doubters and naysayers to be soreheads looking for someone to blame . . . Cullen Baker consumed the same amount of redeye as he had when the gang's luck had been good.

But Johnny *was* disturbed by Baker's fierce urge toward senseless violence. He killed to see men die. More victims began to fall to his guns not for what they did or didn't do but for what they might do or simply because Baker didn't like their looks.

"I had a bad feeling about him" was Baker's ever more frequent excuse for burning down a victim who was too slow in handing over his valuables, or unlocking a cash drawer or similar lapses that were normal reactions of men being robbed at gunpoint.

Johnny had no stomach for killing unarmed men. He'd had more than enough of that with Quantrill. It was needless cruelty and to his way of thinking, smacked of something yellowbellies would do . . .

A particularly relentless and efficient manhunt by the sheriff of neighboring Albedo County who had invaded Moraine County with a small army of well-armed deputies and auxiliaries served Johnny as a pretext for leaving the band. It was an illegal incursion, a charge that bothered the venturesome lawmen not at all. And an outlaw shot dead during an illegal incursion is just as dead as though the operation had been authorized by the highest law in the land.

Ordinarily Cullen Baker viewed the departure of a gang member under any circumstance as akin to desertion, but the sheriff's big-caliber cleanup left no alternative but to temporarily disband the gang. Riding en masse as a group was an invitation to detection and slaughter by the militant lawmen. Only by going it alone or in twos or threes could the outlaws hope to slip the ever-tightening dragnet blanketing Moraine County.

Cullen Baker announced his intention of setting out for Deep Hollow, Moraine County's ultimate backcountry swampland fugitive refuge. Even the river pirates, smugglers, gunrunners, and the like who thronged the county gave the Hollow a wide berth save as a last resort.

Lawmen who entered Deep Hollow sometimes returned but never with the wanted men they originally sought. Baker would retreat into the backcountry. If

the sheriff and his men followed him, well and good—
they would be done for. If not, Baker would remain
in hiding until the sheriff tired of the chase and returned to his home county, to emerge at the right time
to assemble a newer, even more formidable gang.

Johnny Cross decided to return home to Hangtree
County. He invited Bill Longley to join him and try his
luck on Johnny's old stomping grounds but Bill declined, saying that he, Bill, intended to stick with Cullen
Baker and attempt to shelter in Deep Hollow.

So one rainy steamy morning Johnny Cross said so
long to his fellow gang members and loaded a knap-
sack containing all his worldly goods in the bottom of
a pirogue—a kind of lightweight shallow-draft dugout
canoe ideal for traveling the narrow inlets and back
channels of the swampland. Johnny set out to slip the
iron ring of armed men encircling that stretch of the
Blacksnake that includes Clinchfield and Halftown
and win his way to dry land, escape, and the road to
Hangtree.

After countless perils and many wide-ranging detours taking him far afield from his intended goal,
Johnny returned to the Cross Ranch, discovering that
his family was dead, the ranch house a burned-out ruin,
and the spread a scene of weed-grown desolation.

He settled in and set out to rebuild his life. His quick
gun, sharp wits, and raw nerve, and that most elusive
but vital component of success called *luck*, had come
together to win him an abundance of good fortune.

When he now thought at all of those desperate days
with the Cullen Baker gang in Moraine County on the
Blacksnake—and he did so rarely, being inclined to
look ahead, not back—he reflected with wry amusement that it was all to the best that Bill Longley had

declined his invite to accompany him back to his hometown.

Because given Bill's nature, and the nature of Hangtree, the two would have mixed like oil and water, which is to say not at all.

Given the fact that Bill was a killer and a drunkard, and given Johnny's newfound feelings of responsibility toward the continued well-being of the people of Hangtree—well, most of them—it was not unreasonable to assume that Johnny Cross might someday find it necessary to kill Bill Longley. Which would be a shame for he genuinely liked Bill.

So Johnny had mused idly and infrequently when the return of Bill Longley seemed an astronomical impossibility.

The overwhelming likelihood was that Bill was dead or in jail. Dead, more likely, because a wild maverick like Bill Longley if jailed would soon manage to get himself killed, by his fellow inmates, his jailers, or possibly even by his own despairing hand.

Johnny Cross now tried to put the puzzle together with the pieces he had, which were few, some of them at secondhand from the original source:

Bill Longley was not dead, he was very much alive—shot up some, but alive. Shot by the command of that bad *hombre* Loman Vard, himself shot dead by Bill Longley.

But what strange twist of fate could set Bill Longley and Loman Vard so much at odds as to want to do each other to death?

More, who throws a rope with a loop so wide it snares not only Bill and Vard but even that most mysterious fellow himself, Sam Heller?

Last night Sam had sent a rider from town out to the Cross Ranch with a note from Sam to Johnny.

The note said simply that Bill Longley was in Hangtree with a message for Johnny, that Bill had been shot, his injuries serious but not critical, and that he was resting at the Golden Spur.

Don't know how much rest he'll get there, Johnny thought sardonically, not with all those good-looking young whores and high-line whiskey on tap.

Johnny Cross saddled a fast horse that same night and raced to town, going to the Golden Spur.

Damon Bolt and Mrs. Frye were talking with crusty old Doc Ferguson when Johnny arrived. Doc Ferguson described Bill Longley's wounds, saying that Bill was now resting and couldn't be disturbed, a stiff dose of laudanum having put him into a deep, much-needed sleep.

Johnny suggested that Bill should be put under guard in case new attempts be made to kill him; Damon Bolt said this had already been done.

Johnny went to Sam Heller's bungalow on the outskirts of town but Sam was not there. Johnny then went to see town marshal Mack Barton at his jail office; Barton was out and his assistant deputy Ellis was his usual clueless self and no help in filling in the background.

Damon Bolt offered Johnny a free room at the Golden Spur, but Johnny declined with thanks. Too much temptation at the saloon. He took a room at the Cattleman Hotel, Hangtree's best, where he had a troubled night's sleep.

Johnny put the time to good use by taking care of some banking business and other errands that required his presence in town.

Mid-afternoon of the second day after Bill Longley's arrival in Hangtree saw Johnny Cross's return to the Golden Spur to see how Bill Longley was getting along.

It was a slack time in the saloon's working hours. The lunchtime beer-drinking crowd was long gone and the early evening drinkers had yet to arrive. The gaming room was quiet.

A handful of solitary drinkers stood at the brass-railed long bar in the main room. Johnny Cross quietly took his place among them.

Sipping his whiskey, he caught sight of his reflection in the wall-mounted mirror behind the bar. The image in the looking glass was that of a young man in his early twenties, medium height, compactly built. A handsome man with clean-cut features and a friendly face.

There was something unusual about his being clean shaven in a frontier society where some sort of facial hair on males was almost universal.

The years with Quantrill of living rough in the field, too often long haired, bearded, and filthy, going months between baths and a change in clean clothes, a condition too often repeated in the year and a half of being on the dodge after the war, had made Johnny hunger for a fastidious cleanliness in his later civilian life.

He wore a dark flat-crowned hat, a jacket of such dark blue hue it seemed almost black, a slate-gray button-down shirt, black jeans, and boots. A low-slung gunbelt held twin holstered Colt .45s.

He slapped a coin down on the counter, ordering a shot of whiskey and a beer. "Have one for yourself, Mr. Morrissey."

"Thank you, Mr. Cross," the barkeep said, drawing

Johnny's order and setting it down on the bar, then drawing the same for himself. All customers were "Mister" to Morrissey whether they bought him a shot or not.

Rumor had it that he was related to John Morrissey, New York City's famed heavyweight boxing champion, a rumor the barkeep would neither confirm nor deny. In any case Morrissey was a one-punch knockout bartender, as more than a few abusive drunks had found out the hard way.

A minority opinion of too-wise owls held that the barkeep was actually the real John Morrissey, who had faked his own death and gone west to thwart assassins from the Gangs of New York who had targeted him in a deadly vendetta.

Johnny drank his shot-and-a-beer, tingling with its restorative warmth.

"Himself would appreciate a word with you, Mr. Cross," Morrissey said in a low voice for Johnny's ears only. By "Himself" Morrissey was referring to saloon co-owner Damon Bolt.

"I'll see him now, if that's convenient," Johnny said.

"He's in the office," Morrissey said.

Johnny Cross went down the center aisle between the gaming room and the long bar main room, following it to a closed door in the rear wall under a flight of stairs. He knocked on the door panel.

"Come in," said a voice on the other side of the door.

Johnny went in, closing the door behind him.

The room was a combination office and study, well furnished. Within were Damon Bolt and Mrs. Frye, co-owners and proprietors of the Golden Spur. Johnny took off his hat and held it down by his side at the sight of Mrs. Frye.

"Good afternoon, John," Mrs. Frye said. She was serious faced, but her voice held purring warmth. She was the only one of Johnny Cross's circle of friends and acquaintances to call him "John." Perhaps that was why she did it.

Mrs. Frye's straight brick red hair was parted along the middle of her scalp and reached down to her strong jawline. Her body was long, sinewy, supple, and eel-like. She was doing her bookkeeping, poring over entries in the saloon's ledger, steel-nibbed ink pen in hand. He had always found her subtly disconcerting to his well-balanced sensibilities. She had a presence, a sense of sensuous power held under restraint. A kind of confidence borne of her wide experience of the male animal in all the bizarre extremities of his unrestrained behavior. A longtime prostitute, procuress, and brothel keeper, she had insights into human nature best not inquired into too deeply. In matters of manners and deportment she was always impeccably correct.

"Miz Frye," he said, meeting her coolly appraising gaze and holding it for a few beats before breaking eye contact.

"Damon," Johnny said, turning his face to the gambler.

Damon Bolt acknowledged the other's greeting with a tight nod. "Johnny."

He sat behind a desk on the far side of the room, facing the door. Mrs. Frye sat at a corner table, examining the ledger. Windows were set in the short wall behind Damon Bolt, the curtains closed. A well-padded leather couch lay along one of the room's long walls.

The space was shadowy, the desk lamp already lit. Red candles burned in a bronze candelabra set on Mrs. Frye's table.

Damon Bolt was a gambler who looked like a Romantic poet. He had a high forehead, ravaged-looking face, and raven-black hair and mustache. His was the paleness characteristic of folk of the nighttime world such as card players, saloon girls, drunks, bartenders, and the like. He was thin, too thin.

Damon Bolt was a professional gambler and celebrated duelist from New Orleans. A cut-glass decanter stood within Damon Bolt's easy reach on a green baize desk blotter. His hand was wrapped around a tumbler the size of a water glass. It was half-filled with a liquid the color of mahogany wood; its reddish-brown contents were alive with fiery red glints.

"Behold the awful truth, Johnny," he said, holding the glass tumbler up to the lamp so its light shone through. "I play while Mrs. Frye handles such dreary chores as keeping the books."

"What's a chore to others is a joy to me," Mrs. Frye said, not looking up from her ledger.

"Only as long as you stay in the black," the gambler countered.

"Yes, there's that. Going into the red is not a happiness."

"No worries on that score while you're keeping the books, my dear."

"Unless you drink up the profits . . . always a risk with you, Damon."

"You see how it is, Johnny? My vices keep our house suspended on a tightrope between prosperity or ruin," Damon Bolt said. "Oh, well, as long as I'm going to imperil our enterprise, I might as well have help doing it. Sit down, please, and join me in a drink."

"Thanks, don't mind if I do." Johnny took a seat in a chair across the desk from the gambler.

Damon Bolt set a second water glass on the desk blotter and began filling it from the decanter. When the tumbler was half-filled Johnny said, "When."

The gambler kept pouring until Johnny said, "Whoa!"

Damon Bolt paused, decanter at the ready. "It's very good brandy," he said.

"I've got a busy day and night ahead," Johnny said by way of explanation.

"As the poet said, 'Strong drink fortifies,'" the gambler insisted.

"You've got the quote wrong," Mrs. Frye said. "It goes, 'Wine gladdens the heart, but strong drink is a mocker.'"

"I like my version better, Mrs. Frye. Strong drink fortifies."

Johnny Cross was of the opinion that the gambler was already well fortified, fortified to a fault actually, but he wisely kept his opinion to himself.

Mrs. Frye must have been of the same belief. "Stop trying to get John drunk. He's concerned about his friend Bill and wants to see him."

"Yes, yes, of course, I forgot. Thoughtless of me." Damon Bolt picked up the tumbler, reached across the desk, and set it down in front of Johnny.

They drank. It *was* good brandy, Johnny thought, drinking deeply. Very good brandy. Damon Bolt's glass was nearly drained at a gulp.

Johnny Cross got down to business. "What about Bill Longley? How is he? Can I see him now?"

"He's all right, Doc Ferguson says he's going to be okay. He'll heal up fine," Damon Bolt said.

"He's already healthy enough to go bothering my girls," Mrs. Frye said.

"That sounds like Bill, all right. A good sign, I reckon," Johnny said. "But I'll have a word with him, tell him to stop making a damned pest of himself."

Mrs. Frye laughed, waving the notion away. "Don't worry about it. He's not mended enough yet to be dangerous. Besides, the girls are after him as much as he's after them, maybe more. He's something of a handsome young devil at that."

"Don't let him hear you say so; Bill's already got a swelled head about himself where the ladies are concerned," Johnny said.

"He can look all he likes but no touching. The hospitality of the house only extends so far. After that the proceedings are conducted on a pay as you go basis, strictly for cash," Mrs. Frye said.

"That let's Bill out. In all the time I've known him he's never had much more than a couple of copper coins to knock together," said Johnny.

"He does now," Damon Bolt said. "Vard's gang rode, not walked. They left behind eight very good horses. Sam Heller decided to split the windfall with young Longley. Heller left the horses with Hobson at the livery stables to sell on a consignment basis.

"There were two horses Hobson wanted for himself so he bought them paying cash on the barrelhead. Sam Heller left Longley's share of the money with us.

It's in a sealed envelope in the safe. And Longley's due for more when the other horses are sold."

"Best you hold on to that money for a bit," Johnny suggested. "Bill's laid up in the Golden Spur with a bunch of money and nothing to spend it on but whiskey and women. I've got a hunch that it won't be too very long before Bill's back to going without a dime in his pockets—but he'll have a hell of a lot of fun getting there!"

Mrs. Frye stood to escort Johnny Cross upstairs. The girls had their rooms on the second floor and there were private rooms there, too.

The head of the staircase opened on the center of the second floor landing at the rear, north wall. A balcony with gallery extended along three walls: the rear wall and two long walls. The house girls' rooms lay mostly along the rear wall, with private quarters for Damon Bolt and Mrs. Frye in separate unconnected rooms along the west wall.

Bill Longley's recovery room lay along the east wall.

Johnny Cross and Mrs. Frye exited the ground floor office and went to the foot of the staircase.

"No need for you to bother, Miz Frye, I can find the way to Bill's room," Johnny said. *Lord knows I know my way around the girls' rooms upstairs, I've been there enough times.* He smiled to himself.

"It's dangerous for a man to be upstairs alone and unescorted," Mrs. Frye said coolly.

"Your girls are safe from me," Johnny said.

"Ah, but are you safe from them? The girls corner a handsome man like you alone and we might not see you for a few days and then in heaven knows what condition."

"You're joshing, Miz Frye," Johnny Cross said, "aren't you?"

"Um," she said, shrugging. She smiled, showing lots of white-glowing teeth in the mid-afternoon shadows.

Mrs. Frye started up the stairs, Johnny Cross following. He couldn't help watching her high, firm heart-shaped bottom outlined against her long straight skirt. There was something hypnotic in the way her buttocks rolled beneath the taut fabric, slim hips swaying. Nothing vulgar or exaggerated about her movements, just the enticing rhythm of a fine healthy adult female body in motion.

Mrs. Frye paused at the top of the stairs, a hand resting on top of the corner post of the staircase's handrail. Glancing over her shoulder down at him through heavy-lidded green eyes she said huskily, "See anything you like, John?"

He swallowed hard. "Now, Miz Frye, you know it's not nice to tease the animals." It would have sounded better had his voice not cracked in midsentence.

She laughed throatily. "Is that what I'm doing, John?"

"One thing I'm sure of, Miz Frye—you always know what you're doing."

"I'll take that as a compliment," she said. "Rest easy. I'll be good, I promise." She drew an invisible X over her left breast. "Cross my heart."

Mrs. Frye waited on the landing for him to join her. When he stood alongside her she started forward, Johnny falling into step beside her. They turned right at the end of the landing, moving along the eastern gallery past a wall lined with closed doors.

It was quiet, almost hushed in the upstairs area. The house was open for business should a customer appear, but prospects were slim at the hour of three o'clock on a weekday afternoon.

A man sat slumped in an armless wooden chair parked outside a room door in mid-gallery. Presumably the guard posted to protect Bill Longley, Johnny thought.

The guard had managed the seemingly impossible feat of sleeping in a chair designed for discomfort, a straight-backed wooden chair with no arms, and no seat cushion. The man who had met and mastered the challenge was Earl "Cousin" Cozzens, an unlovely specimen of masculine squalor and incompetence.

Cookie, the Golden Spur's able cook was indeed Earl Cozzens's cousin and had gotten him a job at the Golden Spur doing mostly maintenance and donkey work, for which he had a modest ability.

Cousin Cozzens enjoyed a kind of minor celebrity due to his role in a messy drunken shoot-out some weeks earlier at the Doghouse Bar, a low dive on the dirty side of town, south of Trail Street—way south . . .

*During the course of a chair leg-swinging, ear-biting, crotch-kicking exhibition of impressively dirty fighting, Cousin had been lucky enough to lock up with his opponent just as the latter managed to haul a horse pistol out from behind the bib front of a pair of filthy denim overalls.*

*Clutching the thick wrist of the other's gun hand in his pawlike mitts, Cousin wrestled his foe to the sawdust-covered floor, the two of them rolling around underfoot of the dive's bloodthirsty patrons screaming and shouting their excitement.*

*Suddenly the gun fired once in a roaring blast of noise that was followed almost immediately by a howling scream of pain.*

*The frantic crowd fell dead silent. In the absence of sound the lone screamer's sobbing shrieks produced a blood-chilling effect.*

*The next instant, the crowd erupted in helter-skelter flight to escape the scene of the shooting. They poured out the doors, front, side, and back. They jumped out the windows. The Doghouse Bar being a one-story ground-floor structure, none of the jumpers was too badly hurt.*

*In less time than it takes to tell it, the dive was emptied out of all but the two combatants, Cousin and his opponent; the bar's owner and his helper, jealously watchful of the liquor supply to make sure it remained intact; and a handful of drunks too stupefied, bemused, or uncaring to disappear with the rest of the gunfire-shy crowd.*

*The screaming was getting on Cousin's nerves. He looked around in search of its source.*

*It came from his former foreman, who now stood on his knees holding his maimed hand upright, blood jetting from a hole that had been formerly occupied by his thumb. He had been grievously disabled by accidentally shooting off his own left thumb during the fight for the gun.*

*Candlelight glinted off the horse pistol where it stuck out of a sawdust mound on the floor.*

*Cousin scuttled to it on hands and knees, scooping it up and fisting it to triumphantly stick it in the face of the foe. The now one-thumbed man recoiled with a yelp, falling over on his side.*

*Cousin was on his feet, stalking the other, a triumphant leer on his face.*

*The Man with One Thumb bumped into a wall, having*

*run out of crawling space. He was cornered.* "Don't kill me please please don't do it please—"

*Cousin thumbed the hammer back, cocking it with a loud click.*

"No. D-don't!—"

*Seated alone at a small round-topped to one side of Cousin and his imminent victim was a small, slight old man with shoulder-length snowy white hair and matching billy goat beard.*

*He made eye contact with Cousin as the latter's finger tightened on the trigger. He shook his head no.*

"Why not?" *Cousin asked.*

"They'll hang ye," *the Ancient said reasonably.* "You don't want to dance on air swinging on a rope under the Hanging Tree."

"You've got something there," *Cousin said, easing off the trigger and lowering the hammer into place.*

*Town marshal Mack Barton arrested both men. For some reason he didn't like the looks of the one-thumbed man. Digging through an old pile of Wanted circulars, he discovered One-Thumb was an axe murderer from Pingry, an agricultural settlement some twenty miles distant from Hangtree.*

*He'd been working as a handyman on a farm owned by a widow with two children. One night he killed them all with an axe and stole $7.97, all the money he could find on the premises. He took a broken cuckoo clock, too.*

*One-Thumb was hanged not in Pingry but Hangtree, the event drawing a big turnout.*

Cousin Cozzens's supposed ability with a gun had led to his being posted as one of the guards assigned to protect Bill Longley.

Now, Cousin dozed on a chair outside Bill Longley's

room, his tailbone perched on the chair's unpadded wooden seat. Spindly legs stretched straight out in front of him, blocking the aisle. Cousin's head lolled, mouth hanging slackly open. He snored lightly.

More sounds came from within Bill's room, muffled by the closed door. A man and woman were talking low voiced, the woman occasionally giggling.

Mrs. Frye's eyes glinted with green sparks. She held a forefinger upright in front of her lips, signaling Johnny to silence.

Advancing on noiseless feet, she closed on Cousin. He was right-handed, his pistol stuck in the top of his pants on the left-hand side, worn butt-forward for a cross-belly draw.

Standing to one side of Cousin, Mrs. Frye leaned over him. Her left hand was held poised palm-down above his face while her right hand hovered scant inches from the gun butt.

All at once she snaked the gun out of his waistband and clamped her other hand over his mouth, muffling the startled outcry caused by his rude awakening.

"Don't speak," she said in a husky stage whisper. "Don't make a sound."

The awakening grew ruder still as Mrs. Frye pressed the gun muzzle against the underside of Cousin's chin, tilting his head back, his eyes bulging.

Mrs. Frye held Cousin there for a good half-minute, which must have seemed infinitely more prolonged to him.

"Bang! You're dead," she whispered. "That's what happens to those who sleep on guard duty. If I were a real killer, your brains—what there is of them—would be splattered all over the wall.

"I'm going to take the gun away now and I don't

want a sound out of you. Not a peep, understand? Otherwise I'm going to be very angry. Very very angry. Nod yes if you take my meaning."

Cousin bobbed his head. Mrs. Frye straightened, removing the gun muzzle from under his chin. Cousin slumped in his chair like a leaky wineskin.

"Sit in your place and don't get in the way," she told Cousin.

Mrs. Frye turned toward Johnny, so Cousin couldn't see her face. She winked broadly at Johnny.

Johnny Cross was vastly relieved, having been unsure of just how far Mrs. Frye would go.

Mrs. Frye reversed the gun in her hand, proffering it to him butt-first. "You friend Bill might not take it so well if he saw me enter with gun in hand," she said.

Johnny nodded, taking the gun and sticking it under his belt, under his jacket flap, out of sight but certainly not out of mind. Safely put away where it couldn't get into mischief.

Mrs. Frye knocked smartly on the door, turning the doorknob and opening the door at the same time.

"Coming in, dear, it's Mrs. Frye with a visitor," she called out cheerily, bustling into Bill Longley's room.

Johnny Cross hung back, letting Mrs. Frye take the play.

Bill Longley was sitting up in bed, reaching for a young woman in a state of partial undress who stood by the side of the bed, playfully fending him off.

Mrs. Frye came breezing in, and Bill and the girl froze in place. Mrs. Frye closed the door.

Outside in the gallery, Cousin Cozzens looked at Johnny Cross. Johnny shrugged.

"I guess I overplayed my hand, sleeping on the job," Cousin said unhappily.

"I reckon maybe you did," Johnny agreed.

"Kin I have my gun back?"

"When Mrs. Frye says so."

Cousin nodded.

The bed in Bill Longley's room was big enough for two, or even three or more. It had an ornate shiny brass headstand and footstand, looking for all the world like sections of a big birdcage.

Hanging from one of the headstand's knobbed bedposts was a twin-holstered gunbelt with a gun in each holster. It was Bill Longley's own gunbelt and guns, the ones Sam Heller had returned to him.

Bill had vowed to himself that any who tried for him, badman or lawman, would be greeted with hot lead burning through their vitals. No recovery room for them! When Bill Longley opened fire he shot to kill and rarely missed his mark.

This part of Texas was new to Bill Longley, yet he had already made his mark on it. From what he'd managed to pick up from Sam Heller and others, Loman Vard was a pretty big noise in this part of the state.

He *was*, Bill thought to himself. Now Vard was no more and his gang had gone down that same long road to nowhere with him and it was Bill Longley who had sent them there. Yes, he'd had some help from Sam Heller . . . honesty compelled him to admit that, if only to himself.

Heller was the damnedest Yankee he'd ever seen, no doubt about that. Try though he might, Bill could not get a handle on him. Sometimes Heller made noises like a lawman but no lawman could kill like that. He went about killing with cool competence and deadly efficiency. A true Northerner in that!

Yet what strange whim or impulse had motivated Heller to cut Bill in for half of the plunder in the form of the Vard gang's horses? Sharing out half of such a rich prize when he didn't have to? Was he loco? Bill could have seen the sentiment in it if not the logic if Bill had saved Sam's life, but that's not the way the deal went down. The reverse was true: Sam had saved Bill's life when Vard had him nailed six ways to sundown.

The gang's horses hadn't even all been sold off yet, according to Damon Bolt, who had told Bill the news of this unexpected windfall. Hobson, the livery stable owner, had agreed to sell the majority of the animals on consignment, meaning that it could be weeks if not months before Bill saw his share of the money.

Luckily Hobson had wanted two of the horses for himself, Vard's horse and Big Taw's quarter horse. The two best horses in the lot, Bill had to agree. Vard's mount was a superb Thoroughbred with Arabian and Spanish blood, while the quarter horse was an outstanding example of the breed, strong and fit with classic lines.

This outbreak of honesty and, yes, even honor must be contagious. Bill Longley found himself actually consenting to Damon Bolt's offer to hold it in the gambling room's safe vault until such time as Bill should actually need it. All except some petty cash for immediate necessities, which he now had on hand.

Bill Longley found himself half-hoping that Damon and friends would try to steal the cash so as to restore his, Bill's, lack of faith in humanity.

And yet Bill also found himself hoping that Damon

Bolt and, yes, even that damned Yankee Sam Heller would prove out to be, in this world of bent and crooked men and women, that rarest of rarities in town or country: straight dealers and square shooters.

In the meantime, fast recovering and with vigor returning, Bill Longley found other interests with which to occupy his time.

Such as Dallas.

"Dallas," actually.

Not the city but the woman who was known only as "Dallas." She was one of Mrs. Frye's "girls." A high-line, high-spirited sporting girl who plied her trade at the Golden Spur. Her room was just a few doors down the gallery from Bill's.

Convenient.

Especially since Dallas was a luscious brunette with a mass of curly chestnut brown hair pinned up to the top of her head, crowning the dark-eyed face of a fine-featured vixen. She was twenty years old, slim, leggy, high bosomed.

Dallas had helped take care of Bill when he was too weak to get out of bed. Now that he was on the mend and feeling better, he was trying to get her into bed. He had arranged for her to come to his room in mid-afternoon when the Golden Spur was at ebb tide, quiet and practically empty.

Bill also made arrangements with Cousin Cozzens, guarding his room at this particular time. A silver dollar from Bill's stock of petty cash bought Cousin's ready compliance to go along.

Dallas really was a sweet thing. Her skirt and petti-coats were bunched up around her slender waist.

Bill was reaching for her when Mrs. Frye came sailing into the room.

Bill was outraged though he knew better than to show it. Where was Cousin? This was the very sort of interruption Bill had paid him to watch out for.

Dallas jumped away from the bed to be confronted by her boss. The young woman was in a considerable state of disarray. Loose bobbing curls framed her red face. Her lip rouge was smeared around her mouth.

"My apologies, Miz Frye. It's all my fault," Bill said, forcing a halfway grin. "Miss Dallas stepped in to see how I was getting along. She looked so good I tried to steal a little kiss."

"Where? Down her blouse or under her skirt?"

"Please, Miz Frye, you're going to make me blush."

"I doubt that. I know how a man's mind works, Bill, but don't overdo it. There'll be hell to pay with Doc Ferguson if you open up your wounds."

"Yes, ma'am."

"And don't give me that 'Yes, ma'am' crap. You're not a boy and this isn't a schoolhouse."

"You're going to make me blush again, Miz Frye."

Mrs. Frye turned her attention to Dallas. "We'll iron this out later. For now go to your room and freshen up. It's getting on toward working hours."

"Yes, Mrs. Frye." Dallas used her hand to brush back wayward bobbing curls that hung over her eyes.

"And stop sulking or I'll slap that pout off your face," Mrs. Frye said.

Dallas bit her lip, nodded, and went out of the room.

Mrs. Frye was alone with Bill. "If you're well enough to try and make one of my girls, you can pay for the privilege. There's no free rides in this house."

"I understand. Sorry."

"Okay. It's done and forgotten. As they say, boys will be boys, or something."

Mrs. Frye went to the door, gripping the doorknob. "You've got a visitor. I'll send him in presently, give you time to catch your breath and wash your face, there's lip rouge smeared around your mouth."

"Thank you kindly," Bill said.

She went out into the gallery, closing the door behind her. Johnny Cross and Cousin Cozzens were there, Cozzens still seated on the chair.

Mrs. Frye put her hands on her hips. "On your feet, Cozzens. Don't you know it's impolite to sit while a lady is standing?"

"You told me to sit here and not move, Miz Frye."

"Ah, so you can follow instructions. Maybe there's hope for you yet. On your feet."

Cousin rose. Standing, he was a head taller than she, even though his head was now bowed.

"You're lucky Damon thinks you're lucky, Cozzens."

"How's that, Miz Frye?"

"You shoot a drunk in a barroom brawl and he turns out to be a fiend who's got all North Central Dallas in a panic. So Damon thinks you're lucky. Turns out you bring in a lot of new customers who want to take a look at the man who shot the thumb off the axe murderer.

"Damon thinks that's lucky, too, so he wants to keep you around. That's gamblers for you. But that's what's keeping me from firing your ass out of here. So maybe Damon is right and you really are lucky, who knows?"

"Uh, thank you, Miz Frye. Thanks. I really 'preciate it, thanks, thank—"

"Stop it, Cozzens."

Cousin shut up.

"From now on you'll stand your watches and I do mean stand," Mrs. Frye declared. "No more chair for you till further notice. Savvy?"

"Yes, Miz Frye. Should I put the chair in another room so it's out of the way?"

"Leave it where it is so the other guards can use it. Why should they suffer? They can use it, you can't. Don't you use it."

"Yes, Miz Frye."

"Nobody in this house lays down on the job but my girls, and for them it's what you might call in the line of duty. Nobody, but nobody sleeps on the job."

Mrs. Frye opened the room door and stuck her head in. Bill was drying his face with a hand towel; there was a pile of them on the bedside night table.

"You can go in now," she said, opening the door wide.

Johnny Cross stepped inside.

"*Johnny!* Johnny Cross!"

Hey, Bill, long time no see."

"Man, you're good for sore eyes." Bill was excited, face shining. He looked like he was ready to jump out of bed. "What I went through to see you!"

"I'll pull up a chair and you can tell me all about it," Johnny said.

"I'll leave you two to get on with your man-talk," Mrs. Frye said. "You're probably planning a dozen or so murders."

"At least," Bill Longley said.

"The hell of it is, I believe you." Mrs. Frye went out.

# NINETEEN

Three gunmen were under the gun. Their names were Park Farner, Hector Sime, and Justus Pike.

Three rebels who'd gone up against the Power and lost.

Now they must face Death. Not die, necessarily, but play dice with the devil with their lives as the stake. And the name of this particular devil was—Barbaroux.

Trial by Combat, if you will.

In Moraine County on the fever-haunted swamps of the Blacksnake, Commander Rufus Barbaroux now honored the duel and pandered to his own personal prejudices by combining personal combat with an even older tradition: the absolute power of life and death over their subjects once held by the Caesars of Imperial Rome.

A power he reserved for himself as heir of the Imperium by right of mastery of his own self-created Province of the Trans-Mississippi.

Tonight he would exercise that power for the amusement and edification of his Inner Circle, the ruling cadre of the Combine, the vehicle by which he maintained his rule over much of the Blacksnake.

The arena in which the Games would be staged was the Great White Boat, a floating fortress in which Barbaroux made his headquarters. She had begun as a grand steamboat back before the war in the days when steamers were the first and last word in trans-Mississippi travel.

The riverboat had been built in the late 1840s, the heyday of the grand steamers. Christened the *Sabine Queen*, she was a proud member of a great fleet of such steamboats that coursed up and down the great length of the Mississippi River.

The *Sabine Queen* was a medium-sized specimen of its type and class. Her modest dimensions allowed her entree to tributaries and branches where larger steamers could not go. Her size was ideal for the Blacksnake River, which had a number of shallow passages and narrow channels.

It also worked to Barbaroux's benefit, for the U.S. Navy was unable to send its warships or even lighter gunboats upriver to blast out him and his forces for fear of their vessels becoming mired or snagged to be pried open and taken apart by Combine forces.

The Blacksnake River was tight in some spots, shallow in others, both in more than a few places. The *Queen*'s draught was shallow enough to traverse the river.

The upper works looked like a fairy castle, its multidecks flanked by twin black smokestacks. Recently painted, she gleamed all white and shining, but the river and the swamp worked against it constantly. Relentless humid heat rotted woodwork and rope lines, blistering the paint work and peeling it off the boards.

Swamp foliage smeared her sides, streaking them with green stains.

The *Sabine Queen* was moored at the largest wharf at the Clinchfield docks. It was night and the boat and wharf were all lit up. This was done for two reasons: security and Barbaroux's mania for grandeur.

The security issue was paramount. Commander Rufus Barbaroux was the most hated man on the Blacksnake, in all Moraine County.

Barbaroux had commissioned artist Dean Valentine to paint his portrait. Valentine, like the poet Lord Byron, was "too good looking to be good." Unlike Lord B., Valentine had talent not genius.

A revealing exchange between artist and patron had taken place during their most recent sitting several days earlier, before the Night Court . . .


*During one of the artist's breaks, Barbaroux went to the window. He stood there looking out, hands clasped behind his back, rocking back and forth on his boot heels.*

*The window commanded a view of the wharf to which the* Sabine Queen *was moored. It was a typical midmorning dockside scene, bustling with activity. Work gangs loaded and unloaded cargoes. Pallets were stacked. Tarry rope lines thick as a man's forearm were wound on windlasses.*

*Barbaroux kept a lot of sailors employed in the care and maintenance of the* Sabine Queen. *Sailors were used to hard work and the regular grind of chores.*

*A lesser number of pirates, mostly river rats but also some blue-water free-booters, were also part of the boat's company. The pirates were lousy on shipboard chores but adept at the business of storming other boats, raiding ports, and conscienceless killing.*

*"Look at them, the swine,"* Barbaroux said, turning away from the window. *"They're making more money now than they've ever seen, even before the war, and yet they'd cut my throat and stick my head on a pike if they dared."*

He seemed quite cheerful despite it all, or perhaps because of it.

*"Is it really so bad as all that, Commander?"* Valentine asked in a conversational tone.

*"Worse! They don't dare lift a finger against me. Why? Because they know that no matter what feeble plan their pea-brains might hatch out, it would effectively be destroyed by my counterstroke, whatever that might be.*

*"I have a contingency plan for every emergency. Their mutinous efforts would result only in a cruel and unusual death for each and every conspirator, no matter how obscure. A death, may I say, that will be memorably grotesque, to serve as an object-lesson for the rest of the men."*

*"Of that I've no doubt, Commander—"*

*"'Let them hate me, so long as they fear me,'"* Barbaroux ringingly intoned. *"Quick, my educated friend—who said it?"*

Valentine pretended to think it over before replying. *"I'm pretty sure it was one of the Caesars, but which one? Not your illustrious ancestor Nero, it just doesn't sound like something he'd say."*

Barbaroux claimed descent from Nero, citing the emperor's family name *"Ahenobarbi"*—*"bronze beard"*—with his own family name of Barbaroux, which translates as *"red beard."*

He also had a chestful of ancient documents, genealogical charts, registers of the lineage of the crowned heads of Europe, their deeds, charters. Patents of nobility and whatnot. All of which added up to exactly nothing in the way of solid proof but did nothing to prevent Barbaroux from making his reckless claims.

*"Titus made a lot of conquests during his reign and he*

*was known for crushing rebellions with the upmost severity—
witness his destruction of the Temple in Jerusalem—so I'll say
that the source of the quote was—Titus."*

*"An inspired guess, Valentine, very good—really quite
good," Barbaroux said, eyes shining. "Also quite wrong."*

*"You have the better of me, Commander, as usual. I don't
pretend to have your expertise on Imperial Rome. To end the
suspense, then, who said it?"*

*"Tiberius!" Barbaroux crowed triumphantly.*

*"Ah, Tiberius . . . yes, that would figure," Valentine said,
thoughtful, or seeming to be. "With your permission, Commander, may we return to the sitting? You're usually so busy
that I don't get many chances to paint you, and I'd like to take
advantage of the morning light . . ."*

*"Of course." Barbaroux rubbed his palms together in a
brisk hand-washing gesture before moving to take his place in
the sitter's area.*

*Valentine took up palette and paintbrush, hugging to him-
self the sure and certain knowledge that Barbaroux was
wrong.*

*The quote was from Caligula.*

The *Sabine Queen* this night looked something like
a wedding cake set atop an upside-down cake pan. The
wedding cake was the multi-story white-painted superstructure of the steamboat, that is, all her works above
the deck. The cake pan was the boat's shallow-draught
hull, which allowed it to cruise upon shallow waters
where other boats were unable to go.

Rufus Barbaroux's point of origin had never been
pinpointed, but the area had been pretty well narrowed
to the Caribbean. One rumor circulating was that
Barbaroux was a descendent of a pirate colony founded

somewhere in the Caribbean by the buccaneering Lafitte brothers, Jean and Pierre, who'd helped General Andy "Old Hickory" Jackson win the Battle of New Orleans against the British back in 1814. The brothers' freebooting ways proved obnoxious to members of the young republic who ran them and their pirate horde out of the Louisiana Territory.

Rufus Barbaroux was holding Night Court from his throne in the Grand Saloon of the steamboat *Sabine Queen.*

He was surrounded by members of his entourage, including Flossie and Jonquil, his favorite concubines; the painter Dean Valentine; and Malvina the Gypsy Fortune-Teller and her "niece" Tanya.

Tanya seemed like a nice girl. She was in her early teens with an oval face, wide dark eyes that were quite striking, and tawny golden skin. She was tall, thin, leggy, with wavy dark hair reaching down well past slim shoulders.

Yes she seemed like a nice youngster, quiet, soft spoken, polite, but— Too good to be true?

But then Valentine was the suspicious type. He hoped Tanya wasn't as nice and innocent as she seemed. If so, she was in the wrong place. But then how nice and innocent could anyone be who was associated with Malvina?

Malvina was a horror who looked every inch the part.

Oddly, when Valentine had that thought about the Gypsy Witch, Malvina gave him a dirty look. Eerie coincidence, that. Unsettling, almost as if she could read his mind.

Valentine looked away, telling himself that perhaps

he had been incautious enough to let his distaste for Malvina show when he'd been looking at her.

Malvina was a trickster like others of her fortune-telling ilk. No trickery about her off-putting appearance, though, she'd come by it honestly. Her face looked like an apple that had withered and dried in the sun.

Worse, she looked like she'd died and come back to haunt the living.

None of Barbaroux's followers were allowed to stand higher on the platform than the level of his head when he was seated on the throne.

There were two exceptions . . . his favorites Flossie and Jonquil were exempt from the rule.

Two hard-faced, lithe-bodied fancy ladies, gowned, feathered, and frilled, they stood flanking Barbaroux on his high throne chair, bracketing him like bookends upholding some not-so-slender volume.

The assembled guests now crowded as close to the throne and its occupant as Barbaroux's personal elite bodyguard would allow.

Overhead, above the area fronting the throne, a wagon wheel chandelier hung suspended on a length of chain secured to rafter beams high aloft. Big fat candles—wax candles, the most expensive kind—were set in holders regularly spaced around the rim of the wheel. Tapered glass sleeves shielded the candles from gusts of wind that might snuff out the flames.

Torches blazed in iron holders fastened along the hall's long walls, thin spirals and snakes of smoke curling off blazing torch heads, climbing to the heights of the hall before becoming lost in the shadows.

Barbaroux motioned for a flunky, only to have five

of them rush to the foot of the platform to attend to his wants.

"Bring up the prisoners," he commanded.

All five started to dash off to obey, some already elbowing the others in their zeal to obey.

"Halt! . . . *Stop!*" Barbaroux shouted.

The quintet slammed to a dead halt as if they'd hit an invisible wall.

"It doesn't take five, just one of you go," Barbaroux said.

"You!" he called out, stabbing the air with a pointing finger at the server he wanted, the one closest to a bulkhead door in the sidewall. "You go!"

"Yessir!" The chosen one took off like a streak, the other four glaring daggers at his back as he hastened to the exit.

The prisoners were being held below decks in the brig. It should have taken fifteen to twenty minutes for a guard detail to return, so naturally it took the better part of an hour.

The guests didn't mind; they busied themselves with eating and drinking. Presently they began to eat less and drink more.

Finally the guard detail arrived. A door opened in the portside wall. Four guards entered the hall, marching two by two, shoulder to shoulder.

Then came the prisoners, three sorry looking individuals chained hand and foot, in manacles and fetters. Chain links rattled and dragged on the wooden floor.

Two more guards brought up the rear. Council members, Combine functionaries, and other lesser folk hurriedly got out of the way of the guards and prisoners as the former hustled the latter to the foot of the throne.

The prisoners were Park Farner, Justus Pike, and Hector Sime.

Farner, the youngest of the three, was twenty-five. He was powerfully built, a marvel of muscular development. Long thick straight brown hair fell past his broad shoulders.

Justus Pike, forty-four, stood several inches above six feet. He was raw boned and long limbed. His hair was an inky-black pompadour, streaked with gray at the temples. He looked a lot smarter than he was.

Hector Sime, midthirties, had arched high eyebrows that gave him a permanent look of surprise. A thin well-trimmed eyebrow mustache adorned his upper lip.

Their stance was none too steady; they were shaky on their feet. But then anyone might have been unsteady in their place.

Barbaroux's invited guests gathered around the captives. A mood of wolfish expectation among the spectators began to make itself felt.

Aarn Bildad, a master of legal hocus-pocus and double-talk when such was required to slap a thin coating of legality over some Combine proceeding, addressed the throne:

"No need for a trial, Commander, it's an open and shut case: Pike, Sime, and Farner shot and killed one of our tax collectors, Hull Chavis, and stole his weekly receipts. What's more, to add insult and injury to the crime, the act was committed at the Wahtonka Road tollgate."

Barbaroux gripped the armrests of his throne, leaning forward to stare down at the three accused men. "You astonish me, Mr. Bildad."

"I was astonished myself, Commander."

"You mean to tell me that not only have we lost Hull Chavis, a dedicated collector for the regime brutally shot dead by daylight on Wahtonka Road, but that these marauders had the audacity, the effrontery, to commit this despicable outrage on the site of the Wahtonka tollgate station itself?"

"I blush to admit that that is the case, Commander."

"The bloody deed was done—when? After operating hours?"

"No, sir. Hull Chavis was shot dead and his revenues robbed, as near as we can tell, at four o'clock of that weekday afternoon—"

Commander Barbaroux held his hands out from his sides in a gesture of incomprehension, as if beseeching the heavens for divine guidance.

"I don't understand. I'm bewildered. A tollgate operator's duties comprise more than collecting tolls; there is a basic law enforcement component here that obligates toll station operators to suppress violent crime against any user of a Moraine County toll road. This court would like to speak to the operators of the Wahtonka toll station at the time of the killing and robbery. Have you taken steps to make them available for questioning by this court?"

"Our office has taken these steps, Commander." Aarn Bildad couldn't help look smug when making the affirmation to Barbaroux.

"I'm afraid I don't have the names of the toll station operators at hand, Mr. Bildad. Will you be so good as to call forward those on duty at the Wahtonka Road tollgate when Hull Chavis was shot dead and robbed?"

"Gladly, Commander." Aarn Bildad made a show of cupping his hand, putting it to his mouth as a kind of voice amplifying megaphone and shouting:

*"Call Hector Sime, Justus Pike, and Park Farner forward to the stand!"*

There was a moment of bewilderment on the part of the crowd, people exchanging uncomprehending glances.

Aarn Bildad's broad grin was the tip-off that cued the audience and clued them in that tonight's session of Night Court would be a wild one even by the fast and loose rules of Commander Barbaroux himself.

The spectators began to whoop and shout as the truth of the matter sank home to them.

Determined to wring the last drop of fun from the situation, Barbaroux played it straight. "Is it your understanding, Mr. Bildad, that long-serving revenue collector Hull Chavis was shot, killed, and posthumously robbed by the three tollgate operators on duty at the time: Park Farner, Hector Sime, and Justus Pike?"

"That's the way of it, Commander," Aarn Bildad said.

"Anything else you'd care to present in the way of evidence, Mr. Bildad?"

"Just this, Commander." Aarn Bildad held up a canvas moneybag, the standard type and model used by Combine revenue collectors in making their rounds. "The posse found this in possession of Justus Pike at the time he, Sime, and Farner were at the docks trying to charter a boat to ferry them downriver to the next county."

Bildad held the moneybag up for all those in the Grand Saloon to see. "As is painfully evident, this sack is looking mighty thin. A notebook found in Hull Chavis's possession at the time of his death—"

Here Aarn Bildad brandished a leather pocket notepad, holding it out from himself at arm's length in plain view. "This notepad, containing a column of figures in Hull Chavis's handwriting, notes the totals received at each of his stops and adds up the amounts for a sum total of over six hundred dollars."

Outraged buzzing and shocked angry murmurs sounded in the hall at the size of the amount.

Aarn Bildad said, "Let me remind my fellow citizens here tonight that under the dynamic new system of Collective Individualism instituted by Commander Barbaroux, this money is *your* money. Farner, Sime, and Pike stole this six hundred dollars from *you.*

"And if it had been you carrying that money instead of unfortunate Hull Chavis, who leaves behind a widow and two young children without a daddy, it would have been *you* who was shot down like a dog and left to die alone in the dirt of Wahtonka Road last week!

"Do you want to know what Farner, Sime, and Pike were doing while Hull Chavis was bleeding out with two bullet holes in his guts?!"

*"Hell, yes!"*—*"Damned straight we want to know!"*— *"Tell it, Aarn!"* were just a few of the responses shouted out by some of the more vocal members among the irate spectators.

"Pike, Sime, and Farner were over to Halftown, living it up on the six hundred dollars they stole from y'all, drinking, gambling, and wenching!" Aarn Bildad thundered.

It took some time for the clamor to be quelled and order restored so Barbaroux could pass sentence on the accused. He rose to stand on the platform, looming over the three defendants, looking down at them.

"Do any of you have anything to say in your own

defense before sentence is passed and justice is done?" he asked.

"Them two did it," Justus Pike said, stepping forward, rattling his chains. "They shot poor ol' Hull and kilt him dead. I didn't kill nobody, I didn't kill nobody!"

"What did you do to stop them, Mr. Pike?" Barbaroux queried.

Pike was wringing manacled hands. "What could I do? Their two guns against one of me and I ain't no killer—"

"You took your share of the loot and lived it up while Hull Chavis lay dying in the dirt," Barbaroux pointed out.

Silence. Pike had no reply.

Hector Sime stepped up. "I have something to say."

"Speak, Mr. Sime," Barbaroux decreed.

"How many—" His voice broke and he started again. "How many men—and women, too—have you and your damned Combine left dying in the dirt since you took over the county, and before that, too?!"

Angry uproar sounded from the crowd, shouts demanding that Sime be shut up, trying to shout him down. The noise was quelled when Barbaroux raised his hands for silence.

"Let him talk, he has a right to be heard. Every man, no matter how bad, deserves that much when he has to look death in the face," he said.

Sime's voice quavered when he heard that last part about looking death in the face, but he swallowed hard and tried to continue. "You steal big so you get to lord it up over everybody else, being all high and mighty. We stole small and got caught so now we got to pay.

"You stole the whole county, so nobody can tell you where to get off. You're stealing everything that ain't nailed down. When Moraine County is squeezed dry you'll move on to the next one that's ripe for the plucking and let that one fall into your lap.

"But what do the rest of us do when the town is plucked clean and dying on the vine and we're dying with it? Us boys just wanted a little piece of the pie. You're eating the full twelve-course banquet and sticking us townsfolk for the check. It ain't right! We just wanted something for ourselves, a little pittance, that's all we done."

"You killed a man," Barbaroux said gravely.

"How many did the Combine kill taking over? A hundred, two hundred more like, maybe more. That's not counting the folks that starved to death because they got run off land the Combine wanted.

"How many more will you kill before you're done?" Sime demanded.

"This isn't getting us anywhere," Barbaroux said irritably. "You've had your say, man. Stand down and be done with it; we're done with you."

Barbaroux's gimlet-eyed gaze came to fall on Park Farner. "And you?"

Farner said, "I reckon you had your fun playing cat-and-mouse with us, putting on a show, making like you didn't know we was working Wahtonka station when Hull Chavis got burned down.

"Sooner or later somebody's gonna play you the same way and you see how you like it.

"Sure, I gunned down Hull Chavis because I told him not to reach and he reached, going for a gun like he thought protecting money that's gonna wind up in your pocket was worth dying for. Man that dumb ain't gonna live long nohow."

"Are you finished?" Barbaroux asked coldly.

"Give me a gun and I'll do my talking with that!" Farner said.

"Ah, a show of spirit. So much the better, adds spice to the game," Barbaroux said, smiling frostily. "Better sport than we dared hope for."

He motioned to the guards to remove the prisoners to the sidelines, off center stage, which he was once more commandeering for himself. "Judgment must be rendered," he said. "I don't pass sentence, *we* pass sentence. One man, one vote. You know how it works."

Barbaroux demonstrated dramatically, graphically, by showing them the actions. "Thumbs-up, Life!"

The hand reversed, thumb pointing downward to earth and the grave.

"Thumbs-down, Death!"

"I'll cast my vote now," Barbaroux said, turning turns thumbs-down: "Death!"

"Now it's your turn, friends," he went on. "Thumbs-up or thumbs-down, Life or Death, how rule you?"

The crowd voted; they were Barbaroux's crowd, handpicked by him. They were mostly ambitious strivers with no limits who saw which way the wind was blowing and wanted to get a piece of the pie before it was all gone. Barbaroux never doubted they would vote the way he wanted and they didn't disappoint:

*"Thumbs-down!—Death!"*

Barbaroux ordered the guards in the detail to remove the prisoners' chains. Keys were fitted into the locking slots of manacles chaining their hands, fetters binding their feet. Presently the prisoners—the condemned, to call them rightly—were unbound if not free.

Farner stomped his feet, trying to restore their circulation. Pike stood there huddled and trembling, looking more bewildered than anything else. He looked like he was going to cry but managed to keep himself together.

Pike sidled over to Sime. "Hey, what for you think they took the chains off, Sime?"

"Maybe they want us to make a break for it so they can shoot us," Sime spat.

Pike gave a start. "You think they would?"

"You like hanging better than being shot?" Sime's tone was hostile, sarcastic.

"No talking," a guard snapped.

"You heard the man. No talking, dummy," Sime said.

"That goes for you, too," the same guard said to Sime.

Farner unchained made the guards nervous. He was too big, too hostile. They grouped around him, ready to swarm if he moved wrong.

A guard with shifty eyes stood on Farner's left, facing him. He stood still but his eyes kept shifting around like two black olives rolling around in an empty jar.

Barbaroux stood at the head of the red velvet–colored platform holding his arms up in the air signaling for attention. He got it. He waited for the hubbub to die down before speaking.

"My friends, to be just, justice needs to be seen being done. Tonight, you have voted in solemn conclave to purge our community of three extraordinarily vicious individuals: Park Farner, Hector Sime, and

Justus Pike," he said. "To that end, we will now put on a demonstration.

"Your safety is our paramount concern. Our public works crew will now clear a space on the main floor of the hall. Please move to a safety area to watch the demonstration. Thank you."

The public workers were part of the boat's permanent party, a work detail of ten men. They wore blue uniforms and flat white caps trimmed by a free-hanging black ribbon.

They eased the guests to the sidelines to clear a center area fronting the throne at right angles to the long, central axis of the hall and boat as it ran from stem to stern, aft to bow.

The new area was roped off on all four sides. Lengths of thick rope were strung to upright stanchions nailed in place to wooden pallets placed at regular intervals along the perimeter, enclosing the space. Workers were posted inside the enclosure to keep out the curious.

Woven hempen mats were set down on the floor in the center of the enclosure. Several heavy barrels were placed upright on the mats. The upper lids were removed, revealing that the barrels were filled with sand.

These curious preparations caused the humming conversations among the onlookers to buzz louder.

Barbaroux stepped down from the platform, entered the enclosure, and went to an area on the side where the three prisoners were being kept.

Farner, Sime, and Pike were closely guarded, the members of the detail hemming them in. The guards were so tense they all but vibrated. They put their bodies between the prisoners and Barbaroux to forestall any of them making a lunge at the Commander.

Barbaroux addressed the prisoners, speaking loudly enough to be heard by the crowd of onlookers who now lined the perimeter of the roped-off area to see what would happen next.

"Farner, Sime, and Pike— You challenged me before, challenged the righteousness of this court to condemn you to death—well and good!

"The fact remains that you have been so condemned and the sentence will be executed forthwith—*you* will be executed forthwith.

"Yet you need not necessarily die. I now give you a choice between certain death and a chance to live. What do I mean? In ancient days our ancestors determined the rightness of a cause by the honorable institution of Trial by Combat. Simplicity itself. Two contending parties fight to the death. Whoever lives is the winner: He is vindicated and his cause decreed righteous in the eyes of the law, justice, and his fellow men.

"I now propose that you three defend your cause— which is nothing less than your right to rob and kill without punishment—defend it with your lives.

"Our champion, he who will defend our cause, will put his life on the line to uphold our honor, our in- alienable right to punish robbers and killers with the supreme penalty of death.

"You three have the right to fight a duel to the death against our Champion of Justice. In the interest of fairness, the combat will be fought not with swords or similar exotica but with the weapon with which you are most familiar, the six-gun. The very weapon with which you committed the crime that brought you here. Fitting, no?

"Should you win, you will be pardoned, free to go

from this place with no reprisals, no further action taken against you by us. What say you, aye or nay? Will you duel with six-guns to the death with our champion?"

The condemned men put their heads together for a hurried conference.

"What'll we do, what'll we do?" Pike fretted.

"Do what you want, yellowbelly. I know what I'm going to do. I'll take the gun," Sime said.

"Bah! It's all a trick," Farner scoffed, sneering.

Pike's head whipped around this way and that as he followed the back-and-forth between Farner and Sime.

"Trick or not, I'd rather die by the gun than the rope. Hanging's a hard way to die, Farner."

"You can't trust that red-bearded bastard, Sime!"

"I know. I'd still rather take a bullet than the rope."

"You might have something there."

"So you'll give it a go?" Sime asked.

"Like you said, it beats hanging," Farner said.

"What about me, fellas?" Pike asked.

"You can go to the devil for all I care," Sime said.

"I was scared before, that's why I said what I did. I'm not scared now. Besides," Pike went on, "three guns are better than two."

"Well—all right," Sime said, not liking it but feeling he had no other choice.

"Thanks," Pike said, heartfelt.

"Just don't screw up anymore than you have to," Sime added.

Barbaroux once more came to the fore. "Well? Your decision?"

"It's a go," Sime said.

"You're in, all of you?" Barbaroux eyed each man in the trio, one by one.

"All," Sime said curtly.

"Excellent!" Bright spots of red color shone in Barbaroux's cheeks. He enthusiastically rubbed his palms together in a hand-washing motion.

He turned to face the onlookers massed at the rope line. "The condemned have accepted the challenge, the duel is at hand!"

Loud cheers, happy faces.

The crowd was intrigued by the Trial by Combat. It is doubtful whether even the thrill of a triple hanging, which ordinarily would have been something to see for them, could have been so novel and exciting.

Barbaroux was joined by Cutlass and Mr. Spivey, two of his sidemen.

Cutlass was built like a circus strongman. He was shaved bald with a thick black mustache. A set of three gold rings piercing an ear added to his piratical appearance.

Mr. Spivey embodied a completely opposite physical type. He was small, shrunken, and prematurely aged looking. His eyes were watery, his expression leering.

"The firearms, friend Cutlass, if you would be so good," Barbaroux commanded.

Cutlass opened a canvas sea-bag secured at the mouth by drawstrings. Reaching in with an oversized hand, he hauled out into the light three gunbelts with holstered guns. They were looped over one of his brawny arms.

Barbaroux addressed the prisoners but again pitched his words loud enough for the crowd to hear. "You recognize these items, gentlemen? They are gunbelts, your gunbelts, complete with the guns you were wearing when you were taken."

"It looks like them," Sime allowed grudgingly, the other two nodding in agreement.

"I promise you that these guns are in fine working order and have not been tampered with in any way. What's more, they have been fully reloaded with fresh ammunition. In fact, I will now prove just that," Barbaroux said. "Set the gunbelts down on the table prepared for that purpose, Cutlass, there's a good fellow."

Cutlass deposited the gunbelts on a card table standing to one side of the barrels of sand, and stepped away from them.

Barbaroux went to the table, taking up a black leather gunbelt with twin-holstered .44s. He drew a gun from its holster, setting down the gunbelt.

"A good gun," he mused. "Your gun, Mr. Farner. You're the two-gun man here."

"If you say so," Farner smirked.

"Now now, Mr. Farner, don't be coy. If you're not going to enter into the spirit of the thing, we can just hang you as a prelude to the Trial by Combat."

"That's my gun."

"Good. I will now prove it's in perfect working order," Barbaroux said. He spun the gun's cylinder so that it revolved on its axis until a chamber clicked into place. "Observe: The spin was perfectly random, it could have stopped at any chamber."

He raised the gun, pointing it at a glass-shrouded candle mounted on the leading edge of the wagon wheel chandelier hanging suspended over the exhibition area.

Barbaroux pulled the trigger. A shot sounded. The glass candle cover disintegrated as did the candle behind it, snuffing out the flame. A crystal shower of broken glass sprinkled down to the floor.

After a pause, the spectators applauded.

Barbaroux holstered the gun. Drawing the other gun from the belt, he crossed to a sand barrel. "The previous mode being somewhat rough on the lighting, the sand barrel will suffice for this next and the others."

Barbaroux spun the cylinder to select a chamber at random. He held the gun pointed downward at the sand in the barrel.

The gun fired with a crashing boom, tiny flames lipping the muzzle. A cloud of gunsmoke appeared.

"Watch closely please, to make sure there's no chicanery, no sleight of hand," Barbaroux said, playing to the crowd. He signaled to a pair of public workers who'd been standing nearby, off to the side.

They came forward, taking their positions at the sand barrels. One held a large square of fine-meshed metal wire screen held in a wooden frame, a screen box. The other held a medium-sized pail.

The worker with the pail made a show of holding it high and turning it upside-down to demonstrate that nothing was hidden inside. He shoved the pail into the sand barrel the gun had been fired into, scooping out a goodly portion of sand. He upended the pail into the wooden-framed metal screen, which his partner held over an empty barrel, and poured the sand into it.

The partner shook the screen box back and forth, sifting the sand through the mesh into the catch-barrel beneath. The full load of sand was sifted through the screen to no result.

The man with the pail scooped up a fresh load of sand and dumped it into the screen box, sifting it through. Again to no appreciable result.

A third try yielded a hit.

Nestled in the screen box was a fused lead lump, misshapen and deformed. Barbaroux picked it up, holding it aloft between thumb and forefinger for all to see. "Behold! The lead ball from the .44, showing the effects of being fired into the sand! Proof positive!"

Applause and cheers from the crowd. Barbaroux repeated the sand barrel test with Sime's and Pike's weapons, proving them out.

Some public workers cleared away the sand barrels. The crowd's buzzing increased in volume and tempo as the showdown neared.

"It's no small thing to put a gun in the hand of a condemned killer," Barbaroux said, resuming his harangue of the crowd, "no less three at once. The public has got to be protected, and I can't think of a better guardian than Norris Nye!"

Barbaroux gestured toward a man standing atop the bleachers set against the portside wall. Norris Nye was a thin towheaded man with silver hair and a white goatee. He cradled a rifle in his arms across his chest.

He was flanked by two other riflemen posted a few rows below and to the sides of him.

"Norris Nye was a decorated sharpshooter for the Confederacy—"

Wild cheers, hand clapping, and foot stomping burst forth from the crowd in the loudest and most enthusiastic acclaim so far this evening. It was peppered by shouts of, "Hoorah for Dixie! Hoorah for the Confederacy!"

Barbaroux let the ovation run its lengthy course before continuing:

"Norris Nye is one of the boat's company on the *Sabine Queen* and we're proud to have him. Don't think that I'm relying on the goodwill or sportsmanship of our three condemned killers to honor the rules of the Trial by Combat, friends.

"I put my trust in Norris Nye and his two brother sharpshooters whom you see posted in the bleachers. Each will have his rifle aimed at the heart of one of the evildoers. Should they violate the rules of the Trial or show any sign of training a weapon anywhere but at our champion, they will be shot dead."

That got almost as big a cheer as Norris Nye's service for the Lost Cause.

"You've seen the villains in our showdown, but where is our champion? Who will defend the honor of the blindfolded lady with balancing scales and a sword, Lady Justice?" Barbaroux demanded.

*"I will!"*

The voice came from a shadowed alcove to one side of the bleachers. From out of that patch of black darkness emerged a man who strode into the light of the roped-off area.

The stranger was tall and thin, reedy, with long arms and stiltlike legs.

He wore a dark hat with a round-topped crown and stiff round brim, a type of hat favored by circuit-riding preachers and similar religious personalities, and a lightweight dark brown duster overcoat, which reached down to midthigh.

Under the duster he wore dark clothes, good clothes but unprepossessing—no flash in them. Pants were worn tucked into the tops of knee-high riding boots.

Under the hat was a sharply drawn visage with thin-featured birdlike features. Dark eyes were set in a face with a knife-blade nose and thin lips curving down at the corners.

He wore two guns down low; the guns fitted butt-out in the holsters. He halted well short of the prisoners in the enclosure, turned toward Barbaroux.

"Who might you be?" Barbaroux called out to the newcomer. "Your name, sir?"

"Sexton Clarke," came the reply.

A stir rippled through parts of the crowd, caused by widely scattered individuals who knew the name and repute of Sexton Clarke. But the response was muted and absorbed by the vast majority of the assembled that knew not Clarke.

Born and raised in Tennessee, Sexton Clarke had made his name in the Oklahoma Territory, Rocky Mountain States, and the Great Southwest. He was new to the Texas Gulf Coast area, which generally knew him not.

Yet.

"Do you stand for justice?" Barbaroux continued.

"I do," Clarke said.

"Sexton Clarke, my friends! He used to bury corpses in the churchyard for a living not so very long ago. Now he makes them dead and leaves the burying to others."

"Sexton Clarke . . . ever heard of him, Sime?" Farner asked.

"No," Sime said, slowly shaking his head.

"He's supposed to be a gunfighter? Looks more like a choirmaster."

"Barbaroux didn't bring him in because he's easy pickings, count on that." Sime sounded worried.

"The rules of the Trial by Combat are simple," Barbaroux was saying. "Kill your opponent and live— lose and you die.

"What could be fairer?"

He turned to the condemned. "Your guns await, gentlemen. Take them. But don't be so foolish as to try to get ahead of the game. Be mindful of Norris Nye and his two fellows, each charged with covering his man and dropping him with a shot to the heart if there's a violation of the rules."

"What's to stop your riflemen from shooting us while you claim your hired gun did the work?" Farner demanded.

"Where's the sport in that? Or the justice?" Barbaroux countered. "It's not hard to tell the difference between a bullet hole from a rifle or a six-gun; many here can do it and all will have access to what bodies there are to satisfy themselves as to the fairness of the trial."

"Trust a cheat to complain the loudest about cheating." Sexton Clarke laughed.

"I'll kill you for that," Farner said.

"No, you won't," Clarke said calmly.

"Let me at them guns," Farner said. He, Sime, and Pike went to the table where the guns were laid.

Mr. Spivey, shrunken and apelike, stood near the table off to one side of it. He had a baboonlike snout and the exaggeratedly long upper lip of an orangutan. He also had a sawed-off shotgun holstered in a rig under one arm.

He drew it while the three condemned men were reaching for their gunbelts. "Hey, laddies," he called to them.

Farner, Sime, and Pike glanced behind them to see who was making the noise. They saw Spivey holding a double-barreled sawed-off shotgun leveled at them.

He stood out of the line of fire of the riflemen in the bleachers.

"Okay you flotsam, pick up your gunbelts and put them on," Spivey said. "Do it slowly and carefully. You're covered so don't do anything stupid. I'm itching to cut loose with my scattergun. Any of you scum even looks like he's thinking of reaching ahead of time and I'm gonna open up!

"I reckon one double-barreled load of buckshot can take out all three of you at once . . . That'd make a pretty good show all by itself, eh?"

"One I'd like to see," Cutlass said.

The condemned men buckled on their gunbelts, careful to keep their hands well away from their guns.

They formed up in a row, squaring off against Sexton Clarke. They stood shoulder to shoulder with about an arm's length between each one. Farner took the middle position with Sime on his right and Pike on his left.

"He's only one against three . . . one of us is sure to get him," Pike said, swallowing hard.

"That'll be me," Farner said through clenched teeth.

"What a shame I have to die with such idiots," Sime muttered.

"Huh? What'd you say?" Farner demanded.

"Let it pass," Sime said tiredly.

The scene was set for the showdown. Sime, Farner, and Pike faced off against Sexton Clarke. They were covered, doubly covered by sharpshooters posted in the bleachers and Spivey standing in close with the sawed-off shotgun.

Rufus Barbaroux had withdrawn to the relative safety of the red velvet–covered platform. He sat in his throne flanked by Flossie and Jonquil. Full-breasted and long-legged, platinum-haired Flossie with skin white as milk, Jonquil dark and swarthy, her flesh golden-bronze.

Sime stared Sexton Clarke in the face. "If you're looking to do some soul-saving you came to the wrong place, preacher. I been hell bound a long time now and neither of these two birds with me are any better."

Sexton Clarke laughed softly. "I'm no preacher but I'll be glad to say a few words over the bodies."

"We're fast, too!" Farner blustered. "There's three of us and only one of him. Cut loose on him all at once and one of us is sure to bring him down."

"Keep telling yourselves that," Clarke said.

"Shut up, you!" Pike shouted.

Clarke nodded. "The time for talking is done, yes. Actions alone speak. This is the proving ground—the killing ground."

"You just shut up, you hear!" Pike was near hysterical.

"Hold, gentlemen. Not just yet, if you please!" Barbaroux thundered.

A door in the bulkhead behind and to one side of the platform opened, shafting a fan of dim yellow-brown light into the Great Hall. Framed in the doorway were Malvina and Tanya, the withered crone and the lithe, limber, young girl.

Tanya belonged to Malvina in some way, though whether by kinship or some less wholesome channel was known only to them. No family resemblance could be seen between the two but this was not surprising; the withered living mummy that was Malvina bore little likeness to few among the living.

Malvina stood behind Tanya, holding her slim

shoulders with clawlike hands. Tanya wore a colorful satin sash tied around the top of her head and held a violin case cradled in her arms.

Malvina eased the grip of her spidery fingers, releasing the girl. She had been holding back Tanya to mute her youthful enthusiasm and keep her from running out front too soon.

Now that Barbaroux motioned for her to come to him, Tanya dashed forward, violin case banging against her thin chest as she ran.

She circled around to the front of the platform. Halting in front of Barbaroux, she dropped a sort of curtsy, head bowed, but looking up from the tops of her eyes at the Commander.

"Rise, child," Barbaroux said, smiling down at her. Tanya rose.

"I see you've brought something for me. May I have it?"

She handed him the violin case. Someone groaned at the sight of it. Barbaroux didn't see the offender. He hoped one of his spies had so he could make the boor suffer later.

He nodded, dismissing Tanya. She hurried back to Malvina.

Barbaroux opened the case, removing a violin and bow. Violin, not fiddle. An expensive violin from the looks of it. Its glossy exterior shone a bright golden-brown, its finish mellowed by time.

Barbaroux held the violin in one hand and the bow with the other. He spoke to the combatants in the showdown. "Now to get on with the trial. I will play a short musical piece—"

This time the crowd knew what to do—clap dutifully, which they did, if a trifle unenthusiastically. Some

Combine flunkies worked the visiting guests, motioning for applause, which swelled in volume.

Barbaroux basked in the acclaim, which to his lights ended too soon. But the crowd was waiting for a gunfight, bloodshed, and death.

"When the last note of music sounds, go for your guns," Barbaroux said. "Warning!—I caution you, make sure the violin has sounded its last note before shooting. This is imperative, a matter of life and death—yours.

"He who reaches for a gun before the music stops will die, shot by the sharpshooters. Be very sure that while playing I have not paused for a rest. These are the conditions I have set. Reach before the music ends, die! When the music does stop, shoot!

"Do you understand, challengers?"

The three condemned bandits nodded yes.

"Don't just nod, say it," Spivey cued them from out of the corner of his mouth.

"Understood!" Sime shouted, speaking for the three of them.

"Good. And you, champion?" Barbaroux prompted.

"I savvy, Commander," Sexton Clarke said.

Farner's hand twitched with the effort of keeping it from reaching for his gun.

Barbaroux had rosined up the bow and put the violin in place resting on his left shoulder. Setting bow to violin strings, he began to strike up a tune. He played from memory, with no sheet music to guide him, a short piece, one of many known to him by heart.

It was not a happy tune. This was no joyful noise. It was slow, ominous, a kind of funeral dirge.

Barbaroux was a passable amateur musician, a little better than average perhaps but no more. He was able to carry a tune, "but not far enough away," as some wit later observed to a few trusted comrades.

He hit some bum notes and clinkers along the way to conclusion. Knowing the lusty appetites and short attention span of his creatures, Barbaroux planned to keep it short, but after the first sixty seconds of the unhappy droning issuing from his violin, the crowd stirred restlessly.

Not all of the crowd was overawed by Barbaroux. Some, but not all. There was a sizable group of hard-cases who resented the Commander's high-handed ways. But the money was good, whiskey and whores were plentiful, and pesky lawmen were all but absent. So the rebellious swallowed their distaste for now and soldiered on.

Not so Sexton Clarke, waiting for the last notes to sound before shooting. His long fine-boned face looked mournful, but his spirits were dancing at the prospect of the kill.

Kills.

It was a habit he'd picked up during his years as a churchyard gravedigger, when strict employers insisted he maintain proper decorum not only during burials but whenever Clarke was on church property. He'd schooled himself to keep a solemn expression on his face night and day, on duty or not.

The three robbers' attitudes were mixed.

Farner's face was a mask of hate, a silent snarl with teeth bared.

Sime had a faraway look in his eyes, as if his thoughts

were already beyond this world. He knew Barbaroux hadn't staged this game to lose it.

Pike was fighting the fear. His eyes were ringed with white circles, his hands trembled, and his flesh oozed cold sweat. He felt doomed. But he was determined to play the man and see the duel through to the end without funking. He would not let his partners down, he told himself.

The music shrilled on, its high notes tearing at the nerves, its long low notes telling of dreariness and sorrow. And that was just the effect it had on the on-lookers.

Its effect on the duelists was infinitely more intense. Locked in a gunfight to the death, they strained to hear the onset of combat in the final notes of a haunting tune unknown to them.

It was not the shivering Pike who broke first but rather Sime, seemingly the most balanced and stable of the robbers.

Barbaroux sawed at the violin, sobbing notes rising and falling, with no sign of a climax.

"Make an end to it!" Sime suddenly shouted, startling many, including his sidemen. But he was near the breaking point where he couldn't take much more of this.

"This is worse than being shot!" he added.

A few gasps rose up from the crowd. A smile quirked the corners of Clarke's mouth, his only reaction to the outburst.

There's one in every crowd, as the saying goes, and this one was Tom Ingster. So taken by surprise and delight was he at Sime's voicing of his own sentiments, that he broke out laughing.

A Tom Ingster laugh was no quiet thing but a loud,

rude guffaw—a braying horselaugh, loud, ringing, insulting.

A rift opened around Ingster as those in his vicinity sought to distance themselves from the offender, to show that they were not he. Ingster was seen by spying eyes. Aarn Bildad had a hasty word with Cutlass and Spivey.

Cutlass moved to the rear of the hall, taking up a watchful post. He stood with his back to the wall, a vantage point that allowed him to survey the crowd and all the exit doors in case Ingster tried to make a sneak.

Barbaroux decided to skip ahead to the finish. It was a short piece but he cut it shorter, rushing into the last passage, sawing streams of notes into a crescendo.

The end of the piece was near. Sexton Clarke knew it, the robbers knew it, the audience knew it.

The volume peaked, Barbaroux ripping out a last ringing note from the violin, then abruptly breaking off into silence, ending his playing.

He stood motionless, right hand holding the bow well clear of the violin strings. Like all others in the hall, his attention was focused, riveted, on the duelists.

The last note was still echoing in the air when the combatants reached.

Clarke's gun leaped into his hand before any of the bandits could get their guns clear of the holsters. His speed was awesome, dismaying his foes.

Farner's face fell into slack-jawed stupefaction.

"Oh, hell," Sime said, now recovered from his outburst.

Pike vented a shriek of berserker rage.

The robbers clawed for their guns, Pike drawing first.

Clarke took him first, placing a shot square in the

forehead. A black-red disk appeared on the flesh where Pike had been tagged.

After a beat, blood jetted from the head wound as Pike was going down. At that, Pike's gun was in hand and he went down firing off a shot, which missed Clarke and buried itself in the ceiling.

Farner drew, leveling his gun. Clarke dropped a slug into him, hitting him in the side, knocking him off-balance.

Farner staggered, still shooting. Clarke put a quick one into Farner's knee, sweeping the leg out from under him and knocking him down. Farner howled with pain.

Sime had his gun out and working, drawing a bead on Clarke. He was too eager, his first shot missing. Clarke sidestepped and Sime's next rounds whipped through a patch of empty air where Clarke had been.

Clarke threw two rounds into Sime, hitting him above the belt buckle. Sime folded, collapsing, gun dropping from his nerveless hand.

Farner wriggled around on the floor like a broken-backed snake, whiplashing, trying to bring his gun into line with Clarke. The last thing he saw in this world was Clarke standing there calm as you please, pointing a gun at him.

Clarke smiled with his lips, a chilly little smile for Farner as he sent a bullet crashing into his brain.

It was done, leaving Sexton Clarke undisputed master of the field. Three robbers lay dead, while Clarke was untouched.

After a stunned pause, the crowd broke into raucous clapping, cheering, and whistling.

Barbaroux cheered louder than anyone, whooping

in triumph. After all it was his champion who had won, and in such devastating fashion.

Clarke acknowledged the acclaim, lowering his head in a solemn bow to his patron, a furiously clapping Barbaroux.

Mindful that it never hurts to play up to the crowd, Clarke also acknowledged their acclaim with several head-bobbing bows in their direction.

After which he turned to face his dead foes, taking off his round-brimmed preacher's hat in a gesture of respect—or was it contempt? Or both?

Only Clarke knew.

He put his hat back on, went to the black-welled alcove that hid the portside door by which he'd first entered, and exited the same way.

Public worker crewmen appeared to take away the bodies. Spivey signaled them to stop. They stood waiting.

"Avast, mates. Not yet, not yet. Wait till I tell you," Spivey said.

With loving care Barbaroux returned violin and bow to their case, closing it. Tanya scooted out to take the instrument, Barbaroux descending several platform steps to hand it into her thin upraised arms where she stood on the floor.

Aarn Bildad hurried over to him, identifying Tom Ingster as the man who laughed.

Barbaroux climbed back to the top of the platform and stood there looking out into the crowd, scanning its ranks. He unbuttoned the flap of his holstered pistol, hand resting on the gun butt.

Knowing what was about to happen, the spectators near Tom Ingster surged away from him, leaving him isolated and alone.

Barbaroux's icy blue eyes locked with Ingster's, the offender who had laughed so rudely while he was playing.

Ingster raised his arms palms-out, as if in appeal. "W-wait a minute, I didn't mean nothing by it—*don't!*"

Barbaroux drew and fired, tagging Ingster in the middle. He methodically squeezed slug after slug into Ingster's midsection, shooting it to pieces. Ingster was dead before he hit the floor.

The shooting won a fresh round of cheers from the crowd, which Barbaroux happily accepted, soaking them up. They didn't know about music but they knew what they liked. It showed that despite his highfalutin airs, the Commander at heart was a regular fellow, as much as the least of them.

So they thought, and it served Barbaroux's purpose for them to think so. "The common touch," for so he thought of it, was another tool in the art of command.

When the tumult died down, Barbaroux delivered Ingster's epitaph: "Some people just don't appreciate good music!"

That drew laughter and cheers, even as those cheering hoped that they had heard the last of Barbaroux's music for some time.

The Commander delivered one last parting salutation, savoring another triumph: "Remember! Cullen Baker hangs in Clinchfield Gaol in eight days! Eight days! Don't miss it, be there!"

Barbaroux made his exit trailing cheers.

"That's the last of them for now," Spivey told the cleaning crew, indicating Ingster. "Take him away with the others."

Barbaroux went off to look for Sexton Clarke. He had a gift of gold for him, a bonus for his fine work.

Barbaroux also appreciated Clarke's tact in quickly leaving the scene so he, Barbaroux, could occupy center stage in dispatching Ingster, the swine.

He shook his head in wonderment, marveling at Clarke's speed and accuracy with a gun. The pistol fighter had more than lived up to his reputation.

"And Clarke's working for me, my own private gunfighter!" Barbaroux said to himself, exulting. "Nobody can beat him! Who is faster?!"

# TWENTY

*Seven days until Cullen Baker was hanged. Seven days to hell!*

Johnny Cross and Bill Longley came to the Torrent, that narrow swift-running river at the southwest corner of Albedo County in East Texas. The site held a lot of memories for Bill. It was where he had helped Cullen Baker run his barge, where Cullen and Julie made their home with Bill bunking in a nearby shack.

Memories. Hard work, good times . . .

Johnny and Bill were on the far side of the watercourse, on horseback, trailing downstream. It was early morning but already the air was thick, close, stifling. It would only get hotter and more oppressive as the day wore on and the sun rose high.

Swarms of insects buzzed the riders. Insects were the plague of the swamps. One of them.

Riding alongside the Torrent helped. There was something clean about its racing waters that seemed to clear the air around it. A fine misty spray arose from its surface.

"I hate the swamp," Johnny said.

Bill kept himself from smiling.

Johnny Cross was a man who could endure hardship as few men could and generally he was the last to utter a complaint. Bill knew that, he had ridden with Johnny before.

But Johnny made no secret then and now that he was no friend of the Blacksnake River swampland, declaring that the time he'd spent there in the early months after war's end was one of the most miserable times of his life, because of the locale.

Johnny had been on the dodge then, running both from blue-clad Federal troops and local lawmen, and Moraine County was a good place for wanted men to lay low and hide out. That's when he was riding with Cullen Baker, also wanted, as was the very young Bill Longley, then in his midteens but still a blooded Yankee-killer.

"Bet you never thought you'd be coming back to the Blacksnake," Bill said.

"Never. Only saving the life of a man who saved mine—more than once—could bring me back," Johnny said.

They'd come a long way in a short time. Johnny had spent the better part of a week in Hangtree waiting for Bill to recover so they could set out on their desperate trek. Bill healed fast but you couldn't rush these things. The trek was desperate because they were racing to save Cullen Baker from hanging. Execution Day was set for the first of the month.

Johnny had spent the time wisely by readying for the trip. One of his hardest and least pleasant tasks was convincing Luke Pettigrew not to come along. Luke was his longtime best friend and now partner of the Crossbow Ranch, formerly the Cross Ranch but renamed to reflect its changed status. He and Luke had pooled their resources and gone into cattle ranching in a big way. The boom for Texas cattle was on and growing daily.

The hell of it for Johnny was his fear that Luke would think he was being cut out of the play because he was missing one leg, his left leg having been taken off below the knee by a Yankee cannonball during the war. The charge was baseless. Johnny and Luke had shared many death-defying adventures together since they had returned home from the war. There was no one Johnny trusted more to side him than Luke.

But this go-round was different. It stretched back to a time Johnny wasn't very proud of, when he'd ridden with the Cullen Baker gang in Moraine County after the war. Hunted, starved, and pushed to the edge, Johnny had hit back hard whenever he could. He'd killed a lot of men in that time and some of them hadn't deserved it. He didn't want Luke to know the truth of that. Luke had a rough idea of what it was like for Johnny at that time, a very rough idea, but the devil was in the details. And how! Johnny wanted to keep such knowledge from Luke, for it shamed him.

They'd had different wars, Johnny and Luke. Luke had been in the regular Confederate Army, wearing the uniform and serving with Hood's Texans. He'd fought in some of the most hellacious battles of the war, experiencing fear, privation, and the grisly horrors of combat. After losing his leg he'd survived the hell of a Yankee prison camp.

But Johnny Cross had ridden with Quantrill in the Border States. Here was guerrilla war at its most bitter and horrendous. When they spoke of a war that set brother killing brother, the Kansas-Missouri war was the one they meant. It was a dirty sneaking war where each side sought to outdo each other in atrocity. Johnny had seen the massacre of unarmed men, had taken part in such massacres, rationalizing it then as paying the Yankees back in kind for their war crimes.

Then came the sack of Lawrence, Kansas, a Yankee abolitionist center that had been a thorn in the side of Missouri slaveholders for a long time. Quantrill's raiders had hit that town like Huns, shooting down unarmed men and boys by the score, plundering, robbing, raping, burning. This wasn't war; it was crime, land piracy. Johnny had kept out of the worst that day and done what he could to mitigate the horror but it was little enough compared to the grand scale of the bloodletting. That lifted the scales from Johnny's eyes and he knew that for him a change was going to come, had to come.

Quantrill's band had come apart toward the end, with Bloody Bill Anderson and several others splitting off to form their own ever more murderous, monstrous outfits. Johnny stuck with Quantrill almost to the finish and barely missed being encompassed by the guerrilla leader's doom on his last flailing raid. War's end brought no peace to the survivors of the band. No amnesty for them, the Union declared.

Johnny took it on the run, shooting his way south across the map. He'd been alone, friendless, starved, and hunted by bounty men, Home Guards, and vigilantes of all kinds when he surfaced on the Blacksnake in Moraine County. He was at the end of his rope when a chance encounter threw him in with Cullen Baker. He'd found a friend in Baker and a home of sorts riding with the gang. It was good to have allies to side you and back you with their guns and their lives knowing you'd do the same for them. Too bad it had no higher goal than robbing and killing.

Johnny had gotten out but he had no illusions. You could like Cullen Baker, ride with him, have some laughs, and get drunk with him. Especially that last. The gang leader had a prodigious thirst for alcohol and a prodigious capacity for it.

There was no hiding the fact, though, that Cullen Baker was a stone-cold killer. He had a mean streak and when he got drunk, which was almost all of the time, someone was likely to die. Cullen wouldn't and didn't think twice about burning down an unarmed man. That went against Johnny's grain. He'd killed unarmed men during the war until after Lawrenceville, when he swore there would be no more of it. Nothing more yellowbelly than shooting an unarmed man, by his lights.

Cullen Baker was a killer and Bill Longley, too. Johnny liked them both in many ways, but he had no illusions about them. He was unsure whether saving Cullen Baker's neck this time was a good thing or a bad thing, but he knew he had to try. He owed Cullen a debt for the times he had saved Johnny's life. This would even up things and then Johnny could call it quits.

But there was no way in hell he was drawing Luke Pettigrew into this go-round. Luke was clean and Johnny had no intention of getting him dirty with mud from a part of his, Johnny's, life that he'd hoped was dead and buried. This was all about Johnny's past sins catching up with him, and the burden was his alone.

There was more. This year the railroad would reach Abilene, a cowtown a-building that spring of 1867. The

Crossbow Ranch had plans, big plans, to make a cattle drive to Abilene come summer, sell the herd for top dollar to the big-time beef merchants who planned to ship the cattle east by rail to the ever-hungry markets of the North.

There were things to be done: preparations made, cowhands hired, cattle rounded up and branded, and countless other items big and small in readiness for the big drive north. The ranch at this critical time could get along without Johnny or Luke but not without both. One of them was needed to be on site ram-rodding the enterprise, and since this was Johnny's mess it was his call to clean it up.

"If something happens to me the ranch will still go on as long as you're here, Luke. But if something happens to both of us the ranch is finished and that can't be, we've got too many folks depending on us," Johnny had argued. He'd won the argument because he was right, but that didn't make Luke any happier. Or Johnny, either.

"Besides, it'd be a good thing to have one of us who's not tangled up in law," Johnny added.

"You're not tangled up in law. You're a free man, you got a pardon," Luke countered.

"I'd like to keep it, too, and I'll do my best, but on a venture like this there's no telling what might happen. I need you here on the outside, where you can hire lawyers and whatnot if I need them."

"Dang that Bill Longley! I almost wish he hadn't made it to Hangtree," Luke said bitterly.

"But he did, so it must be that that's the way it was meant to be," Johnny said. There were times he felt the same way though, that it would have been better all around if Bill had fallen short of his goal and

Cullen Baker was hanged on schedule without Johnny being any the wiser.

Thinking like that wasn't getting him anywhere. He had a job to do and he'd best set his mind on doing it—and quick!

Adding to Johnny's miseries was the fact that the one man Johnny really wanted to talk to had dropped out of sight. Sam Heller had gone for parts unknown and Johnny Cross couldn't get a line on him, not past a certain point.

Damon Bolt knew some things and Hangtree town marshal Mack Barton knew some, too, and between them Johnny was able to put together a partial chronology of Sam Heller's comings and goings:

On the same night Sam brought Bill Longley to town, he rode out to Fort Pardee, a cavalry post thirty to forty miles northwest of Johnny's ranch, itself a good half-day's ride west of Hangtree. The fort was on the far side of the Broken Hills range, also known as the Breaks. It was sited on the eastern edge of the Llano Estacado, the Staked Plains, where it guarded the trails from Comanche raiders.

Captain Ted Harrison, commander of the post, was a good friend of Sam's. The captain had worked with him to get Johnny his pardon.

Fort Pardee was where Malvina the Gypsy, working as a cook in the mess hall, had poisoned over a hundred troopers dead as part of a plot to sack Hangtree town and county. The Army wanted Malvina bad. So did Sam Heller. He'd lost a lot of friends and acquaintances to the mass poisoning.

Bill Longley said Malvina was now associated with Commander Rufus Barbaroux in Moraine County. Bill had talked about Malvina during his fever dreams and Sam Heller had heard.

Sam had spent a day and a night at the fort before returning to Hangtree. He hadn't been in town long, and while he was there Johnny missed him. Sam had told the owner of the small bungalow in town that he rented that he was going away on a trip. He paid three months' rent in advance and said that if he hadn't returned within that time the owner was free to rent it out.

A curious fact: Hobbs the livery stable owner said that during the short time Sam was in town, he, Hobbs, had seen him riding a roan horse. Hobbs and Johnny both knew that Sam was greatly attached to his gray steel-dust horse Dusty. Johnny reckoned that Sam had boarded the animal at Fort Pardee and gotten the roan there, too. Was he going somewhere where he couldn't or didn't want to take the gray? Where?

Johnny had a pretty good guess on that score, but he kept it to himself.

Sam Heller rode east out of town. There the trail vanished. Sam started out on the road to Weatherford but he hadn't gone through it, there being no reports of a one-man tornado making a return visit to that town. He must have detoured around the town entirely. Johnny and Bill had later done the same, not having the time to waste taking the town apart. Pity.

"What's that Sam Heller all about?" Bill Longley asked. "He's got a strange way of operating for a bounty hunter. He left a lot of beef on the hoof behind at the dry lake. Vard had to have a price on his head, and some of them other boys must have been worth money, too."

"Sam doesn't walk away from money lightly. If he

did he must have had a good reason," Johnny said. He didn't tell Bill much of what he knew about Sam and more of what he suspected. That was none of Bill's business.

"I'll tell you this: Sam Heller is a most mysterious fellow, and no mistake," Johnny Cross was content to say.

"Not a bad fellow at that, for a Northerner. He sure saved my bacon," Bill said.

"He does that sometimes, gets those impulses, whims. Another day he might have left you on your own to sink or swim."

"I could almost like him if he wasn't a Yankee."

"He's a good man to have on your side in a fight," Johnny said.

Johnny Cross and Bill Longley were now traveling light, having sold the string of fast horses they'd used to race cross-country from Hangtree to the marshy lowlands of the Sabine River. They'd sold the animals well outside Moraine County limits for a fair price.

"No sense selling them on the Blacksnake, too many horse thieves there to make a square deal," Bill had said at the time.

Yes, they were traveling light now to quicken the pace, but not so light that Johnny had shed the several bags of gold coins he'd brought from home. They were wrapped in cloth to muffle their telltale jingle stowed away in Johnny's saddlebags.

Johnny had learned early on that gold was just as much a weapon of war as guns and bullets and sometimes more effective.

Johnny and Bill would have made a strange sight to those uninitiated in the ways of the swamp. They'd smeared a thin coating of mustard-yellow clay on their faces, necks, and forearms, the exposed parts of their bodies. Found locally, the clay offered some protection against the noxious hordes of mosquitoes and other insect pests. It was an old swampland remedy.

But the two had left their hands below the wrists bare of clay except for the very thinnest of coatings on the backs of their hands, to avoid interfering with the speed of their gunwork—a gunman's remedy.

They made an eerie sight, those two, a pair of yellow-faced phantoms flitting through the shadowy trail along the south bank of the Torrent.

They were in Albedo County but still in the territory Barbaroux had staked out for his own. They had not yet come across any sign of Combine presence yet.

"We're almost there," Bill said. "The crossing is just yonder."

Ahead, the river vanished around a bend. Johnny and Bill rounded the curve, coming into a fresh view. They reined to a halt, sizing up the scene.

Here was a fairly straight and narrow stretch where the river narrowed to the width of a stone's throw. The narrowing made the water run still faster.

This crossing lay below, in the middle ground. A small sturdy dock marked this side of the landing. A high-sided wooden flatboat barge was moored here at the near end, the south bank.

A length of thick rope cable hawser was strung from one side of the river to the other, hung from a set of twin posts at either end. The rope was strung in a continuous loop. It dipped low, sagging at the midpoint so it hung close to the water.

"We're in luck," Johnny Cross said, "the ferry's still running. Looks like it's under new management."

A couple of figures were grouped at the landing.

They took notice of the newcomers, turning to face them.

Johnny rested one hand on top of the saddle horn and the other hand atop the first. He turned his yellow-clay masked face toward Bill.

"A word before we go down to the crossing," he said. "You got a quick temper and a gun to match, and I don't fault you on that score. Lord knows I'm not the one to go pointing fingers. But it might not be a bad idea to walk soft for a while until we get the lay of the land. Our mission is to break Cullen out of jail. Let's not get sidetracked."

"Anything you say, Johnny. You're running this shindig."

"Let's ride in."

They started forward. The trail followed a slight downward slope toward the landing.

"See those two docks, one at each landing? The towers on both banks? The barge? We made that, Cullen and I," Bill Longley said, prideful.

"You done good, they're still standing," Johnny said.

"Yes, and to think they've been stolen outright by a pack of no-accounts!" The edge in Bill's voice was as distinctive as the warning buzz of a rattlesnake.

"Hold on before you fly off the handle. Folks have got to make a living. Could be the new bargemen saw something that looked good and made the most of it. Can't blame them for that. Land's lying fallow . . . some man's gonna sew a crop there," Johnny said.

"It makes me mad, that's all!"

"Hell, what doesn't?"

"Not much," Bill confessed with a halfway grin. "You sure have changed, Johnny."

"How so?"

"Time was you'd shoot a man for looking wrong at you. Now . . ."

"You can't fight the world, I learned. Now I try to pick my fights."

"Getting pardoned might have had something to do with that," Bill said.

"Could be," Johnny said, face clouding.

"Hey—hope I didn't say anything out of line; I didn't mean nothing by it."

"Let it go. Who knows if that pardon'll be any good once we're done here?"

"Sorry, I know you put everything on the line to help Cullen."

"So did you."

The conversation had gone where Johnny didn't want. Thinking about consequences would only jam up his natural moves, and that could be fatal in a game like this.

He and Bill rode down the mild slope to level ground, closing on the landing. They could smell it.

"The new proprietors ain't too keen about cleaning up after the horse droppings and what all," Johnny said.

"It's a damned pigsty!" Bill was indignant. "They've let it go to rot and ruin."

"What do you care? We're just passing through, remember? What we want is to get to the other side so we can do what we came here for."

"Right, Johnny, right. I'm okay now. But to see something you helped build with your own hands not only stolen but run down into the ground—it makes me see red."

The figures at the landing—they numbered five— were lazing around under a shade tree. Two of them rose and went to the trail and stood facing Johnny and Bill, watching them come on.

Of the three remaining under the tree, two of them were passing a brown jug back and forth. A third sat off by himself, leaning against the tree trunk. He looked like a hogshead barrel fitted with a head and limbs. He stared at the sky, dull eyed.

"I know them," Bill said in a low voice. "The Clewtes brothers." *Klootz*, he pronounced it. "Purley's the younger one with the long greasy hair, Reese's the older meaner-looking one. Back shooters the both of them."

"They know you?" Johnny asked.

Bill nodded. "They'll think I'm long gone, if they think of me at all. They'll not be looking for Bill Longley, they've got no reason to. And with this yellow clay smearing my face—I should pass muster."

"We'll find out," Johnny said. "Too late to turn back now, not that I'm of a mind to. Let me do the talking. You stay in the background so they don't get too good a look at you."

Bill pulled his hat brim down so it partly covered his face. He and Johnny reined in, halting.

The Clewtes brothers exchanged glances, then started forward to palaver with the newcomers. Purley's smile was as oily as his hair, which fell in curly black ringlets past his bony shoulders.

Reese had a big outthrust jaw and small round eyes set too close together. "Howdy, gents," he said.

"'Morning to you," Johnny said.

"Fixing on making the crossing?"

"How much?"

"Two bits. Each."

Bill snorted, outraged.

"Something wrong with your pard there?" Reese peered at Bill, trying to get a better look at him.

"Your prices, maybe. Two bits a throw seems awful hard," Johnny said.

"So's riding," Reese Clewtes said, laughing humorlessly. "Take you till nightfall to get to Clinchfield by land. That's where you're going, ain't it? Clinchfield?"

"You sure ask a lot of questions. You a bargeman or a lawman?" Johnny said.

"Lawman! That's a good one!" Purley Clewtes guffawed, a real jackass braying. "Imagine taking you for a lawman, Reese!"

Reese smiled tightly. "No more lawman than you, stranger."

"Reckon we'll get along then," Johnny said.

"We will if'n you got four bits to cross over with," Reese said.

"I'm studying on it."

Purley cupped a hand to his mouth, calling to the two passing the jug around. "Rafey, Guy! Here's a good one: this yere pilgrim just asked if Brother Reese is a lawman!"

Rafey and Guy were in their early twenties. Rafey was short, his dark curly hair thinning on top. Guy had black hair combed in a pompadour, thick straight brows, dark eyes.

"Reese a lawman? That's a caution," Rafey said, not laughing or cracking a smile.

Guy didn't say anything; he was busy drinking. Rafey reached out, trying to wrest the jug from the other. Guy turned away from him, putting the jug out of Rafey's reach, fending him off with a straight-arm.

The big man under the tree kept on staring at a blank patch of sky.

"Four bits for two seems a mite steep. How about giving us a play on a double rate?" Johnny asked.

Reese Clewtes's rheumy chuckle bubbled in his lungs. "Knock down on the price? You're lucky we ain't charging extra for the horses. No dickering, we got to make our Combine tax."

"Combine tax? What's that?" Johnny said, playing dumb.

"Hear that, Reese? He wants to know about the Combine tax!" Purley Clewtes slapped his knee over that one, he thought it was so funny, or else made out like he did.

"Combine's the outfit that runs the river, mister," Reese said. "Everyone on the Blacksnake pays a Combine tax. Storekeep pays to keep his store open, fisherman pays to fish, farmer pays to farm . . ."

"Sporting gal's got to pay if she wants to turn up her legs and ply her trade," Purley chimed in.

"All must pay," Reese said, "that is, if'n they want to stay healthy."

"Sounds expensive," Johnny remarked.

"It ain't cheap," Reese agreed. "There's money to be made here, though, if'n you know how."

"How?"

"Hire on with Barbaroux."

"Who's he?"

"You never heard of Barbaroux? Man, you must have come from a long way off!" Purley marveled.

"A fair piece," Johnny said noncommittally.

"On the dodge, are you?"

"That's a hell of a question."

"That's a hell of an answer," Purley cracked. "Tells me all I need to know."

"Barbaroux runs the Blacksnake and everything on it," Reese said.

"That's who he is, that's all," Purley seconded.

"I hear tell Barbaroux's allus' looking for fast guns. You any good with those?" Reese said, indicating Johnny's twin-holstered guns.

"Reckon I can hit a barn door if I'm standing close enough to it," Johnny said.

"Don't crack too much, do you, mister? Well, that's fine. Your business is your business," Reese said.

"And I ain't paid no Combine tax on it, either," Johnny said.

"You just got here," Purley pointed out.

"My business is running this here ferry," Reese began.

"And mine, Brother," Purley said quickly.

"I said my piece and named my price. Take it or leave it . . . your choice. Ferry across or ride on, it's all the same to me," Reese said. "I got bigger fish to fry than to stand around jawing with you. I want to get some of that whiskey before it's all gone."

"Too late! I drank it all!" Guy shouted, then started giggling.

"You sure did, you blamed hawg," Rafey accused, angry and red faced.

Guy giggled all the louder.

"We'll barge," Johnny said.

"Well, good! Climb down from them horses and we'll take you across the river," Reese Clewtes said.

Johnny and Bill dismounted, the latter keeping his horse between himself and the Clewtes to further hamper their getting a good look at him.

"Long as you got the fare, that is," Reese added, holding out a hand palm up.

Johnny fished some coins out of a pocket in his jeans and let them trickle from his fist into Reese's hand, which closed around them like a trap being sprung.

"Done!" Reese cried, making the money disappear.

"Your pard don't say much," Purley said.

"Cat got his tongue once and he never got it back," Johnny said lightly. "'Course, it's only the fish with the open mouth that gets hooked."

"Where does that leave you, talking for two?" Reese needled.

"Me? I'm the sociable type," Johnny said blandly.

"You look familiar—we ever meet before?" Purley said, squinting at Bill.

Bill shook his head no.

"He don't get around much. Simple," Johnny said, significantly tapping the side of his head.

"We got one of them, too, and damned if'n we don't' need to put him to work," Reese said. He called out to the big man sitting under the tree. "Stubb, Stubb! Haul ass over here, you big dumb ox!"

Stubb kept on staring at the sky, as if he hadn't heard.

*"Stubb!"*

"I'll git him," Purley said. He hurried over to the tree and began kicking Stubb, saying, "Up, you blamed idjit, up!"

Stubb rose to his feet. Purley took him by the arm and hustled him down to the waterside.

Stubb was built like a fireplug, short, squat, and solid. A head shaped like a cinder block was set atop a massive upper body, itself supported by stunted bandy legs and gunboat-sized feet. His muddy eyes looked like two shards of brown glass and held about as much understanding.

Rafey and Guy got up and ambled over to the riverside.

The barge was a rectangle-shaped raft, its deck of plank boards nailed down to thick logs that supplied the buoyancy. A chest-high board rail fence enclosed the sides. It wallowed low in the water, wide enough for two horses to stand abreast.

A hinged gate and upraised loading ramp stood at both short ends, fore and aft. Reese Clewtes opened the gate at the near end and lowered the boarding ramp so it connected with the embankment.

Stubb hopped on board the raft, sending it shuddering under his weight. The horses were boarded with some effort; they didn't like the closed confines, the unsteady footing. Johnny and Bill and the Clewtes brothers came on board.

The barge wallowed low in the water.

"Sure we'll make it?" Johnny Cross asked.

"Never lost one yet," Reese said. "Of course, there's always a first time. Don't fall off, that current will suck a man right straight down to the bottom no matter how strong a swimmer he is."

"We'll chance it if you will," Johnny said.

The crossing cable was strung across the river on two towers, one on each side. Each tower had a wagon wheel mounted vertically on it. Metal wheel rims had built up edges circling them to provide a groove for the cable to nest in. The cable hawser was fastened to both tower wheels in a continuous loop, like a giant clothesline.

Stubb took up a place at the barge's forward end. Purley Clewtes raised the shore-side loading ramp and closed the loading gate, securing them. He and Brother Reese stood at the aft end.

Rafey and Guy remained on shore, watching.

"Here we go! Hold on to your horses," Reese shouted.

The Torrent's waters, swift and murky, tore at the barge trying to rip it downstream and would have done so if not for the tow rope and a second, anchor rope tethered to the upstream side float and spanning the river.

Even so the barge bulged out downstream, straining at the traces.

The Clewtes brothers stood at the shore end wielding long poles to push off from the bank. Mighty Stubb took hold of the towrope with oversized pawlike hands, their insides rough as pine bark.

"Heave, heave!" Reese shouted.

Stubb hauled away at the towrope, the brothers poling. The barge creaked slowly away from shore, the Clewtes setting the poles down on the barge deck.

Once the boat was under way Reese and Purley took up posts on the upstream side rail to haul away at the towrope along with Stubb.

Johnny and Bill stood on the downstream side for balance, holding the reins of their horses, the animals standing between them and the bargemen.

Stubb did the lion's share of the work, hauling away, encouraged by Purley slapping and thumping him.

"Put your back into it, Stubb, damn yeh! Break your back on it, yeh lazy ox!" Purley shouted.

Reese contrived to bump against one of the heavily laden saddlebags slung down the flanks of Johnny's horse. "Them bags sure are heavy, mister—what you got in them?"

"Rocks—for ballast," Johnny deadpanned.

"Ha ha! Like I said, Brother Purley, this one don't crack too much!"

There was a steady creak, squeak, and thrum of the cable sliding along the tower wheels. Progress was slow, the barge inching across the water, moving by fits, starts, and jerks into the mainstream.

The process kicked up a lot of spray. Some splashed on Bill's face, washing away much of the yellow clay covering it, a fact of which Bill was unaware.

Purley glanced at Bill, then froze, staring him in the face. "Lawd almighty, Br'er Reese! As I live and breathe, it's Bill Longley!"

"You don't say," Reese remarked too casually.

"Bill Longley! I thought they run your ass clean out of the county!" Purley shouted.

"Life sure is funny," Bill said.

"Sure is," Purley said. He reached for a knife and Reese reached for a gun.

Johnny Cross snaked out his gun, beating Reese to the draw. He opened up on the other. This was gun-fighting at its most raw, standing face to face with the opponent, blasting away at point-blank range.

Johnny squeezed a couple of shots in Reese's middle.

"Oww! You've killed me, mister!" Reese Clewtes folded up, hands to his sundered belly, gun falling to the deck. He rocked backward hard against the board side rail. Boards cracked, splintering.

The horses danced in place, rocking the barge. Purley Clewtes came up behind Johnny, knife held upraised to strike.

Bill Longley shot Purley. Purley cursed, backpedalling, knife still held high. Bill shot him again, this time in the head.

Purley turned, falling against the downstream rail fence.

Stubb loomed toward Bill, massive arms outspread, oversized hands reaching. His expression was totally blank, an unintended poker face. No light showed in his dull brown eyes, inexpressive as wet pebbles.

Stubb tried to wrap a crushing bear hug on Bill, one that would have crushed his ribs and snapped his spine.

Bill sat down hard, dropping below and clear of Stubb's arms before they could close around him. The planks were wet with an inch of water, soaking the seat of his pants.

Stubb's arms snapped shut on empty air. Bill reached up, jamming his pistol barrel hard against Stubb's belly, pumping slug after slug into him.

Muzzle flares caused Stubb's shirt to burst into flame, charred, blackening. Sizzling black scorch marks ringing the bullet holes' entrance wound.

A big man like Stubb took no little amount of killing.

Stubb staggered back, walking on his heels. His expression was as blank as ever, save that his wide mouth gaped open, loose and yawning.

He wasn't moving fast but he had plenty of weight

and heft working for him. He hit the forward railed gate, breaking the catch. The gate swung open, causing Stubb to fall backward into the water.

The swift rushing current whipped the body away like a shot, sending it hurtling downstream, pulling it underwater and out of sight.

"Lord!" Bill cried, somewhat unnerved by his narrow escape.

On the riverbank Rafey and Guy had their guns out and working, firing at Johnny. Bill was out of sight where he sat on the deck, shielded by side rails and gate. Bill had to do some fast scrambling to dodge the horses' hooves.

Johnny held a gun in one hand and his horse's reins in the other, fighting to control it. The forward gate was busted open, swinging back and forth on its hinges, banging against the raft.

He didn't want to lose a horse to the Torrent. Hell, he couldn't afford it! Not with a couple of bags of gold in his saddlebags.

He didn't want to get shot, either. Bullets from the duo on shore whipped past Johnny's head, too close.

Johnny dropped put two slugs into Guy's middle. The shots came one after the other, one-two, sounding like one big leveling blast.

Guy spun, fell, stretched his length on the grass of the riverbank.

Rafey stopped shooting and did a take when he saw his sideman go down. "Guy!" he cried, anguished.

Setting his jaw, squaring his shoulders, Rafey popped shots at Johnny as quick as he could jerk the trigger. Fury didn't help his aim any, because all he hit was air.

Johnny fired two at Rafey, a sudden lurch of the barge throwing him off-balance. The first shot missed Rafey.

Johnny did an instant correction and the next shot tagged Rafey him in the side, knocking him sideways. Rafey tripped over Guy's dead body and fell to his hands and knees, the gun still in hand. Shouting wordlessly he raised the piece for another try.

Johnny pointed his gun at Rafey and fired.

And then there were none.

"You okay, Bill?"

"Yes—you?"

"They missed."

Johnny and Bill had their hands full for the next few minutes getting control over their horses, gentling them down. Being on the water had made them uneasy . . . the violence, blood, and death really driving them wild.

Presently the horses had settled down, though their ears were pointed straight up and their eyes were wide and rolling.

Order of a sort was finally restored to the raft. It stood in midriver.

"The barge line is gonna need some new proprietors," Johnny said sourly.

"That'll teach those Clewtes not to go taking what isn't theirs," Bill said.

"Too bad Purley didn't recognize you after we got to the other side, now we're stuck in the middle of the river."

"I've got a feeling he suspicioned it might be me early on . . . he was a cagey one."

"I don't mind a little killing but now we have to haul the raft the rest of the way."

"Don't forget I'm a bargeman, too. I've been doing my share of the work with Cullen for months."

"Don't you forget that was before you got shot," Johnny said. "I don't want you ruining yourself hauling away on the line."

"The barge isn't going to move itself," Bill said.

"Let's get rid of this dead weight first," Johnny said, indicating the bodies of the Clewtes brothers sprawled and leaking on the deck planks.

He had Bill hold the reins of the horses, keeping them in check while he took care of the body dumping. He dragged Reese's body to the forward end of the barge, tumbling the corpse into the water, which sucked it away and gone. Purley followed his brother into the river.

Johnny cut a short length of rope from the lariat hung coiled at the side of his horse's saddle. He used it to tie the forward gate closed.

He got a pair of wrist-length work gloves out of his kit and fitted them over his hands. "Got gloves, Bill?"

"Nope."

"Cut some strips off your bedroll and use them to wrap your hands to protect them."

"I don't need gloves, I'm a ferryman," Bill said. He held up his hands palms out. "I didn't get these calluses sitting in the shade drinking dandelion wine."

"They look like they've softened up some. You've been laying off the job for a month or more," Johnny said. "Don't get those hands all tore up, you'll need them in good shape for gunwork."

Bill bowed to the logic of necessity, cutting some

strips off the edge of a blanket and wrapping his hands with them.

He and Johnny got into position along the upstream rail, Johnny posted forward and Bill aft behind him. They laid hands on the cable rope and began hauling away. To maximize their efforts they both tugged on the rope at the same time in one synchronous motion.

"Pull!" Bill shouted, calling the cadence, and they both heaved away at the cable line. "Pull! Pull!"

At first the barge seemed motionless, anchored in place. Presently it started to inch forward.

Johnny Cross was medium sized with a trim, athletic build. There was real strength in his well-knit form. Bill Longley was a professional bargeman whose strength was still far from being fully restored, but he had a skilled technique that helped make up for it.

Even so, it was hard, grueling work. The steaming humidity of the swampland didn't make things any easier, though the swift current of the Torrent generated a much welcome cooling breeze.

Johnny and Bill were soaked with sweat before they'd moved the barge more than a foot or two. Johnny called frequent breaks to ensure Bill didn't put a hurting on barely healed wounds.

Heave away, pause, heave some more. The duo fell into a machinelike rhythm, losing track of time, absorbed in the seemingly endless business of tugging away on the cable line to advance the barge to the other side of the river.

At last the forward edge of the barge crunched against the Torrent's north bank. Johnny and Bill rested from their labors.

"Bill, my hat's off to you," Johnny said when he'd finally caught his breath. "That's a damned hard job and no mistake!"

"I never knew just how much of the work Cullen was doing when we were manning the lines; he was doing the lion's share. One lick of this without him is enough to send me right straight back on the owlhoot trail!" Bill said fervently.

Once they were sufficiently recovered, they disembarked. Johnny opened the forward gate. He and Bill lowered the boarding ramp to solid ground and disembarked their horses.

"What about the barge? I'm minded to burn it so no other varmints like the Clewtes can come along and milk it for their own," Bill said.

"Leave it be, leave it be," Johnny said. "Don't close a back door until you're sure you ain't gonna need it. This here barge might come in handy for a getaway after we bust Cullen loose. We can always cut the line and let the barge run downriver once we're safely on the other side. That'd slow up any posse by hours, hours that could be the difference between getting away clean or not."

"You're talking sense," Bill said.

# TWENTY-ONE

This was the clearing on the Torrent's north bank where not so long ago Cullen Baker, his wife Julie, and Bill Longley had lived and worked. There'd been some changes made, not for the better.

The long-standing hunter's cabin that Baker and Julie had used for their home had been burned out. Its stone foundation was now a pen for charred mounds of half-burned timbers and sodden ash heaps.

Bill's one-room wooden shack nearby had been torn down for kindling for a bonfire.

Bill's eyes glistened but their dark irises and pupils were blazing. His face was long, downcast. "Why do people have to be so damned mean? It was a good cabin, and it would have stood for a long time. Folks could have used it, lived in it. Young couples could have sneaked off here for some loving. Hell, let it stand just for a place to get out of the rain . . ."

Yet there had been times not so very long ago when he had gladly and gleefully spread terror by fire when riding with the original Baker gang.

\* \* \*

*There was a roadhouse outside of Halftown where a rival gang congregated. The Baker gang had come by night, using the cover of darkness to douse the outside of the structure with lamp oil and paraffin. Then they put it to the torch.*

*"It's burning like a bastard!" one of the gang happily exclaimed.*

*The rivals tried to shoot it out from inside the roadhouse until the flames got too high, too hot. Then they came out. Some tried to surrender, some tried to run, some to shoot it out, but they were all gunned down.*

*A few stayed in the burning house too long and caught fire themselves, running out of the inferno, human torches screaming. It was a mercy to kill them, put them out of their misery.*

*Cullen Baker had been at the center of things, like always, ramping up the mayhem with a gun in each hand. Firelight outlined his huge shaggy-haired form as he methodically fired a shot first from one gun, then the other, never missing his man.*

*And right beside him was Bill Longley . . .*

"Hey, Bill!" Johnny Cross called. He was on the other side of the burned-out cabin, in a cove of grass that reached into the trees, pushing back the brush.

Something in Johnny's tone set Bill's ears quivering with unease. "What?"

"I think you better see this."

Bill Longley went around the cabin's burned-out wreck, circling around back. He found Johnny standing in a grassy glade ringed by a curved arm belt of woods.

Johnny had his back to Bill, his head bowed and

bared. He held his hat down by his side. He was looking down at something at his feet.

Bill came alongside him, stopping dead in his tracks when he saw the thing:

A grave.

A fresh-dug grave, not more than a few weeks old by the looks of it. The grave mound was sunken. At its head stood a crude wooden cross, tilted to one side.

A thin plank served as the horizontal crossbar. Carved on it was the legend:

JULIE MORGAN BAKER
1851—1867

Bill Longley let out a cry of loss and pain, an anguished howl that seemed to shake the leaves in the trees. He staggered, as if struck a tremendous physical blow.

That was all from him, that single outcry. It was still echoing when Bill shuddered, then slowly drew himself up to full stature. A furious gaze burned in a face set in hard lines that promised no good for the objects of his ire.

Bill Longley was a good hater.

Johnny Cross stood there uneasily, shifting his weight from foot to foot. He didn't know what to say.

He knew this, though, an insight to which he would never give voice:

*Bill Longley had loved Julie, too.*

"Sorry, Bill . . ." Johnny's voice trailed off.

"She was a mighty fine gal," Bill said, his voice husky. "I set a lot of store by her, in a respectful way, her being Cullen's wife and all."

"Sure," Johnny said.

"Julie always had a smile even when things looked blackest. She had a gentle spirit. Seeing her was like the sun coming out after a storm."

"You want some time alone to say a few words over her, Bill?"

Bill Longley shook his head no. "She doesn't need any words from the likes of me. She's one of the angel band now. Let's be doing."

Johnny put on his hat and clapped Bill roughly on the shoulder. "We'll make them pay, hoss."

"Lord, yes!" Bill said feelingly.

A twig snapped behind them. Johnny and Bill whipped around with guns in their hands quick as lightning.

"Easy, gents," a voice said. Standing on the far side of the clearing was its owner, a big woman who took up a lot of space.

She bulked larger than a lot of men and it was all brawn and no fat. A straw planter's hat with the brim curled up at the sides was pulled down over a melon-sized head. Black hair marbled in gray was pulled back into a tight knot at the back of her head. She had dark eyes, an eagle beak nose and a jack-o'-lantern mouth.

She wore a man's button-down shirt, dark and loose ankle-length skirt, laced-up thick-soled boots. She held a double-barrel shotgun pointed down at the ground.

"Easy, Johnny," Bill said. "That's Kate. She's a friend." He eased the hammer down on his gun, holstering it.

Johnny did likewise. "Dangerous game in these parts, sneaking up on folks," he said, his blood still up and running high.

"Lucky I recognized Bill Longley or I might have cut loose on you on general principles," Kate said.

"I stepped on that twig to let you know I was here. Elsewise you'd never have knowed."

Kate advanced. "Combine men tried to put out the word that they'd run you out of the county with your tail tucked between your hind legs, Bill, but I wasn't having none of it."

"Thanks for the vote of confidence. I see Barbaroux's crowd hasn't done for you yet."

"Nor will they. That crowd specializes in dirty tricks and back shooting but they have to find me first, and in the back country that takes some doing," Kate said.

She cut a quick side glance at the gravesite. "So— you know."

Bill nodded. "What happened, Kate?"

"Julie was worn to a frazzle even before Cullen was tooken. After that she had to go into hiding. Barbaroux wanted her; it would have tickled him to torment Cullen that his wife was being held on the Big White Boat with Lord knows what being done to her.

"I looked after her best as I could, but you know running and hiding in the swamps night and day is no life for a young girl. And Julie always was of a delicate constitution. She come down with swamp fever bad. Tore her down. She was already near half-crazy with worry for her man. I tended to her with herbs and such, but I'm no doctor. Afore I could fetch a real saw-bones she was gone. She went to sleep and never woke up. She passed quietly, if that's any consolation."

"Not hardly," Bill Longley said, his dark eyes pits of cold fury.

"Didn't 'speck it would be, ain't hardly no comfort to me, neither, but I'm giving all of it to you, the way it was," Kate said. "Julie was happiest here at the landing for those few months when she was fresh wed to

Cullen, before the trouble started and them Combine hounds came sniffing around looking to fatten their coffers. I laid her to rest here. It was like burying my own daughter."

"You did a real nice job, Kate. I thank you for it. I know Cullen would thank you, too," Bill said.

A burlap croker sack with a top strap was slung over one of Kate's broad shoulders. She reached into it with her free hand, pulling out a tight bouquet of wild-flowers. "I come by when I can to leave some small remembrance. I saw two strangers standing by the grave. Y'all seemed respectful else I'd have just blowed you away with this here scattergun and picked through the pieces later. Danged if the bad penny himself hadn't turned up again in the form of that young hellion Bill Longley! I knew you'd be back sooner or later, but I didn't know when."

"I had to take a long hard ride, Kate."

"And this is what you brung back, huh?" Kate said, indicating Johnny Cross. "You're almost too blamed fast with the plow handles, Bill, but danged if your friend here didn't shade you on the draw when you both reached.

"Still . . . seems like a lot of time and trouble to go to to fetch back just one man even if he is a fast-draw artist."

"Not just any man, Kate," Bill said, corners of his lips quirking in the phantom of a smile. "He's a friend. Friend to me and Cullen, good friend."

"Who be you, stranger?" Kate demanded.

"Johnny Cross, ma'am."

Kate's eyes narrowed, then got a faraway look as if peering through shades of memory. "Johnny Cross," she repeated. "'Pears to me I recollect the name at that. You was in that first Cullen Baker gang a couple of years back."

"That's right," Johnny said.

"Yes, I heard of you. You look a tad undersized for the hell-raising, fire-eating Johnny Cross the barroom idlers used to talk up, if you don't mind my saying so."

"Say what you please, it's a pleasure to hear a body speak her mind straight out."

"You won't get much of that on the Blacksnake. Not now."

"Johnny got reformed, Kate," Bill said.

"You sure picked a hell of a time to do it, mister. Not that this whole blamed county couldn't use some reform. And you aim to do it?"

"No, ma'am," Johnny said, "I came here to help out two friends, Bill and Cullen Baker."

"If you want to help Cullen you'll have to act fast and then some more. He's slated to hang in seven days," Kate said. "Seven days!"

"Then Bill and I had best be about our business. Pleased to make your acquaintance, ma'am," Johnny said.

"Call me Kate, friend," she said, extending a pawlike hand that looked like an oversized mitten. "Shake!"

"Go easy on him, Kate, he's going to need that hand," Bill said, only half-joking.

Johnny shook hands with Kate. She shook like a man, a bone-crushing power in her grip, held in restraint.

"Saw you looking at these mitts of mine," Kate said. Her shirtsleeves were rolled up to the elbows, baring brawny forearms thick with scar tissue down to the fingertips. "I catch and sell crawdads to earn me some spending money. That's why they call me Crawdad

Kate. Them critters don't come without a fight . . . they always nip you with their claws a moment afore they go to the cooking pot."

"Can you blame them?" Johnny said.

"Not at all! I'd do the same in their place." Kate laughed, then she got serious fast. "I'm gonna do what I came here to do, if you'll give me a moment." She wasn't asking, she was telling.

Kate went to the gravesite and put her shotgun down. She took the bouquet from her sack and laid it down on the mound at the head of the grave. She got down on her knees, folded her hands, and prayed silently to herself, her lips moving.

Johnny and Bill drifted away a bit to give her some privacy. Kate wasn't long, only a moment or two. She rose, brushing dirt off her knees, and took up her shotgun, all business now.

"I take note that them egg-sucking dogs the Clewtes brothers and their chicken-thieving friends seem to have absented themselves from the locality kind of sudden," she said.

"They retired from the barge business," Johnny said dryly. "Seems they couldn't handle the freight."

"Well you're off to a good start and no mistake," Kate said. "But the Clewtes and their ilk are mighty small fry compared to the Commander in the Big White Boat, Not to mention Warden Munday in Clinchfield Gaol. The place is a fortress."

"No nut too tough to crack," Johnny said.

"I admire your spirit if nothing else, but what're you gonna use for a nutcracker?" Kate asked.

"Guns and gold, and plenty of both."

Kate eyed him with new interest. "You got?"

Johnny nodded yes. "I've got the gold, the gold will get the guns."

"You ain't just whistling Dixie, son. Let's get to where the deals are made," Kate said.

"Deep Hollow," Johnny said. It was not a question. This was not his first time on the Blacksnake.

Kate nodded. "Any reason why we can't get started now?"

"The sooner the better."

"My mule's tied up in that clump of trees yonder," she said, gesturing at a grove in the far side of the clearing. "You boys saddle up and we'll be off directly."

Kate started tromping off in that direction taking big-legged strides. Bill called her name, bringing her to a halt.

"You reckon Cullen knows about Julie?"

"It's no secret she's gone, Bill. Her resting place is in plain sight. Anybody who came to the Crossing couldn't help but see. Julie being who she was—wife to Cullen Baker—word was sure to spread like wildfire. The prison grapevine being what it is," she added. "Word is sure to have reached Cullen. Even if they're keeping him apart from the other prisoners."

"They lit a fire that won't quit," Bill said darkly.

"They figure to quench that fire by killing Cullen Baker," Kate said. "In seven days."

# TWENTY-TWO

"Time to get down to the nut cutting," Johnny Cross said. "Let's deal."

He and Bill Longley sat at the Big Table of the Council Flatboat in the bayou backcountry hideout of Deep Hollow.

It was night. A sputtering kerosene lantern sat at the center of the big table, an oblong slab of cypress wood the size of a billiards table. Seated there with Johnny and Bill were some of the Powers of Deep Hollow, that last refuge and redoubt of the most wanted, most desperate, or purely most ornery folk on the Blacksnake:

George St. George, leader of the night runners, a band of river pirates.

Swamp cat Belle Nyad, one-eyed hellcat who served as acting chief of the Skinner Kondo River Rats smuggling gang.

Albert "Gator Al" Hutchins, part Tonkawa Indian and speaker for the small but potently lethal tribe of Tonks and their blood-kin, a force to be reckoned with in the swamp.

"There's others in the Hollow just as dangerous and

with even larger followings, but you can trust these three," Crawdad Kate had confided earlier to Johnny Cross when he and Bill Longley were plotting whom to bring in on their plan to save Cullen Baker.

"I know George. He and I did some work together the last time I was in Moraine County," Johnny said.

"Oh? Who'd you kill?"

"Nobody important, just some thieves who stole a fish cannery payroll and kicked when we stole it from them. Nobody hollers louder than a thief who's being robbed. George is a good man. I hope we can do business."

"He's your best bet. He's liable to throw in just for the chance to get at Barbaroux."

"Why's that, Kate?"

"The Commander killed his kid brother. Or had him killed. Same thing."

"Little Ned? They killed Little Ned?" Johnny said, shocked. "Why, that young'un wasn't even old enough to wear a gun!"

"When you was last here, maybe. But they grow up fast in the swamp, and a few years can make a big difference. Poor Neddy was sweet on some Halftown gal that Barbaroux had his eye on and she looked on the boy with some favor. Too much for the Commander. One of his Combine gunmen picked a fight with Neddy and shot his eyes out," Kate said.

"That's a damned shame," Johnny said feelingly.

"George did for the shooter all right—fed him alive piece by piece to the gators, so I heard—but he held Barbaroux responsible for the killing and is sworn to get him. Yes, George St. George is a pretty sure bet for any go that'll sting the Commander."

"Well, I've got a whopper for him."

"Swampcat Belle and Gator Al both have good reasons to hate Barbaroux," Kate continued. "His Gun Dogs river police sank Belle Nyad's steam-powered boat.

"And the Commander is pure hell on the Tonks, swore a blood oath to wipe them out to the last man, woman, and child. Any Tonk the Combine takes they kill out of hand. That puts Gator Al Hutchins right square in your corner."

Kate continued. "One more thing about those three, you can trust them. Once they're bought, they stay bought. No worry about them selling you out to the Combine."

"Sounds like a basis for negotiations," Johnny said. He asked Kate to come to the meeting but she declined.

"I'll help set it up but it's your bit, you do the talking," Kate said. "Everybody in the Hollow—hell, on the Blacksnake—knows about Cullen Baker. He gave Barbaroux a real hard time, killed a lot of Combine men. Then the Combine tricked him, lured him into a trap when he went to meet some folks he thought were friends. They took Cullen alive. Tried him in a show trial in one of Barbaroux's kangaroo courts and sentenced him to hang. You say George St. George knows you—that'll help. Belle and Gator Al know Bill, so they'll give you a fair hearing at least. The rest is in the horse trading. You've got to give them something they want. It may be gold or guns or who knows what."

"You'll find out tonight at the meet," Bill said.


Deep Hollow was way out in the bayou backcountry. A number of paths led there: by horse, on foot, by water. It was easier to get into than to get out of alive, especially if the folk there were against you.

The local Tonkawa tribe first fled to the Hollow to escape far-eastward ranging Comanche bent on wiping out the whole Tonkawa nation. Next came runaway slaves, indentured servants, and fugitives from the law.

Now the Hollow was in crisis because of the recent influx of several hundred refugees fleeing the wrath or tyranny of Barbaroux. The permanent colony in the swamp was never equipped to handle such numbers.

Whole families by the score were living in primitive lean-tos, tents, and hovels. Food shortages were common. The refugees lived on the edge of starvation. The swamp was full of fish and four-legged varmints, but the foragers had to range ever farther afield to take some daily catch for their cooking pots.

The refugee camp of Deep Hollow was a powder keg waiting to explode. Bad for them but good for Johnny Cross, according to the hard logic of necessity. Folks with nothing to lose are more likely to get up on their hind legs and scrap, particularly if they think they've got a fighting chance.

Johnny meant to give them that chance. He was not the only one.

There was the Major, for instance.

Johnny couldn't help but notice a considerable number of repeating rifles in the hands of the hard-core swampers, the river pirates, smugglers, and thieves who'd already been long established in the Hollow before the current influx of newcomers.

The weapons were new model Winchester 1866 repeating rifles, pretty much state of the art in the killing trades. To Johnny's eyes they looked like U.S. Army issue. He and Bill did some discreet asking around: Where did the rifles come from?

The Major, came the reply. The Major was the source for the Winchesters. The way the newly armed gun toters said his name, you could almost hear the capital letters: "The Major."

Who was the Major?

The Major had first appeared little more than a fortnight ago, partnered with Captain Quent Hazard, the craftiest, most dangerous smuggler on the river. Hazard was at the very top of the list of men Rufus Barbaroux would most like to hang.

Captain Hazard's credentials were impeccable, gaining the Major access to the higher-ups in the Hollow. The Major would deal only with the bigs and damned few of them, only those Captain Hazard would vouch for personally.

The higher-ups were more than ready to come in when they saw the Major's deal: crates of Winchester Model 1866 repeater rifles and ammunition to match. The swampers were used to getting the worst firearms on the river. Barbaroux had decreed a death penalty on anyone selling weapons to the Hollow.

Then along comes the Major with more and better hardware than ever before seen in the swamp, and at bargain prices, too.

The swampers figured that was because the ordnance was stolen, from a bluebelly army arsenal somewhere. So much the better; it only made the deal all the sweeter. They bought every box of rifles and ammunition the Major had to offer.

And the supply was plentiful. Captain Hazard was making three runs a week. It seemed like the Major was intent on flooding the hardcore element of Deep Hollow with first-class weaponry.

Whoever the Major was, he was sure enough in the anti-Barbaroux business, Johnny Cross said to himself. He very much wanted to meet the Major.

All in due time. First, the palaver with George St. George, Belle Nyad, and Gator Al Hutchins.

The council flatboat was just that, a keelboat-type barge moored in the middle of a bayou lake. A one-story cube-shaped cabin was built in the center of the barge.

The participants had been rowed out to the barge early at night, at moonrise. A steamy haze hung over the lake, blurring the outlines of the swampy nightscape. The moon was a fuzzy yellow crescent shining through the trees.

Before the meet began, Johnny Cross went off to one side with George St. George.

George St. George was long, lean, lithe. His hair was combed straight back from his forehead. A pair of pistols was tucked into a cummerbund-type red sash worn low around his middle, pirate style.

"Johnny Cross, long time no see," George said.

"So you're still alive and kicking," Johnny said. "Glad to see it."

"Likewise. Thought we'd seen the last of you here on the river."

"That's what I thought, but . . . here I am. Listen, George, this is apart from anything else, the meet and all. I heard about Little Ned. It's a damned shame. You know I always liked the boy."

"I know it," George St. George said, smiling sadly. "Little Ned . . . once he got his growth, or thought he did, he couldn't bear to be called that, Little Ned.

He'd fly into a rage when I forgot. But he was and always will be Little Ned to me.

"I couldn't side him always. You know how it is. He wanted to stand on his own two feet, and it was right that he did. But it wasn't right that that redheaded son in the Big White Boat had him killed over a no-account slip of a Halftown gal." George sighed before continuing.

"I swore I'd get him and I will. But it ain't easy. Barbaroux surrounds himself with an iron ring of shooters. Gun one down—and believe me, I've gunned down plenty—and more rise up to take their place. But I'll get him, no matter what."

"I believe it," Johnny said. "I've been studying on how to give Barbaroux a bloody nose . . ."

They went inside, into the cabin. It was dim, hot, close, and smoky. A lone kerosene lamp sat in the middle of the big cypress table that the players sat around. The chairs were a mixed bag, no two alike and not a one comfortable. It helped keep meetings short.

Johnny Cross sat at one end of the rectangular table, with Bill Longley seated on his right. George St. George sat opposite Johnny at the far end of the table. Belle Nyad sat on his right and Gator Al Hutchins on his left.

Bunches of slow-burning dried punk reeds were scattered around the space. Their smoke was harsh and burned the throat, but it seemed to keep the swarming mosquitoes at bay.

Belle Nyad looked the very picture of a piratical femme with a black eye patch worn over the left eye. She was a raven-haired wench, her looks hard but comely, her body ripely curved. A silver earring pierced her left ear. From it hung a thin silver chain several inches long, attached to the top of an acorn-sized silver skull with a death's-head grin.

She was acting chief of Skinner Kondo's River Rats gang. Kondo was a legendary terror on the river. In recent years a crippling wounding had laid him low, but not so low that he wasn't a figure still to be respected and feared.

Belle Nyad was not to be underestimated, either, not if she could lord it over Kondo's crew of cutthroats, Johnny reminded himself.

Gator Al Hutchins was a long-limbed, raw-boned giant with a thatch of thick coarse dark hair streaked with gray, high cheekbones, bright eyes set back deep in their sockets, and a slash of a mouth. In the Indian manner his face was free of facial hair save for his brows. He wore a wildly out of place black top hat of the type swells wore to the opera and theater. It clashed oddly with his necklace made of alligator claws.

He was a power among the Tonkawas, themselves a power in the swamp.

George St. George, Belle Nyad, and Gator Al stared with poker faces at Johnny Cross.

Johnny was a direct actionist. He slammed a leather pouch the size of a quart bottle down on the table. It hit with a heavy *thunk* in which was mixed the resounding ring of metallic coin. The impact jarred the kerosene lantern, making its oily flames dance.

The pouch was open at the top. From its mouth spilled a rush of gold coins, fanning out across the tabletop. It was one of the bags of gold Johnny had brought from Hangtree.

The space suddenly brightened with the golden glow reflected from the mass of coins, throwing weblike golden highlights on the faces of George St. George,

Belle Nyad, and Gator Al, all of whom leaned forward as one, alert and intent, quivering like hound dogs on point.

"I aim to bust Cullen Baker out of Clinchfield Gaol before he hangs," Johnny Cross said. "Now what's it going to take to get y'all to come on board?"

The horse trading began. It ran long and hard, the back and forth frequently heated. This was serious business. In the end, the answer to Johnny's question was:

Gold, of course. But not just gold.

Belle Nyad wanted gold and revenge on the Gun Dogs, Barbaroux's elite river police, for sinking her boat.

Gator Al wanted gold and his people who were being held in Clinchfield Gaol freed.

"I want to sink Barbaroux," George St. George said. "Busting open Clinchfield Gaol is just what's needed to set him up for the kill. And I want gold, too. I'd do this just for the doing, but my people need to be paid for risking their lives."

"Done!" Johnny Cross said.

# TWENTY-THREE

*Six days until Cullen Baker was hanged.*

"See Sharkey at the Dead Drunk in Halftown," George St. George advised. "He's smart—smart enough to know that he's next in Barbaroux's gunsights. He's exposed in Halftown, out in the open. No swamp to hide in. He may want to come in. If he does, he'll be a big help. If not, he'll keep his mouth shut. He wouldn't give Barbaroux the time of day if his life depended on it."

That night, Johnny Cross set out for Halftown.

The Blacksnake River ran south-southwest through Moraine County. It ran south until reaching a boggy peninsula on the north bank known as Pirate's Point, where it took a sharp curve to the southwest.

Clinchfield town, capital of the county, lay downstream of Pirate's Point, nestled in the crook where the land thrust out into the river. From there the Blacksnake ran southwest before joining the larger Sabine River, which ultimately emptied into the Gulf of Mexico.

Halftown lay a few miles upstream from Pirate's

Point, off the south bank. It was sited on an oval-shaped almost-island, connected to the mainland by a narrow spit of ground.

Halftown began as a pirates' base founded by Jean Lafitte. Now it was a settlement of roughly a thousand souls. In most ways it was a typical river port. A sheltered safe harbor for waterborne traffic, its shore thick with docks and warehouses where goods were loaded and unloaded day and night.

The waterfront district was a gridded maze made up of unpaved streets and crooked alleys. River Street, the main drag, bordered the dockside area. A row of warehouses and storage sheds lined the shoreline side of the thoroughfare.

The other side of the street was crowded with wooden frame buildings that served the needs of the rough men who plied their trade along the Blacksnake. There were rooming houses and flophouses, eateries and saloons, gin mills, gambling houses, low dives, brothels, and suchlike.

Halftown was still a smugglers' paradise and thieves' market, dealing almost exclusively in contraband and stolen goods. It was a hard place, rowdy and violent. Shootings were common, virtually an everyday occurrence.

The hordes of blue-clad Federal occupation troops whose presence was such an oppressive reality throughout the former Confederacy had yet to be seen in Moraine County. The Federals' resources were stretched to the limit trying to garrison the big cities and vital towns of the Southland.

While most of Dixie wore the yoke of Yankee occupation troops, Moraine County was under the thumb of Rufus Barbaroux.

The powers in Halftown were the brotherhoods, gangs, and clans of smugglers, dealers in stolen goods and river-borne crime. These were commercial associations dedicated to turning a profit. Open hostility to Barbaroux might be a costly mistake, some argued. Barbaroux was a power in the land, a big operator with big ideas and a not so small army of gunmen.

Clinchfield was Barbaroux's and Halftown was next on Barbaroux's list. He was already in the opening stages of a massive offensive against the thieves' haunt.

By any measure Halftown was dangerous by day, doubly dangerous by night. The farther one traveled from the center of the waterfront district, the greater the threat.

The Dead Drunk lay on the outskirts of town, at the westernmost edge of River Street where the warehouses played out. It was set on a long pier stretching out into the water.

Johnny Cross came to the dive not by land but by water, seated in the middle of a pirogue. With him were George St. George and Roe Brand, a strong supple youth who was one of Gator Al's most trusted men.

The watercraft was something like a hollowed-out dugout canoe but lighter and with a more shallow draft. Roe Brand was perched at the stern, wielding a double-bladed paddle, George St. George at the bow.

It was a sultry night with a welcome breeze on the river blessfully blowing the mosquitoes away, mostly. A hazy sickle moon sliced through scudding clouds.

A lone pier extended some fifty-sixty feet out into the water. It was solidly built, rugged and foursquare, a wooden tongue thrust deep into rushing black waters. It was supported by pilings that rose ten feet above the water's surface.

Sharkey's saloon was a one-story rectangular-shaped building, its short ends parallel to the shoreline. It squatted at the end of the pier, solid and chunky. Sooty yellow-brown light fanned out of square-shaped windows. The place was alive with crowd noises.

"Sounds like a racing mill wheel when the river's high," Johnny said.

"Milling out money," said St. George.

Roe Brand wielded the double-bladed paddle deftly, each blade knifing cleanly into the water without a splash. The pirogue closed on the pier. The river current was buffered here by the rows of upright columnar pier pilings.

A wooden raftlike float was chained to the pilings on the pier's downstream side. A ladder hung down the side of the pier, ending a few feet above the side of the float nearest to it.

The pirogue glided alongside the float, nudging it with a gentle bump. Restless churning splashes sounded in the darkness under the pier.

"What's making all that noise?" Johnny asked.

"Gators," Roe Brand said.

"What I thought," Johnny said dourly. Being on the river held both the risk of drowning and being eaten by alligators.

"The Dead Drunk tosses its garbage over the side. The gators hang around for the free meals," George St. George said. "Every now and then a body goes over the side. The gators know it and wait for it."

"That's nice," Johnny said.

"Helps keep the river clean," said Roe Brand.

Johnny thought the pirogue seemed mighty frail, a lightweight wooden shell skimming atop the surface of the water. "Looks like it wouldn't take much for a big ol' gator to capsize this boat," he said.

"Not much," Roe Brand cheerfully agreed.

St. George uncoiled his folded legs from the bottom of the boat, rising to step nimbly onto the float.

He reached out a helping hand to assist Johnny in climbing out of the boat. The pirogue wallowed unsteadily despite Roe Brand holding on to the side of the float to maintain balance.

Johnny Cross had traded his boots for moccasins on this boat ride. The mocs were more practical for the lightweight, thin-shelled pirogue. He had feared that with boots on he was liable to accidentally step through the bottom of the hull.

He clambered up onto the float without mishap. He had good moves, sharp and catlike.

"I'll be waiting on the upstream side of the pier," Roe Brand said. "Can't stay here without attracting attention."

"We'll be there later," St. George said.

"Luck." Roe Brand pushed off from the float to gain some way, back-paddled to turn the pirogue around, then cut a curving course into the river and around the end of the pier.

George and Johnny went to the far side of the float where the ladder was. George climbed first. Johnny waited for the other to reach the pier before starting up himself. That ladder looked none too sturdy.

Johnny climbed, testing each rung before trusting his weight to it. It was a relief to feel at last the solid deck planking of the pier underfoot.

The saloon's out-shore end stood ten feet from the end of the pier. The ladder had put Johnny and George behind the back of the building.

Johnny tried the back door. "Locked. Reckon Sharkey don't want nobody leaving without paying."

"No one gets served without paying first. Not even the dead can leave without first settling up their bill," said St. George.

The pier was wide, leaving six feet of clear space on both sides of the building's long walls. The duo walked shoreward, going around to the saloon's front where there was light and people coming and going.

Nailed to the cornice of the flat roof was a wooden painted signboard showing a crude cartoon of a man's face with X's for eyes and a cloud of little circles that were supposed to be bubbles floating over the top of his head. Placed around the face were painted clusters of whiskey barrels and kegs marked XXX. Some upright, others overturned.

No words were needed to identify the waterfront dive known far and wide as the Dead Drunk.

A man sat on the plank boards to one side of the front entrance, slumped against the wall, his face buried in his hands.

Johnny's gaze scanned the scene on the mainland at the ratty western end of River Street. "No sign of Bill and the others yet," he said.

"They're coming by land, takes longer than the river route," George St. George said.

"No Gun Dogs, either."

"They'll be here. Crabshaw and Marston won't be able to resist the bait. No doubt some dirty little Judas has already gone on the run to them to give them the word."

A young man came slinking out of the saloon's front entrance. He was skinny, shifty eyed and sunken faced, with greasy blue-black hair and a three-day beard. He seemed weighed down by the big-caliber pistol holstered at his side. The buckle was set at the tightest notch, but the gunbelt still seemed in danger of slipping down his scrawny hips.

"Speak of the devil!" George St. George said, stepping back into the shadows before the newcomer could see him.

"That's Blue Fane, a mangy mutt who wants to run with the big dogs, the Gun Dogs," the swamper said low voiced so only Johnny could hear. "He's been sucking around them lately, trying to get in. He is also, I'm sorry to say, a cousin of mine."

Approaching hoofbeats sounded. A band of nine riders appeared out of the darkness, pulling up opposite the pier.

Sharkey's two guardsmen posted at the hitching rails stiffened, moving off to one side.

The men dismounted, one staying behind to hold the horses' reins while the others took up a stance facing the saloon. They were heavy with six-guns. Grim, purposeful, they looked like they had a job to do.

"Enter the Gun Dogs," George St. George said softly.

"Things are breaking faster than we figured on," Johnny said, sounding like he relished the prospect of action.

"The big dogs are here, Crabshaw and Marston. The fat tub of guts is Pigfeet Crabshaw and the one tricked out like a medicine show barker is Tully Marston.

"They started out as gunrunners, believe it or not. Pigfeet Crabshaw was the ramrod and Tully Marston had the guns. They used to run them into the Hollow, among other places. They sold old junk guns—throwaways—for top prices. Tully's the one they call 'Miracle' Marston. Like the saying goes, 'If the gun works, it's a miracle.'" George St. George paused a second before resuming.

"Barbaroux let them stay in business long after he cracked down on all the other gunrunners. We reckoned it was because they were spying for him, keeping an eye on the Hollow where he couldn't reach.

"Now they're his river police. They've got a steam-powered launch they use to cruise the Blacksnake. That's the one that sank Belle's boat. It's moored now at a slip farther east on River Street."

"Convenient," Johnny Cross said.

"Yes, isn't it?" said George St. George.

"Marston and Crabshaw are both awfully fond of their own skins," he went on. "They let the lesser lights in the crowd do the real fighting. They won't make a move until the rest of the outfit gets here. Which should be soon because we know they're all in Halftown."

"How many more?" Johnny asked.

"Ten, maybe," George St. George said.

"Is that all? No sense waiting for Bill and the bunch, we might just as well clean up on them ourselves."

"I believe you'd do it, too, Johnny," George said, quirking a smile.

"And you!" Johnny replied.

"I will if I have to, but no sense in us hogging all the fun. Let's see what jumps."

Blue Fane started at the sight of the Gun Dogs. His face lit up like he was glad to see them. He hitched up his gunbelt and took a few quick steps forward, a hand raised in greeting.

"Blue!" George St. George said sharply, stopping the other in his tracks.

Blue Fane's hand hovered over his gun butt. George

stepped into the light where the other could see him. Fane's hand jerked away from the gun as if it had been scalded.

"Hey, Cousin George, I didn't see you there." Fane frowned. "Ain't you taking a chance, coming out in the open like this?"

"No," George said flatly. "A word of friendly advice, cousin. Think twice before pressing your luck tonight. I'd hate to have to go to your funeral and say nice things about you that I don't mean."

"Huh? You got me all wrong, George—"

"You're all wrong for sure, but you got that way all by your own self. I said my piece. You can go, Blue— now."

Blue Fane got, scuttling away down the pier, holding his gunbelt up with one hand to keep it from falling down as he hurried away.

"There he goes, straight to Crabshaw and Marston to tell them I'm here. I'm not trying to put on any big brag, but I do believe that'll make them pull in their horns and sit tight until they've got more numbers," George said.

"Let's step inside for a minute," Johnny said, "I've got a hankering to see the famous Mr. Sharkey before the fireworks start."

They went into the saloon. Stepping through the doorway was like walking into a fifth wall: noise. The place roared, sounding like a riot in a boiler factory. Everybody was shouting at the top of their lungs, it seemed.

The big main room was crammed with tough waterfront denizens: riverboat men, fishermen, crabbers, dock workers, and warehouse strongbacks.

There was no shortage of women, either, most of

them professionals ranging from hard-bitten slatternly harridans to comely fresh young things new on the market.

Despite the crush of bodies, folks made way for a burly dockworker type, a hulking brute with bulging muscles and an arm-swinging swagger. He elbowed aside those too slow to get out of the way, and if any of those so roughly handled was minded to take offense they thought twice about it and swallowed their protests. He kicked a cripple aside and knocked an embracing couple sprawling.

"If that ain't the limit!" Johnny Cross said, disgust showing plain on his face.

It must have been Johnny's expression of hostile contempt that caught the brute's eye, for the latter was too far away to have heard his comment. He changed course, bearing down toward Johnny.

"Bigger Wright, bully brawler of the docks," St. George said, identifying the oncomer fast closing on them.

Collision was imminent, but Johnny was not minded to step aside.

"Gangway, runt!" Bigger's gruff growl was silenced and his progress immediately arrested by the sight of a gun leaping into Johnny's hand and leveling on his belly.

Bigger was a brawler, not a gunfighter. He realized he was out of his league in a county now swarming with killer gunmen who would rather shoot than punch. His eyes widened in a face suddenly oozing cold sweat.

"Next time be polite," Johnny said loud enough for Bigger to hear.

Pistol-whipping was widespread among gun-toters

of the day, but Johnny generally disapproved of the practice, holding that a gun was a complex mechanism with a lot of moving parts that could be knocked out of line when used as a club.

But he reckoned that it would do no harm to use the pistol not to hammer but to thrust. That's what he did, jabbing the gun barrel hard and straight on into Bigger's belly just below the rib cage, into the solar plexus.

"*Whoof!*" Bigger went slack, folding at the knees, eyes bulging, mouth vainly sucking for air in a face suddenly ashen gray.

He dropped to his knees but it was only a way station en route to the sawdust-covered floor. He flopped around like a fresh-landed fish, holding himself. He rolled on his side, curled up, legs together, knees bent.

Johnny holstered his piece. In the space now opened by Bigger's downing, he caught sight of those he had come here to meet:

Belle Nyad, Gator Al, and Wake Spindrift, all seated together at a nearby table. The table was against the downstream-side long wall. The trio was positioned around the table so that Gator Al faced front, Belle Nyad viewed the middle ground, and Spindrift kept an eye on the rear of the saloon. Nobody was sneaking up on them.

"Over there, George," Johnny said, indicating the trio with a slight nod.

"I see them."

The two went around Bigger, angling toward the table where their cohorts waited.

From a vantage point near the bar from which he directed operations, Niahll Sharkey motioned to some nearby staffers.

"He's drunk!" Sharkey shouted, grinning wolfishly: "No place here for a man who can't hold his liquor!—Throw him out, lads!"

A pair of grimly efficient toughs hopped to it, hurrying to carry out the boss's orders.

At a hefty two hundred and fifty pounds, Bigger was not dead but surely dead weight. The bouncers each grabbed one of his arms and dragged him across the floor and out the front door to the accompaniment of ragged cheers, catcalls, and whistles from various members of the crowd.

The bouncers returned presently, rubbing their hands together with the air of men who have performed a task well done.

Johnny and George St. George took seats at the table. A handful of bottles and some wooden tumblers were laid out on the tabletop.

"Nicely done, sir! You got that gun out fast," Wake Spindrift said to Johnny. A small wisp of a man with prematurely gray hair and a long sensitive face, he was one of George St. George's most trusted henchmen.

Johnny waved a hand in modesty.

"I'm disappointed," Belle Nyad said. "I thought you were going to shoot him."

"Bloodthirsty wench, ain't she?" Gator Al said, grinning hugely.

"That's why I'm here," Belle said.

"I didn't want to jump the gun and start the party too soon. And I don't want to waste any rounds. Ammunition is liable to be at a premium directly," Johnny said. "The Gun Dogs are here."

"Ahh," Belle said with a shiver of sensual pleasure.

Johnny Cross was always a gentleman or at least he tried, but he couldn't help stealing a peek at Belle's tight red satin blouse whose open V-neck revealed a deep plunging cleavage.

"About time those pups got here. We've been showing ourselves long enough," Gator Al said, strong horse teeth chomping down on a foul-smelling cigar butt.

"All their crowd isn't here yet, or at least they weren't a few minutes ago," George St. George said. "They're most likely still being rounded up out of the whiskey bars, gambling hells, and brothels of River Street."

"What about our people? Are they in place?" Wake Spindrift asked.

"Not yet," George had to admit.

"Bill Longley won't let us down," Johnny said.

"But he's just one man of a dozen," Spindrift said.

"Crawdad Kate is driving the wagon, and she'll get through," Belle said.

"You women always stick together, don't you?" Gator Al laughed.

"We have to—there's no depending on you men," Belle retorted.

Gator Al laughed louder.

"We all have to depend on each other or Cullen Baker ain't the only one liable to hang," Johnny said.

A young-old man, slight with thinning hair, eased his way through the press of the crowd toward their table.

"Here comes Slip Rooney, one of Sharkey's people . . . Wonder what he wants?" Spindrift said.

Slip Rooney set an unopened bottle of whiskey and two tumblers down on the table . . . "Compliments of the management," he said. "Sharkey liked the way you handled Bigger."

"Much obliged. Tell Mr. Sharkey we said thanks," Johnny Cross said.

"Why don't you tell him yourself, Mr. Cross?"

"You know who I am?" Johnny was a bit surprised.

"Sharkey does." Slip Rooney grinned. "That's him over at the end of the bar." He indicated a feisty-looking bantamweight with a jet-black pompadour and blue eyes.

Johnny caught Sharkey's eye from across the room and mouthed the word, "Thanks."

Sharkey nodded, giving Johnny a jaunty two-finger salute.

"Sharkey would appreciate a word with you—at your convenience, Mr. Cross," Slip Rooney said.

"Tell him I'll be over there in a minute, soon as I wet my whistle with some of this whiskey he sent us," Johnny said.

"I'll do that," Slip Rooney said, withdrawing and making his way to Sharkey to give him the word.

Johnny uncorked the bottle, filling a tumbler first for George St. George and then one for himself. "Red whiskey," he said. He raised the tumbler. "Mud in your eye."

He tossed back his drink and George St. George did the same.

"Damned good, too," Johnny said, smacking his lips. He refilled the tumblers and threw back a second drink.

"Ahh," he said, pushing back his chair and rising. "Reckon I'll have that talk with Sharkey now."

"This could be good," George said, "or nothing at all. You never know which way Sharkey's going to jump."

"Help yourself to some of that red whiskey, y'all," Johnny told the other three at the table.

"We already had a pretty good start on you," Wake Spindrift said, declining with a wave of his hand.

"Speak for yourself, son—I don't mind if I do," Gator Al said, reaching eagerly for the bottle.

"Ladies first," Belle said, snatching it up first. She raised the bottle to her ripe red mouth, taking a long pull of the contents.

"Who said you're a lady?" Gator Al groused.

Belle set the bottle down, red lips glistening. "I'm sure you wouldn't call me anything but a lady," she said, casting a cold hard look from her lone eye at Gator Al.

Gator Al hefted the bottle, dubiously examining its fluid level. "A lady would have left more for me."

Johnny went to Sharkey.

"Come this way, where we can talk a bit," Sharkey said, raising his voice to be heard over the saloon clamor, and motioning to Johnny to follow.

Johnny trailed Sharkey along the length of the long bar toward the rear of the building. Coming out around the bar's far end they entered a short passage and went into a dimly lit storeroom reeking of alcohol fumes. The noise level was significantly lower.

"A pleasure to make your acquaintance, Mr. Cross," Sharkey said, thrusting out a hand.

Johnny shook it. "The same applies, Mr. Sharkey."

"It's just plain Sharkey, lad."

"Call me Johnny."

"That was nice work, the way you took down Bigger. But it won't be so easy taking down Crabshaw and Marston and the Gun Dogs. Not to be nosy, but would you mind telling me your plans on that score?

"I'm just asking on behalf of my establishment here. I'm not too keen on seeing it turned into a battlefield, y' understand. I lose enough customers through the usual shootings, stabbings, and brawls without hosting a private war that's none of my affair. I'm saying this in all friendly respect, mind. No hard feelings but you must see my concern."

"I surely do, and I'd like to set your mind at ease. My friends and I mean to kill the Gun Dogs but we'll do it outside. We've no intention of turning the premises into a shooting gallery."

"Well that's grand, Johnny. I like how you handle yourself, and I'll tell the world that George St. George is as fine a boyo as you'll find on the river. But an innkeeper can't afford to take sides, not in a private grudge fight. Even though it's my belief that Crabshaw and Marston are a pair of low-down stinking polecats who ought to be blown sky-high along with all their bullyboys and good riddance to them!

"That's my own personal belief, mind, and I can't let it affect my business."

"Like you said, Sharkey, no hard feelings."

"I'm glad you're taking this so well, Johnny. And since we've reached a basis of mutual understanding, I'm sure you won't take it amiss if I inquire when you and your friends might be moving along? I don't want to be inhospitable, but the Gun Dogs are liable to become mighty antsy and I wouldn't want them coming in the saloon looking for you."

"Say no more, we'll drink up and be gone."

"You're a gentleman, Johnny, and I don't mind saying so. It's rare to find someone who sees the other fellow's point of view."

"We didn't come to get your place shot up, Sharkey. Just let us get set and we'll clear out."

"Take as much time as you need, son," Sharkey said

magnanimously. "But not too much time," he added quickly.

Johnny readied himself to go. "I'm on my way, I'll tell the others what's going down," he said. "One more thing, though—"

"Yes? and what might that be, lad?" Sharkey asked.

"You said this is a private fight. But is it?"

"How do you mean?"

"Barbaroux already ate up all of Clinchfield, you know that. And from what I've seen the Combine is starting to crowd Halftown pretty hard. How long before he comes for you?"

"There's wisdom in your words, Johnny boy, and don't think I haven't given the matter some hard thought on more than one sleepless night. I've got no use for Barbaroux and his highfalutin ways, carrying on like he's the King of England."

From the venom with which Sharkey said this last, it seemed there was no lower, more insidious comparison in his way of thinking.

"And Lord knows," Sharkey continued. "I don't hold with the likes of his pet, Malvina the Conjure Woman, with her poisonings and heathenish deviltries; it's a stench in the nostrils of the righteous. You've put your finger on the problem and no mistake, Johnny. What to do about Barbaroux? I've thought and I've thought about it for some time now."

"What did you decide?"

"I decided that I don't know what to do," Sharkey said sadly.

"Well, if you should want to get in on some action, send word to George in the Hollow. But don't wait too long," Johnny cautioned, "things are going to start breaking fast. Real fast."

Johnny went out of the passage with Sharkey following. When they entered the main room, Slip Rooney hurried over to Sharkey to whisper something in his ear.

"Wait a minute, Johnny, this concerns you," Sharkey said, "you and your friends. Seems the Gun Dogs have a couple of men out back on the pier."

"That's good to know. Thanks, Sharkey."

"I'm sticking my neck out a wee bit here, but I can't abide those scoundrels sneaking around the place like weasels nosing into a hen coop. There's a side door out of here if you've a mind to use it. You just might surprise a few of them boyos."

"Believe I'll take you up on that offer. Let me get George first," Johnny said.

"I'll be waiting," said Sharkey.

Johnny went across the room to his table, moving easy and confident, betraying no great haste. He didn't want to draw attention to himself if the enemy had spies in the saloon, as they well might.

The foursome at the table looked up at him expectantly.

"The Gun Dogs are starting to crowd the play. They've got a couple men prowling the back of the pier. We don't want any guns at our backs when we make our play. We need to take back the initiative," Johnny said, smiling, his manner relaxed as though he was just passing the time with some friends.

"George and I will take care of the back shooters— quietly if possible but definitely with dispatch," he went on. "Then we'll go on shore and get behind the

Gun Dogs. We'll send Roe Brand to tell you when we're in position. Come on out and we'll get the ball rolling."

"Sounds like a plan," Gator Al said.

"It's a go," said Wake Spindrift.

"That gives us time for another drink," Belle Nyad said.

Johnny Cross and George St. George took their leave of the others and went to Sharkey waiting at the far end of the bar.

"Slip will unlock the door and let you out—once you're outside he'll lock it and it won't be opened again," Sharkey said. "That's as much as I can do . . . I'd like to do more but I can't. I'm in no position to go against Barbaroux openly."

"Thanks for all you have done," Johnny said.

"I won't shake hands or make any sign you're going—too many spying eyes around."

Johnny nodded. "See you."

"Good luck, men," Sharkey said.

"And good hunting," he added.

Slip Rooney went into the passageway, Johnny and George St. George trailing. At midpoint a short jog opened on the right-hand side, more of an alcove than anything else. At the far end of it stood a barred door.

Slip Rooney lifted the bar and opened the bolt. He eased the door open . . . it opened outward. He stuck his head outside and looked around. He stuck his head back inside, nodding.

George St. George stepped outside first.

Johnny pressed a coin into Slip Rooney's hand. "A bottle for my friends at the table."

"You've given me too much," the other said.

"Keep the change," Johnny said, "and tell Sharkey thanks."

Johnny went out, easing the door closed behind him. There was the sound of a bolt thudding into place and the bar being reapplied to the door.

The door opened on the upstream side of the pier. The light was low, the yellow crescent moon shedding more of a glow than the weak light filtering through the saloon's small square oil-papered windows. Mists rose off the river.

The two stood with their backs to the wall for a moment, getting used to the night's dimness and gloom.

Johnny looked left, looked right, looked left again. "Pier's clear on this side," he said low voiced, "but there's supposed to be a couple of Gun Dogs nearby."

"I'm ready for them," George St. George said, patting his sheathed belt knife.

"Let's get set for a getaway before we make our move," suggested Johnny.

"I'm with you there," George agreed.

Torchlight flickered at the landward side of the pier, much of it blocked by the saloon's bulk, keeping this side of the pier in heavy shadows, which hid the duo from the Gun Dogs gathered on land.

The upstream side was where Roe Brand was waiting in the pirogue. Johnny couldn't see him at first.

George St. George vented a trilling chirp, the uncanny imitation of a night bird's call.

From somewhere near shore came the return reply of a bullfrog's croaking. Its source was no bullfrog but rather Roe Brand, whose pirogue was hidden under some brush overhanging the shoreline.

The boat pushed out into the river, gliding into view in near-silence, making for the pier's edge.

"That birdcall was pretty good," Johnny said admiringly.

"One of the things you pick up in the swamp," George said offhandedly.

Roe Brand backwatered with the paddle, halting the pirogue below where the other two stood at the pier's edge.

"Throw me a line, Roe," George rasped in a stage whisper.

Roe Brand set the paddle safely inboard and picked up a length of coiled rope that lay in the bottom of the boat and had been brought along for this purpose. It had thick knots at each end for weighty casts.

Holding on to one end of the line, he pitched the rope underhanded, upward and out. The end hit the edge of the pier and fell back into the water. Roe Brand gathered up the line and tried again.

George snagged the line, taking in some of the slack.

Johnny stiffened.

"I'll rig this end of the line— What's up, Johnny?"

"Thought I heard something."

"I didn't hear anything . . ."

"I'll take a looksee while you tie the rope."

Johnny light-footed it along the wall to the building's rear near the end of the pier, the place where the sounds seemed to have come from. He paused at the rearward edge of the saloon's wall just in time to hear deck planks creak under the weight of footsteps. He peeked around the corner.

A man was on the apron of the pier. He stood smoking at the downstream side, his back to Johnny.

The dark figure's head was tilted forward, looking down at the floating raft and river traffic. He puffed away at a hand-rolled cigarette, a dome halo of orange light pulsing around his head with each puff.

Gun Dog or not? Johnny couldn't tell. He hung fire, not ready to commit to action. He didn't want to do in some poor soul who came out here for a smoke.

The smoker reached the end of his cigarette, flicking the still-lit butt out into space. Its orange speck of ember arced out and down, going dark when it hit the water.

The stranger turned and began walking landward along the downstream side, vanishing behind the building.

Johnny went back the way he came. George St. George had finished throwing a loop over the top of a piling, securing the line. It descended straight down to the water where Roe Brand sat in the pirogue, holding the opposite end of the rope.

"Well?" George demanded.

"It was a fellow taking a smoke, but damned if I could tell if he was a Gun Dog or not," Johnny said. "This is a trickier proposition than I thought. How do you tell a Gun Dog from an innocent person?"

"I know most of those sons by sight," George St. George said thoughtfully.

"Kind of dark out here though. Reckon we'll have to make the rounds of the pier. Whoever tries to throw down on us is a Gun Dog."

"That could get kind of noisy—"

"*Hey!* . . . *What're you two doing?*"

The harshly barked query came from a thickset looming figure that hurried toward them from landward on their side of the pier.

"Now that sounds like a Gun Dog," George said dryly.

"I believe you're right," Johnny agreed.

"Sounds like a Yankee, too."

"Don't he?"

The newcomer was not the smoker Johnny had seen but a different fellow, a big man wearing a derby hat that would not have looked out of place in Manhattan's notorious Five Points where the gangs of New York thronged and battled but which seemed out of place on the Halftown waterfront.

The figure resolved into a big blocky bruiser with a paintbrush mustache and a fat lit cigar stuck in a side of his mouth. "What're you doing back here?" he growled.

"My pard's getting sick over the side here, can't hold his liquor," George St. George said easily.

Johnny took hold of a piling top and held on with both hands, standing in a bent-legged crouch with his head hanging down over the water.

"You don't belong here!" the derby wearer accused.

"What do you want him to do, get sick inside? That ain't sanitary, mister," George said reasonably.

"Come out of there into the light so I can get a better look at the two of yez," Derby Hat said.

"What light? It's dark out here," George pointed out.

"What's it to you? Making noises like a lawman!" Johnny said, slurring his words. "Folks come to Halftown to get away from that kind of thing!"

"I'm Wyler Hemphill for what it's worth and when I say jump, you jump!"

"You a Gun Dog?" George said silkily, moving toward Hemphill.

Hemphill grabbed for his gun. His mistake was not having it drawn and cocked before bracing Johnny and George.

George already had his knife in hand as he lunged for the burly tough and ripped him up the middle.

The shock paralyzed Wyler Hemphill, freezing him in place. The lit cigar dropped from his gaping mouth, falling to the planks of the pier.

They two were so close that George could feel Hemphill's foul-smelling breath on his face. Wyler Hemphill was dead on his feet.

Johnny helped ease the corpse to the planks.

"That was nice work, George," he said.

George wrenched his knife free of the corpse. The blood was inky black in the moonlight.

"A Yankee Gun Dog! How low can Crabshaw and Marston go?" he wondered aloud.

"Psst!" Roe Brand hissed from below. "Y'all all right up there?"

"Yes, yes," Johnny said.

A cloud covered the moon, veiling the scene with still more rolling darkness.

Footsteps approached, coming from the riverward side of the pier.

Johnny and George stood with their backs to the wall, flattening themselves as much as possible. There was nothing they could do about the body of Wyler Hemphill. In the absence of moonlight it looked like a pile of rubbish strewn on the boards.

Not far from the truth at that, Johnny thought.

A figure appeared, moving landward along the up-stream side of the pier, a blacker man-shape emerging from blackness. It called:

"Wyler? That you? It's me, Custis . . . You back here? Yo, Wyler!"

The topmost pointed tip of the crescent moon began slicing through the clouds, loosing thin sheets of pale moonlight.

Something in Custis's outline looked familiar to Johnny. Custis was the cigarette smoker he'd seen earlier.

"Wyler? . . . Damn! So dark here I can't see a danged thing!—slippery, too," Custis said, talking to himself, unaware he was treading in Wyler Hemphill's blood.

He stumbled over the dead body, narrowly avoiding a fall. "What in the Sam Hill—!"

The sickle moon tore free of the clouds, releasing a flood of moonlight that revealed the savaged corpse sprawled at Custis's feet.

"Oh, Lordy!—*urk!*"

Johnny was behind Custis with a length of rope in his hands, part of the slack of the line tied to the piling. He hooked it over Custis's head and neck, using it as a strangling cord to garrote him.

Johnny leaned back hauling on the rope, bending Custis backward, lifting him so that his kicking feet were in the air.

A quick knife thrust by George slipped under the rib cage stabbing Custis in the heart, killing him in-stantly and ending his misery. The body joined Hemp-hill's on the planks.

"Is that the last of them on the pier?" George asked.

"One way to find out—we got to make the circuit,"

Johnny said. "I'll do it. You stay here and make sure nobody finds the bodies. Or better still, let's drop them in the water."

"Not yet. That'll drive the gators wild."

Wyler Hemphill's derby hat had rolled clear of the corpse and lay several feet away.

"How d'you think I'd look in one of those citified hats?" George St. George asked.

"Like a danged fool," Johnny replied.

"That's what I thought . . ."

Johnny started landward, accidentally kicking the derby off the pier into the water. "Oops."

He moved alongside the wall to the front of the saloon. Standing in the shadows, looking around the corner, he surveyed the scene.

Things were much the same as before on the pier fronting the Dead Drunk: amorous couples, groups of men, drunks. The people were different but the types were the same. Johnny detected in none of them the taut readiness of professional gunmen on the job.

Bully Bigger was nowhere to be seen . . . he had either gone off under his own power or been taken away. Or maybe he fell off the pier into the water. Johnny didn't give a damn as long as he was gone.

At the landward end of the pier the Gun Dogs were massed facing the saloon. Their reinforcements had not yet arrived. If they glimpsed Johnny Cross glide through the idlers lounging outdoors, it meant nothing to them. They didn't know him from Adam.

Johnny followed the downstream side of the pier riverward, encountering no one else, no hostiles, friendlies, or neutrals. He had this side of the pier to himself. Rounding the rear of the building, he rejoined George St. George.

The two of them dragged the bodies one by one away from where they'd been killed and out to the back of the saloon before dropping them over the side. They didn't want them becoming gator bait too close from where they would use the rope to lower themselves to the pirogue.

Two successive splashes raised waterspouts. After a pause the river surface below began to heave and stir with restless unease as gators thrashed out from under the pier, drawn by the scent of fresh blood and meat.

Johnny and George climbed down the rope into the pirogue, which bobbed on the waves churned up by the gator onslaught farther riverward.

Wyler Hemphill's derby was perched jauntily atop Roe Brand's head.

"How do you like my new hat?" he asked proudly. "Found it floating in the water, one of them newfangled big city jobs . . . sharp, huh?"

"You look like a danged fool," George said sourly.

"You're just jealous 'cause you didn't find it first," Roe Brand sassed him back. He piloted the pirogue to the shore, where Johnny and George St. George set foot on land.

A burlap croker sack was secured to one of the boat's thwarts, suspended by it to keep it clear of water sloshing in the bottom of the hull. Roe Brand untied it, handing it to Johnny. It had heavy, metallic rattlings sounding from its contents.

Johnny set the bag down on dry ground and reached inside. It was full of loaded revolvers. He was already wearing twin Colt .45s holstered to his hips. He now stuck two more guns in the top of his pants, one on the left, the other on the right. A third gun was jammed into his waistband at the small of his back.

Standard practice for a veteran pistol-fighter. Reloading takes time, which could spell the difference between life and death when the action is hot.

George St. George helped himself to a couple of extras, sticking them in his belt and covering their butts with his shirt.

"Loaded for bear," Johnny Cross said, smiling thinly. "Let's go."

# TWENTY-FOUR

Johnny Cross and George St. George lurked in the shadows of a line of trees on a low knoll on the embankment a stone's throw west of the Dead Drunk's pier.

They surveyed the scene. The Gun Dogs now numbered not their original nine but rather seven men.

"Reckon they miss Custis and Hemphill yet?" Johnny wondered.

"If they don't, they surely will when the shooting starts," George said. He looked east along River Street, a ribbon picked out by moonlight. "No sign of our folks yet," he said, frowning.

"Nor of the rest of the Gun Dogs," Johnny pointed out. "I like our odds."

"Just as long as our friends come out of the saloon before enemy reinforcements show."

"Roe Brand should be at the float by now."

"Even if he is, we couldn't see him from here."

"We'll see him once he's on the pier," Johnny said.

"Can't miss him in that damn-fool hat of his," said George.

River Street lived by night, and even here at its

westernmost end there was a steady flow of traffic on horse and foot, made up of the players of the half-world of bars, dives, gambling hells, and sporting houses.

With the uncanny instinct that folks have for smelling out a fight, a fair-sized crowd was building along the riverbank at the eastern sidelines of the pier, close enough to see the coming action but far enough away from the Gun Dogs to be out of the line of fire, hopefully.

"Battle always pulls them in," George observed.

"Hell, I'm that way myself—I'd go a far piece just to watch two dogs fight," Johnny said.

"Me, too."

"Folks always like to watch a fight . . . as long as they're safely out of it."

Johnny caught sight of two figures at the edge of the crowd who struck a note of familiarity—and more. "See those two duded-up *hombres* standing off to one side, George?"

"The ones surrounded by a passel of fancy gals? Can't miss them."

"I know them."

"You do?"

"One I know personally, the other I know by sight. The one I know by sight is a dangerous man: the one with the preacher's hat on."

"That parson-looking fellow? Dangerous?" George St. George snickered. "What's he gonna do, bore you to death with a sermon?"

"That's Sexton Clarke," Johnny said flatly.

"Huh!" George's smile fell. "You sure?"

"I saw him fight a duel a few years back in Fayetteville. Killed two men with two shots. He's lightning fast."

"So that's Clarke! I heard of him, sure. Barbaroux

sent for him to handle your pal Cullen Baker, but the Combine was lucky enough to take Cullen alive before Clarke reached town. I heard he was living on the Big White Boat . . .

"This change anything, Johnny?"

"It might," Johnny said thoughtfully. "Sexton Clarke's an odd duck. He has whims, fancies. Holds a mighty high opinion of himself, thinks he's the best—the fastest on the draw."

"What do you think?"

"He's good—damned good—a quick gun. But that don't mean somebody else can't do better. I'll say this for him, he's no back shooter. When Clarke comes at you, he comes straight on and he makes sure you know he's coming.

"I misdoubt me that he'd mix into a brawl to help out the Gun Dogs, thinks he's too good for that. Like I said, he ranks himself almighty high. But you never know," said George.

"If he does get in, leave him to me."

"Be my guest, Johnny. You're our specialist in triggernometry," George St. George said. "What about the other fellow, the one with Clarke?"

"That's Valentine. No, really, that's his name," Johnny said. "He's harmless. Well, not exactly, but he'd draw only to save his own life. He's an artist fellow, paints pictures. Pretty good, too."

"He makes a living doing that?!" George asked, incredulous.

"Sometimes. He's also a card shark, thief, and confidence trickster. Lives off women's earnings, too, when he can get it. A decent enough fellow."

"Friend of yours?"

"We had some laughs together. I wouldn't trust him any farther than I could throw him. One thing's sure, though: Whatever jumps, Valentine will keep out of it."

"He's a handsome son, I'll give him that. Look at them fancy gals hanging all over him."

"Val's a ladies' man, sure enough."

Roe Brand appeared on the pier.

"There's Roe," George St. George said.

Roe Brand flitted across the front of the building and went inside.

"The storm'll break when our friends come outside," Johnny said. "Best we get set for the kill."

"Yes," said George.

Johnny and George came off the knoll, keeping to the shadows out of the circle of flickering light created by the torches Sharkey had posted at the hitching posts where his patrons tied up their horses.

The two guards on site stood off to one side from the Gun Dogs, pointedly not interfering with them, making a show of neutrality.

Should the Gun Dogs move directly against the Dead Drunk, the guards' reaction would be decidedly different. But for now they were sticking to Sharkey's hands-off policy where private fights were concerned.

Johnny and George came off the knoll behind the long row of hitched horses. They were at the east end of the row, a few paces from the foot of the long pier. George St. George stood on Johnny's left to screen him as much as possible from Sexton Clarke and Valentine.

The two from the Big White Boat, like the rest of the gathered onlookers, were focused on the Gun Dogs and the saloon on the pier.

"Sexton Clarke being here changes things, George," Johnny said. "We can't count on him staying out. I think he will but let's not risk both our skins having him at our backs when the shooting starts. Clarke was no back shooter when I saw him last, but folks change."

"So?" George asked.

"I'll go ahead like we planned and brace the Dogs. You hang back and keep an eye on Clarke. If he reaches, kill him."

"That's a hell of a plan! The two of us going up against them is how it's supposed to be, how it should be—"

"Like I said, Clarke changes everything. I'd rather go up against all the Dogs alone than have Clarke at my back with a gun. Anyhow I won't be alone. Our three from inside plus Roe and me makes five against seven."

"As long as the rest of the Dogs don't show too soon. I don't like it, Johnny—"

"You said I was the expert so trust my judgment. This is how it has to be. I've got one advantage going in: I know about Clarke but he doesn't know me, not by sight."

"Valentine does, you said."

"If Val puts me on the spot, I'll know I have you covering my back, George."

"All right, I'll do it, but—hell!"

"Don't try to beat Clarke's draw—you won't. Have your gun out and ready and if he shows fight, kill him. No warning, shoot him in the back if you have to."

"That sticks in my craw."

"Hell, George, you was in the war, right?"

"You know I was!"

"You still are. It don't matter which way the enemy is facing when the shooting starts, you drop him. We ain't playing here, this is for high stakes. Don't get squeamish on me," Johnny said.

The stubborn look left George's face, the set of his jaw relaxing. He sighed.

"You're right, of course. It's a go. I'll cover Clarke and your artist friend. In case he turns out to be not such a friend after all."

"Good man," Johnny said, clapping the other on the shoulder. "By the way . . . how attached are you to your cousin?"

"Not so's you'd notice, not at all. Blue's throwing in with the Dogs, he takes his chances same as everybody else," George said. "Don't think twice if it comes to burning him down . . . it's nothing to me."

"Good to know."

"Something else you should know, Johnny. That snotty-looking son standing next to Crabshaw is Viper Teed, the gang's fastest gun. Take him first."

"I will."

Motion at the saloon front caught Johnny's eye. "Here we go," he said.

Gator Al Hutchins, Belle Nyad, and Wake Spindrift came out of the saloon, their attitude one of seeming naturalness.

The Gun Dogs stiffened at sight of them, hands hovering over gun butts. They started to spread out, forming up in a rough semicircular arc facing the newcomers.

The crowd stirred, instinctively moving herdlike farther off to the side to get out of the line of fire.

Seemingly uncaring as to what was happening at

the landward end of the pier, Gator Al drank from a bottle held up-tilted to his guzzling mouth by a hand that was not his gunhand.

He, Belle, and Spindrift started forward, walking three abreast.

Gator Al was a giant standing a head taller than Belle and a head and a half taller than Spindrift, and that was without the extra height added by his rakish top hat. A sidearm was worn holstered on one hip and a tomahawk hung down on his other side by a rawhide loop connecting pommel to belt.

Belle Nyad's trim middle was cinched by a thin, wide black leather belt. A Blacksnake bullwhip hung coiled by a clasp on the cincher hanging down along the curve of her hip. She never went about without it. She was expert with the bullwhip, having been schooled in its use by the acknowledged master Skinner Kondo, once overseer on her family's now-lost plantation and before that a leading regional slave-driver.

A machete-sized saber hung from the cincher on Belle's opposite hip.

Tucked into the top of the cincher was an unusual double-barreled over-under pistol featuring a wide-mouthed snub-nosed barrel on top and a regulation-sized pistol barrel below. The top barrel was loaded with a shotgun shell, the lower barrel was sized for the six cap-and-ball rounds loaded in the cylinder. The piece had two triggers, one for the shotgun attachment and the other for the six-gun.

Wake Spindrift wore a pair of .44s in twin shoulder holsters somewhat concealed by a baggy tropical-weight linen jacket. The guns were fitted butt out. A short-barreled pistol lay in a jacket pocket and a six-gun in a hip pocket of his baggy pants.

The trio came on, advancing along the pier at a deliberate pace.

Behind them, Roe Brand eased out of the saloon's entrance, fading off to the downstream side of the pier and taking up a post there. His job was twofold: to back up the trio but more importantly to guard against any other back shooters who might emerge from the saloon or pier.

Gun Dog ramrod Pigfeet Crabshaw, huge and gross, showed a head shaped like a smoked ham. The grizzled hairs of his short salt-and-pepper beard stuck out like bristles on a boar's hide. He hitched up his gunbelt.

Tully "Miracle" Marston, lesser of the two copartners, had longish auburn hair and a same-colored handlebar mustache with the tips upturned. He was something of a dandy with a bottle-green swallow-tail coat with a black spiderweb pattern, white shirt with ruffled front, loud plaid pants, and custom-made cordovan boots.

He held a high-crowned hat in front of him, one hand inside the high top, the other holding the brim. "I don't see Custis and Hemphill," he fretted.

"If you could see 'em somebody else could, too, and that's not what we want," Crabshaw reminded the other. "They're there . . . they'll show when the shooting starts."

"I'd feel better if they showed before the shooting," Marston said.

Crabshaw cursed disgustedly under his breath, Marston choosing to ignore it.

Viper Teed laughed. He was the outfit's top gun, a gangly youth with a permanent sneer curling his upper lip.

Marston glared at him. Viper smirked back. Marston looked away first. Viper laughed again.

"Spindrift's the fastest," Crabshaw said out of the side of his mouth. "Take him, Vipe—when I give the go and not before."

"That shoulder harness of his is too slow, I'll drill him before his guns clear leather," Viper Jones said, thumbing the rawhide safety loops clear of the hammers of his low-slung holstered guns, palms resting on their butts.

"That goes for the rest of you, no shooting till I say so," Crabshaw said.

Murmurs of assent and nodding heads signaled the Dogs' obedience to their master's voice.

A Dog to one side of Viper unconsciously squared his shoulders in anticipation of the coming clash. Another widened a bent-knees stance, hand hovering over his gun.

The Gun Dogs numbered not seven but eight, their number having been augmented by Blue Fane, George St. George's cousin.

"I still say we should wait for the others," Marston said apprehensively.

"They must have got held up . . . they'll be here directly," said Crabshaw. "And even if they don't, so what? We here can take 'em. Hell, Vipe alone could probably take all three."

"I surely would enjoy that." Viper Teed smirked.

"I don't like it," Marston insisted.

"Here they be, coming at us. What're we supposed

to do, step aside and let 'em go by because the rest of the bunch ain't here?" Crabshaw said.

"Well, no—"

"You want to tell Barbaroux they got away because you didn't like odds of three-to-one? That'd really put us in solid with the Commander."

"You made your point, Pigfeet," Marston said coldly.

"We muff this and there's nothing for us but to clear off the river fast! Barbaroux ain't one to forgive failure or have you forgot?" Crabshaw pressed.

"I said you made your point!"

"Good."

The trio of Gator Al, Belle, and Spindrift reached the midpoint of the pier between them and the Gun Dogs and halted. Gripping the empty bottle by the neck, Gator Al pegged it at the Gun Dogs.

It landed at their feet, shattering into pieces. A Dog nicked on the shin by a glass shard cursed.

"Call that friendly? I don't," Crabshaw called out, taunting.

"That's 'cause we ain't friends," Gator Al said.

"No . . . we ain't."

Marston's anxious expression was offset by the lewd gleam in his eyes as he looked Belle Nyad up and down. "Evening, Miss Belle, you're looking fine to-night. Glad to see you recovered from that little dunking in the river we gave you when we sank your boat," he said.

"You'll be joining it soon at the bottom of the river," she said evenly.

"Those swivel-mounted guns we had sure 'nuff made all the difference. Too bad you didn't have any or things might have come out different."

"After tonight I'll take yours."

Pigfeet Crabshaw spat. "You got a mean mouth, Belle. You're carrying a gun. Don't expect special treatment because you're a woman, not when you go around insulting folks."

"Why don't you shut up?" Wake Spindrift asked quietly, a gentle smile on his face.

"Make me," Crabshaw said.

Johnny Cross started forward, walking easy, hands down by his sides, near his gun. He left St. George standing off by himself, alone in the shadows on the west side of the pier entry, with Sexton Clarke and Dean Valentine on the east side.

George was opposite Clarke and slightly behind him. His gun was in hand and held along his side pointing down, screened by his body from Clarke in case of the unlikely event of Clarke's taking a chance glance in his direction.

Or maybe not so unlikely. These ace gunfighters sometimes seemed to have a kind of sixth sense or animal instinct for menace in their vicinity.

Johnny walked on, drawing abreast of Sexton Clarke and Valentine standing at the edge of the crowd. They were watching the faceoff on the pier and Johnny passed them without any eye contact. An electric thrill tingled along his spine at having Clarke at his back.

He went to the foot of the pier and kept on riverward along its center, pulled by an inexorable trajectory toward the Gun Dogs.

Through spaces in the Dogs' line, Gator Al, Belle, and Spindrift saw Johnny coming on.

"You're in our way, Crabshaw," Gator Al said.

"Funny, we was thinking the same about you," said Crabshaw, venting a low, mean, dirty laugh.

"Now—stand aside!" Gator Al demanded.

"Or else what?" Crabshaw returned.

The confrontation was at the trigger point. That's when Johnny Cross came to a halt about a dozen feet away from the Gun Dog arc and said, "Hey!"

A couple of the Dogs were so keyed up over the coming fight that they jumped at the unexpected intrusion. Others stiffened, not liking a stranger at their backs during a showdown.

The crowd buzzed at sight of the intruder.

"Who's that?"

"Don't know him—you, Slim?"

"Never seed him before."

"Why, he's just a kid!"

"So's the Viper."

"He can't be bucking the Dogs . . . can he?"

"There's easier ways of committing suicide!"

"I'd like to know him better—he's handsome," sighed Risha, a comely young sporting gal fresh on the street.

"Shut your mouth, slut!" snarled Chazz, her thick-featured escort.

"Who're you to be callin' me names?" Risha demanded, turning on him. "We ain't married . . . Thank the Lord!" she added in a too-audible aside.

A couple of nearby bystanders laughed.

Chazz raised a hand, saying, "Keep running your mouth and you're gonna get a beating, Risha— *Wha'!*"

He recoiled from the thin sharp-pointed stiletto Risha had pulled from somewhere on her person and now held pointed at his belly. She looked like she knew how to use it and was ready to do so.

"You want some of this, try layin' hands on me, Chazz," Risha challenged.

Chazz threw his arms up into the air but not before backing several paces away from Risha, out of lunging reach of that too-sharp-pointed knife of hers.

"I'm through with you, gal . . . we're quits!"

"Ya' think?" Risha spat with a short bitter laugh.

Chazz scuttled away in red-faced confusion, saying over his shoulder, "Find yourself another honey man!"

Derisive laughter pursued him, not only Risha's, but from others who witnessed the back and forth.

When she was sure Chazz was gone and not coming back, Risha made the stiletto disappear by reaching into a side-slit in her dress and returning the dagger to its sheath clipped to a lacy round garter band holding one of her stockings up.

"Not much honey in that fellow," Risha said, "and less man!"

A gaggle of other River Street sporting ladies who had gathered to watch the fight now grouped around her.

"You're better off without him, Risha, you can do better," said Marie, a fellow working girl and sympathetic friend.

"Don't I know it! He talked big about getting me on the Big White Boat, but he couldn't even get himself on."

A third lady in the group looked around cautiously before saying, low voiced, "From some of the stories I've heard, girl, you're better off never setting foot on that boat—and that goes for all of us!"

The Unknown—for so Johnny Cross was to Gun

Dogs and onlookers alike—had created quite a stir by horning into the middle of a showdown. Or perhaps not entirely unknown, for a gleam of recognition showed in Valentine's keen artist's eyes, which he quickly hooded.

Sexton Clarke seemed too interested in the newcomer's dramatic entrance to have taken note of his companion's fast-stifled reaction. An amusing development, if the youngster showed fight!

The Gun Dogs were in a tricky situation. They didn't want to take their eyes off the trio they'd come to get, but they had to see who was at their backs. When they saw the intruder was one lone man, little more than a fresh-faced kid from the looks of him, their spirits instantly revived.

They wouldn't have felt so well had they known George St. George was behind their backs, but he was well out of sight keeping to the shadows and keeping watch on Sexton Clarke.

Crabshaw stood angled so he was at a tangent to both Johnny and the trio. He stood with thumbs hooked into the top of his gunbelt, trying for a posture of dominance.

He stared Johnny slowly up and down, then hawked up a glob of phlegm and spat it on the planks at Johnny's feet. He would have spat on Johnny's boots if he could have reached that far.

"This ain't none of your business, sonny," he said, making a contemptuous shooing gesture. "Now run along and roll your hoop somewhere else before you get hurt."

That won some laughter from his men and some in the crowd.

"I'll roll *you*," Johnny shot back, pulling some oohs

and aahs from the onlookers—a reaction that was not a happiness for Crabshaw, Marston, or the Dogs.

Viper Teed, prickly and with a short fuse to start with, started to burn, his face flushing. He held his peace because he held Gator Al, Belle, and Spindrift—especially Spindrift—as the threat and the newcomer as a suicidal clown.

Marston stuck his horn in. The trio worried him but not this loco kid. "I don't know if you're drunk or what, Junior, but if you're putting on a show to impress that swamp cat"—here he indicated Belle Nyad—"you're fixing to get yourself kilt over nothing, because she plain flat-out don't like men! Got no use for them, haw haw haw!"

"You're a fine one to talk about manhood, Miracle Marston," Belle returned. "As for that tub-of-guts partner of yours, I doubt if Pigfeet could even find his under all them belly rolls!"

The crowd was more shocked than amused by this effrontery. An intoxicated woman hooted shrill laughter until a quick-thinking companion clapped a hand over her mouth and dragged her deeper into the crowd and out of sight.

"That's killing talk, Belle," Marston said, face red and swollen.

"Let her have her fun," Crabshaw said, waving it off with a dismissive gesture. "It'll give us all something to remember her by."

He glared down at Johnny. "As for you, kid, since you're so set on getting your guts shot out, start something!"

"Let me have him, chief," Viper Teed begged, face

twitching, hands clenching and unclenching over his guns.

"You the one they call Viper?" Johnny asked, knowing the answer, raking the other with a coolly hostile gaze.

"He's mine, Crabshaw! He—"

"Hold your horses, Vipe. That's an order," Crabshaw said, holding up a meaty hand with palm showing.

Viper Teed restrained himself with difficulty, all but jumping out of his skin in his eagerness to kill.

"Now I get it! It all makes sense to me now why some young pup sticks his nose into our business," Crabshaw said, his manner smug and knowing. "He wants to be you, Vipe! The kid thinks he's fast and wants to build a reputation by burning you down!" Crabshaw ripped out a huge belly laugh.

"Very funny," Viper Teed said tightly. "Somebody's going to die laughing!"

"Ha ha," Johnny said.

Viper Teed almost drew then, held back only by the last of his fast-shredding discipline. Crabshaw or not, he would reach the breaking point in a span of heartbeats. Crabshaw knew the signs, knew he'd better slip the chain of his most dangerous Gun Dog and let him tear out the throat of this arrogant challenger.

"Take him, Vipe!" Crabshaw said.

Viper Teed went for his guns.

Something slammed him, sending a great confusion descending upon him. His guns were in his hands, clear of the holsters, leveled on the challenger, but strangely the Viper couldn't recall pulling a trigger.

Yet there had been gunfire, two shots coming so

quickly together that they seemed as one. Loud, too, like a thunderclap or a bomb going off.

The noise of it staggered Viper Teed. He was standing still, he thought, while the world around him reeled and swayed.

The stranger stood opposite him, upright, a gun in his left hand. It was pointed at Viper Teed, smoke curling from the muzzle.

The Viper, frowning, confused, opened his mouth to wonder aloud, *What in blazes is going on?*

A mass of red blood spilled from his open maw. Viper Teed looked down, saw a rapidly blossoming bloodstain on his left breast.

Viper Teed had never gotten off a shot, and the confusion that had fallen on him was the last of life rushing away from him. He was dead before he hit the pier planks.

Echoes from the double gunshots rang out in the stunned silence.

Then things started moving again:

"Crabshaw!" shouted Gator Al. He held the tomahawk in his hand poised for throwing. He called out Crabshaw's name because he wanted to turn him around to make a better target.

Crabshaw gave his head a toss as if literally shaking off the stupefaction that had seized him at seeing his top gun shot dead. Hauling his hogleg clear of the holster he turned toward Gator Al to burn him down.

He was the recipient of a hurled tomahawk in the face. There was a *thunk* as the tomahawk struck home square in the middle of Crabshaw's forehead.

Crabshaw's reflex trigger pull sent a bullet thudding into the planks underfoot. He lurched sideways as he went down, barreling into one of his men and causing him to blow a shot fired at Wake Spindrift.

Spindrift's arms were crossed over his chest as his hands plunged under his jacket to haul out the twin-holstered .44s he wore under each arm. Those hands came out shooting, pumping lead into the Dog who'd shot at him and missed, throwing him into a crazy Dance of Death.

Three Gun Dogs slapped leather, drawing on Johnny Cross.

Johnny had a gun in both hands now. He dropped into a crouch and cut loose on his three foes, squeezing off shots alternately from the gun in his left fist and his right.

Each shot told, hitting a man. The three Dogs wheeled like spinning tops as they whirled down into oblivion.

Tully Marston still held his hat in front of him with a hand inside its high crown. He held a gun inside. Seeing Gator Al drawing his gun, Marston opened fire, shooting through the top of his hat into the other's torso, emptying his gun into him.

Gator Al backpedaled and went down, gun in hand. His torso was shattered, red life leaking out of him from a line of bullet holes in his chest.

Raising himself up on an elbow, he brought his gun in line with Marston.

Marston frantically worked the trigger of his concealed gun, receiving only a series of metallic clicks for his pains. He'd already emptied the gun into Gator Al.

Gator Al grinned savagely as he thumbed back the hammer of his piece.

Gun and hat fell from Marston's hands as he saw

death coming for him. He threw his hands in front of his face and shrieked wordlessly.

Before Gator Al could fire, a slug took off the top of his head.

It had been fired by a Dog gunman on the left of the line facing the Dead Drunk.

He was shot by Roe Brand standing at the downstream side corner of the saloon front. The Dog hadn't even seen Roe there.

The Dog swayed with the impact of being hit. He jerked a few shots at Roe, missed. Roe fired, not missing. The Dog cried out, spinning off-balance, angling to one side. He hit the pier safety rail hard and broke through it, falling off the side into the water.

He was still alive when the gators got him.

Tully Marston couldn't believe he hadn't been hit. He giggled at the stroke of luck that had reprieved him from death at Gator Al's hands. A tremendous roaring blast swatted him like a fly.

He'd been blasted with buckshot from the shotgun attachment of Belle Nyad's over-under pistol. It well nigh cut him in half.

Wake Spindrift cut down a Dog shooting at him from the right-hand side of the pier. Spindrift advanced slowly, guns blazing in both hands.

The Dog's life dissolved in a mass of bullet holes, blood, and gunsmoke.

Spindrift stumbled, shot from behind. He staggered forward, trying to stay on his feet. A second shot brought him to his knees.

The shots had come from the Dead Drunk, from either a Gun Dog who'd been planted there earlier and escaped notice, or from a Barbaroux partisan and assassin.

The back shooter stood sideways in the doorway, hanging back so he was out of Roe Brand's line of fire. He shot again and Spindrift flopped facedown.

His gun swung toward Belle as she turned to fire, but she would never get her gun around in time.

Johnny caught the play and snapped a few well-placed shots into the man in the doorway. The back shooter crumpled, falling in a heap across the threshold.

Belle slammed a few rounds into his body to make sure of him.

The Gun Dogs had been all but cleared out. Only Blue Fane remained. His eyes seemed ready to pop from their sockets as he looked around for his comrades and saw only the dead and dying.

He'd had enough. He dropped his gun, cried, "I'm hit!" and threw himself flat on the boards, unmoving.

Belle Nyad saw him go down in the absence of gunfire. She crossed to Blue Fane, pointed her gun at his head.

"Quit playing possum. Look up or I'll put a bullet in you," she said.

Blue Fane put hands flat on the planks, raising his upper body, lifting his head and craning his neck. "Please—don't shoot—"

Belle put a bullet in his skull.

"*Now* you're hit," she said.

Johnny Cross looked at her.

"I like a clean slate," Belle said.

Johnny nodded. Hell, why not? Had things gone the other way Blue Fane would have done his share of the killing.

A haze of gunsmoke hung over the pier, the smell of gunpowder heavy in the air, momentarily overpowering the somewhat rank river scent.

Gator Al was dead, Wake Spindrift badly wounded. But the Gun Dogs on the pier were all dead.

Johnny looked around. The crowd of onlookers had gone to cover when the shooting started. Neither Sexton Clarke nor Valentine was in sight.

Johnny pulled first one of the guns stuck in the top of his pants, then the other, fitting them into empty holsters. He wanted fully loaded pieces to hand in case something jumped. The guns he'd been using he stuck in his waistband. He hated to throw away good guns.

The Battle of the Pier was over, but the action was not yet done.

A commotion was developing on River Street.

A freight wagon appeared in the east, driving west. A long freight wagon pulled by a team of six horses yoked in tandem.

Crawdad Kate was at the reins. The wagon's hopper was covered with canvas tarpaulins, concealing its cargo. Kate drove at medium speed with no signs of undue haste, nothing to excite suspicion.

The wagon was being rapidly overtaken by a dozen hard-charging riders sweeping along the street at a breakneck pace. They were not chasing the wagon, they were in a mad rush to get to the pier.

They were the main body of the Gun Dogs, having finally been dragged half-sober from the whiskey bars, hauled away from the gambling tables, or rousted from whatever whores' beds they'd been sporting in.

They were coming to reinforce their comrades already present at the Dead Drunk to take Gator Al Hutchins, Belle Nyad, and Wake Spindrift, they thought.

Their mad plunging haste was spurred by the sound of gunfire crackling over the water that they'd heard while riding to the pier.

They knew Crabshaw and Marston would raise holy hell about their not being present for the action, even though it wasn't their fault. The surfacing of the three swampers had come as a surprise while the Gun Dogs were off-duty and at liberty to raise hell in the sin bins of River Street.

Informants had come to pass the word that the much-wanted threesome was to be found in the Dead Drunk. Crabshaw and Marston had roused what men they could and hurried to the pier, leaving henchmen behind to round up the rest of the bunch and get them in place pronto!

The reinforcements now came charging along, riding in a column by twos as they raced west on River Street. The pier neared but a maddening obstacle lay athwart their path: a long freight wagon moving in the same direction at moderate speed.

Good riders all, the oncoming Gun Dog column now began to come apart on command, dividing from head to rear.

The wagon was in the middle of the road with room to pass on both sides. The Gun Dog column executed a maneuver by which the double-ranked column would split in two, dividing into two separate single files.

One file would pass the wagon on the left, the other on the right. Once the wagon was successfully cleared, the twin files would reunite to reform the double column and complete the ride to the pier.

The head of the column closed on the rear of the wagon, the lead rider on the column's right peeling off to the right of the wagon, the lead rider at column left peeling off to the left of the wagon.

The next pair of riders in tandem performed the same operation, and the riders behind them, and so on, unzipping the double column into a pair of singles files fast flanking the wagon. A right smart maneuver.

The lead riders drew abreast of Crawdad Kate. Kate grinned at the rider on her left. She drew a double-barreled sawed-off shotgun out from under a blanket covering her wide lap and blew the lead horseman out of the saddle.

Then she reached over in the opposite direction and did the same to the rider on her right.

The pair of fear-maddened lead horses quickened their pace, pulling ahead.

The shotgun blasts gave the signal for the real massacre to begin. The canvas sheets covering the wagon's hopper were thrown back, revealing a cargo of murder-minded gunmen crouched down on the floor bed rising to do mayhem.

They were a mixed band of swamper Nightrunners, River Rats, and Tonkawa Indians and breeds. There were five on the left-hand side of the wagon, five on the right. They were armed with repeating rifles, shotguns, and six-guns.

They cut loose at point blank range on the Gun Dog riders flanking them. The opening salvo sounded like the height of a Fourth of July fireworks display going off. Twin sheets of lead raked Dog riders off their horses and out of life.

Bill Longley was there, broad-brimmed hat jammed on his head, a gun in each hand, blasting away. Flaring gunfire underlit his dark-eyed face making him look like a grinning young demon from hell.

The slaughter was sudden, brutal, and thorough. Not a Gun Dog rider escaped.

Kate reined the wagon to a halt. Swamper gunmen jumped down to the ground to deliver the coup de grâce, the death stroke, to the downed Dogs.

As always when there was killing to be done, young Bill Longley was at the fore.

The Gun Dogs' weapons were taken and their valuables stolen.

The pier was in sight. Kate drove the wagon to it, the others could easily follow on foot. She reined in at the pier. The first of their band that she saw there was George St. George.

"Sorry we're late but it couldn't be helped. A bridge was out and we had to go the long way around," she said.

"Looks like you made a good job of it anyhow, Kate," said George, glancing toward the massacre site.

Swamper gunmen began filtering into the sight, some carrying extra rifles and belt guns looted from the dead Dogs.

The crowd of onlookers who had taken cover when the shooting started at the pier had scattered to the four winds when the melee erupted on River Street. They were nowhere to be seen, including Sexton Clarke and Dean Valentine.

Johnny Cross made a point of looking for those two but they were gone like all the others. "Just as well," he said to himself, not being particularly minded at the moment to mix it up with ace *pistolero* Clarke.

Bill Longley caught sight of Johnny and hurried to him. Bill's face was lit up with unholy glee at the mass slaying he had been a part of.

"I knew you'd come through all right, Johnny, never doubted it," Bill said. "Sorry I missed the show."

He started to explain about the wagon having to detour but Johnny waved it away. "Knowing you, you'd have run here all by your lonesome if that's what it took," he said.

"I would have, too!" Bill agreed.

No way the swampers were leaving their dead behind. The Tonkawas among them bundled the body of Gator Al Hutchins in a blanket and reverently loaded him into the wagon bed.

Wake Spindrift, seriously wounded by two bullets in the back, was carried to the wagon and made as comfortable as possible.

"Looks bad," George St. George said, mouth downturned.

"How bad?" Johnny asked.

"Real bad."

"Hope he makes it."

"We all do."

"He's a good man."

"The best."

"I should have been with you, then this might not have happened," George St. George said, making a fist and smacking it against his palm.

"Wake was shot in the back from some skunk inside the saloon. Nothing you could do about that. Roe Brand was posted for just that sort of thing, but the shooter covered himself out of the line of fire," said Johnny.

"Still . . ."

"If Sexton Clarke got in on the play at our backs, neither of us would be here."

"But he didn't."

"We know that now but there was no way of knowing it then. Trust me: We haven't seen the last of Clarke."

The swampers readied to go. They dared not linger for fear of a chance encounter with a Combine patrol. The gunmen piled into the wagon and Kate gathered up the reins.

Johnny looked around for the two armed guards Sharkey had posted on the saloon patrons' horses, but the duo was long gone. Sharkey and company and his customers remained safely battened down inside the Dead Drunk, none having emerged since the slaughter in the street.

Johnny and Bill cut four horses out of the line at the hitching post: two for themselves and two more for Belle Nyad and George St. George. They would ride on horseback to avoid overloading and slowing down the wagon.

Roe Brand would make his getaway by water, by the pirogue that he'd tied up to the float. It was his boat and he would no more abandon it than Johnny would have thrown away a good gun.

Johnny gave Roe Brand a fat fistful of greenbacks. "Tell Sharkey this is for the horses. We'll leave them at the landing but Halftown is so full of thieves they may not be there for too long. In any case, this should cover the damages.

"Pay the man and get out fast, no telling when the Combine will come along to stick their noses in."

"I'll be gone in a flash," Roe said, double-timing it toward the saloon.

Johnny Cross, Bill Longley, George St. George, and Belle Nyad mounted up. Johnny and George rode west, following River Street where it became a wagon trail snaking through bosky rises and hollows en route to the landing. They would scout for danger along the path.

Kate set the team in motion, following the moonlit ribbon of dirt road in the direction taken by Johnny and George. Bill and Belle brought up the rear.

All reached the peninsular landing without incident. It fronted a cove where a steam-powered launch waited to ferry them to Deep Hollow.

The shallow-draught flatboat steamer had formerly belonged to the Gun Dogs. When the Dogs moved out of Halftown in force, a crew of swampers had overpowered the undermanned skeleton guard left behind at the boat slip, fired up the steam pressure, and piloted the boat to the prearranged rendezvous at the landing site.

While the swampers boarded the steam launch, Johnny and George hung back with a few others, guarding the site until departure.

"Here's something for you, Johnny. You know what this landing's full name is?" George asked.

"Nope, can't say as I do," said Johnny.

"Hangman's Knot Landing— What d'you think of that?"

"Could be a sign or omen . . ."

"Maybe, but what kind, good or bad?"

"Remains to be seen," Johnny Cross said. "But I'll tell you this, George: We set out tonight to give Barbaroux a bloody nose and we sure enough did!"

"But we got bloodied, too," said George.

"We'll just have to hit him harder the next time," Johnny said.

# TWENTY-FIVE

Once the shooters were long-gone, those who had earlier made up the crowd of onlookers began to emerge from their places of cover.

Staffers and patrons of the Dead Drunk came out to examine the devastation with stunned eyes.

Revelers from points east on the more brightly lit good-time sections of River Street came out to see the scene of slaughter for themselves.

Among the first to come into the open and dust themselves off were Risha, Marie, and a few other sporting girls in their immediate circle.

"Pretty yourselves up, ladies," Marie said, fussing with her hair, patting her curls back into place. "We could do some serious business tonight. There's nothing like a killing to make men's blood run hot."

"If that's true than tonight's work should put the brutes into a state of monstrous excitement," said Tally, a dark-eyed blonde with thin straight hair. "I never seen such killing!"

"Could be, so keep your eyes open for serious prospects, girls," Marie said.

"Hey! Wasn't that Bill Longley there at the end?" asked Jonelle, a plump brunette.

"Naw, he got run out of the county a long time ago," scoffed green-eyed Dawn.

"It was him sure enough," Marie declared flatly.

"It surely was!" Risha seconded. "Before him and Cullen Baker had their troubles I used to see Bill on the street here all the time . . . I know him when I see him."

"Never you mind about the likes of Bill Longley, dearie," advised Suze, short haired, hard faced, wiry. "He's right there at the top of the list in Barbaroux's bad book—he ain't long for this world."

"'Pears to me he's done all right so far," Risha said.

"He can't last. He'll hang like his friend Cullen Baker is gone do next week."

"I don't know about that, Suze. I'm gone keep on rooting for Bill anyway."

"Careful where you say that, Risha. You can trust us, but let something like that slip where some Combine spy can hear you and he'll go telling tales on you and then you won't be so happy."

"Think I care a fig about that?" Risha said saucily.

"You'd better," Marie chimed in. "Suze is telling you true. High or low, it ain't healthy to say you side with an enemy of the Commander."

Nearby was a mound of cast-off broken paving stones behind which Sexton Clarke and Dean Valentine had taken cover when the action got hot. They were now on their feet, brushing the dust from their clothes.

"This evening's entertainment turned out to be more amusing than I anticipated," Sexton Clarke said.

"Quite a show," Valentine agreed dryly. "I'm surprised you didn't mix in, Clarke."

"Why should I?"

"You're Barbaroux's top gun, I should think you'd want to protect his interests."

"Let me set you straight on that score, my artistic friend, so there'll be no misunderstandings between us," Sexton Clarke said, holding up a single admonitory finger. "I'm no ordinary brawler or gunman, I'm a specialist—a *duelist*. Barbaroux has an army of men to fight his battles . . . though if these so-called Gun Dogs are a sample of the caliber of fighting men in his employ, he had better look to hiring on a more professional grade of recruits.

"I was brought in to take care of Cullen Baker. By sheer bad luck—his and mine—Baker was taken by what they laughingly call 'the Law' in these parts. Baker's bad luck because he's doomed to hang, my bad luck because I missed the chance to match my gun against his and kill him. Cullen Baker is a name not without a certain repute and it would have added fresh luster to my laurels to mark him among my list of conquests."

"I certainly didn't mean to minimize your professional abilities, Clarke. No offense meant, I'm sure you understand."

"None taken. Yes, Baker's bad luck is mine, too. Being shot dead by me in a fair duel would have been a far better and more honorable way to die than hanging by the neck from a rope until dead. Pity."

"Cullen Baker is fast—very. I know, I've seen him in action."

"Have you? You interest me, Valentine. Do go on."

"It was on the south Arkansas border when they were having a militia war about a year ago. Baker burned down a couple of gunmen in a saloon brawl.

He's trigger quick and a dead shot drunk or sober—when he was sober, which wasn't too often."

"Tsk-tsk. Another gunfighter who needs to bolster his courage with the bottle. I don't think much of such men," Clarke sniffed.

Valentine thought it was more complicated than that but kept his opinion to himself.

"Friend Barbaroux now keeps me on retainer to handle the next high-ranking triggerman that comes along and dares to defy him," Clarke went on. "And there will be such a one, and more than one, in such a contentious place as this. I welcome that day and long for a challenge to my abilities . . . Perhaps we saw such a one tonight," he added.

"Oh? Who?" Valentine asked, mindful to display a merely casual interest. He had to play this angle carefully to avoid raising Clarke's suspicions. Valentine knew Johnny Cross right off but preferred to keep his knowledge to himself.

"Surely you must have noticed: the young man with the left-hand draw who took Viper Teed and several others. Not that the Viper was anything much and the others were worse, but the stranger displayed a smooth technique," Sexton Clarke said.

"Do you know him?" Clarke asked, turning his gimlet eyes on Valentine to look him square in the face.

"No," Valentine denied blandly.

"Odd . . . from the look on your face I thought you recognized him."

"He looked like someone I thought I knew, but when he moved into the light I saw it wasn't him."

"So?" Clarke shrugged. "In any case his identity cannot remain a mystery for too long. Not after this, tonight. So much killing will raise a big stink."

"No doubt about it."

"I'll tell you this, Valentine: That youth with the left-hand draw is a professional gun. His technique, way he handled himself and his weapon . . . the signs are unmistakable. To me, at any rate.

"I wonder if he has come to the Blacksnake to kill me? That would be truly amusing. I'd welcome the chance to exercise my talents. Despite the Commander's lavish hospitality on his Big White Boat, and the unexpected novelty of such amusing diversions as tonight, I long to be back in action, doing what I do best."

"You like to live dangerously, Clarke."

"Not really. False modesty aside, for one of my skills, the risks are minimal. But exhilarating! When and if the time comes for me to try out that youth with the left-hand draw, the encounter will be exciting for me but not very dangerous at all."

Valentine took a light tone. "Speaking as a devout coward, I prefer to dodge the gunfights and enjoy living the good life on Barbaroux's floating pleasure palace."

"Far from me to dispute your candid self-assessment, Valentine," Clarke said, smiling thinly. "We might as well be on our way, there's nothing more here of interest."

He set off toward River Street, Valentine walking alongside him.

Did Clarke believe his denial about knowing the identity of the slayer of Viper Teed? Valentine wondered. Hard to tell. Clarke was a cool one, iron nerved, under control, giving away little or nothing. In any case he hadn't pressed the point, which Valentine counted as a win, if only for now.

Because of course he did know Johnny Cross, knew

him personally and knew much of his back history. But for reasons known only to himself, Dean Valentine had decided to give away nothing about the Texas gun to Sexton Clarke.

He hoped he could make it stick.

"Hello, handsome men!" Came a cooing female voice. Risha, Marie, Jonelle, Dawn, Tally, and Suze crossed paths with Valentine and Sexton Clarke, intercepting them.

"Hel-lo!" Valentine said, beaming.

"Ladies," Clarke acknowledged, politely touching the brim of his hat and smiling one of his thin milk-and-water smiles.

"Y'all looking for some female companionship?" Marie demanded.

"Not any more," Valentine purred.

"Yes, that would top off a most amusing evening," Sexton Clarke agreed.

# TWENTY-SIX

*One day until Cullen Baker was set to hang—One Day to Hell!*

Clinchfield Gaol sat on the same promontory as Clinchfield town but was a mile west of it. It had been built on Pirates' Point by Spaniards, the original Old World colonists in the region. The Gaol was a castle-style fort of reddish-brown sandstone formed up into walls, towers, battlements.

Since Rufus Barbaroux controlled the county, you could say that Clinchfield Gaol belonged to him. Though a prison for over a hundred years, it was stuffed to overflowing with Barbaroux's foes. Clinchfield Gaol was a hellhole.

Now came a bloody sundown, the sun sagging into the west with a scarlet blaze. The tall black gallows in the prison yard stood outlined against the red sky.

Cullen Baker eyed it through the small square barred window in his cell on Hangman's Row, the place where condemned men were kept.

Baker often kept his face pressed against the bars

for hours at a time day and night, not least because it afforded a taste of fresh air in this foul-smelling prison.

He watched the sunset, almost certainly the last he would ever see. In the prison yard the executioner's assistant headed a work detail testing the gallows drop in anticipation of the Big Day tomorrow.

Warden Munday was one of Barbaroux's creatures. The Commander had put him in charge of Clinchfield Gaol and given him a free hand to run it as he liked. That is, just as long as he kept it to Barbaroux's liking. That meant overcrowding in filthy inhumane conditions, starvation diets, and a regular regimen of torture and brutality for the inmates.

Cullen Baker suspected, hell, *knew* the real reason for the needless test was to satisfy Warden Munday's inexhaustible lust for tormenting Baker in a relentless attempt to break him.

Munday stood outside Baker's cell watching the condemned man as avidly as Baker was watching the sunset.

Under ordinary circumstances Munday wouldn't have stood so close to the cage wall on the aisle, but since Baker was at the window on the far side of the cell the warden counted on his abilities to evade any sudden lunging attack by Baker reaching through the grids. Munday had a healthy respect for Cullen Baker's violent abilities, diminished though they were by weeks of harsh confinement.

Warden Munday was a compact-sized man of below average height with a well-conditioned athletic physique. Thinning hair was combed back from the forehead and parted in the middle, a close-cropped beard the color of dried dung covered the lower half of his face.

His eyes were narrow horizontal slits dotted by brown dots, his nose a fleshy lump, his thin-lipped mouth another horizontal line with an upper lip so thin as to be virtually nonexistent.

Cullen Baker was a big man standing a few inches over six feet and built like a hardworking farm hand with powerful upper body development. He'd lost some twenty-five to thirty pounds on the prison diet but he was still big, if hollow cheeked and raw boned.

He stood with his back to Munday, so the warden couldn't see his face. Munday would have liked to study it closely, searching for any signs the condemned was breaking under what must be the tremendous strain of knowing he was doomed to die by hanging on the morrow.

Cullen Baker was a hard nut to crack, Munday had to give him that.

Not even learning of the death of his young wife seemed to put a dent in his iron self-control, despite Munday's sneering and mocking revelation of the same, an elaborate presentation into which he'd put great thought and work and of which he'd had high hopes of cracking Cullen Baker.

Baker showed as much outward emotion as if he'd been told it was raining outside. In the end it was Munday who feared he himself was breaking.

Life in Clinchfield Gaol was hard to start with, but there were countless ways of making it far worse for even the toughest inmates.

There were limits on Munday, unfortunately: no maiming, broken bones, or mutilation. Commander Barbaroux had been very clear about that. Cullen Baker had to be whole and intact when Execution Day arrived. Barbaroux intended to put on a show for himself and his cronies when Baker was hanged.

Cullen Baker must go to the gallows knowing, *knowing*, that it was Barbaroux who put him there and was present there at the hanging to gloat over his death throes. Only then would the triumph of Barbaroux be complete.

So within those limits Warden Munday went to work on Cullen Baker, continually taunting him, baiting him, orchestrating a host of indignities and torments to increase his sufferings. Munday wanted him broken to the point that Baker showed a yellow streak when he went to swing by a rope and dance on air.

Munday knew Barbaroux would be pleased by such an outcome. The Commander tended to express such pleasure by a bonus in gold. Trouble was, Cullen Baker didn't break easy, he was a hard nut to crack. And highly dangerous.

Early on during his stay at Clinchfield Gaol a couple of guards had gotten too close to Baker while trying to give him a beating. Instead they had gotten the beating, Baker busting them up so bad they had to be hospitalized in the infirmary. One guard, Hankus, had only come back on shift three days ago and still walked with a limp. The other had yet to return, quite possibly never would.

Others who had been on-scene said Baker would have beaten the two to death if not for reinforcements clubbing him into insensibility.

That was Cullen Baker: natural-born killer.

Now Munday waited, as Baker watched the drop test. The moment of truth was near.

The scaffold was a ten-foot-high wooden deck centered by a hinged trapdoor. Beside and above the trap loomed the actual gallows itself, an inverted U-shaped topbar—from whose center hung a length of yellow hempen rope stretching down to what would roughly be the height of the condemned man standing atop the closed trapdoor.

The executioner's assistant supervised the detail while three guards did the donkey work. The trio manhandled a two-hundred-pound heavy-duty canvas sandbag into place, setting it upright on its base on the trap below the dangling noose. The sandbag was a stand-in for the condemned man.

The executioner's assistant hooked up the noose to the upright sandbag, cinching it tightly about a foot below the top, making sure it was secure.

He took up a stance beside a vertical metal lever handle protruding up through the wooden deck adjacent to the trap. The lever controlled the trapdoor through a series of metal rods, pins, and joins running beneath the deck.

The guards stepped back moving well clear of the trapdoor.

There was a pause, the guards glancing up at the barred window behind which Cullen Baker stood. They well knew that cell and its occupant.

The executioner's assistant threw the lever, triggering the spring-catch mechanism holding the trapdoor hatch in place. It made a sound like a giant mousetrap being sprung.

The hinged square hatch opened swinging downward. The heavy sandbag dropped through the now-open hatchway, plummeting earthward. Its speedy descent abruptly ended when it reached the end of its rope.

It jerked to a halt a few feet above the ground with

a deep-booming *Whomp!* that was the signature of a resounding impact shivering gallows and scaffold, a loud booming noise that was as much felt as heard even in the depths of the prison.

Rare indeed was the inmate behind those walls who could hear that sound without shuddering.

Yet Cullen Baker was such a one. No slightest flinch or wince did he betray, to the infinite disappointment of Warden Munday.

The dangling sandbag hung swaying pendulum-like, its taut hempen rope creaking.

The warden held himself too well under control to show any sign of disappointment or annoyance that his ploy had once again failed. Yet the taste of such failure was bitter gall and wormwood to him.

The exercise was over.

The guards went down the scaffold staircase and under the deck, hefting the sandbag and wrestling the noose clear of its top. The executioner's assistant hauled the rope up through the trapdoor, then closed the hatch and locked it in place, resetting the mechanism.

The three guards had more donkey work to do. The sandbag could not be left outside overnight, for fear of damage by the elements. Warden Munday was a real stickler about the proper care and maintenance of Clinchfield Gaol property, as he was about every other single rule and regulation concerning the operation of that tightly run prison.

The guards lifted the heavy sandbag onto a four-wheeled handcart and push-pulled it across the yard.

Cullen Baker laughed loudly, a harsh cawing sound. "Work, you sons, work!" he shouted down to the guards below.

The guards grinned up at him.

"Does me good to see y'all doing some honest work for a change," Baker called.

"I'm looking forward to hauling away your dead carcass come tomorrow," a guard replied. "That won't be work . . . it'll be a pleasure!"

Baker's laughter cawed again, harsh and mocking. The guards worked the cart through the door and inside. The turnkey slammed the door shut and locked it.

"Still the tough man, eh, Baker," Warden Munday said to the inmate's back. It was not a question.

Cullen Baker turned, facing the other. Mindful of the dangers of a sudden lunge by the prisoner, Munday quickly stepped back from the cage.

Baker took note of that and grinned. The warden hated him more than ever before but didn't let his feelings show, smirking instead.

Cullen Baker folded his arms across his chest and leaned back against the wall as if to demonstrate there was no threat to the warden from him. Munday wasn't buying and continued to keep his distance from the cage.

"Starting to sweat yet, Baker? Your time is almost done," he taunted.

"It'll be a pleasure to get out of this hole," Baker said.

"You'll be trading it for a hole in the ground, an unmarked grave in the prison burying ground."

"I'll save a space beside me for you, Warden."

The warden ignored that. "Not very pleasant, hanging. I've seen even the toughest cry for their momma when the hangman tightens the noose around his neck. I wonder how you'll hold up, Baker?"

"Wait and see, Warden."

"Take it from one who knows, hanging's a chancy thing, Baker. You never know what's going to happen until the trap's sprung. It seems straightforward enough: The rope goes around your neck, a relatively quick and clean death compared to some. Nothing compared to some of those lawmen you gut-shot."

"Lawmen, hell! They was crooks with badges—Combine crooks. They'd have done the same to me or worse if they could."

"So you said at the trial, but a jury of twelve good men said different and found you guilty of murder many times over."

"That was no trial, that was a trained dog act. Everyone on the jury was a hand-picked Combine man or one of their friends or kin."

"Why tell me, Baker? This is no appeals court. You hang tomorrow. Appeal your way out of that," Warden Munday said.

Munday continued his taunting. "By the way, don't be too sure about hanging being a quick death," Munday added. "Things happen sometimes, strange things. If the hangman doesn't set the noose just right, you slowly strangle to death instead of a swift death from a broken neck. Very very slowly. I've seen them take five, even ten minutes a-dying when that happens. A tough man like you might take a very long time, eh, Baker?"

"You'd like that, wouldn't you, Warden?"

"Nonsense, it's a matter of no difference to me."

"We both know better."

"Tomorrow noon we'll find out what's true and what's not. I'm looking forward to it," Munday said.

Cullen Baker shrugged, he was through talking.

Munday took a different tack. "This being Execution Eve you get the customary last meal of the condemned man. What'll you have?"

"A big fat juicy steak, fried potatoes, some cut-up tomatoes, corn bread—"

"You'll get fried chicken and like it, Baker."

"How about a bottle of something with a kick to it?"

"I know your reputation as a drunkard and bar fly, Baker. This past month must have been mighty thirsty for you. Too bad! No alcoholic spirits allowed inside Clinchfield Gaol. You can have milk or water."

"Mighty cold comfort, Warden. You must be trying to kill me off before the hanging."

"Wouldn't think of it. I want you cold sober when you go to be hanged. I don't want you to fall down the stairs to the gallows and hurt yourself."

Munday made ready to leave. "Eat hearty, Baker. You've got to keep your strength up for your appointment with the hangman."

# TWENTY-SEVEN

Cullen Baker hadn't slept well or easily any night since his capture, and tonight, his last night, was certainly no exception. He spent a lot of time standing at the window watching the stars come out and the rising moon climb into the night sky.

He now lay awake on his back on his bunk watching a patch of moonlight creep slowly across the ceiling. The hour was late; the moon was declining in the western half of the sky and the stars shone through scudding clouds and mists rising off the river.

Cullen Baker was not one to regret the deeds of a misspent life. Indeed he held his span to be far from misspent. He reveled in it. He'd lived hard, raw and hellbent for leather and he meant to go out the same way.

Often he thought of Julie. There'd been other women, lots of them, other wives even, but Julie rose foremost in his mind.

"'Tain't likely I'll see her where I'm going," he said to himself with a quirked smile.

More time passed, physical and emotional fatigue, boredom and lack of stimulation taking its toll. Cullen Baker drifted in and out of a light troubled sleep. He

passed from wakefulness to slumber and back again.
Perhaps he only dreamed that he was awake.

Whatever they were, his dreams were not pleasant,
if the expressions crossing his sleep-dulled features
were any indication. There were frowns, grimaces,
sneers, tooth-gnashing snarls, and such.

One dream took on a vivid immediacy.


*Back in the war for a time he rode with the Independent
Rangers of the Arkansas Confederate Home Guard—that's
what they called themselves but in reality they were one more
of the many ragtag, bobtailed bands of marauding bandits
preying on the folk of the region be their loyalties Union or
Southron.*

*One day near war's end the band came across a group of
several dozen refugees, men and some women, trying to flee
Perry County for points west.*

*Most likely they were in search of some place where they
could find something to eat—"good luck on that"—but there
was no luck to be had for the hapless fugitives when the Home
Guard came across them trying to cross the Sabine River.*

*They were trying to flee . . . flight meant disloyalty to the
Cause, disloyalty meant death.*

*The Independent Rangers caught the refugees right in the
middle of a river crossing when they were most vulnerable.*

*"They's goin' over to the Yanks!" one of the band shouted.
That's all it took to spur the Home Guard into opening fire,
cutting the hapless fugitives down, men and women alike, no
mercy.*

*Cullen Baker had been in the thick of it that day as always,
doing his share of the killing and more, and now it seemed
that he was there again, reliving the experience with a sensa-
tion of stark reality.*

*Crackling waves of gunfire, screams of dying men and women, river water splashing, spraying, the river turning red, guns going bang bang bang!*—

Cullen Baker came awake—

Or had he?

He was lost in confusion for a moment. He knew he was awake on his bunk in his death cell in Clinchfield Gaol, no doubt about it. But the racketing gunfire from his massacre dream continued to sound unabated.

"That's no dream!" he said out loud. "Awake or asleep, I know gunfire when I hear it and I'm hearing it now, plenty of it—!"

Hangman's Row was in tumult, awake and riotous. Inmates were shouting, screaming, beating against the bars of their cages with fists and feet.

Cullen Baker jumped to his feet and stood at the window.

*Fire!*

The guards' barracks was ablaze, a sight to gladden any inmate's heart.

"It's a breakout!" shouted one of the condemned men on the row.

Cullen Baker knew the man was wrong; it was a break-in.

Gun battles raged all over the prison yard, a yard already littered with dead bodies. There was shooting and furtive movements on the battlements, too.

Suddenly a volcano seemed to erupt at the main gate, secured by a pair of massive ironbound oaken doors. Those impregnable doors ceased to exist, disintegrating into glare, pressure, fragments, noise.

A tremendous blast or rather series of blasts made

rolling thunder to herald the explosion of the main gates.

Sunfire at night blossomed into white-hot fury where the gates had been, so bright that Cullen Baker had to look away to keep from being dazzled by the glare.

Clinchfield Gaol shook from the blast like an earthquake. Dust shaken from the stones rained down from the ceiling of Hangman's Row. Echoes resounded across the Point and over the waters. The blast cloud rose to the heavens, blotting out the stars. A rain of debris fell, throwing down crushed rocks, pulverized portals, twisted iron bars, and dust.

"Hot damn! Somebody just blew the gates!" shouted a denizen of the Row, exulting.

The block guard was so scared he didn't know what to do. He was as jumpy as a frog in a pot of boiling water. The iron access door was locked from outside and he lacked the key, sealing him in on Hangman's Row.

The smoke cleared, revealing a hole in the wall where the main gate had been.

A band of mounted men, several dozen of them, armed and shooting, came pouring through the gap into the yard.

"Who are they?" one of the condemned cried.

"Whoever they be they's no friends of Clinchfield Gaol!" crowed another.

That was certain. The invaders poured in, shooting down guards on sight, trampling them under horses' hooves, even cutting them down with cavalry sabers. The guards downed some of the invaders but not enough.

The riders were the second wave of the invasion. The first wave, the advance guard of skirmishers, had made their entrance earlier. They had come quietly, covertly, secretly. That's why the fighting had begun not outside but inside the gates.

The skirmishers had fired the barracks. Now they were inside the prison, having secured a beachhead within the main building. Shots and screams sounded somewhere deep within the structure.

The condemned men of Hangman's Row reacted to the onslaught:

"Shoot-a-mile! Kill 'em, burn 'em down, the dirty dogs!"

"Oh, what I wouldn't give to be down there, in on the killing!"

"Lord, we gone burn alive!"

"Grow a pair, yellowbelly—we's doomed to die so at worst we lose nothing and take our enemies with us!"

"But I don't want to burn—"

The shooting sounded closer now, nearing if not yet actually inside the west wing.

"Sounds like they's on the ground floor!"

Finally there came what Cullen Baker had been listening for though he dared not hope: the racket of oncoming attackers below, rising up the stairwell to the second floor. Steady sustained bursts of gunfire drew ever nearer.

Outside the iron door came the muffled rattle of a key ring, the sound of a long-handled key being thrust into the lock, its bolts being thrown.

The iron door flung open. A handful of armed men came bustling in, hustling a captive turnkey into the central aisle with them.

One of them shot down the block guard who had

fled to the corridor's end and stood cowering with his back to the far wall.

Another held in one hand a hooded lantern throwing a tight beam of light, and in the other a gun held pressed against the turnkey's head.

"Take us to him or I'll blow your brains out!" the gunman commanded.

"That's it! This is his cell!" croaked the turnkey in a fear-choked voice.

The intruders clustered in front of Cullen Baker's cage. They were a fearsome-looking bunch, faces blackened with soot to blend in with the darkness of night, devil masks with slitted eyes and grim mouths.

The turnkey fumbled with the key ring, trembling fingers sorting through the keys in search of one that would open the Hangman's Row cages.

"Open it up, damn you," a second raider menaced, prodding the turnkey with a gun.

"He's stalling," said another. "Kill him and try the keys yourself."

"No, wait! Here's the key, and it opens all the cells in the row," the turnkey cried.

"Don't kill him till we're damned sure it's the right key," a second raider said.

The key rattled in the lock, unsealing it.

"That's it!"

"Don't kill him," said the raider holding the lantern and a gun. "Let him unlock the rest of the cells. He can do it faster than we can. A couple of y'all go with him."

"Right!" a third raider said, grabbing the turnkey by the scruff of the collar and hustling him to the next cell in line. A fourth raider went with them.

The lantern holder worked the beam so that it fell

on the cell's occupant, revealing Cullen Baker. "Let there be light," he said.

"Get that out of my eyes," Cullen Baker barked, squinting against the glare.

"Sweet natured as ever," the second raider said, chuckling.

"Must be him," said the lantern holder, "ain't nobody else that ugly!"

Cullen Baker squinted against the lantern's glare. "By the Lord, is that young Bill Longley I hear?"

"You're not just whistling Dixie," said Bill Longley. "What, did you think I wasn't coming?"

"I never doubted it," Baker said.

"I brung a few friends along—"

"So I see."

"Including one you might remember."

The lantern holder held the lamp under his face, under-lighting it to reveal his features.

"*Johnny Cross!*" Cullen Baker shouted.

"Howdy, hoss," Johnny said.

"You never looked better."

"Wish I could say the same about you. You don't smell so good, neither. Best save the handshakes and backslapping for later, though, we ain't clear of ol' Clinchfield Gaol yet."

Lantern light revealed that Cullen Baker was barefoot, a condition in which Hangman's Row's condemned were kept.

"We're gonna have to get you some boots," George St. George said.

"To hell with that! There's only one thing I want—a gun!" Cullen Baker answered.

"What I figured," Bill Longley said, handing the other a six-gun.

Baker's big fist closed around the gun butt. "Ahh." He sighed, like he was sinking into a luxuriant hot bath.

"Let's get a move on, we got plenty more killing to do before first light," Johnny urged.

"I know where to start," Cullen Baker said, grim-faced, eyes alight with unholy joy.


Johnny Cross had put his head together earlier with George St. George, Belle Nyad, and the Tonkawa tribal elders who took the place of their fallen spokesman Gator Al Hutchins.

Forty swampers were recruited for the raid on Clinchfield Gaol. They came from George St. George's Nightrunners, Belle's River Rats gang, and the Tonkawa braves.

Forty guns: fifteen skirmishers, five blasters, twenty for the cavalry.

Niahll Sharkey decided to come in after the massacre of the Gun Dogs. He supplied dynamite and blasting powder.

The advance guard of skirmishers was a mixed band that included Johnny Cross and Bill Longley, George St. George, some smugglers, River Rats and Tonks, not least of whom was Roe Brand. Among them were several tough swampers who'd served time in Clinchfield Gaol and knew the layout inside out.

The forty guns massed outside the prison in the dead of night. They rode recently stolen horses, one of the easiest items to come by in the thieves' market of Halftown. Their people had earlier stolen them from various horse thieves.

This advance guard went in first.

Tonkawa archers silently picked off the night guards patrolling the fortress's rampart walls. Grappling hooks with lines attached were used to scale the walls.

The bowmen used fire arrows to set the guard barracks on fire. This resulted in flames, heat, smoke, and panicked guards, many of whom ran out into the yard unarmed and in their nightclothes.

The fire and shooting cued the blasters outside to do their work. They were headed by Niahll Sharkey, a dynamiter of no small expertise. Sharkey had done demolitions and explosives work for the Confederate Navy during the war.

He supervised four sidemen in rigging the barrels of black powder designed to demolish the main gates. When shooting started within the walls, he lit the fuse. The resultant blast blew the portals to pieces, making a massive breach in the enemy's defenses.

The way cleared, a twenty-man cavalry force stormed the yard, riding and shooting.

At about the same time, Johnny Cross used a couple of bundles of dynamite to blow a hole in the front entrance of the prison's main building. He and the skirmishers bulled their way inside, gunning down prison staffers and guards.

Johnny led half his force into the ground floor of the west wing, leaving the others behind to secure the main building and begin freeing the general prison population from their cells.

Helping to break the inmates out quickly was the fact that as soon as they were freed they were set to work performing the same service for their fellows still behind bars.

With all the blasting and shooting a number of fires broke out in the main building, adding urgency to the mission of freeing the prisoners.

Johnny and his band shot their way into the west wing, taking several guards and turnkeys alive. One turnkey was pressed into service at gunpoint into securing the keys for Hangman's Row and using them to open its iron door and free the condemned men, Cullen Baker first and foremost . . .

Now Johnny Cross, Bill Longley, Cullen Baker, Roe Brand, and several others roamed the second floor of the main building, cleaning up on whatever prison personnel they found there. Dead bodies of guards and staff littered the stairs and landing and were scattered throughout the complex.

The raider band now padded stealthily down a long hall at the front of the building, a hall lined with closed doors behind which lay dark rooms. The skirmishers proceeded with guns in hand.

Night lamps were few and far between with frequent patches of black darkness. Johnny Cross kept hold of the hooded lantern in his left hand, using it to light the way, while his right hand fisted a gun.

"You know the way to the warden's office, Cullen?" Bill Longley asked in a low voice.

"I should, I been in there enough times," Cullen Baker rasped. "Munday liked to call me on the carpet so he could work the prod on me. Now I'll call on him."

"I know you got to do what you're gonna do, Cullen," Johnny began.

"I got to!"

"Well let's make it fast."

"The whole blamed shooting match is like to burn down around us!" said Roe Brand, eyeing the thickening smoke piling up on the ceiling.

They came to a closed door in the center of the hallway, a thin faint line of light leaking through the slitted gap at the bottom of the door.

Stenciled on the door in gilt letters several inches high was the legend OFFICE OF THE WARDEN.

Below that in smaller letters: *KNOCK BEFORE ENTERING*.

Cullen Baker raised a hand, motioning the others to halt. "This is my play, boys," he whispered, "so whatever happens don't interfere."

"All right," Johnny Cross said softly, hanging back with the others while Baker moved to the fore.

Standing well to one side of the door, back flattened to the wall, Cullen Baker reached out with his free hand to try the doorknob. The door was locked.

Baker rapped his knuckles smartly against the door panel, quickly pulling his hand clear.

"Warden Munday?" he called mockingly. "Oh, Warden, you in there—?"

From within the office a volley of bullets came in quick succession, ripping through the door panel at chest-height.

"Looks like he's home." Cullen Baker grinned. He shot the lock out of the door, straight-arming the door open while keeping himself under cover.

Another volley of shots came sizzling through the open doorway, cratering the wall on the far side of the corridor.

In the dimly lit sanctum of his spacious office, Warden Munday crouched behind a massive golden oak desk blasting away to no effect save to further impact the opposite wall. Several guns were laid out on his desktop, ready to hand.

Baker hunkered down, reaching around with the pistol to draw a bead on Munday. He fired, tagging the warden in the shoulder.

Munday grunted, shaken by the impact. He'd been hit high up on his gun arm, which now dropped to his side, useless. The gun slipped from his nerveless fingers.

Munday threw himself across the desktop, his other hand grabbing for one of the guns laid out there but clumsily knocking it out of reach instead.

Cullen Baker stepped into the room, gun pointed at Munday. Munday lurched upright, standing crouched, dead arm hanging at his side. His leaden-gray face was clammy with cold sweat. The enlarged pupils of his eyes looked like black buttons.

Cullen Baker spoke: "Like you said, Warden—*you never know what's going to happen until the trap's sprung.*"

He shot Munday twice in the belly.

"Owww!" Munday crumpled, trying to hold himself together with his good arm. He backpedaled into the wall, then slowly sank to the floor, sitting down on it. A smeary blood trail marked his downward path along the wall.

Cullen Baker circled around to the far side of the desk, never taking his smoking gun off Munday.

The warden's eyes were glazing and his lips gummy. He began, "Listen, Baker—"

"Here it comes," Cullen Baker said, rolling his eyes in disbelief.

"I'm valuable to you alive . . . hostage . . . bargaining chip . . ."

"You?—you're nothing. What good is a jailer without a jail? Clinchfield Gaol is coming down around your ears, Warden, or ain't you noticed? But you'll go before it."

"Money, gold—I can get it . . ."

"Take it to hell with you."

As if accepting his fate, Warden Munday gathered his last remaining reserves of strength and life, sneering. "You'll never change, Baker . . . You're an animal, a stupid brute animal with fast reflexes and no brain."

"Maybe so, but I'm alive and you're dead, just about. I was minded to do something fancy and cut up capers like hanging you on your own gallows, but we're plumb out of time, so I'll stick to what I know, something plain and simple," Cullen Baker said.

With that, he aimed his gun again, and fired.


"I'm back," Cullen Baker proudly announced.

Johnny Cross tied a bandana around his nose and mouth to protect against smoke, as did the others of the band. All but Cullen Baker who had no kerchief. He remedied the lack by tearing one long sleeve off his prison shirt and binding it across the lower half of his face.

They rushed onto the second-floor landing and started downstairs. Smoke was thick in the stairwell, the treads of the steps hot against Baker's bare feet.

Reaching ground level they rushed out through the hole where the front doors had been before Johnny Cross blew them up earlier with dynamite. It was a relief indeed to stagger away from the smoky structure and breathe fresh air—as fresh as swamp air, thick, humid, and overlaid with the reek of rotting vegetation, ever gets.

The general prison population had all been set loose, the last of them streaming toward the gap in the main gates and outside.

Cullen Baker meant to set fire to the gallows but he was too late. It had already been put to the torch and was now burning brightly.

The raider band joined the mass exodus fleeing through the gap in the prison walls where the main gates had been.

Once outside, Bill Longley was drawn up short by the sound of baying somewhere in the brush, a distant rising chorus of howling. His face twisted into a mingled expression of fearful expectancy and disbelief.

"Something wrong, Bill?" Johnny Cross asked, frowning.

"Listen! You hear that?"

The sound of howling rose up again, ringing in triumph, stirring as the clarion call of a trumpeting band. Shivers ran along Bill's spine.

"That? That's nothing, just a pack of hunting dogs that treed a 'coon or something," Johnny said dismissively.

"I reckon," Bill said, not believing it.

"Come on, shake a leg and let's get out of here, we still got plenty of work to do this night," Johnny said.

He and Bill joined the flight from the burning wreck of Clinchfield Gaol.

A pack of hunting dogs? Bill Longley knew better. *He had heard the hellhounds.*

# TWENTY-EIGHT

"The *Queen*'s coming out!"

A different kind of uproar seized the Clinchfield docks later that same night, particularly at the wharf where the *Sabine Queen*, the Big White Boat, was moored.

On receipt of the startling intelligence that Clinchfield Gaol was under assault, Commander Barbaroux's well-armed and heavily manned steamboat made ready to set forth and do battle.

Barbaroux had the vessel kept under steam day and night and so it was always ready for action. With news that Clinchfield Gaol was being attacked, fireboxes were heaped high with fresh kindling and paraffin sprayed on them to quickly goose the boilers up to full steam.

The boat's permanent party fighting force armed themselves while civilians and all nonessential personnel made a mass exodus from boat to wharf.

The *Queen* disgorged several dozen devastatingly attractive sporting ladies in various stages of undress, but neither Flossie nor Jonquil was among them. Barbaroux's favorite concubines would ride into battle with their master.

The wharf was thronged with cooks, pot scrubbers, musicians, maids and manservants, entertainers, gamblers, vendors, and a variety of hangers-on. Each one represented dragging weight, which must not be allowed to slow the *Queen*'s race to the assault.

It being the wee hours of the night, many of the discharged had been roused from their beds and swiftly herded along the ways and down the gangplanks to shore, adding to the air of dazed confusion that hung over the mass.

One who was not confused was Dean Valentine, who on hearing the alarm swiftly dressed and threw his most important valuables into a carpetbag. Here was a modest horde of recently acquired wealth, including the amassed weekly fees paid him in gold by Barbaroux for his role as in-house portraitist, along with whatever else he could win at the card tables, chisel from slower-witted passengers, or steal.

Not that Valentine feared their loss by their going down with the ship, for he held the well-nigh universal opinion on the Blacksnake, certainly among Barbaroux and his creatures, that the *Sabine Queen* was unbeatable and unsinkable.

No, Valentine rather feared the theft of his loot by some member of the steamboat's crew, as piratical a bunch of rogues, cut-purses, and cutthroats as he had ever seen massed in one vicinity. If there's one thing a thief hates most of all, it's being stolen from.

Valentine stood on the wharf, gripping his carpetbag by the handle, dividing his focus between watching the *Queen*'s hurried preparations for departure and eyeing the array of lithe and lissome lovelies who had been summarily evicted from their cushy berths on the boat and herded on to the wharf.

Standing off to one side of the crowd, Valentine watched the steamboat get under way. Black smoke chuffed out of the tops of the *Queen*'s twin stacks, flames licking out from their mouths like muzzle flares. Mooring lines were cast off. Dual side-mounted paddle wheels began to turn and churn, beating up trails of white water on the river's black surface.

The steamboat surged forward, moving away from the wharf, gathering speed and momentum as it plowed a course into the mid-Blacksnake. The multi-decked boat looked like a giant white wedding cake trimmed and frosted with strings of beaded lights as it powered into dark night and blacker waters.

"Impressive sight, no?"

Valentine gave a slight start as a familiar voice murmured behind him. He'd thought he was alone on this part of the wharf but apparently not. Glancing over his shoulder, he was not surprised to find Sexton Clarke behind him.

Clarke moved forward to stand alongside Valentine. The gunfighter's round-topped, flat-brimmed preacher's hat was perched on top of the back of his head at a tilted angle, giving it the appearance of a black halo. He held a traveling bag in one hand, the hand that was not his gun hand.

"You've a light foot, Clarke, I didn't hear you come up."

"A soft tread can be an asset in my profession, Valentine."

"So?"

"So," Clarke said. "A majestic sight, the *Queen* under way in dead of night. It must appeal to your artistic sensibilities."

"More so if I hadn't been so rudely roused from my

bed. In any case, my landscapes, er, waterscapes here, are few and far between. I'm a portraitist," Valentine said.

"Ah, even the painterly set is given to specialists. It's much the same in the duelist's trade."

"No river battles for you, eh, Clarke?"

"Heavens, no!" Clarke said, giving a mock shudder. "Noisy and disagreeable, with the additional danger of drowning."

"No swampers will ever sink that boat."

"Still, a person might fall overboard."

"It must be a sight to see—from safely on shore."

"Strange things are in the air, Valentine. Less than a week ago, the Gun Dogs were wiped out. Tonight, Clinchfield Gaol is under siege, or so they say. Clinchfield Gaol, think of it! Who would be rash enough to assault that grotesque pile of stone?"

"Maybe the same ones who massacred the Dogs," suggested Valentine.

"Perhaps. They won't find it so amusing when the *Queen* opens fire with her cannons. Those big guns can reach far inland," Clarke said.

Valentine nodded agreement.

"Yet it seems beyond doubt that our redoubtable Commander is experiencing considerable unrest in his vest-pocket kingdom." Sexton Clarke smiled as if he found the thought not unpleasing. "What next, I wonder?"


Clinchfield Gaol and Clinchfield town were both sited on the east bank of Pirate's Point, the famous peninsula extending from the north bank of the Blacksnake deep into the river. Clinchfield Gaol was set inland near the point's southern tip, with the town laying a mile or two to the north.

When Clinchfield Gaol was cracked open, the liberated prisoners mostly fled riverward to the point's east shore. Nothing but tangled overgrowth and boggy marshland lay in the opposite direction.

A dirt road ran along the eastern shoreline from its southern tip to Clinchfield town and beyond to where the point joined the embankment.

The mass of the freed prisoners fled to this shore road because it was the surest and easiest route to travel, especially by night. Many of the freed inmates were from Clinchfield and hoped to find aid and shelter there with family, friends, or sweethearts. A sizable minority of the inmates hailed originally from Halftown. They knew their only hope of reaching Halftown safely was by water. In Clinchfield were boats that could be stolen or stowed away on. These inmates, too, were impelled along Shoreline Road toward the town.

As for the rest of the prisoners who came from various sites along the river, they followed the others, hoping there was safety in numbers.

They moved on Clinchfield en masse, knowing it was where Barbaroux's headquarters were sited, even though the Commander had put huge numbers of them in jail not for crimes of theft or violence but rather for anti-Barbaroux activities, organizing, or even remarks overheard in the wrong places.

Shoreline Road was also the most dangerous route because it would come right under the guns of the *Sabine Queen*. But the prisoners fled to the road, and east toward Clinchfield for a very good reason: They had no place else to go.

The forty Swamper raiders who'd busted Clinchfield

Gaol wide open had had their numbers thinned by about a fourth during the storming of the fort. The survivors, too, headed for Shoreline Road but for a different reason than the newly liberated inmates: They had a rendezvous to keep there.

The *Sabine Queen* came on. Rufus Barbaroux was up in the wheelhouse, the steamboat's nerve center and operative "brain."

The Commander's eyes glittered, his face shiny with excitement. His complexion was flushed almost as dark as his red hair and beard. He wore a white commodore's hat with gold braid on the visor and a blue coat with massive oversized gold braid shoulder boards and gold stripes on the sleeves.

The real captain, the one who actually steered and piloted the *Sabine Queen*, wore a plain cloth cap with a narrow-brim visor and a dark coat. He stood at the wheel, steering the steamer on course south along the point.

Ahead Clinchfield Gaol burned, making a throbbing red blur of light in the sky farther on and inland. In the east the sky was paling. Dawn was near.

The prison fortress's firelight bathed Shoreline Road with a smoky red glow, revealing masses of men thronging the road heading east, the freed inmates. They looked like a column of ants.

Barbaroux eyed them through the monocular telescopic viewer held screwed to one bulging twitching orb. "Prison break! I cannot image what that ass Munday is all about, but clearly he has lost control of his command. He'd better be dead if he knows what's good for him."

Gripping the bell-mouthed speaking tube as if it were a snake he was holding by under its head, he barked, "Commander here! Attention, attention! Tell the forward gun crew to open fire on those men on the road!"

In her cubbyhole of a cabin on the upper deck of the *Queen*, Malvina the Conjure Woman worked the Tarot cards trying to forecast the future. Her future.

The cabin might as well have been a hole in the wall or dismal cave in the forest. It was dim, crowded, and messy. It stank of old crone, wood smoke, incense, and a variety of oils, powders, and potions contained in rows of stoppered flasks and bottles set along the walls.

Malvina sat cross-legged on her bunk, shrunken head and narrow stooped shoulders wrapped in a brightly colored shawl embroidered with suns, moons, stars, and mystic signs.

She worked the cards by candlelight. Her ancient face was that of a living mummy, her hooded dark eyes were bright as a snake's and as alive with venom and malice. Clawlike hands with skeletal fingers handled the oversized deck of Tarot fortune-telling cards.

She laid out the cards on her bunk before her in a cross shape. Up came the next card in the shuffle, and she turned it over to reveal it:

The card called the Emperor—Barbaroux, surely. Next came the Wheel of Fortune—self-explanatory, really. Big events were in play.

The next card: Death. Not necessarily a card of ill omen according to the arcane lore of Tarot, it could mean death to the foe, the enemy. Or spiritual death.

It could mean just plain Death. Its meaning could only be interpreted in the context of the other cards in the reading.

Now the final card in the configuration, the one signifying the ultimate result of the question.

It showed a lightning bolt striking a castle, overthrowing towers, striking it down: the Tower. A card of complete and unmitigated disaster.

Malvina hissed with dismay. Cabin walls pressed in around her, trapping her. Too late to get off the boat now . . .

The *Sabine Queen*'s bow had been turned into a gun deck. A medium-sized naval cannon was mounted there. A five-man gun crew labored over the piece, readying it to fire.

It was loaded with separate gunpowder packet and canister shot. A viciously effective anti-personnel weapon, the shell was filled with metal shrapnel. When it burst, a cloud of white-hot metal shards would erupt, tearing flesh, blood, and bone to pieces. Devastatingly effective at close range, it was of varying effectiveness farther off.

The piece was sighted in on the masses of men fleeing east on Shoreline Road. The gun crew chief gave the command:

*"Fire!"*

A crewman touched the lit end of a length of corded match to the touchhole, igniting the powder. The cannon boomed, spitting shell, fire, and smoke, recoiling on its wheeled carriage.

The shot arced over the water, zeroing in on the Shoreline Road.

*Whoosh!*

It missed its target, impacting harmlessly on the wooded slope above the road and its teeming mass of escaped men.

"Too high!" the gun crew chief shouted. He had to

shout because he and the crew were partly deafened by the cannon's roar. "Lower the sights a degree or two, no more, and try again!"

"Aye-aye, sir!"

None of the escapees was hurt by the first shot, which passed harmlessly overhead to detonate against the side of the hill. But the effect on morale was immense, throwing the mass of men into a panic.

They were men kept caged for months—starved, beaten, and abused—many of them barely able to stay on their feet and keep going. You wouldn't have known it by the way they broke into a run at the first burst, scrambling in all directions, shouting, scattering.

The gun crew chief ordered, "*Fire!*"

The shell was low. It hit the water and bounced, skimming across the surface, taking another bounce to hit some few yards below the road.

"Lord, did they free us just to kill us here?" one man cried aloud.


Waiting, waiting for the *Sabine Queen*. That's what the *Gator Al* and its crew were doing.

The watercraft was the steam-powered launch recently stolen from the now-defunct Gun Dogs. In the last six days it had been worked on around the clock, night and day in Deep Hollow, refitting and refurbishing it, making it a deadly new weapon.

It now sat floating in the waters of a cove in the south shoreline of Pirate's Point at a site several hundred yards north of where the road from Clinchfield Gaol connected with Shoreline Drive.

The nameless cove was sheltered, virtually hidden

by overgrown drooping boughs of cypresses, willows, and water oaks.

That was its name: Nameless Cove.

It was large enough to hold a barn or boathouse. It had neither but what it had was a boat: the *Gator Al.*

The steam-powered launch was oblong-shaped with a slightly curved convex bow. It was a shallow-draught craft with minimal freeboard allowing it to go into water of only a few feet's depth. Its long roller-shaped stern paddlewheel could be raised clear out of the water and the craft transported by man-powered long poles for short distance should the water become too shallow for the paddlewheel. Gun Dog patrols used to use it to nose far into the backcountry bayous, lakes, channels, and sloughs.

A bow-mounted eight-pounder swivel gun was the something extra that had sunk Belle Nyad's boat in the run-up to the Battle of the Pier. After being stolen by the swampers, the steam-powered launch was under new management.

Something new and lethal had been added by the swampers to the watercraft: It had a stinger now.

Battened to the bow was a three-sided sharply tipped skeletal metal spike ten feet long. Its three long axes were metal railroad rails scavenged from a long-defunct branch line connecting the Blacksnake and Sabine Rivers. The line had gone out early in the war but stretches of intact track remained. Such a stretch had yielded the three rails.

Deep Hollow smiths and ironworkers, most of them recent fugitives from Barbaroux's tyranny, used a framework of crossbeams and trusses to brace what looked like a narrow three-sided metal obelisk tapering to a sharp point: the Ram.

This tapered obelisk-like construction had then been fastened to the steam launch, bolted and battened to the stoutest beams and ribs for extra strength and security.

The craft was partly shielded against ordinary small-arms fire by the strategic placement of cotton bales to protect the crew. The tied-down bales would stop rifle bullets though they were ineffective against heavier shot.

Here was the swampers' secret weapon against Barbaroux's mighty *Sabine Queen*.

One finishing touch remained. The launch was renamed *Gator Al* in honor of the recently slain Tonkawa leader and warhorse. The name was painted in large black letters on both sides of the bow.

Belle Nyad and a select crew of River Rats would put it into action. Having recently lost her own steam-powered boat to Barbaroux, vengeful Belle was the natural choice to make the run.

She wouldn't have it any other way. And since it was likely to be a suicide run, no one cared to dispute the point of pride with her.

Now Belle and her River Rat crew of Harry Sauder, Pol Philpott, Crazy Chester Coughlin, and Mantee made final preparations for the assault.

Belle alone would be making the run all the way, but the others would jump overboard well clear of the *Sabine Queen*.

For *Gator Al* was not only a ram, it was a floating bomb. The bow was packed with kegs of black powder and bundles of dynamite wired together and rigged with waterproof marine fuses.

The explosives were so arranged in the bow as to become a shaped charge, fitted in a fan-shaped iron funnel whose large end was wedged into the front of the bow and whose small end emerged just below the crude instrument panel holding the wheelhousing and steam-engine control levers.

The iron funnel was shaped like a giant megaphone, the idea being that the blast would be directed forward and outward in a tight fan.

Such was the concept, anyway.

Yet something old and new—someone old and new—had been added to the mix, overshadowing even the volatile, lethal, lusciously shaped Belle Nyad.

This was Skinner Kondo.

Skinner Kondo, near-legendary founder and master of the River Rats. In his day he'd been a slave master, blue-water and river pirate, brawler, lover, thief extraordinaire, and killer many times over.

The acknowledged master of the Blacksnake whip, he'd once been able to use the bullwhip's thirteen-foot-plus length to use its tip to flick a fly out of the air—a mosquito, even. Not to mention taking the eyes out of a man's head or flaying the skin off his bones.

At one time overseer of the Nyad family plantation, he'd taught young Belle the technique of wielding the bullwhip as a deadly weapon. An apt pupil and quick study, she became expert with the Blacksnake but could never surpass master and mentor Kondo.

When war came, Skinner Kondo reformed the River Rats gang, bedeviling Yankee and Confederate forces alike with his outrageous smuggling ventures and bold plunderings along the river.

But a chance minee ball fired from a sentry's rifle during a routine warehouse raid had struck Kondo low on the spine, shattering it into fragments and paralyzing him below the waist, spelling finis to his active depredations.

His body was a half-inert hulk, but his cunning brain was more active than ever, craftily hatching out master plans for rapine and plunder that were masterpieces of the marauder's art.

Belle Nyad became his mouthpiece and go-between, relaying his orders to the gang, bringing their information to Skinner Kondo. Her unparalleled ability at smelling out planned treachery and killing the betrayers before the betrayal, and her mastery of violence and the arts of murder, established her dominance over the gang.

But this night, tonight, Skinner Kondo had finally come out. It had taken four able strongbacks to carry him from a wagon on Shoreline Road down the slope to Nameless Cove.

He now sat lashed in place to a forward thwart in ready reach of the launch's spoked control wheel, a hulking bald-headed long-bearded two hundred and fifty pound man-monster. Dead below the waist, he still retained tremendous upper body strength.

His mind was made up.

"I'm taking my last ride, Belle. I'll pilot the ram into the *Queen*. I've outlived my time and I want to make myself useful once again and go out in a blast of glory. That's how I want it and that's how it's going to be."

Belle tried to talk him out of it but before she could even get started he held up a bear paw–sized palm out, his signal that discussion was ended.

"I have spoken," he said, voice rumbling like water rushing through underground pipes.

That was that. Nothing for it but to continue making the launch ready for the run.

Skinner Kondo took out a cigar from an inside breast pocket. It was fat and about a foot long. He bit off the end and spat it out, then stuck the cigar in a corner of his mouth.

"I'll use this to touch off the short fuse," he said. "Light me up."

Belle struck a match, holding its flame to the end of the cigar while Skinner Kondo puffed away, setting it alight.

There was a fallback device in case the cigar went out or failed to light the fuse. A wide-mouthed single-shot pistol lay ready at hand to touch off the fuse.

Strongbacks Pol Philpott and Mantee shoveled kindling into the firebox, driving the pounds-per-square inch pressure gauge up so that the needle kept flicking into the red danger zone. The steam engine shuddered against its mountings from the force at which it was being driven. The launch trembled to be in motion like a twelve-horse team straining at the harness in eagerness to be off.

"We're in the redline!" Belle shouted.

"That's where we got to be to make this work!" returned Crazy Chester.

Through swirling river mists and fog the *Sabine Queen* swam into view, running lights shining like blazing jewels.

"There she blows!" Crazy Chester cried.

The crew clambered aboard, taking their places, Belle throwing herself down on a thwart beside Skinner Kondo.

Kondo held up a warning hand before Harry

Sauder could enter the launch. "Not you, Harry! You stay here."

"What the hell, Skinner?!" Sauder said, face collapsing like a new bride's soufflé.

"This damned gang's gone need a leader if Belle don't make it back and you're the best man for the job."

"Hell, Skinner, I want to go with you! We been together for years—why break up a winning combo now—?"

"I have spoken! It's done."

"Aww . . . hell."

The *Sabine Queen* neared.

"Let's go!" Skinner Kondo roared.

Belle threw the lever, which caused the steam-power plant to engage the drivetrain of the stern wheel. The steamroller-like construction churned water, the launch lancing forward out of Nameless Cove and into the river.

"So long, Harry! See yah in hell!" was Skinner Kondo's farewell salute to his old comrade-in-arms.

# TWENTY-NINE

The *Blackskimmer* rounded the point's southern tip, making for the *Sabine Queen*.

Named for the predatory swamp bird notorious for stealing the catches of other birds right out from under their beaks and claws, the *Blackskimmer* was a steam-powered cutter, long, fast, sleek, and low in the water, an ideal smugglers' craft. No boat on the river could catch her.

She was armed with swivel-mounted guns fore and aft and her crew of six plus her captain were all first-class fighting men as well as veteran sailors.

The *Blackskimmer* was skippered by Captain Quent Hazard, the most skilled pilot and smuggler on the river. He had been a blockade-runner for the South during the war, trading valuable contraband cotton for much-needed medicines and ordnance, as well as such luxuries as fine brandies, wine, and cigars.

After the war he continued to ply the smuggler's trade, specializing in gunrunning. He'd been a particular thorn in Barbaroux's hide but continued to elude Combine patrols, spies, and informers.

Hazard's trade had risen dramatically in recent weeks as a result of his association with the Major, that shadowy figure with a steady and inexplicable supply of Winchester repeating rifles and ammunition.

Expert in his trade, Hazard knew at first sight that the crated ordnance had come from some U.S. Army arsenal, though no open thefts of same had raised a hue and cry or even been acknowledged by the authorities. This would hardly be the first time that a conspiracy to defraud the government of its lawful property had been carried out by insiders.

The pay was good, the business was brisk, and Captain Hazard asked no questions as he stepped up his schedule to run guns into Deep Hollow several times a week. It was obvious, though, that whoever he was and for whatever reasons, the Major was the front man for an outside effort to arm a resistance against the reign of Commander Rufus Barbaroux.

Now Hazard and the *Blackskimmer* were on a different kind of mission, a combat mission. The Major was paying the freight and the pay was good. More, to Hazard it felt good to get into hot fighting action once more.

Mysterious though the Major's origin and motives might be, the man himself was a real vital presence of flesh and blood. He was on board the *Blackskimmer*, too, along with Shrike, his omnipresent Tonkawa sideman.

In preparation for the mission, a shooting platform had been built and attached toward the boat's stern. It was not unlike a crow's nest set atop an eight-foot-tall four-sided scaffold made of sturdy wooden beams and diagonal cross-braces. The square-shaped platform atop it measured four feet on a side and had a three-foot-high safety railing.

The construction was lightweight, sturdy, and well secured to the boat.

The Major was up on the platform now, armed with a Winchester Model 1866 repeating.

He was none other than Sam Heller.

Sam Heller was an undercover operative for the Department of the Army, originally commissioned by General Ulysses S. Grant himself to suppress foreign and domestic subversion in the West. Sam was a contract agent with virtual freedom of movement and action and a wealth of extraordinary powers and resources to draw on. But then, he was an extraordinary man.

His long-term mission had brought him to Hangtree, Texas, a town set squarely on the frontier line between civilization and savagery. Its vital strategic location made it the focal point of a number of ongoing conspiracies involving Comanche raiders, *Comanchero* gunrunners, private marauder armies, would-be bandit kings, and worse.

Sam had gotten on the trail of Malvina from the moment he first delivered Bill Longley to safety in Hangtree. Call her Conjure Woman, Gypsy, Witch, or whatever, the fact remained that she was a cunning, vicious mass murderer who had slain a hundred troopers or more at Fort Pardee by the use of poison in the mess hall.

She had not done this on her own hook but in the pay of Jimbo Turlock, leader and master of the so-called Free Companions private marauder army. Malvina was Most Wanted by the federal government in general and the Department of the Army in particular. More, she knew things. The Army's top intelligence officers very much wanted to interrogate her about her knowledge of and participation in various subversive plots to destabilize the West and Southwest.

Sam had gone from Hangtree to nearby Fort Pardee to confer with his local contact, the post's commanding officer, Captain Ted Harrison. While there he secured the services of Shrike, a Tonkawa Indian who scouted for the post and with whom Sam had worked in the past. Shrike's Tonkawa origins would prove useful indeed in the swamps of Deep Hollow with its long-standing Tonkawa settlement. Shrike could talk to the tribes people in their and his own language.

Sam had left his beloved horse Dusty in the safe-keeping of the Fort Pardee stable master, wanting to spare the animal the rigors and dangers of a trek to the East Texas Gulf Coast. Dusty would be well cared for in Sam's absence and in the event that he did not return.

Sam procured a handful of Army horses and set off with Shrike on the long trans-Texas journey. Along the way they stopped at an Army post farther east that had access to a telegraph wire. Sending various coded messages to his contacts in the Department of the Army and the Secret Service, he gained much valuable intelligence about the situation on the Blacksnake in Moraine County.

Malvina's presence among the entourage of Commander Rufus Barbaroux was verified. With his murky origins, extensive assets, wide-ranging connections high and low, and his overweening ambition, Barbaroux was just the sort of problem Sam had been set to solve as part of his undercover assignment. The All-Highest of the Department of the Army agreed, and charged Sam with the imperative: "*Smash Barbaroux!*"

Sam Heller held a presidential warrant, a powerful

document that served as a kind of *Open, Sesame!* to a veritable Aladdin's cave of potencies and powers. It enabled him to procure the crates of new rifles and ammunition needed to set up his gun-running operation into Moraine County.

Captain Hazard was the best at the smuggler's trade on the Blacksnake and Sam suborned him to transport the weapons to Deep Hollow. Shrike's advance work with the Tonkawa tribal elders and their front man Gator Al Hutchins proved invaluable in establishing a secure working relationship with the larger community of prickly, suspicious, and opportunistic Hollow bigs such as George St. George's Nightrunners and Skinner Kondo's River Rats gang.

Sam stayed in the background as much as possible in his role as the Major, source and supplier of the hardware, using Captain Hazard as his front man to oversee the details of taking on firearms cargo, transportation, and sales.

Johnny Cross's arrival on the Blacksnake and his plot to spring Cullen Baker from Clinchfield Gaol proved to be the spark to detonate the powder keg that was Moraine County.

The crisis had arrived. The showdown was nigh— on the Blacksnake River.

Time for Sam Heller to take a personal hand in the matter. Which is why he was now posted on a shooting platform on Captain Hazard's *Blackskimmer* as it was fast closing on the *Sabine Queen*.

Sam secured his position with a canvas safety strap around his waist, to prevent his falling off the platform in case of rough waters.

The instrument for Sam Heller's deadly marksmanship was his mule's leg, the chopped sawed-off version of the Winchester Model 1866, now fitted with an extra-long barrel and add-on wooden stock to transform into a long gun.

Sam forewent the use of a telescopic sight, knowing the lenses would be adversely affected by moist river fogs and hazes and turbulent splashing sprays. He could do what he had to looking through the rifle's open sights.

Back in the war, sharpshooters on both sides frequently specialized in picking off gun crews manning cannons in the field artillery. Big guns fall silent when there's no left alive to fire them.

Sam now set his sights on the *Sabine Queen*'s gun crew, currently shelling the escapees on Shoreline Road. The gun crew needed light to see by to effectively perform their operations. However dim and well shaded, that wan glow allowed Sam to see them.

Not an easy shoot. Apart from the low light there were conditions of distance and the pitch and roll of the *Blackskimmer* as it arrowed toward the Big White Boat. But Sam Heller was a marksman supreme, an expert.

The platform was too unsteady to shoot from a standing position and the platform too small from which to fire prone. Sam took up a sitting position, wedging himself in a rear corner of the platform with his back braced against an upright safety rail.

He shouldered his rifle.

The *Queen*'s gun crew chief at the bow gun again gave the command: *"Fire!"*

The crewman with a length of lit match cord reached for the touchhole to set off the charge.

Sam's bullet drilled through him. The would-be igniter fell down dead on deck.

There was a moment of stunned surprise for the chief and his crew.

"I'll do it myself!" said the gun crew chief. He knelt beside the dead man, who featured a big bullet hole in his chest. The chief pried open the corpse's dead hand and took from it the match cord, which was still lit.

Crouched almost double, the chief moved toward the bow deck cannon, reaching out, extending the orange-embered tip of the match cord toward the touchhole.

*Wham!*

The chief reeled under the crushing impact of the bullet that killed him and fell down dead.

The three remaining gun crew members flattened themselves on deck.

"Where's that shooting coming from?"

"On shore?"

"Whoever it is, that's a helluva shooter!"

Up in the wheelhouse Barbaroux looked down in disbelief. "Fools! What're they waiting for?" he fumed.

"Reckon they don't want to get shot," the pilot at the wheel said between puffs of his pipe.

"I'm paying them to get shot, damn them!" Barbaroux rushed to the forward area, throwing open a viewport to one side of the spoked steering wheel. Thrusting his face into the round open space, he shouted down to the crew at the bow, "Shoot, you blasted idiots! Shoot!"

The gun crew trio conferred.

"The gun's all loaded and sighted in, it just needs a simple touching off that's all."

"We've already moved on, the original sighting's no good."

"Shoot it anyway, we'll hit something. And if we don't, so what?"

"You shoot it."

"All right, I will!"

The volunteer crawled on hands and knees to the body of the slain crew chief. The match cord had dropped from his hand when he was struck. It lay nearby, still lit.

The volunteer crawled around the chief, reaching for the match cord. "I got it . . ."

*Bam!*

Down he went. He died right away, facedown, bleeding on deck.

"He got it, all right," one of the two gun crew members said.

"This's a death trap, I'm getting out of here!" said the other. He got to his feet and scuttled off to the port side, disappearing behind a stanchion.

In the wheelhouse, Barbaroux demanded, "Where's that shooting coming from?"

"That boat there," the pilot said, taking the pipe from his mouth and gesturing with the stem at the *Blackskimmer* moving along about a hundred yards off the starboard bow.

"I don't believe it, nobody could hit with such accuracy at that distance on a moving boat," Barbaroux said. Nevertheless he took up his telescoping spyglass, set the view piece to one bulging outraged eye, and peered through the lens.

He focused the lens image, bringing into view the

rifleman who sat atop the boat's shooting platform gunning down his mouth.

"Bah!" Barbaroux set down the spyglass.

The last bow deck gun crew member was antsy, whipping his head from side to side, looking this way and that as if seeking a safe exit.

Barbaroux saw him doing it. He recognized all the signs of a man under fire losing his nerve and ready to run. Barbaroux had run many times himself but never mind that. He lifted the flap of his holster and took out his pistol.

The last gun crew member got his feet under him and shakily rose to a half-crouch, steeling himself to make a break.

Barbaroux extended his gun hand through the open porthole and fired a shot into the deck to one side of the gun crewman.

The gun crewman jumped. A follow-up shot tore into the deck on the other side of the gun crewman, pinning him in place.

"Do your duty or die!" Barbaroux bawled, face red as a sizzling brick oven.

Squaring his shoulders, the gun crewman swallowed hard and advanced stiff legged on the match cord length, bending forward and picking it up. He held the ill-fated match cord at arm's length as though it was the problem, not the sharpshooter. It was still lit.

He started toward the cannon—

*Slam!*

The last gun crew member joined the other three dead bodies lying sprawled across the bow deck.

Sharpshooter Nye and his two marksmen came out on deck for a rifle duel with the shooter on the *Blackskimmer*. A well-placed round from *Blackskimmer*'s forward-mounted swivel deck gun blew the *Queen*'s three riflemen sky-high.

"Now what the hell do we do?" Barbaroux wondered aloud.

The Ram steam launch *Gator Al* plowed a dirty white furrow across the dark river surface on its collision course with *Sabine Queen*. The Ram itself skimmed the surface, rising out of the water like a skeletal iron horn.

The launch was now closer to Barbaroux's steamboat than to the shore. Its course was meant to take the *Queen* amidships.

The laboring steam engine pounded and thrummed, shaking the boat and all in it. Belle Nyad was at the wheel, holding the course straight on. Her long black hair streamed behind like inky tendrils. Her lone eye gleamed wild but her face was set in masklike rigidity. Smooth, cold, impenetrable.

The airstream struck tiny orange sparks from the lit end of the cigar that Skinner Kondo held clamped between massive jaws. "I been saving this seegar for something to celebrate!" he shouted. "Now, this— Can't think of a better use for it!"

Mantee and Crazy Chester threw the last of the split logs into the firebox. Pol Philpott cupped a hand to his mouth to amplify his voice. "Pressure's so far into the red the boiler might blow before we hit!"

"That'd be a hell of a note!" Skinner Kondo laughed.

"She'll hold long enough!" Crazy Chester cried exultantly.

Seemingly random splashes began to kick up in the water around the boat, but they weren't random at all.

They were rounds being fired at the launch by the *Queen*'s defenders.

Stray bullets began to whip and zing through the air around the onrushing launch. The crew ducked their heads.

The level and accuracy of the firepower increased as more shooters on board the *Queen* took notice of the launch closing on it. Bullets made thudding ripping noises as they buried themselves in the protective cotton bales bulwarking the attack boat.

"Keep your heads down!" Belle cautioned, taking her own advice.

Crazy Chester waved away the threat. "Aw, they couldn't hit the broad side of a barn—"

A bullet caught him right below his left eye. He fell in a heap to the floor of the boat.

"I warned him," Belle said grimly.

"They don't—didn't—call him Crazy Chester for nothing," Mantee said. His head was hunched way down low, below the gunwales.

"He's bleeding all over the boat," Pol Philpott complained.

"So what?" Skinner Kondo said.

Philpott thought that over for a few beats. "I see what you mean."

"Time to light the fuse," Skinner Kondo said. He leaned forward from the waist, cigar in hand.

The fuse protruded from the narrow end of the iron funnel holding the explosives. It lay below the curved panel where the wheel was set. Skinner Kondo pawed the air near the fuse but it remained unlit.

He sat up straight, a study in frustrated fury. "I can't reach it! You do it, Belle, I'll hold the wheel!"

Belle Nyad took the cigar he proffered and ducked

down low, below the bottom of the panel. The orange disk at cigar's end looked a bit wan, so she puffed until it was hot and glowing.

The fuse was not a single cord but a number of fuse cords all coiled together. Belle held the cigar's hot tip to the end of the fuse cord. After a heart-stopping pause, a sputtering hiss announced that the fuse had been ignited. It shed tiny orange specks like a minia-ture fireworks sparkler.

Belle cautiously raised her head. "It's hot!"

She went to throw away the cigar but Skinner Kondo caught her wrist before she could make the cast.

"That's a hell of a waste of a good smoke!" he said, taking the cigar from her and sticking it back in his mouth.

An ever-mounting clangor was composed of the yammering steam engine, sounding as if it were about to shake itself apart; the roaring hiss of the straining boiler; the relentless churning of the stern paddle-wheel; and the ever-increasing volume of enemy fire.

"They're pouring it on . . . They know we got some-thing here and they're right, haw haw haw!" Skinner Kondo roared, gleeful.

He maintained his grip on the wheel, fending off Belle Nyad's attempts to take the helm. "I got it, it's all mine now," he said.

The *Sabine Queen*'s multi-decked superstructure rose up ahead like a giant white wall. It blotted out the riverscape, filling the crew's field of vision.

"Jump, boys, jump!—*now!*" Skinner Kondo urged.

Mantee threw himself over the port side, and Pol Philpott exited via starboard into the river.

The *Queen* was so close that the faces of excited crewmen appeared as pale ovals amid the gloom.

"You too, Belle!—*out!*" Skinner Kondo said.

"I'm sticking! We're taking this ride together to the end!" she cried.

"That's sweet," he said. He grabbed her arm, hooked his other hand between her legs, effortlessly hefting her into the air and pitching her headfirst over the side.

A quick glance back revealed the reassuring sight of Belle's head breaking the surface of the water. Did she call his name? Skinner Kondo couldn't be sure, not amid the racketing engine noise and the crackling fusillade of bullets tearing into the boat.

Skinner Kondo leaned forward, puffing the cigar, bear paw hands clutching the wheel spokes as the *Gator Al* passed the point of no return.

"Most fun I've had in years!" he growled. Since the shooting that had left him dead from the waist down, in fact.

*"Here I go!"*

A slug tore into him, drilling deep into his barrel chest. He rocked with the impact but kept his grip on the wheel. A second, then a third round tagged him. Skinner Kondo growled, throwing them off like water—

Impact!

The *Queen* didn't have a lot of freeboard between her waterline and gunwales, her shallow draught being a major factor in her ability to navigate the Blacksnake.

The tip of the ram lanced the *Queen*'s hull about a foot above the waterline. Wood splintered and cracked, hull planks breaking as the launch's momentum drove the ten-foot ram half its length deep into the boat's side.

The crash had nearly torn the ram loose from the launch, to which it remained attached by a handful of creaking straining bolts.

Skinner Kondo still lived, the vital force in the magnificent ruined hulk of his once powerful body refusing to surrender despite three mortal bullet wounds and the terrific shock of the crash.

Combine shooters lined the starboard rail, leaning over the side to blast Skinner Kondo with rifles and handguns, literally riddling his body with bullets.

The shooting stopped. He sagged slumping at the helm, only the ropes binding him in place holding him even partly upright. His grip loosened from the wheel, hands loosening, opening, then falling away from the spokes.

He looked dead but wasn't, not quite. His head tilted back and he looked up at the paling stars in the sky overhead. "Got me, yah dirty sons . . . but watch out for mah Sunday punch."

Had he whispered it or just thought the words? Skinner Kondo didn't know. What difference did it make anyhow?

The bomb blew.

In her cubbyhole of a cabin, Malvina the Conjure Woman, the Gypsy Witch, raised her hands over her head, shaking tiny wrathful fists at heaven.

The rolling thunder of the blast's aftermath shuddered through the now wounded *Queen*.

Malvina slowly lowered her hands and opened them, covering her face with them. "*Undone! Overthrown!*" she shrilled.

A happy accident of the bomb blast—happy for the attackers, that is—was that the concussive force and pressure waves ripped the ram free of the launch, driving it deeper into the hole with pile driver power, widening the hole in the hull considerably so that it now reached below the waterline. River water began pouring through the expanded opening.

*Sabine Queen* took on water fast, quickly developing a noticeable downward tilt to starboard, while the port side steadily, inexorably rose.

The steamboat was stalled, dead in the water. There was flooding below decks. When the gang of boiler stokers saw water come rushing in, they abandoned their posts and rushed on deck for fear of drowning.

Barbaroux missed a bet there. Had he thought of it in time he would have had the hatches sealed so the stokers, engine tenders, and pipe fitters had to keep working the pumps to keep the ship afloat or else drown like rats.

By the time he had that brainstorm, it was too late. The machine-tenders had already fled beyond his reach to all points on the ship.

With *Sabine Queen* crippled, the swamper boarding party flotilla rounded the tip of the point to come sailing into view.

It was made up of several dozen small craft of all varieties: flatboats, keelboats, barges, launches, rowboats, pirogues, dugout canoes, skiffs, and more.

Each boat was filled with well-armed fighting men out for blood: smugglers, River Rats, Tonkawa Indians, Sharkey's people, and a horde of unaffiliated individuals who bore a grudge to the death over the tyranny of Barbaroux.

They numbered several hundred men in all. Not all were of the boarding party, a large number of them were boat handlers needed to sail their craft alongside *Sabine Queen* to allow the fighters to board her.

*Blackskimmer* went to pick up the crew of *Gator Al* who'd gone overboard before the crash and blast.

The steam-powered cruiser slowed to a halt near Belle Nyad. Because of her nearness to the *Queen*, she was the last to be picked up, after Mantee and Philpott had already been retrieved.

Those on board the *Queen* now had more important things to do than waste time shooting at a rescue boat that was not actively engaging them. They were in the fight of their lives . . .

Belle swam the short distance to the boat. Somebody reached down to help her aboard. She gripped the rescuer's hand.

Sam Heller hauled Belle out of the water and set her down on deck. Her wet garments clung to every curve and hollow of her superbly formed body.

"Well, hel-lo!" Sam said.

# THIRTY

*"Repel all boarders!"*

Barbaroux shrieked the command, wildly waving a cutlass over his head as he attempted to rally the crew of *Sabine Queen* for a counterattack.

The boarding party flotilla attacked from the starboard side. That was a natural: The starboard side was lower down in the water, making it easier to board. Of course they had to stay well clear of the hole in the side, which was taking in so much water so fast that there was danger of a boat's being caught in the suction and helplessly pinned to the hull.

The stern side wheel, now stilled, served as a stairway to the main deck for boarders, its paddle spokes functioning as so many steps out of the water and on to the boat.

That was one way of access. Most of the boarders preferred to clamber out of their boats and up the starboard side, throwing feet on deck.

Among the first boarding parties to storm its way into Barbaroux's wounded floating palace was a longboat marshaling the formidable combined firepower of

Johnny Cross, Bill Longley, and Cullen Baker. Busting open Clinchfield Gaol was only a warm-up exercise for these three.

Now came the Big Killdown.

The longboat was a large streamlined rowboat capable of carrying fifteen. Crowded up at the bow out of the way of the oarsmen, the Texas pistol fighters were already in action, mowing down Combine reinforcements rushing to starboard.

An oarsman used the hook on the end of his gaffing pole to grip the steamboat's starboard gunwale, bringing the longboat alongside the *Queen.* The rush was on as the boarders came scrambling out of the boat, lusting to fight and kill, with the Texas trio at the fore.

Similar scenes took place along the starboard side from bow to stern.

Bill Longley lost his balance on the tilted deck, starting to slip and fall. Johnny's free left hand shot out, grabbing Bill by the arm and steadying him.

"Thanks! With that tilt it's like being drunk," Bill said.

"You should be right at home then," Johnny quipped.

"This is one place where going barefoot comes in right handy," said Cullen Baker.

Johnny's right hand fisted a gun. He raised it to shoot a charging Combine man in the face, erasing the other's features in a red splash.

"Yee-hah!" Bill Longley crowed.

"Remember: When we find Barbaroux, he's mine," Cullen Baker said, breathing gustily, the kill fever working on him.

"I'll tell you how we find him," Johnny said, putting a hand on Cullen Baker's arm. "Look where the fire-power is heaviest, that's where he'll be. He'll be the best guarded. Then we come at him from a different direction, one Barbaroux won't expect."

"He's mine," Baker repeated, a stubborn mulelike cast stiffening his features.

"You got him," Johnny said, Bill nodding assent. "And Sexton Clarke is mine."

"Clarke? That little preacher-looking pissant Barbaroux sent to kill me? I'll kill him, too."

"He's mine, Cullen," Johnny said seriously. "I done staked my claim and already laid the ground work in on him. Don't cheat me of my fun."

Cullen Baker was silent.

"Cullen . . ."

"All right, Johnny, he's yours."

"What the hell, Cullen? How many people can you kill at one time?" Bill Longley said, only half-joking.

"I don't know, but I aim to find out."

The *Sabine Queen* was warm with swampers and Combine men locked in mortal combat, shooting, slashing, stabbing, hacking, clubbing, and even using their bare hands.

Below decks, the boiler exploded, loosing a tremendous explosion amidships. The cylindrical, torpedo-shaped boiler blasted vertically upward like a rocket, tearing through the main deck and the next deck above, inflicting huge damage to the superstructure.

A number of fires had broken out on the boat, taking their toll of lives and adding to the chaos. Dawn was breaking, the sky lightening in the east. This only fanned the fighting frenzy on both sides, attackers and defenders. There was more light to kill by.

The Grand Saloon was where Commander Rufus Barbaroux made his last stand, ringed by a hardcore element of his elite personal bodyguard.

The site was brightly lit by chandeliers, rows of wall-mounted flambeaux torches, and ornate many-branched candelabras scattered throughout the big room. They were the illuminants of the nightly revels in the hall, gone unsnuffed because of the surprise attack on Clinchfield Gaol and its fast-developing aftermath.

The floor tilting down toward starboard gave the scene an unreal, hallucinatory quality. A pall of gray-brown smoke gathered in the great hall, fruit of one or perhaps several unseen fires burning throughout the boat. The lights looked blurred and hazy through the smoke. Things were getting hot for Barbaroux, both literally and figuratively.

*Sabine Queen* was really starting to burn. The forward bulkhead of the Grand Saloon was ablaze, a solid wall of fire. The heat was terrific. Tongues of flame began to lick their way aft along the walls while serpents of fire wriggled their way along the high ceiling.

Smoke was thick in the space, eyes stinging, throat searing, choking. Yet to set foot outside on deck meant death, for out there the boarders had gained the upper hand.

Bodies of Barbaroux's bodyguards piled up as swampers crowded the Grand Saloon from all sides not already cut off by fire. They shot down Combine men from around doorways and through windows.

Most of the growing number of corpses belonged to Barbaroux's men, with more swamper attackers making themselves felt with each passing moment.

A tentacle of flame lashed out at Barbaroux. Involuntarily crying out, he ducked barely in time to avoid being smacked by it but lost his commodore's cap, which went rolling away down the tilted floor.

His once iron ring of bodyguards had been winnowed away to a single thickness, with gaps steadily opening as more of his protectors were gunned down from barely glimpsed shooters flitting from cover to cover through ever-thickening smoke.

The Commander recoiled, jumping back to avoid being run down by a screaming human torch. The burning man rushed past, leaving footprints of fire across a priceless Persian carpet. The floorboards were hot underneath Barbaroux's feet.

*Time for me to make an exit—undignified, perhaps, but necessary,* he said to himself. He couldn't have said it aloud to save his life because he was coughing too hard from the choking smoke.

Leaving what little remained of his personal bodyguard behind to fend for themselves, Barbaroux beat a hasty retreat aft, stumbling past the throne platform, through a passageway and into a shadowy back room.

Set in the opposite wall was a bulkhead door accessing the stern of the boat. Barbaroux pressed against it, eyes red and burning, body sweat drenched, panting and gasping for breath like a sow trying to haul itself out of a too-deep mud wallow.

Gathering his reserves for a breakout effort, he flung open the door—

Only to be confronted by Cullen Baker standing on the other side.

Barbaroux froze, paralyzed by shock and fear, the gun in his holster forgotten. Not that it would have done any good.

Cullen Baker had his guns out and leveled, pointing at the Commander.

"Well, Barbaroux!" he said, a towering pillar of cold rage.

He shot Barbaroux in the belly. Barbaroux lurched, staggering backward.

"That one's for Julie—my wife," Cullen Baker said.

He fired again.

"Oww!" Barbaroux cried, going down. He hit the floor with a thump.

He looked up, eyes wide and scary. Cullen Baker stood over him. He shot Barbaroux in the right elbow, then the left. Shot him in the right kneecap, then the left.

"Those were for me," he said, smiling.

"*Cullen, Cullen!*" Someone was calling his name, softly, insistently.

"*Cullen! It's me, Bill! Bill and Johnny!*"

Cullen Baker looked back, seeing Bill Longley and Johnny Cross standing outside, sticking their heads around the edges of the door frame to peek inside.

"What're you whispering for?" Cullen Baker demanded, frowning, his thick-featured face knotted up like a fist.

"We didn't want to surprise you," Bill said in a normal tone of voice.

"Didn't want to get shot by you," Johnny added.

"Oh. That makes sense," Cullen Baker said, tension flowing out of his face.

Johnny and Bill stepped inside and took a look at Barbaroux.

"Help . . . help me . . ." Barbaroux mouthed the words but lacked the strength to say them.

"Sure you shot him enough?" Johnny said.

"Enough for him to last a while and suffer," Baker said.

"C'mon, Cullen, we've got to get out of here," Bill urged. "The boat's sinking and the fire's rising."

"Finish him off and let's go," Johnny said.

"Like hell! Let him burn," Cullen Baker said.

Johnny shrugged. "That's your business, ain't nothing to me."

Away they went, the three of them, in search of a friendly boat and escape. Roe Brand saw them and gave them the high sign, steering them to a flatboat waiting off the starboard stern.

"Don't fall in," Roe warned the Texas trio as they readied to board the boat. "The water's full of gators!"

They climbed down into the flatboat very carefully indeed.


Barbaroux lay on his back, agonized, and moaning. Fire had reached the back room, the ceiling was a mass of flames, sagging ominously in the middle. Fiery flakes and chips rained down from it, its underlying framework creaking and straining.

He became aware of the nearness of a presence—

Tanya, Malvina's creature, silent, wide eyed, staring down at him.

"Faithful to the finish, my last follower," Barbaroux mumbled.

Dropping to one knee, Tanya began turning out his pockets, her small slim hands swiftly and expertly lifting his hefty overstuffed billfold, several modest-sized pouches of gold, and a diamond and emerald stickpin, making them hers.

She coveted his ornate gold and diamond rings and tried with all her might to pry them off his fat fingers, but they were too tight, too deeply sunken to come off. If she'd had a knife she would have cut off his fingers to get the precious jewelry, but she didn't. Was there time for her to find a blade?

No! With a heave and a groan the flaming ceiling started to give way, black cracks spiderwebbing through it, swelling out and down, bellying out.

It looked like it would all come down but at the last instant it held—just.

Tanya's eyes were wide indeed, showing white rings around dark brown irises and swimming pupils. The spooked orbs seemed to fill the upper half of her face.

She rose, darting out the door, not looking back.

"Oh, what an artist is lost to the world!" Barbaroux sobbed.

The blazing ceiling gave way and came down, engulfing Commander Rufus Barbaroux in an Eternity of Flame.


Malvina the Gypsy Witch had run out of space and time. She stood huddled at the rail of the uppermost deck of the superstructure on the starboard side.

Starboard because it was much lower than the port side, which was correspondingly thrust higher into the air as the opposite side sank lower in the water.

Still it was a dauntingly long drop to the water below, a drop that would have given a well-conditioned adult in the prime of life pause, not to mention an incredibly ancient crone who labored when she took a breath.

But taking the high jump to the river far below was one of only two options Malvina had left. It was that or burn to death in the blazing inferno now turning the superstructure into a fiery witch's cauldron.

There was nowhere else to run. Heat, flames, smoke surrounded her on all sides, leaving her only a tiny patch of untouched deck on which to cower. It was a race to see which would get her first: the fire or the building collapsing around her. If the latter, the fire would still get her anyway.

She would have jumped sooner but the waist-high safety rail balked her. She lacked the strength and agility to climb it and jump from the top rail.

Now the rail itself was on fire, its uprights and horizontal top rail entwined by vines of flame, the wood charring and blackening.

On the water, Hazard's *Blackskimmer* stood a safe distance off *Sabine Queen*'s starboard, idling, afloat in place.

The other boats on the scene, filled with members of the victorious swamper boarding party, were getting away from the sinking burning steamer as fast as they could.

Crew and passengers of *Blackskimmer* stood at the rail watching the singular human drama being enacted as Malvina reeled and swirled on the top deck, a black-clad spidery looking thing staggering amidst sheets of red flame that sought to consume her.

"The Conjure Woman!" Belle Nyad exclaimed. A blanket provided by the cutter's crew was worn wrapped over her shoulders.

"Can you go in closer, Skipper?" Sam Heller asked.

"I could but I won't," Captain Hazard said.

"How much . . . ?"

"Not a matter of money, not this time," Hazard said, shaking his head. "When the *Queen* goes under, as she will any minute now, she'll create a whirlpool that'll suck in anything too close and take it down to the bottom with her. I don't mind risking my neck, but I won't risk my boat!"

The safety rail had almost burned through. Malvina took a last desperate chance. She took a few steps back to gain headway, as much as she dared with the flames so close. She wrapped her long black shawl over her white-haired head and living mummy face. She took as deep a breath as her withered lungs and crabbed shrunken rib cage would allow.

Hugging her upper body she scuttled as quickly as she could at the charred blazing safety rail and bumped up against it.

The rail gave way, falling out and down, Malvina falling after. Trailed by folds of her fluttering dark robes, she plummeted downward like a black comet.

She hit the water, raising a spout twice her height. A column of silver bubbles marked her descent into blackwater depths. Rippling circles radiated outward from the point of impact.

A long pause followed.

"Gone! It's over," Captain Hazard said.

"And good riddance," added Belle.

Just when it seemed the world had seen the last of Malvina, she surfaced, floundering and flailing, spitting out water and sputtering.

A mighty unease thrashed below the surface, ringing her. A mass of gators surrounded Malvina, arrowing in for the kill.

Razor-fanged maws gaped, each of them snapping shut on the Conjure Woman. Already maddened by the excess of blood in the water, the gators dragged her under and tore her to bits.

"Whew! Now it's over," Captain Hazard corrected.

Sam Heller swore softly under his breath, shaking his head. "She had a lot of answers," he said.

"Now they belong to the gators," Belle Nyad said. "So does she," she added.

"The Witch Woman, the Fortune-Teller. She must not have seen this in her future," Captain Hazard remarked.

"It was all a lie. Just like everything on the Big White Boat," Belle said. She moved away, standing near the steam engine to bask in its radiant warmth.

Captain Hazard nudged Sam with an elbow to the ribs. His voice pitched low so only Sam could hear as he said, "What matter a dead old crone when a live young beauty walks among us, all fire and silk, eh, bucko?"

Sam began giving some considerable thought to the remark.

On the flatboat commanded by Roe Brand, George St. George was enraged that Barbaroux had escaped his personal vengeance.

"Cullen Baker got him. That beats feeding Barbaroux to the gators," Johnny Cross said.

"You might have something there," George said thoughtfully.

The sun came up, all scarlet and seething, giving promise of a sunrise as bloody looking as had been the previous day's sunset.

The *Sabine Queen* went down, a squalid smoking hulk swallowed whole and without a trace by the Blacksnake.

# THIRTY-ONE

Johnny Cross was going home.

He'd said his good-byes. Cullen Baker was a free man . . . as free as any man could be with his appetite for destruction and bottom thirst for raw whiskey. But at least he wouldn't hang. Not this time, anyway.

Bill Longley was going to stay in Moraine County for a while with Baker. There was still plenty of Combine men and supporters who had yet to clear out of the Blacksnake. Hunting them down promised to be great sport and profitable, too. That crowd had stolen big while Barbaroux was in the saddle, Bill said.

He and Cullen Baker would form a partnership to hunt them down, kill them, and take their stolen loot. A third of it was Johnny's if he cared to throw in with them . . . all he had to do was say the word and the Texas Trio would be back in business together, hellbent for leather!

"Much obliged, but I've got to move on," Johnny had said.

It was time. He'd been lucky to come out of this shooting scrape as lightly as he had.

The new regime in Clinchfield was friendly and then some. Niahll Sharkey had been made provisional town mayor by voice vote acclamation. Sharkey swore that he'd doctor the official record so as to keep Johnny Cross's name well out of it so there would be no comeback from the law, which suited Johnny just fine.

"So soon?"—that's what Cullen Baker and Bill Longley had chorused the day before when Johnny told them he was moving on the morrow. They wanted him to stick around for at least a week of drunken roistering and general hell raising, if not a month.

Johnny didn't need a conjure woman fortune-teller to foresee the future if he stayed around much longer. The volatile combination of Cullen Baker, Bill Longley, whiskey, and guns would inevitably lead to fresh trouble, violence, more killings. Which Johnny didn't need. He'd had enough Days of Blood for a while.

"I've got a ranch to look after and business to tend to. The roundup's coming up if it ain't gone down already. Seems I've been away so long I can't hardly remember," Johnny said.

His funds could use some beefing up, too. He'd spent gold like water financing the breakout. Naturally he made no complaint of this to Bill and Cullen. That was his affair. Besides, what good was money if not for spending? He considered it well spent and there's an end on it.

It would be just like Cullen and Bill to commit some big-money robberies to pay him back and they would be none too fussy about who they took it from or how or who got hurt. Johnny didn't want to be responsible for that.

So they gave him a big bustout going-away party

yesterday, all day and late into the night. Cullen and Bill were undoubtedly still sleeping off that epic drunk. Johnny had drunk his share and more but nothing like the other two.

Nothing, not even a king-sized hangover, was going to stop him from pulling out this day. He planned to take a boat from Clinchfield down the Blacksnake to the junction with the Sabine River, then downstream to Sabine to catch an Overland Stage back to Hangtree.

It was early in the morning of this departure day when Johnny Cross checked out of the Clinchfield Hotel and stepped out onto the veranda, pausing to take a look-see.

The sky was light but the sun had not yet risen. Pools of pale blue-gray shadows lapped at the bases of the buildings fronting the town square. The early morning air was about as cool and fresh as it ever got in swampy Clinchfield on the river, but he could still feel a mass of heavy-aired heat astir, trying to muscle in.

He angled across the square to the livery stable where he settled up the bill for boarding his horse. The boat was a ferry equipped to carry livestock, so he was taking the animal with him. The horse was saddled up and brought to him.

Johnny rigged his traveling bag to the saddle, securing it to a side ring with a length of rope. He mounted up and rode out of town to take the road to the docks. The road was on a rise overlooking the riverfront. Tall thin cedar trees lined the inland side of the road.

The ferry wouldn't leave for an hour or two, but this was a good time to be out and about, the air hazy with river mists that the slow-rising sun had yet to burn off. Moisture dripped from trees and bushes, and the grass was wet with sparkling dew.

Johnny slowed the horse as he neared a junction where the road from town met the road down the slope to the riverfront.

A lone rider stood beside his horse where the two roads met. He stood facing Johnny, watching him come on.

As Johnny neared, the other stepped into the middle of the road, barring the path. Even without his signature preacher's hat, his identity would have been known to Johnny: Sexton Clarke.

It just had to be him. And it was.

Johnny reined to a halt.

Clarke stood easily, feet spread slightly more than shoulder-length apart. His hands hung at his sides, his guns worn holstered with the butts facing front in that characteristic style he favored.

"Good morning, Mr. Cross," he said.

"Clarke," Johnny said, acknowledging the other's presence with a tight nod.

"So you know who I am," Clarke said with a thin wintry smile.

"And you know of me," said Johnny.

"Only by repute. I prefer a more personal encounter."

"Why?"

"Frankly this whole Blacksnake venture has been something of a setback for me. I intend to salvage something out of the situation."

"You're still alive," Johnny said pointedly.

"So are you," said Clarke. "For now."

"That's the way of it, eh, Clarke?"

"That's how it must be, Mr. Cross. Stop here for a bit so we can talk."

"Talk?"

"Well . . . you know," Clarke said, his smile widening.

"I reckon so," Johnny said. "You'll have me at a disadvantage when I get off the horse."

"I won't make my move till you're ready—it wouldn't be sporting."

"Can I count on that?"

"You have my word."

"Your word, huh? Well, I'll get down anyway," Johnny said.

The smile left Sexton Clarke's face.

It was Johnny's turn to smile at him. He stepped down from the saddle, holding the horse's reins in his right hand, left hand resting near the gun holstered on his left hip.

"No call for you to be disagreeable. I'd like this to be conducted as an affair of honor, a duel between two gentlemen," said Clarke.

"I'm no gentleman," Johnny said.

"We'll duel all the same."

"You're a strange bird, Clarke. You want to kill me for no good reason except to shine up your reputation, but I mustn't be 'disagreeable.'"

"I like to keep it civilized," said Sexton Clarke, as if that explained everything. Hell, to Clarke maybe it did, Johnny thought.

"We'll play a little game, Mr. Cross—a game of death."

"And any gun can play," Johnny said.

Clarke shook his head. "Oh, no, not just any gun. One has to reach a certain level of high skill to ante up in this game. When I saw your gunwork at the pier last week, I knew you'd make a worthy opponent. I didn't know who you were then but I've since found out, me and the rest of Moraine County. You've been busy, Mr. Cross.

"The man who broke Cullen Baker out of jail and helped down Rufus Barbaroux, that would-be Caesar of the Blacksnake . . . That's won you a full measure of acclaim, far and wide."

"I didn't do it by myself," Johnny noted.

"No false modesty, please. I've made inquiries. I know you were the driving wheel behind Barbaroux's downfall. You're not only a champion-quality pistol shot but a thinker, a planner. That's something rare in our line of work. Impressive."

"Stop, Clarke, you're making me blush."

"Joke if you like, you can't rile me. I'm the master of my emotions. It's a matter of will, self-control, mental discipline. At the moment of truth, a cool head can mean the difference between life and—"

"Are you trying to talk me to death?" Johnny broke in.

"Ah, you're doing it again, trying to goad me into losing my temper. Can't be done," said Sexton Clarke, unruffled. "Yes, we're talking about you. You've already achieved some renown, but your part in smashing the Commander and the Combine puts your name at the top of the lists. You're quite the celebrity—*famous.*"

He all but drooled when he said the word "famous," rolling it around in his mouth like it was honey-sweet. "And the man who kills you will be even more famous."

"Meaning you, Clarke?"

"None other."

"Suppose I don't feel like playing?"

"That would be a disappointment, Mr. Cross," Clarke said feelingly. "It would turn a duel of honor into a mere vulgar killing."

Johnny's laughter was short and mirthless. "Can't have that! I'll tie up my horse first . . . you don't mind?"

"Not so long as that's all you do. I'm sure I don't have to tell you not to, er, jump the gun so to speak, by reaching for a weapon before we've formally squared off for the duel," Clarke said.

"Don't worry, there'll be no tricks—not by me."

"Who's worried? I like to see these matters conducted with a degree of civility and decorum, that's all."

Johnny led the horse by the reins to the side of the road, never fully turning his back on Clarke. He tethered the animal to a low-hanging branch, then turned to face Clarke.

"Thanks," Johnny said. "This way I won't have to go chasing an untied horse spooked by gunfire. You know—afterward."

"Such confidence," Sexton Clarke mocked.

Johnny started toward him, moving easily, hands beside his holstered guns.

"That's close enough," Clarke said sharply when Johnny was a half-dozen paces away.

"All right," Johnny said, halting. "You want a showdown, Clarke. You've got it."

Sexton Clarke crossed his arms so each hand would be making a cross-belly draw of the guns worn butt-out on each hip. His eyes glittered in a face exultant with the certainty of ultimate triumph.

"This is a mere formality, Mr. Cross. Going through the motions of the actual duel, that is. But that's the only way to keep the record straight. I'll let you in on a little secret . . . the outcome is preordained. I can't lose! Remember, I saw you at the pier that night. You can't beat me with your left-hand draw. I've seen it *and*

*I know I'm faster.* You've been a dead man from the moment we came face to face!"

"So it's really not a fair duel after all," Johnny said evenly.

"Who knows? You might get lucky," Clarke smirked. "You won't, but what else is there for you to do but try? Try, and fail . . . I owe you a debt of gratitude, though. Thanks to you I'll have a second chance to kill Cullen Baker, the job which brought me to this swampland hell-hole in the first place. I'll leave the Blacksnake with two celebrated scalps on my belt, yours and his!"

"No, you won't. You'll die here," Johnny Cross said. "*Now!*"

He and Clarke slapped leather, Johnny drawing and shooting *with his right hand.*

Three shots sounded: two that Johnny put into Sexton Clarke's chest, and one that came a beat later, too late, the wild shot Clarke fired as he was already toppling and going down.

Johnny advanced on Clarke, approaching him as cautiously as if he were a cornered rattlesnake. But there was no fight left in Clarke and damned little life, and what there was of that latter fading fast.

Clarke lay sprawled on the ground on his back, the expression on his face one of raw shock and disbelief.

Johnny kicked the gun out of Clarke's hand, Clarke had only managed to draw the one in the split-second before Johnny's two slugs tagged him in the chest.

Clarke's watery eyes bulged, his mouth gaped open. He tried to form words, failed, then with a supreme effort tried again. "What—how . . . ?"

"I saw you kill those men in Fayetteville years ago. You didn't see me but I saw you. So I knew you that night on the pier when I saw you again," Johnny said.

"I knew you were watching so I drew with my left hand. I'm faster with my left than most men are with either hand. I'm not bragging on it, it's just the way I was made. But my right hand is the dominant hand. I'm faster with the right than with the left. You never saw my *fast* draw till now."

Sexton Clarke's eyes were wide and staring. The last thing he saw were the two gold coins that Johnny pressed down on his still open eyes, covering them, blacking out the fading light of the dying gunman's vision.

The next person to come upon Sexton Clarke would be greeted by a sight uncommon weird, an image half-comic and half-grotesque: a corpse with what seemed to be a pair of shiny gold coins for eyes, a prize specimen of what's called *gallows humor.*

"Buy yourself a funeral, gravedigger," Johnny Cross said.

# THIRTY-TWO

The steam-powered ferryboat bound for Sabine on the Gulf Coast chugged out of Clinchfield harbor. Its shrill whistle hooted an earsplitting series of blasts, echoes booming across open water. The boat surged south into the wide bay south of Pirate's Point.

Standing at the rail watching the Clinchfield docks' waterfront slowly recede were Johnny Cross, Sam Heller, and Dean Valentine. They smoked and drank.

Sam thoughtfully drew on his corncob pipe, Johnny set fire to the end of a long skinny cheroot of the type he favored, and Valentine puffed away at a long fat cigar, venting clouds of aromatic smoke.

"From the Commander's private humidor, a special blend custom-made to his order," Valentine noted with satisfaction. "Barbaroux said that each cigar was specially hand rolled on the taut round thighs of Cuban virgins working in the Havana curing sheds."

"Go on," Johnny scoffed.

"That's what he said," Valentine insisted.

"Makes a nice story."

"And a damned good smoke."

The three passed a bottle around, drinking from the neck.

"That's good brandy," Sam said after taking a long pull at the contents.

"Some of the Commander's finest," said Valentine.

"I suppose the grapes were stomped under the bare feet of French mademoiselles selected for their youth and beauty," Sam said, straight-faced.

"That's not bad," Valentine said appreciatively, chuckling. "Your *amigo* is quite droll, Johnny."

"He's as much fun as a fire in a crowded circus tent," Johnny said off-handedly. "Sounds like you and Barbaroux were great chums, Val."

"The Commander didn't have friends, only people who did things for him. If you were useful you could do all right for yourself. He lived *rich*. A fellow could live high off of his leavings."

Johnny held out a hand palm-up. He upended the bottle over it. After a pause a few scant drops oozed out. "Gone," he said.

"I had a couple bottles in my bag but that's the last of it," said Valentine.

"There's a common room on the boat; it's got a bar and a food stand," Sam said.

"But the quality! . . . Or lack of it. What a comedown, to go from vintage French wines and brandies to common-room six-snake whiskey. Worse, I'll have to pay for it instead of getting room, board, and alcohol as a perk for painting the Great Man's portrait."

"Quit your bitching, Val, you're lucky to clear out of Moraine County with your hide intact," Johnny reminded the other.

"Too true. Barbaroux's associates have become marvelously unpopular overnight."

"They was always unpopular, it's just that now the Combine's exploded folks can do something about it."

"They're doing it, all right. Pity the local pitchfork brigades can't or won't distinguish between Barbaroux's thugs and killers and an innocent painterly dauber like me. The good people of Clinchfield were looking at me like they were measuring me for a rope to throw me a necktie party so they could watch me dance on air."

"Can't say I was surprised to find you on the first boat out, Val. The bad penny always turns up, they say."

"Funny, I was thinking the same about you."

"Speaking of bad pennies, my friend the Major here makes three," Johnny said, indicating Sam Heller.

"Ah, yes. The celebrated gunrunner," Valentine said, eyeing Sam with new interest.

"I'm retired from that line of work," Sam said.

"You must have made a lot of money, the way those Winchesters were flooding the Hollow."

"Not me. At those prices, we were practically giving the rifles away. Which was the idea. Middlemen like Sharkey and George St. George were the ones who really turned a profit."

"I thought you'd be in the chips."

"You don't see me chartering a yacht to sail to the Gulf, do you?"

"Oh," Valentine said, losing interest, the greedy gleam going out of his eyes.

Johnny laughed. "Listen to yourself, Heller! Less'n a month in the gunrunning game and you sound like all the other tired businessmen crabbing about how they're getting whupped in the marketplace, don't know how they're gonna say afloat, drowning in red ink—

"Hell! Let that be a lesson to you. You do better as a gunman than you do as a gunrunner. Sell your skills and stay out of the hardware line.

"Though I sure would like to know how you got hold of all them good guns, so many and so easily . . ."

"A big man at a regional armory went into business for himself. He was going broke trying to keep a wife in the style she was used to and a mistress in the style she wanted to get used to. He had the rifles, I had the customers, so we did a deal. He just got transferred to a post in Walla Walla, Washington, so now we're out of business," Sam said cheerfully.

Johnny's eyes were narrow in a suspicious, skeptical face. "That's the way of it?"

"Sure," Sam said. "And if you don't believe that one I'll tell you a half-dozen more lies before breakfast."

Johnny made a face and a noise ripe with disgust. "Trying to get a straight answer out of you is like watering a tree stump to make it grow."

"How long have you known about my horning in on this Blacksnake deal?" Sam asked.

"I knew you'd be going after Malvina since Hangtree, when Bill Longley told me she was tied into Barbaroux. The way you and every bounty killer and blood hunter was scouring North Central Texas for the Gypsy for the Fort Pardee poisonings, I reckoned you'd make a bee-line to Moraine County.

"As for you being the Major, what with the big hunt for Malvina kicking up a storm, it didn't take much to put those crates of Winchester 66s going into the swamp with that same model you use for your mule's leg. Knowing your last Army rank was Major was kind of a tip-off, too," Johnny said.

Sam shrugged. "That was obvious but that's the kind of job it was so who cares? No time here for a lot of fussy masterminding and sneaking undercover work. It called for dynamite.

"All that work, and at the end Malvina gets away—"

"Into the bellies of a couple dozen gators. I wouldn't exactly call that a clean break," Johnny said.

"And Barbaroux went down," Valentine added.

"There's a satisfaction in that," Sam conceded.

"Look at all them poor blamed jailbirds got busted loose from that hellhole of a Clinchfield Gaol. That was a mercy," Johnny said. "Man, the way they were crowded in there, the filth, the *stink*— Lord!"

He shook his head as if to jar the memory loose. "I felt like Santa Claus giving out presents at the orphanage on Christmas Day when we busted the inmates out of their cells. That was a dirty business and everybody that had a hand in running it deserved to die."

"And they did," Sam said. "I'm not kicking. That was a fine job. Can't say I'm happy with your murdering pard Cullen Baker being at large again, but that was one of the trade-offs." Sam's eyes were icy and his face stony when he thought about Baker. "He's a bad one. You and I will both share in the responsibility for any innocent folks he kills from here on."

Dean Valentine discreetly eased off to one side, putting himself in the background, not wanting to get involved with whatever was behind Johnny Cross and Sam Heller exchanging harsh words. He hoped it wouldn't go any further.

"Hell with that," Johnny flared up, hazel eyes glinting more keenly yellow than brown, as they did when his blood was up and running hot. "Cullen Baker's a full-grown man, he's responsible for what he does, not me."

"You trying to convince me or yourself?" Sam fired back.

"I ain't trying to convince nobody. Cullen's got his good points and his bad points. He's a friend of mine—like you. You two couldn't be in the same room together for more than a minute before there'd be a killing, maybe two. I'm almighty glad you're clearing out of the Blacksnake before that happens. From here on in Cullen starts out with a clean slate. Me, too. Whatever debt I owed him for things he done for me in times past is paid in full. He's got no call on me now. Whatever he does or doesn't do is on his head, not mine. Or yours."

Sam nodded heavily. "My mistake. My apologies. I talked out of turn."

"It's nothing, let it go," Johnny said.

"No, I should have thought before I spoke. I've been in the same bind myself. You start out riding a trail with a friend, a good friend, one you'd trust with your life, and he feels the same about you. Then one day you come to a fork in the road and you take one branch and your friend takes the other and after that everything changes, not necessarily for the better. It can never be the same. You can only hope that things work out and that the path you've chosen won't put you in a showdown with the stranger who used to be a friend."

"You've been there, then. What happened?" Johnny asked.

"Everyone is different. What happened to me need not happen to you. A man's fate is not set in stone or fixed by the stars."

*Or is it?* Sam wondered.

"How did it end?" Johnny pressed.

"Not well," Sam said. He looked away, watching the green ridges of Pirate's Point roll past. He was done talking for now.

Johnny was grateful for the return of Valentine, who eased back to join the other two at the rail when he saw their friction had subsided.

"I saw a friend of yours earlier, Val," Johnny said.

"Who?"

"Sexton Clarke."

"Clarke's no friend of mine, merely a shipboard acquaintance," Valentine said, wiping away the association with an airy wave of the hand.

Sam Heller turned toward the others. "Thought I heard shooting up on the rise right before you came down to the boat. What happened?"

"Clarke decided to stay on in Clinchfield," Johnny said, his face smoothly untroubled.

"Permanently," he added.

"What I figured," Sam said. "Any trouble?"

"He expected me to come at him with my left but I dropped him with my right instead."

"Come again?"

Valentine laughed. "Clarke took an interest in Johnny after the fight at the pier. He asked me if knew who he was, but I lied and said no. Clarke took note of the left-hand draw that Johnny used to take the Vipe. He was almighty confident he could beat that draw."

"But Johnny's a right-hand draw," Sam said.

"Not wanting to shatter Clarke's illusions, I let him go on thinking the opposite. Looks like it all worked out," Valentine said.

"I knew Clarke was watching me that night so I put on a show for him, gunning Viper with my left, kind of laying down a marker for the future if Clarke wanted to play," Johnny said. "To tell the truth, I didn't know which way you would jump, Val."

"I don't go telling tales out of school, especially about an old drinking buddy. '*Auld lang syne*' and all that, don't y'know. Glad it all worked out."

"Clarke knew my name and who I was but not which hand was coming at him. I maybe could have beat him without the edge, but—it didn't hurt. Thanks, Val."

"None needed. Trust in Valentine, friends, and you can't go wrong!"

"Unless you're looking at him across a poker table."

"Ha ha. Johnny's joking," Valentine said to Sam.

"Like hell I am—"

"Hard to believe the *Sabine Queen* is sunken somewhere below us on the bottom of the bay," Valentine said quickly. "Come to think of it, the Commander went down owing me a week's wages for my most recent work on his portrait. It's only fair, though, because the unfinished canvas went down with him. Now the only ones to see it will be the gators, crawdads, and catfish. Which is more than came out for my last gallery showing."

"Barbaroux was crazier than a maverick bull with a mouthful of loco weed," Johnny declared flatly.

"Say what you will about him, Rufus Barbaroux had an appreciation for the finer things in life: the best food and drink, beautiful women everywhere . . . A man of taste." Valentine sighed.

"I reckon the gators would agree," said Johnny Cross.

The ferryboat coursed to the lee of Pirate's Point, crossing the bay en route to the river and downstream.

A lone rider came galloping south on Shoreline Road, racing after the steam barge and overtaking it, a task requiring no great speed for the boat moved slowly across the bay, the pilot warily on the alert for any wreckage from the sunken *Sabine Queen* that might have surfaced to present a threat to navigation.

The rider was a woman, long black hair streaming back behind her. She drew abreast of the boat, passed it, and continued onward for another twenty-five yards or so before stopping. She turned her horse so that it and she faced east, looking across the water in the direction along which the ferryboat must inevitably pass, and soon.

The boat was near enough to shore that the black patch covering the rider's left eye could be discerned.

"Belle Nyad," Johnny Cross said with some surprise.

"Swampcat Belle," Valentine murmured. "She's all woman and then some more but a tough lady—very tough!"

"Belle's not as ornery as she likes to make out, she's quite agreeable when you get to know her better," Sam Heller said.

"How would you know?" asked Valentine, one eyebrow raised.

"Nice of her to swing by to see us off and say *adios*,

it's not what I would have expected of Belle, her being kind of standoffish where men are concerned," Johnny said.

"Sorry to disillusion you, but it's not us she came to see, it's me," Sam said.

"Huh?" Johnny said, genuinely surprised. "You? You mean you, Sam Heller, and Swampcat Belle—?! No sir, it can't be, it just can't be."

"We spent some time over the last day or two getting better acquainted, Belle and I. Quite a gal when you get to know her," Sam said blandly, poker faced.

"Well if that don't beat all!"

Catching sight of Sam, Belle leaned forward in the saddle, waving to him.

Sam took off his hat, swinging it out and down in a grand sweeping gesture accompanied by a courtly bow to the lady, a farewell salute done with such stylish flair as would have done a Musketeer proud.

Belle Nyad blew him a kiss.

"Why you rascal, you!" Johnny exclaimed, shaking his head in bemused wonderment and disbelief.

"Life is full of surprises, no?" Sam said.

The steam barge's course now curved to the southeast, away from the point and out toward the middle of the river, where the current ran strong and deep. Belle Nyad was lost from view as the ferry made its way downstream.

"Never knew you had it in you, hoss. You come pretty danged close there to handling yourself like a real Southern gentleman," Johnny said.

"Coming from you, I suppose that's a compliment," said Sam.

"You're damned right it is. Who knows, there may be hope for you yet!"

"Ah, hope," Dean Valentine said, "the last item left at the bottom of Pandora's box when she set loose all the troubles in the world, back in the days of the Ancient Greeks. Is it Hope that keeps us going in this hard world, or is it an illusion, the last evil left in the box to plague all mankind? Maybe both!"

Johnny Cross and Sam Heller turned to stare Valentine in the face.

"What the hell you talking about?" Johnny demanded.

"You're quite the philosopher, Valentine," Sam said dryly.

"I have to be, to console myself to the loss of Barbaroux's patronage, his free-spending ways and lavish entertainments, the nights and days of good food, strong drink, and women who are too beautiful to be good. Oh, well, life goes on," he said, abruptly brightening up. "What say we go to the common room, men, for a drink or ten and perchance even a friendly game of cards?"

"Now I get it," Johnny said. "Don't let Val's fancy talk fool you, Sam Heller! He's just baiting the hook in hopes of netting a couple of suckerfish. There's no such thing as a friendly game of cards with that sharpster."

"Might as well play a few hands to pass the time," Sam allowed. A pretty fair poker player himself, he was of a mind to trim Valentine out of some of that Barbaroux money.

"We'll have a few drinks, too," Valentine chimed in.

"Who's buying?" Johnny asked skeptically.

"I'll get the first round," Valentine said grandly.

"Will wonders never cease! Let's go, Heller, before he changes his mind," Johnny said.

"Sounds good at that," Johnny agreed. "Let's go."

Off they went, the three of them, in search of ship-board diversion.

On the point, Belle Nyad watched the ferryboat go downriver until it was out of sight. Then she rode away.